THE COVEN

THE MAJOR
After many lifetimes, he has come
to fulfill his final destiny.

THE COUNTESS
As High Priestess, she knows
her touch can save a nation.

THE SPY
He discovers a terrifying secret
in the dark heart of Nazi Germany.

THE PRINCE
In this most sacred of ceremonies,
he is the sacrifice.

THEIR MAGIC MUST PREVAIL
ON THIS NIGHT OF WONDERS.

Also by Katherine Kurtz
Published by Ballantine Books:

THE CHRONICLES OF THE DERYNI

DERYNI RISING
DERYNI CHECKMATE
HIGH DERYNI

THE LEGENDS OF CAMBER OF CULDI

CAMBER OF CULDI
SAINT CAMBER
CAMBER THE HERETIC

LAMMAS NIGHT

KATHERINE KURTZ

BALLANTINE BOOKS • NEW YORK

All rights reserved under International and Pan-American Copyright Conventions. Published in the United States by Ballantine Books, a division of Random House, Inc., New York, and simultaneously in Canada by Random House of Canada Limited, Toronto.

Library of Congress Catalog Card Number: 83-90784

ISBN 0-345-29516-1

Manufactured in the United States of America

First Edition: December 1983

ACKNOWLEDGMENTS

Special thanks are due to the following good folk from both sides of the Atlantic without whom the author's task would have been far more difficult:

Technical advice on military and protocol matters: 1150784 W/O R. A. Pearson, former Sunderland rear gunner serving in 201, 228, and 204 Squadrons.

Astrological expertise: Erin Cameron, B.A.

Consultant on vintage motorcars: Scott MacMillan.

Additional invaluable advice from: Doreen Valiente, John and Caitlin Matthews, Dolores Ashcroft-Nowicki, Michael Howard, Jim Alan, and the many others who also gave their assistance so graciously but who, for various reasons, wished to remain anonymous.

PROLOGUE

It is a matter of historical record that Adolf Hitler had more than a passing interest in astrology and the occult, and apparently based many of his decisions of the Second World War on what the stars told him. We know that the timing for many of his major offensives—the invasion of Poland, his march into the Rhine, the annexation of Austria, the rape of Czechoslovakia—all coincided with periods when his stars were in ascendancy. Nor was he the only high-ranking official of the Third Reich to keep one or more full-time astrologers on his staff.

But there is other tradition, less well known, that suggests that occult factors may also explain why Hitler never carried out his threatened invasion of Britain, though he was poised to do so for many months. It is said by some that the witches of England—whose ancestors claimed to have caused the storm that destroyed the Spanish Armada—joined forces and raised a cone of power to break Hitler's nerve and keep him from even trying to cross the English Channel. We will never know for certain whether this or any of the other measures suggested in this story had any effect—only that, indeed, Hitler never came.

This is how it might have happened. . . .

CHAPTER 1

Oakwood Manor, 2030 hours, 28 May 1940

THE ELDERLY MAN IN THE UNIFORM OF LONG-AGO WARS would have been at home in any elite London club. He was equally at home in the Earl of Selwyn's library, placidly smoking an expensive pipe as he lounged on the arm of an overstuffed chair. The rows of medals on his chest and the brigadier's insignia at each shoulder reflected gold off the cheery flames in the Tudor fireplace across the room. The firelight was the room's only source of illumination.

Only the man's hands betrayed his restlessness, stroking the smooth burl of the pipe's bowl with a thumb and fiddling with it distractedly every time it went out. The hands told the story—and the jaws, clenching and unclenching on the pipe stem and sometimes even chewing, setting the steel-grey mustaches trembling. The crackle of the fire and the drum of rain beyond the curtained French doors, soothing under most circumstances, did nothing to ease the visible tension in the room.

Nor was Brigadier Ellis its sole contributor, though his three companions revealed their nervousness in different ways. Beside him, in the overstuffed chair whose arm he had claimed off and on for the past hour, his granddaughter Audrey sat with eyes closed and head leaned languidly in the angle of one of the chair's wings, apparently at ease—until one noticed the stockinged toe tapping almost imperceptibly against the carpet. Though she, too, wore a uniform, dark blue instead of brown, she had shaken loose her long auburn hair when she came in

1

from duty at nearby Hawkinge. From time to time, the brigadier leaned across to stroke her hair in reassurance, but the tapping of the toe would only pause, to resume almost immediately when he withdrew.

Far more difficult to read was the countess, settled demurely in a Chippendale chair a few yards across from them, her back to the fire. Before the Great War, when she and Audrey's mother were schoolgirls together, the Honourable Alexandra Deville had been a great beauty. Her wartime marriage to the dashing Viscount Jordan, heir of Selwyn, had been a profound love match as well as the social event of a war-lean season. Two sons and a quarter century later, she had not lost the ability to turn heads when she walked into a room.

Tonight, however, even Alix was showing the strain. Working at a knitting project, she looked almost matronly in her sensible Welsh tweeds, dark blonde hair tucked into a neat roll at the nape of her neck and rimless reading glasses perched precariously on her nose. The stiff, oiled wool had already shaped itself into a pair of sleeves as the result of the night's work; the rest of the garment formed a pool of navy blue on the edge of the Persian carpet at her feet. In the center of that carpet lay the fourth of their number, Sir John Cathal Graham.

He lay on his back, nearer the large chair than the countess's, apparently asleep. The pale face was handsome in a ruggedly Celtic way—the closed eyelids slanted at the corners, the jaw slightly pointed and shadowed with a day's stubble of beard. The hands lay motionless along his sides. He appeared far younger than his forty-two years, for the dark hair was untouched by grey; the body, lean and hard.

He wore a black polo sweater that came close around his neck and made his face seem oddly disjointed in the semi-darkness, with loose-fitting trousers of a nondescript khaki drill that had become all too familiar since the war. Something in the very line of his body, even in repose, conjured up images of finely tempered steel, innocuous and even forgettable while safely sheathed but potentially deadly.

The minutes passed. Only the crackle of the fire, Graham's shallow breathing, and the occasional chomp of the brigadier's teeth on pipe stem intruded on the steady lull of the rain. When the countess glanced up from her knitting over the top of her little glasses, the brigadier raised one eyebrow in question. Alix shook her head.

"Nothing yet," she murmured.

With a sigh, the brigadier sucked at his pipe and frowned, then began worrying at the tobacco with a pipe tool.

"Bloody inefficient navy!" he muttered under his breath.

The man on the floor slept on, oblivious.

Dunkirk, Malo-les-Bains, 2045 hours, 28 May 1940

His true name was Michael Jordan, but for this mission they had given him the code name Leo. He thought it ironic from the start. The legendary courage of the beast was the farthest thing from his mind as another shell screamed in close over his head and he dove for cover.

Around him, others were hitting the wet sand and tumbling into trenches even as the explosion rocked the beach. Unspeakable debris rained down on and all around him, but the concussion mercifully dulled his perception of the cries of the newly wounded, at least for a few seconds. As his ears recovered and he slowly raised his head, he began to hear their agonized screams and moans—at least the ones who still could cry out.

He screwed his eyes tightly shut and shivered in the rain, remembering men less randomly slain—had it been only yesterday?

He had worn a German uniform then. He had stripped it off a dead body, the same way he had gotten the British battledress he wore now. He had come upon the scene of calculated carnage as the perpetrators were pulling out. They were seasoned troops of the SS *Totenkopf* Division, with Death's heads on their collars and murder in their hands—men whom even the German army detested and feared. The chatter of their machine guns echoed off the shell of the burned-out farmstead, punctuated by the occasional sharp report of an officer's pistol, long after the white flag of surrender fluttered out of sight behind a half-demolished wall.

He had thought himself inured to the necessity of death on the battlefield, but the cold-blooded execution of a surrendering opponent was outside the code he had always been taught. Beyond the shelter of the farmstead wall, herded together like so many sheep led to the slaughter, he found the bullet-riddled bodies of scores of the Royal Norfolks, their major still clutching the bloody remnants of the white flag. He recognized a few. Many of the men had been shot at close range. Some had not died right away. One died in his arms, too far gone to notice the uniform he wore. He had wept at the unfairness of it all.

Another shell exploded even closer than the last, jarring Michael harshly back to the present even as he tried instinctively to burrow deeper in the sand. Simultaneously, searing pain in his left arm convulsed him into a tight, fetal ball, all other thought or memory temporarily shattered in the stunned recognition that he was hit.

In those first pain-laced seconds, he wheezed with the effort even breathing cost, knowing he must make himself move and head for safer ground or else die right there. His mind knew, but the pain in his arm dominated nearly everything. Feebly, he began the laborious process of getting his feet under him, forcing protesting muscles to move as he willed. One of the men nearby mouthed something at him, but only the urgency came through. He could not make out the words.

Then two men grabbed his arms from either side, and he was running with them—half dragged at first, then staggering and stumbling, miraculously supported, finally tumbling into yet another trench to flatten himself again. He panted with the pain and the exertion as he huddled with his rescuers, ducking in blind reflex as more shells whistled overhead. Though explosions continued to chop up the strip of beach they had just vacated, their new position seemed to be inside the big guns' range. He was no longer cold, but he began to shake again. This time he suspected he was going into shock.

Above the sound of shelling, the murmur of voices and the curt orders of the officers as they prepared to move the men out again gradually broke into his awareness. He thought he could feel blood running down his arm and pictured it steaming where it met the cold, steady rain. But when he tried to look, all he could see in the flare-lit night was a slightly darker shadow staining his already wet sleeve from shoulder to elbow. He knew an instant's panic as he fumbled at his belt for the pouch whose contents were the reason he was in this place of madness, but it seemed to be intact.

His benefactors tugged him to his feet, and they ran again, pain throbbing up his arm and along every nerve with each jarring step and pulse beat. Closer now, he saw, silhouetted against the burning town of Dunkirk, the ships moored along a thin, fragile-looking mole that stretched into the sea. Long, winding queues of battle-worn soldiers extended back from the mole and all along the beach, slowly funneling men onto the narrow walkway toward the ships and safety.

He and his companions joined one of these queues. As he caught his breath and held his wound, trying to stop his bleeding and block the pain as he'd been taught, he wondered what had gone wrong here—never mind the series of disasters that had plagued his own mission.

Could it be that the war was lost already? The British Expeditionary Force (BEF) was leaving France in an orderly but humbling retreat, abandoning weapons, equipment—everything but men. If the Germans pressed their advantage now, an invasion might well succeed. Even if Michael got back with his dearly gained information, would it all be for nothing?

Naval Headquarters, Dover, 2100 hours, 28 May 1940

Vice Adm. Sir Bertram Ramsay, the flag officer ultimately responsible for the Dunkirk evacuation, stood beside the window of his darkened office high in the Dover cliffs and stared into the night.

He could not see far—a mile, at most. A fierce downpour had opened up late in the afternoon, and a drizzle continued to obscure the twenty-two-mile stretch of Channel before him. On a clear night before the war, he easily would have been able to see the lights of Calais, Boulogne, and even Dunkirk itself. Tonight, the blank void beyond the shatter-proof glass gave back only an oddly welcome numbness. Ramsay was very, very tired.

Operation Dynamo—as one of his staff had dubbed the evacuation during its planning stages—had been conceived in the chamber adjacent to Ramsay's office called the Dynamo Room: a deep gallery carved in the white cliffs a century and a half before, when another continental dictator named Bonaparte had threatened an invasion of Britain. During a more recent war—the one that was supposed to have ended all of them—the chamber had housed an electrical generating plant for Dover Naval Command.

Now the room generated another kind of energy: desperation, in the attempt to lift nearly a quarter of a million men of the retreating BEF to safety before they could be overrun or pushed into the sea by the Germans. Allied lines from Nieuport to Ypres and along the Mardyck Canal to Cassel, west and south, were under increasing pressure, being forced into an ever-shrinking pocket whose only outlet was the sea. Ramsay was still stunned by the speed with which Hitler had moved, as was the rest of Europe.

Calais had fallen to Hitler's advancing infantry and panzer divisions two days before. Boulogne was lost. Of the three ports originally included in Ramsay's evacuation plan, Dunkirk alone remained open. And unless Dunkirk could be held long enough to rescue a sizable portion of the BEF, Britain's part in the war would soon be over.

Ramsay sighed and let his gaze drift downward to the harbor, rubbing his forehead and the bridge of his nose with a weary hand. The dark harbor offered little visual difference from the blank display across the Channel, but at least he could rest assured that all was proceeding with reasonable efficiency at this end of the operation. Though the lights of the port were dimmed to the absolute minimum—just in case the Luftwaffe dared a night bombing raid in such filthy weather—Ramsay knew that dozens of ships were going in and out of Dover Harbor, from destroyers and large passenger ferries down to minesweepers, drifters, torpedo boats, and a host of miscellaneous smaller craft. And each carried precious cargo—the rescued men.

The ships traveled close to ninety sea miles to reach their destination even though the French coast lay only a tantalizing twenty-odd miles away. To avoid the treacherous Goodwin and Ruytingen shallows and the even worse menace of the minefields and German-held shore batteries, it was necessary to divert north along a dog-leg course that twice doubled back on itself. An additional danger was the increasing number of German torpedo boats and submarines that had begun to prowl the more northerly regions of the Channel since the fall of Holland. If the trend continued, Ramsay feared his evacuation ships would soon have to abandon the longer but so-far safer Route Y and find another route. Already, he had lost so many men. . . .

He sat down in the swivel chair behind his desk and put his feet up, wondering what it looked like for *them*—gathered on the beaches for rescue and under fire from the enemy. Not for the first time, he wondered whether he had thought of everything, whether he was doing enough, whether he had made the right decisions.

Dunkirk, 2230 hours, 28 May 1940

Michael Jordan had no quarrel with the decisions being made at Dover, though he would certainly have a few choice words for whoever had botched the rest of his mission. If someone had thought to tell the RAF that the Dornier making its way across the Channel to France carried a British prize crew, Michael might at this moment be having tea with his chief, prints of his precious film spread on the table before them while he debriefed.

But the Spitfires had been too efficient, and the intended pickup plane now lay at the bottom of the Channel with its crew. Its loss had left Michael the very awkward task of making his way back across most of Germany and France on his own, now ending in a long queue of British soldiers inching its way onto the narrow East Mole at Dunkirk, as the rescue ships ran the gauntlet of German shellfire. The journey had also included the dangerous and disturbing meeting with Dieter.

A shell burst flung up an enormous waterspout just astern of an approaching drifter, rocking the timber walkway atop the mole and nearly swamping the ship. Michael braced himself on wide-spraddled legs and swore softly, his good arm cradling his injured one. Another explosion farther out shattered the superstructure of a half-sunken minesweeper that had not been as fortunate as the drifter, showering the nearest section of the mole with deadly debris. Michael forced himself to put Dieter out of mind as he and his adopted unit continued doggedly onward.

At least he had gotten his wounds bandaged and stopped most of the bleeding, thanks to the man behind him. But pain lanced up and down his arm every time a movement shifted the shrapnel in his flesh, and he dared not accept morphine if he hoped to remain on his feet and functioning. He tried repeatedly to block the pain himself, but the concentration required was nearly impossible under the repeated shelling.

Resignedly, he shifted his attention to the men directing the loading operation and tried to think about something besides Dieter or his pain. An old destroyer was backing away from the mole. Someone had said they could cram six hundred men above and below decks. As the ship turned north, disappearing almost immediately in the rain, Michael found himself wondering what it was like below—trapped if the enemy should strike on the long run home. The thought was hardly more reassuring than his pain.

Somehow he endured the next hour. He and his companions were among the last to board a battered and battle-scarred destroyer of about the same vintage as the other he had seen— and somehow he managed to keep from getting shepherded below decks. The ribbon on one of the crew caps read H.M.S. *Grafton*—a ship whose record, as well as that of her captain, Michael knew. In happier times, his father had entertained such men at Oakwood.

Somewhat reassured, he let himself sink down exhaustedly between two Royal Marines who appeared already to be asleep. Huddling against them for warmth and shivering in a detached fog of pain and weariness, he was only vaguely aware when the ship backed off the mole and swung her bows toward the north. He felt her pick up speed as she began her zigzag dash up the Belgian coast, heeling crazily when the helmsman would put her hard over to avoid a shell, the klaxon whooping stridently in the darkness and rain.

The sound was oddly lulling to Michael, gradually allowing him to put from mind all the outside sounds and sensations of war—the explosions, the groans of the wounded and queasy around him, and even the hiss of the bow wave curling along the hull. Soon only the whoop of the klaxon remained at the edge of awareness, a harsh but heartening clarion call carrying him at last into merciful semiconsciousness, his good hand protectively covering the pouch at his waist.

Oakwood Manor, 2300 hours, 28 May 1940

The room was colder and darker, but no one had moved to fuel the fire. As the brigadier stood to stretch his legs, the countess also paused to ease her neck from side to side, flexing stiff fingers. Graham finally gave a deep sigh and began to rouse, one hand twitching slightly. The brigadier snapped his head around to stare, pipe in hand, then dropped to a crouch between Graham and his granddaughter. Audrey struck a match and lit a candle on the small table beside her. The countess put aside her needlework.

Almost immediately, Graham sighed again and moved his head, lips parting slightly and tongue moistening long-dry lips as the eyelids began to flutter. He yawned mightily, stretching interlaced fingers taut away from his body. Then, as the arms fell back, the eyes opened—hazel, startlingly luminous in the dimness of the room. He grinned as he sat up and glanced at the three of them.

"He's alive, and he's safe. Not as solid a contact as I would have liked, but under the circumstances, I shan't complain. He's on a destroyer—I think it's the *Grafton*."

As the two women smiled in relief, the brigadier nodded, gesturing with his pipe.

"He's a clever lad, is Michael. Does he have the film?"

"I think so—which is a bloody miracle, considering how many other things went wrong with this mission." Graham yawned again and rubbed his eyes, then sat up straighter and rested a hand easily on the girl's knee.

"Audrey, my love, how do you feel about taking over now? Everything should go smoothly from here on out, but someone ought to keep an eye on him until we're sure. Are you up to it?"

"Of course."

As she rose and moved into the space he had just vacated, Graham shook out a folded afghan that the brigadier tossed him from the back of the chair and settled it over her lower body. She smiled as he kissed his fingertips and touched them lightly to her forehead, her eyelids fluttering and then closing as she breathed out with a soft sigh. As Graham stood, the brigadier and the countess also came to their feet.

"Well, I'd say it was a good night's work, Gray," the older man murmured around his pipe. "I don't envy you what you just did, though."

Graham's hazel eyes held just a trace of amusement as well as warmth. "Aye, the Second Road was a mite crowded this evening. We're not the only ones interested in the outcome of this war." He shrugged. "With any luck, however, I'll not be going out again for several days. If Michael got what I hope he did, my chaps are going to have their work cut out for them. You have the number at Dover Ops if anything should change?"

The brigadier nodded. "I'll try not to bother you unless there's need, though. Wouldn't want them to think the old war horse is trying to horn in on this young man's war."

"I think you've more than earned the right," Graham said with a grin as he flicked a forefinger lightly against the rows of medals on the old man's chest.

The brigadier did not reply, but he smiled in answer and plucked the pipe from his teeth before drawing the younger man into a quick embrace. He did not meet Graham's eyes as he withdrew and settled into the overstuffed chair, his attention now apparently turned inward and to the pipe in his hands, but he did not need to speak in any other way. The friendship of Graham and Brig. Gen. Sir Wesley Ellis extended back nearly a quarter of a century, when a brash but gifted young Guards lieutenant had sought and won the hand of his commander's daughter.

That daughter was more than ten years dead now, her and Graham's only son presently serving with RAF Coastal Command in Hampshire. But the bonds formed with Ellis in the years before and after Caitlin's death went far beyond father and son or comrades in arms or any other more usual human bonding. All of them had sworn sacred oaths together and served a common goal through those years, as they continued to do tonight. Those same oaths and bonds bound all within this room, and a handful of others not able to be present because of the war.

Graham spared a last affectionate glance at the older man, then turned to where Alix waited beside her chair. Behind her, the door from the room seemed faintly misted, though this was not unexpected in light of what they had done.

"Well, I suppose I'd best be off, then," he murmured, taking one of her hands and touching it to his lips in a casual gesture. "Don't worry. I'll see that your Michael gets back safely."

"Does it show that much? I'm sorry. With his father and his brother both at sea, though . . ."

He flashed her a quick smile, but his own son came to mind, flying deadly missions daily, and the thought gave the smile a slightly brittle quality. He saw her flinch and tried to gentle the smile to a more reassuring one.

"Richard," he murmured by way of explanation.

Nodding, she averted her eyes and cleared her throat uneasily.

"I know. We all worry. Speaking of worrying, David is getting a little anxious about setting up that meeting. I've been putting out feelers, but with very little luck so far. Any reassurances I can send him from your end?"

He sighed and shook his head, still cradling her hand, as much for his own comfort now as for hers.

"I'm sorry if I've disappointed him, Alix, but you know I wasn't trained for this kind of thing," he said in a low voice. "That was always David's domain. I can do a lot of useful things, like what I just did out there,"—he gestured vaguely—"but I never expected to have to take David's place in something as delicate as this."

"We never expected war on this scale again, either," she reminded him a little sharply. "A lot of us are having to do things we weren't trained for. Look at Audrey. She should be going to betrothal parties with Peter and planning her wedding, not wearing a uniform and tracking enemy bombers and worrying whether he'll come back to her in one piece—or even whether he'll come back at all!"

He forced himself to glance at the girl apparently asleep on the floor behind him, then reluctantly returned his gaze to Alix.

"I'm not arguing that we don't all have to make sacrifices," he said softly. "God knows, *I'm* not exempt. And I'm not even afraid to die if it comes to that. But if word were to get out, I could lose my military effectiveness and maybe even be locked away. They do strange things in time of war. I think that's what I really dread the most."

"Your cover is safe so far," Alix replied. "The ones I've talked to think it's David and I who are initiating the effort— and even if they knew otherwise, they'd never betray us."

"I'm glad you have such faith. And what happens if we *do* get them all under the same roof?" Graham breathed. "Then all we have to do is persuade them to work together. Fat chance!"

"We can only do the best we can," Alix said stubbornly. "One may still hope for the triumph of reason over paranoia. We've still got two months until Lammas. A lot can happen in two months. If it comes down to the wire, we really only need a week or ten days' lead time. I'll help you all I can, Gray."

"I know you will. It isn't that."

With a grimace of resignation, he glanced at the door, then back at her.

"We've gone over all of this before. I really do have to go. Your very weary son should be at Dover in a few hours, and if Denny and I aren't there to meet him right off the ship, God knows how we'll find him."

"I'm sorry. I didn't mean to keep you." She paused, her face still a little strained. "He *is* all right, isn't he? You weren't just saying he was, to reassure us worried womenfolk?"

He permitted himself a sigh. He had not wanted to tell Alix everything he saw, but he realized it was best if she heard it all now.

"He's definitely alive; I believe he may be wounded."

"Wounded? How badly?"

He shook his head. "I don't know. I'll ring you as soon as I find out. I don't think it's life threatening, but there was definitely an edge of pain. It could have been just fatigue. In any case, he should be at Dover by dawn—and so must I."

He took both her hands in his and kissed them, an intimate yet formal gesture to balance their uneasiness. Then he stood back a pace while she stooped to pick up a letter opener with a dark staghorn hilt. She touched its point to the edge of the rug, then drew it upward and to the left in a long arc above her head as she stood, sweeping parallel down the other side, perhaps a yard from the first tracing. The enclosed space appeared to grow darker as the blade touched the edge of the rug again, the door beyond no longer hazy.

She left the letter opener on the rug at her ending point, then straightened to lay her hands lightly on his upper arms.

"Bright blessing attend you," she whispered, stretching on tiptoes to brush his lips with a kiss.

He held her for a moment. Then he moved through the opening she had cut and headed for the door, casting her a final glance before he closed the heavy panel behind him.

But she was out of mind as soon as out of sight. He was already preoccupied as he walked down the dim-lit hallway and through the long portrait gallery, searching for Michael even now in the Dover of his mind's eye. He could feel the night's tension closing in, as it had not while he walked the

Second Road of mind and soul, and his eyes ached despite the dim light dictated by blackout regulations.

He glanced automatically at a favorite painting of an earlier Lord Selwyn doing homage to a fifteenth-century Henry. The earl's joined hands were clasped protectively between the king's, but for once, the almost mystical significance of the feudal relationship failed to move Graham, for he barely saw it. Apprehension had begun to worry at the edges of his mind as soon as he stepped outside the confines of the circle. Had something else gone awry with Michael?

The door at the end of the gallery opened into another hallway, then into a high-ceilinged entryway, also dimly lit. Denton, his driver and batman of nearly fifteen years, came to his feet immediately—a small, wiry man about Graham's age, wearing the chevrons and crown of a staff sergeant on his sleeve, scarlet staff aiguillette looped around one shoulder of his brown service uniform. Strapped around his waist was an automatic pistol in a gleaming leather holster; a second was tucked under one arm, the webbed belt wrapped neatly around.

"Is he safe, sir?" Denton asked.

"I think so, Denny. At least he's on a ship. Where's—"

Before he could finish the question, Jennings, the Selwyn butler, emerged from another hallway with Graham's jacket—a standard khaki battle-dress blouse such as any soldier might wear, were it not for the colonel's crown and pips on the shoulder straps.

"Thank you, Jennings," Graham murmured, shrugging into the jacket. "I take it I had no calls?"

"None, sir. Would you like a flask of tea to take along?"

Graham pulled a black beret with field insignia out of one pocket and jammed it on his head, taking his sidearm from Denton as they moved toward the door.

"Not tonight, I think—but I appreciate the offer. Just now I need sleep more than tea."

"Very good, sir. Safe journey, then. Remember about the blackout, and you'll want to mind the roadblocks at Ashford."

As the light went out and the door opened, Graham clapped the butler on the shoulder in a gesture of long-standing acquaintance and affection.

"Jennings, you're a mother hen!"

Then he and Denton dashed into the rain, Denton opening

the rear door of the Bentley saloon so Graham could duck inside. Settling back in the red leather seat, Graham put aside his weapon and closed his eyes as Denton came around to the driver's side. What was it, nagging at the fringes of consciousness?

"Back to Dover Ops, sir?"

His eyes popped open with a start. He *was* jumpy.

"That's right, Denny. And if you can help it, don't wake me until we get there. We've got a busy day ahead of us. I hope you got a nap."

He sensed rather than saw Denton's grin in the rear-view mirror; and the driver's "Right, sir" was mostly drowned out by the purr of the motor being eased into gear. By the time the black Bentley emerged from the long, oak-lined drive of the manor, Col. Sir John Graham had already settled into uneasy sleep.

CHAPTER 2

Aboard the H.M.S. *Grafton, 0200 hours, 29 May 1940*

DULL PAIN AND A CHANGE IN THE RHYTHM OF THE engines woke Michael. The ship wallowed a little as she slowed, and in that twilight moment between wakefulness and pain-drugged sleep, he wondered whether they were already nearing Dover. He dismissed the notion immediately as the klaxons sounded and the ship's speaker system bawled for battle stations.

Sitting up, he saw lights in the distant darkness: bright white beams stabbing through the drizzle, illuminating deep Channel swells. Members of the ship's crew and an increasing number of evacuees from the upper decks already lined the rails, some of them preparing to lower lines, nets, and lifeboats. As Michael lurched unsteadily to his feet and made his way nearer the side, he could make out several minesweepers and torpedo boats standing to and playing their lights over the water, picking out bobbing heads and bodies, an occasional life raft, and all too much debris and oil slick. The *Grafton* slowed again, keeping just enough headway to maintain steerage.

They stood to for nearly an hour, they and the crews of other ships picking up the pitifully few survivors and watching nervously for signs of new danger. More ships converged on the disaster scene, for it was squarely in the middle of the evacuation route.

No one knew precisely what had happened. As Michael helped spot, he heard one of the rescued victims babbling about

15

a German E-boat that suddenly appeared out of the mist and began firing. Another, who identified the doomed destroyer as the H.M.S. *Wakeful*, said she had sunk in less than a minute. She had left Dunkirk carrying nearly seven hundred men. Michael recalled how he had wished himself aboard an earlier, unknown destroyer as he waited to board the *Grafton* and shuddered as he realized it might have been the *Wakeful*.

All at once, a tremendous explosion split the darkness, and he was hurtled through the air, hitting the water hard, choking, trying to claw his way to the surface—trying to decide which way the surface *was*. The water was bitter cold, and his whole body shrieked with outrage. He wanted to breathe, needed to breathe, but he knew he must not until the last possible instant. He got his bearings and struck out for the surface, ignoring the protest of his wounded arm, and surfaced to the din of screaming and more explosions.

Sputtering and gasping, he twisted around and tried to see what had become of his ship. He found her, but she was in flames and already down by the stern, her whole aftersection gone. Men streamed onto the decks from below and leaped overboard, not even waiting for boats or rafts or life vests. There were swimmers and bodies in the water all around. He could only watch and tread water dazedly, one part of him numbly seeing to survival while another tried to puzzle out what had happened. Had they hit a mine—or was another German E-boat in their midst?

Suddenly, one of the rescuing minesweepers opened fire—and then the *Grafton*'s big guns spoke, though who was firing them, Michael had no idea. Nor could he decide on their target, though it seemed to be not far from where he struggled in the water. As more explosions shattered the air, the minesweeper turned her bows toward him and, all her guns blazing, began racing toward another, smaller vessel that had emerged from the smoke and flames behind him.

Another German E-boat?

He glanced around wildly, helplessly, for if an E-boat were loose in the middle of the flotilla, it could wreak immeasurable havoc on the heavily laden rescue ships—and had, judging by the condition of the *Grafton*. Of even more immediate personal concern was the minesweeper bearing down on him and half a dozen other men flailing in the water between her and her intended target—but no skipper would weigh those lives more heavily than the stopping of the enemy ship.

He managed to elude the churning propellers as the minesweeper passed close by, as did most of the men in his immediate vicinity, but too late he glimpsed the blue with the red and white on the flag the supposed E-boat flew—a British naval ensign, not the flag of the Third Reich. It was too late for the captain of the minesweeper as well, for she did not turn aside even when Michael began screaming impotently for her to veer off.

Horrified, his lips still moving in futile warning, he watched the men on the target vessel scatter like ants as the minesweeper bore down on them directly amidships, many of them leaping overboard as the two vessels met with a sickening crash and rending of metal and then a series of devastating explosions.

Then he was fighting for his own life as another swimmer latched onto his wounded shoulder and began babbling hysterically, threatening to drag them both down.

Dover, 0300 hours, 29 May 1940

Graham came to with a start as traffic slowed to a snail's pace just below Dover Castle, but it was not that which had awakened him. He had been dreaming about Michael—dark, vivid dreams, akin to what he had seen before on the Second Road, though he could not recall any details. Only a vague uneasiness persisted of something being not quite right, an echo of his earlier forebodings.

He considered trying to retrieve the dream, knowing he could have, under the right circumstances, but he was too far awake now and in too public a place for proper concentration. Denton was totally loyal and discreet, long aware of his superior's less than conventional methods of gaining information, but they were nearing the first of the sentry posts guarding the approach to Dover HQ.

Graham lowered his window as the car came to a stop, squinting as the guards flashed their shielded torches inside and caught the crown and pips on his shoulders. He tried to be patient while they compared his face with the photo and description on his identity card.

Though Graham was considered something of a renegade

in the army, he thought he might well reach general rank by the end of the war—if this thing with Alix did not blow up in his face. Intelligence officers were expected to be a little odd. A man awarded a Victoria Cross (V.C.) at twenty-two could be forgiven a few minor eccentricities, such as an aversion to proper uniforms and a preference for working alone. Twelve years after receiving the V.C., Graham had justified his superiors' sometimes dubious indulgence by earning a knighthood. The reasons were still too classified for the direct knowledge of any but a few very senior generals and a now-dead king—though stories did surface from time to time, most of them wild conjectures.

The Intelligence Service had proven an ideal refuge for a renegade, however. Military discipline and inflexibility, on the one hand, balanced with a large measure both of anonymity and very minimal close supervision. All of this was essential to the other type of work Graham did, generally quite surreptitiously and of the sort that never wound up in official reports. And since he always produced results, his methods were rarely questioned.

Still, Graham had to wonder how his superiors would react this time, were they to learn of the methods he used for the mission now coming to an end on the *Grafton*. Not that they were ever likely to learn the truth. Graham's most recent assignment provided ideal protective coloration for his unique talents. With the outbreak of war the previous year and at the recommendation of a high-ranking naval officer whose predelictions ran in similar directions, Graham had been named to head a special section of MI.6 investigating the use of the occult sciences in warfare—a function barely even tolerated, much less understood, by most of his superiors since they did not believe such things existed but pursued because they knew that Hitler believed. Besides, the Germans had their own department of dirty occult tricks, whether or not it was producing verifiable results. The point was that Hitler *thought* it was—and so Whitehall must have a similar section.

Of most immediate concern at the moment was astrology, though Graham's hand-picked little group gathered intelligence on other occult activities as well. Most of the senior intelligence staff no more believed in astrology than they believed in the rest of the occult, but at least they acknowledged the possible usefulness of astrological counteroffensives for psychological warfare, since Hitler was very much a believer. Michael's mission had to do with such a use.

But the notion that occult forces might be applied to prevent a German invasion would be considered patently absurd, even though the oral traditions of Graham's ancestors and others could cite strong historical arguments for their part in stopping the Spanish Armada, repelling "Old Boney," and even keeping off the German fleet during the Great War. Outside his official function and unknown to his professional staff, Graham was being asked to engineer a repeat of what had been done in Elizabethan and Napoleonic times.

And it must be done in secret, with utter confidentiality on the parts of all involved, because the old witchcraft statutes still on the books from the eighteenth century would make little distinction between what Graham and his people did in the name of their ancient tradition, for the protection of the realm, and what popular opinion tended to lump together as charlatanism, witchcraft, black magic, and satanism. There were vast distinctions, but Graham was loath to attempt reasoned explanations at a time when stories of Nazi black magical practices and atrocities were already too common.

Denton stopped the Bentley again outside the Constable's Gate, where guards once more inspected their identification and shone shielded torches inside the car. Distractedly, Graham drummed his finger tips against the arm rest as they continued into the castle precincts, for he was impatient now to reach the Ops Room and find out for certain about the *Grafton*. Though his ability on the Second Road was usually reliable, he did not like the hints of danger that had teased at his sleep.

But as they crawled past the few cars parked at the foot of the Constable's Tower, something less sinister caught his attention: a familiar-looking Rolls-Royce that had not been there the previous afternoon when they left for Oakwood. Was it possible that William was back at Dover?

"That Phantom II by the tower, Denny—isn't that Prince William's car?" he asked, craning his neck for a better look as Denton glanced in the rear-view mirror.

"It does look like it, sir. They didn't build too many like that. His aide said Monday that he might be back today if the evacuation was still going on."

"His aide?" Graham sat back in his seat with a vexed mutter. "I love the way staff always know our movements before we do."

"Sir?"

"Never mind, Denny. I was just being peevish. I haven't had my tea yet. Ignore me."

"Yes, sir," came the slightly amused reply.

Graham sighed and closed his eyes as the car inched along toward the headquarters car park, reminiscing with affection about the man who owned the Rolls—who, despite his rank, had always seemed almost like a younger, if occasionally exasperating, brother. There were many memories, some of them far too grim for a morning already ripe with the possibility of yet another disaster—for Prince William had worked the Intelligence Service with Graham when he was Michael's age—but the memory that surfaced now brought only a smile.

He grinned as he recalled a night not very many years before when he and the prince had escorted two young ladies on a lighthearted evening on the town and had not returned to the Palace until well past dawn. William's father had been waiting for them, silently fuming.

Both men had been less prudent then—and William retained a regrettable tendency to revert to his earlier playboy behavior with all too little provocation—but Graham, at least, had learned not to encourage frivolity in the King's youngest surviving son thereafter. It was all very well for William to endanger his life when on an active mission—the King had four other sons, after all—but woe be to anyone, relative or subject, who led a member of the Royal Family into public scandal!

Contemplation of scandal brought Graham back to William, so often on the brink of trouble, and he found himself wondering, not for the first time, whether William would be scandalized, were he to learn of the rather unorthodox methods in use to track Michael tonight. Of course, the prince was aware of the official and theoretical scope of Graham's section, as was anyone with even minimal intelligence connections who cared to ask. But he did not think William took it any more seriously than anyone else other than for its pure propaganda value.

Especially with the prince, that suited Graham very well. Even in his early years with the Service, Graham had been careful to cultivate the impression that his interest in and knowledge of such subjects as astrology and so-called psychic phenomena had arisen from a childhood fascination and preoccupation with parlor tricks and stage magic. Skill in sleight of hand, for example, was not without its usefulness for an undercover agent. It was also amusing at government receptions.

This reputation had not hurt Graham when the time came to form the section he now headed or when William asked the occasional too-perceptive question. The prince had shown a passing interest in Graham's "magical" skills and was fascinated by the way Graham's section seemed to be approaching their part of the war effort, but Graham was not convinced that William believed any of it was real. The lack left a gap in an otherwise intimate friendship that had built up over the years. But if Graham's own legal status vis-à-vis the occult was shaky because of archaic laws still on the books, then William's could only be described as precarious, were he ever to become involved. Far better for him never to know, though his royal line certainly had been no strangers to the Old Ways in centuries past—far past, as Graham sometimes had to remind himself.

He opened his eyes with a start and realized that Denton had eased the Bentley into its customary parking space and turned off the motor. The drizzle had turned to a heavier shower, pinging loudly on the roof and the wetly glistening pavement. The weather lent an eeriness and sense of isolation to the very air, increasing the feeling of imminent disaster that had been building since Graham woke.

Then a ship hooted somewhere in the harbor below, and the mood was broken. A guard coughed noisily in the shadows not far away as someone came out of the building, and somewhere in the greyness a door slammed. Graham yawned and tried to ease the tension out of his body as he began buckling on his sidearm— a reflex concession to the awareness that this was wartime and he would have to keep up some pretense of military bearing inside Naval Headquarters. A weary-looking Denton turned in the front seat to glance back at him as he struggled into his mac.

"Shall I wait here or come along, sir?" Denton asked.

"Why don't you catch a few winks, Denny? No sense both of us getting wet. As soon as I find out about his ship, we'll have to go down to the harbor, anyway."

"Right, sir."

Within minutes, Graham was making his way down to the level of the Dynamo Room, pausing several times to flash his identity card at the Royal Marines on duty. As he threaded his way through the honeycomb of smaller tunnels and galleries, nearing the nerve center of the operation, he gradually became aware of the increasing level of noise: telephones jangling, voices, the occasional harsh rasp of a priority buzzer.

The sounds washed over him in an almost physical sensation, grating on already taut nerves as he entered the gallery doorway and excused his way past two WRNS ratings consulting over a handful of signal flimsies. The room was full of navy and khaki uniforms, chaotic sound, the dim spark of lights—red and green and amber—on the status boards that loomed around the perimeter. The acrid bite of cigarette and cigar smoke and the ozone sharpness of too much electrical equipment in the crowded space added to the Dante-esque impression of purgatory.

With a deep breath, he hauled himself up by the psychic bootstraps and headed toward the huge plotting table in the center of the room, where junior officers and ratings of the Women's Royal Naval Service and the Women's Auxiliary Air Force— WRNS and WAAF—pushed battle and ship markers around the map like so many solemn croupiers. Banks of telephones and wireless positions lined the room, aides shuttling the incoming information to the plotters. Graham had been in this room at least a dozen times in the past week and still marveled that they could make any sense of it.

He scanned the plotting table briefly, but it soon became apparent that he would gain little of the specific information he needed from such an overall picture. The table's map was geared to troop positions on land and the location of convoys in the Channel, not to individual ships. The ships themselves were tallied on a series of boards around the room, but he had no idea where to begin looking for the status of any particular vessel.

After a moment of fruitless perusal of the nearest board, he found a staff sergeant he recognized from briefings with the admiral, working at one of the wireless positions. The ruddy Scot's face was haggard and even a little pale, as if he had not slept recently or long enough in the past few days. When he looked up, as Graham unbuttoned his mac in the closeness of the room, it took a few seconds for the identity to register.

"Sir John," the man acknowledged, easing his headset off the ear nearest Graham and making a notation on the clipboard in front of him. "Anything I can help you with, sir?"

"I hope so, sergeant. I need information on a destroyer, the *Grafton*. Can you tell me when she's due in?"

The man riffled quickly through the sheaf of flimsies on his clipboard, pausing several times to listen to his headset and make more hurried notations, to acknowledge, or to murmur a few words of instruction. He shook his head as he looked up again.

"I'm afraid I can't tell you much, sir. She took on fuel yesterday around noon, but I have nothing for her in the past twelve hours." He swiveled in his chair to point across the room with a well-chewed pencil. "Why don't you check with Sergeant Matthews, down the line, sir? I think he's monitoring sea traffic. If something's happened, he should be able to tell you."

As Graham murmured his thanks, the sergeant was already speaking to one of the tugs out in the harbor. Increasingly apprehensive, Graham made his way to the side of the indicated operator, who, as harried looking as his colleague, pushed his headset slightly from one ear and looked up briefly over the top of his glasses, though his hand continued to jot down information.

"Sir?"

"I'm trying to locate the *Grafton*. Do you have an E.T.A.?"

"*Grafton?*" The man grimaced and glanced at the plot board over his shoulder to the right, thumbed a switch and spoke quietly into his microphone, then turned back to Graham as he listened to the response.

"Sorry, colonel. I wanted to be sure I had the latest information. *Grafton* took a couple of torpedoes out near the Kwinte Buoy between two and three this morning. Several other ships are steaming toward the area to assist, but we don't know the extent of damage or losses yet."

"Bloody hell, I was afraid of something like that!" Graham swore under his breath. "Did she sink?" he asked, half afraid that this, too, would be confirmed.

Matthews shook his head. "Not yet, sir. We've lost several ships in that area during the night, but at last report she was still afloat. Until we have some light to work with, though, I'm afraid I can't give you anything more definite."

"I see. How long until we know, then?"

"Several hours, anyway, sir. It's close to five now, coming dawn. But it could be—oh, ten or eleven before any survivors start coming in."

Shaking his head, Graham thanked the man and turned to search the room for someone else who might have more information. Merle Collingwood, one of the naval commanders on Ramsay's staff who had come over to the central plotting table while Graham questioned the two wireless operators, was sipping a cup of tea as he studied the blue line of the Dunkirk coastline. He gave a vague salute with his cup—the gesture of a man who is tired almost beyond functioning—as Graham approached.

"Morning, colonel. You look almost as grim as I feel. Tea?"

"Thank you, no. I don't suppose you can give me any more details on the *Grafton*?"

"*Grafton*." Collingwood sighed and shook his head, looking possibly more dejected than before. "Christ, you don't believe in asking the easy ones, do you? If you know she was hit, you probably know as much as I do already. There's something about one of our own ships firing on another, but it's too soon for details on that yet." He hesitated a beat at Graham's dour expression. "Any particular reason you're asking?"

"A very particular one."

"But you can't talk about it."

"Sorry."

Collingwood shrugged. "No need to apologize to me, Gray. I wouldn't trade places with you intelligence chaps for all the commissions in the Royal Navy."

"Smart man."

Graham glanced at his watch, one hand rubbing at the stubble on his jaw as he considered his next move.

Five to six hours before there was word. He would go mad if he had to spend them waiting in this room. Even less appealing was the thought of waiting in the crush and confusion by Admiralty Pier, where the evacuees were off-loading down in the harbor. The mere psychic din of that much pain and battle shock in such close proximity for so long would addle his Sight for hours, perhaps even days.

Then he remembered the Rolls-Royce parked at the front of the Constable's Tower and the man who owned it. He would wait with William. The prince knew that Graham had been monitoring the progress of an important mission for the past week even if the identity of the agent had never been revealed. He would be delighted to be in on the mission's hopefully successful conclusion. Besides that, the prince could use some reassurance that what he was doing was useful; the past few years had included far too little of that kind of reinforcement.

"Listen, Coll, are you going to be on duty for a while?" Graham asked, looking up at his friend again.

"Through the morning, unless the boss pulls me for something else."

"Good. Could you ring me at the Constable's Tower as soon as you have anything firm on the *Grafton*?"

"Will do."

"Thank you. Also, if any calls should come through for me, can you patch them through as well?" he added, thinking of Audrey and the rest at Oakwood.

"Of course. I'll brief the operators at once."

Graham made his way back through the maze of Naval Headquarters and into the open air without further incident, but he was still uneasy as he collected Denton and walked briskly along the pedestrian path toward the tower, collar upturned against the mist.

The significance of his dream was clearer now, though he still could not recapture any details. His instincts had been right all along; something *had* gone wrong. While he slept, he must have picked up something of the confusion and turmoil surrounding the attack on the *Grafton* and perhaps some of Michael's fear, the brief touch triggered by the earlier psychic contact. Now he longed to go back on the Second Road and try for a more solid contact. Audrey would still be monitoring, of course, but Graham was not certain she could hold onto something this chaotic.

He knew he was foolish even to be considering such a thing. But despite the danger, he found himself examining the terrain in the shadows ahead and looking for a place that was sufficiently sheltered for him to make a quick foray. The matter was becoming urgent, and he dared not do anything of this sort once he reached the tower. The last thing he needed was William asking awkward questions. He did not want to even think

about what he would do if Michael were dead or had lost what
he had been sent for.

"I need a few minutes of privacy, Denny," he murmured,
touching the man's sleeve lightly and nodding toward the shadows beneath a small footbridge to their left. "See that I'm not
disturbed, all right?"

As Denton grunted agreement, Graham headed off into the
darkness, singling out a particularly dense patch of shadow
next to one of the timber bridge supports. He leaned his back
against it and stood there listening for several seconds, hands
slipped inside the pockets of his mac for warmth, then locked
his knees and closed his eyes, consciously drawing a slow,
steadying breath. As he settled into a comfortable level of
trance, he began to visualize himself within a ring of darkly
flickering light.

He knew he should not be doing this. Alix would be furious
if she found out. If the slightest thing went wrong, alone and
outside the bounds of a formal protecting circle, he knew that
the best he could hope for was a blinding headache. He might
also endanger his thus-far meticulous cover if, despite Denton's
efforts, someone came upon him like this—and those were the
more pleasant alternatives. At worst—

He did not even want to think about the worst. The Second
Road was neutral; it did not lead only toward the light. There
were others just as adept as he, and even more adept, who
walked other paths altogether. Hitler himself was said to be an
initiate of one such black tradition that had spawned much of
the racist aspect of Nazi doctrine. Furthermore, Graham's research had uncovered hints that a very powerful black adept
might be actively supporting Hitler—which was one of the
reasons Michael had been sent into Germany a week before.

Michael. . . . He fastened on the image of Alix and David's
younger son and let his Sight go out along the Second Road
again, questing now for the *Grafton* and her six hundred souls,
seeking some hint of their fate.

Michael—slender and sandy-haired and just about the same
age as his own son. Michael—cold and hurting, numbed limbs
flailing in the icy waters of the Channel, chilled in heart as
well as body by the company of corpses floating near him,
though some stirred feebly. . . . Michael—

* * *

Squinting in the glare of a searchlight, Michael raised an arm yet again and prayed that they had spotted him—and that an E-boat or submarine would not. His voice was hoarse from earlier screaming, but he managed a few harsh croaks as he let go of the spar to which he had been clinging and waved his arms again, splashing for all he was worth. This time he was sure they had seen.

His leg throbbed even more than his arm as they hauled him aboard; he had nearly crushed it against a capsized lifeboat earlier when he tried to free a man who was tangled in debris. The man had drowned, anyway. He did not think the leg was broken, but it hurt incredibly as they brought him aboard and wrapped him in blankets and the cold began to recede. Hours seemed to pass before someone came to look at his injuries.

They rebandaged his arm and pronounced his leg probably unbroken, but the pain of both had him almost gasping by now, all the worse for having been held at bay by sheer force of will during the hours in the water. Though he had begun shaking so badly that he nearly bit his tongue, he tried to refuse the painkiller they offered, for he feared to sleep and perhaps have them take away the precious pouch on his belt. He hoped the water had not ruined the contents.

He never felt the needle in his arm—only the slow, drowsy, blessed warmth of morphine creeping over the pain and muffling everything. He dreamed just before he went under, and the dream momentarily shifted into nightmare.

Dark shapes robed in black—masks covering eyes—a black-clothed arm descending, bright blade flashing—and blood welling up, spurting, spraying, spattering—

The nightmare caught Graham by surprise, for he had not even been certain it was Michael he was brushing with his Sight. Just as he tried to pull back from what had been a hazy connection at best, he found himself hurtling along the Second Road and, with a jolt, being dropped into awareness of an altogether different place. It had been triggered by Michael's nightmare, but no trace of Michael intruded here.

Suddenly, he seemed to be hovering outside a dark semi-circle of men in cowled black robes—though he sensed instinctively that these were no benign monks or even white magicians. Beyond an oddly shifting shimmer of not-quite-light, he could barely make out high ceilings, and red, black, and white banners, the folds stirring in unfelt breezes by the light of torches set along the walls. Fat black candles guttered to either side of where he seemed to be.

All at once, a black-robed figure pushed between the others to peer in his direction, the scarred face masked across the eyes. A hand emerged from a voluminous sleeve, pointing a double-edged blade directly at him.

Graham snapped back into his body with a speed that left him queasy and weak-kneed. Clutching at the bridge support to keep from collapsing into the mud, he still caught a backlash that left him gasping. For what seemed like several lifetimes, he could only concentrate on breathing, on slowing his pounding heart, on keeping his mind wiped clean of any telltale ripple that might identify him to the entity that still searched, very near on the Second Road—though physically he knew it was miles away.

Eventually, he became aware that he had shaken off whatever had threatened him and began to breathe a little easier. Other than having reassured himself that Michael himself was still alive, he had no idea just what he had touched. By the time he stood away from the bridge and began making his careful way back to Denton, only memory and the vague throbbing behind his eyes reminded him that something had, indeed, happened. He did not want to think about what it was. Something very horrifying.

And far across the Channel, in a chamber dug deep beneath a castle in the Rhineland, a masked man in cowled robes eased back into the midst of his colleagues and scanned the torch-lit stillness yet again, his gaze narrowing as he searched each taut, apprehensive face turned to his.

"Zeigen Sie mir die Gesichten!" he ordered, though he hardly raised his voice above a whisper.

Instantly, the others removed their masks, standing stonily while he scanned each face anew.

"Was war das?" he murmured then. *"Hatte jemand etwas neben dem Kreis gesehen?"*

No one spoke. No one moved. After another moment's further reflection and more suspicious scrutiny of the men around him, the man in the mask nodded slowly and then gestured with a curt wave of his blade for the others to replace their masks.

A few moments he allowed for everyone to settle again, to gravitate a little closer. Only then did he return his attention to the center of the circle.

Nordic runes flashed in the candlelight as he laid his blade against the upturned throat of a man tied naked and spread-eagled across a rough black altar stone.

CHAPTER 3

*Constable's Tower, Dover Castle,
0530 hours, 29 May 1940*

Graham gave his name to an orderly on duty downstairs, with instructions to forward any calls, then left his mac and sidearm with Denton and headed up to the royal quarters. Wells, the perpetually intense young naval lieutenant who served as William's secretary and aide, met him at the door. The man sitting with the grey dawn at his back turned and rose as Graham and Wells entered the room, his face a blur against the rain-smeared windowpanes.

"Sir," Wells said, "Colonel Sir John Graham is here."

"Why, Gray, what a welcome surprise," said the familiar voice. "Good morning."

"Good morning, sir."

Graham paused to incline his head with proper formality before continuing on toward the light, for Wells was still in earshot. But as soon as the door closed behind him, Graham was met by the always-unexpected warmth of the royal handshake and the bright Windsor smile.

"Good gracious, you look like you could use a cup of tea," his host observed, leading him back toward the table in casual fashion and gesturing toward a chair. "Had a rough night, have you? Not that I look a great deal better, I suppose, but—sit down, sit down. I'll be mother, and you can tell me all about it when you're ready."

As they sat and the fine, agile hands splashed milk into a

china cup and added sugar, pouring strong black tea from a pot engraved with the arms of a former constable of the castle, Graham sighed and let himself slump a little in the chair, appreciating William's discretion. He shaded his eyes against the oddly glaring greyness of the window beyond as cup and saucer were passed across the table, but only as the first cautious swallow trickled down his throat, hot and soothing, did he realize how shaken he still was. He wondered whether it really showed that much or if William had simply been making conversation.

Nor, on closer inspection, did the prince himself look much better for wear, though that fact might have escaped anyone who knew him less well than Graham. Prince William Victor Charles Arthur, Duke of Clarence, K.G., K.C.M.G., and a host of other suitable alphabet soup, was ordinarily a man bursting with vibrant life—perhaps the most energetic of all the royal brothers in a family known for its love of physical activity. An even six feet tall, slender like his brothers but fairer, bright far beyond the necessity of his royal station, this youngest living son of King George V had long ago mastered the royal art of masking his true emotions. Despite that, he looked tired this morning.

At least the cause was likely of an honest sort, Graham reflected, unlike the occasional hints of dissipation in his youth. William had been somewhat frail as a child. An epileptic twin brother had died before their fourteenth birthday, and the resultant coddling of the surviving boy by family, nannies, and tutors had produced a somewhat spoiled young man. Improved health enabled him to enter the Royal Naval College at the expected age, like several of his elder brothers, but Graham knew that the prince's pranks might have gotten a man of less exalted rank quietly written out of the service. Graham had seen the records when William was posted to his section on graduation.

That posting—not entirely a chance occurrence, Graham often suspected—had begun a wary and often exasperating first year for both of them, tempered only by the fact that the two men had taken an instant liking to one another. Graham, only seven years William's senior and by then a rising young major of army intelligence, was ordered to treat his new agent exactly like all the others—so William began by performing all the routine and often boring tasks expected of any young naval lieutenant on his first assignment: copying and filing countless reports for more senior agents; processing mountains of paperwork that made little sense to his inexperienced eyes; occasionally acting as a courier; and, very rarely, working as part of a surveillance team or helping collect an operative from some rendezvous point—so long as it was not too dangerous. Officially, the only impact of his presence felt by MI.6 was that as a member of the Royal Family, he must be sheltered from excessive physical danger and, of course, scandal—even if he was fifth in line for the throne and very unlikely ever to inherit. Unofficially, it is probable that Graham's superiors expected little more of their royal intelligence officer than to serve his time in rank as innocuously as possible until duty called him to more conventional royal obligations.

Such an attitude very shortly began to trouble Graham, however, though he knew better than to defy department policy directly. The more he came to know the prince, the more he became convinced that William was a rare commodity and far too intelligent to waste merely occupying desk space. After an initial breaking-in period during which both of them did a certain amount of testing, Graham began to bear down with increasing pressure, pulling military rank unmercifully and sometimes even bullying to get William to apply himself to his full potential. Over the next few years, an increasingly interested and competent "Lieutenant Victor" took part in a variety of specialized missions with Graham—each one more challenging than the last and some of them far more dangerous than his father or elder brothers would have approved, had they known. William shrugged off the dangers at first, reminding Graham that he was a fifth prince and therefore expendable, but the underlying bitterness in that remark gradually decreased as his faith in himself grew.

By the time William's family became aware of the true scope of his activities, *Commander* Victor had been working closely with Graham for over two years on a project that came to have profound implications for national security. It earned Graham his knighthood almost immediately, but the prince's part remained deeply buried—though eventually, he, too, was admitted to a second order of knighthood. It came as a part of his brother's coronation honors, and in conjunction with his creation as Duke of Clarence on the eve of his planned marriage; but the well-deserved recognition paled when a fatal car crash claimed the new duke's bride-to-be before they could be wed.

This new disaster, following within six months of his eldest brother's abdication—in itself a staggering blow to the adoring William—shook the youngest royal duke almost beyond enduring, canceling out much of the progress he had made in the recent years. Following a near breakdown that left him desolate and uncommunicative, he plunged into the mindless solace of hard work, spending the next year in a whirl of royal appearances, patronages, and unfortunately, a return to the irresponsible ways of his youth, ever on the brink of scandal.

Gradually, he emerged from his depression and modified his behavior. But when he had recovered, His Royal Highness *Captain* The Duke of Clarence found himself no longer permitted to participate in the all too dangerous and sensitive area of intelligence operations—the very work that might have given him purpose and the stability he so desperately needed. The prohibition, from higher than either he or Graham could appeal, had been liked by neither of them, but it had been obeyed. It did not curtail the friendship that had begun under such improbable circumstances so long before and had grown so in the intervening years.

Now Prince William, lost in thought, sat in the brightening Kentish gloom idly smoking a cigarette, almost ordinary looking in the service dress uniform of a Royal Navy captain. He wore only the ribbons of his decorations, as was customary in wartime; only those and the four cuff rings of his earned rank set him apart from any other naval officer. The white shirt under the uniform coat was immaculate, as usual, but the knot of his tie was loosened and slightly askew, and the fair hair needed a comb. Graham wondered whether the prince had slept at all the previous night.

"I needed this," Graham said quietly, savoring another mouthful of the strong, sweet tea and sighing gratefully. "If you never learned anything else while you worked for me, you certainly learned how to appreciate a proper cup of tea. When did you get back?"

William flashed a quick, distracted smile and exhaled smoke as he flicked his cigarette over a silver ash tray.

"Is that all you think I learned?"

"A bit more than that," Graham conceded with an answering smile.

The prince chuckled mirthlessly and inspected the end of the cigarette in his hand.

"I got back last night," he said. "Bertie continues to be amazed that we're still getting men out of Dunkirk, so he asked that I continue my blow-by-blow report from the harbor." He shrugged. "I had nothing better to do."

As the prince turned his head to gaze out the window again, taking another slow, deliberate drag on his cigarette, Graham had to fight down a dual pull of pity and admiration, as he had so often in the past three years. While he sipped his tea, he let the taste take him back to the days before disaster: strong, acidic tea at the harried morning briefings in the old office in Whitehall; the more tranquil tastes of coffee and cognac before the fireplace in William's apartments at the Palace; champagne the night the prince told Graham of his engagement to the shy, demure Caroline-Marie; and, a few months later, neat whiskey—far too much of it—and holding the prince while he wept like a child at the news of her death, grieving with him.

Other memories, less fraught with tragedy: minor explosions of temper in their early days, when William had rebelled against the discipline of Graham's training; apologies, gradually less grudging, when Graham's patience did not snap and William discovered that Graham would not permit him any effort that was not his best, no matter how simple the task; the growing sense of mutual respect and camaraderie, and then friendship.

Long arguments, talks, discussions, both light and serious, sometimes from horseback at Windsor or at one of the other royal estates. And the first time, though not the last, that William's life had truly been in danger and Graham had been responsible.

It had begun as a routine mission. They almost always did. William, who had only been on a few very tame field assignments, was one of four operatives chosen to go with Graham by fast torpedo boat to pick up an agent off the French coast. When the agent did not show, Graham and two of the other men had gone ashore.

An ambush had been waiting. Killing one man and slightly wounding Graham, snipers had pinned down Graham and the remaining agent with automatic weapons fire. Strictly against orders, William slipped ashore to cover Graham and the other survivor as they struggled back to the boat. Once they were all safe, a trembling Graham had sworn both his remaining men to silence and given William a private tongue-lashing that neither of them soon forgot. William had not disobeyed orders again.

The boat and the thought of wounded agents brought Graham back to Michael and the events of the past few hours. He did not think he had changed expression, but something must have shown because William suddenly glanced at him sidelong and raised a speculative eyebrow.

"So, is this purely a social visit, at this hour of the morning, or can I help *you* for a change?" he asked, breathing smoke ceilingward as he stubbed out his cigarette. "You don't have to tell me about it if you don't want to—I'll give you the same option you've always given me—but you've got a ready ear if you want one."

Graham sighed and set aside his tea. He had come here for company while he awaited word on Michael. That need had not changed. But he also needed to understand the new nightmare—wishing that were all it were. Perhaps it was only the figment of an overtaxed, overtired imagination, though he feared not. If only his eyes did not ache so.

Lack of sleep, he told himself, though a part of him knew otherwise.

"You know Leo, that agent I've been tracking for the past week?" he said, massaging the bridge of his nose between thumb and forefinger as he sat back in his chair. "Well, his ship was torpedoed a few hours ago. Ah—Leo is Michael Jordan."

"Michael?" A grieved look flashed across the prince's face. "Oh, bloody hell! Are you sure?"

Graham nodded. "We're sure about the ship. We're reasonably sure that Michael was aboard. The hopeful news is that the ship was still afloat as of a few hours ago. That's about all I know. They'll have started intensive rescue operations with first light."

Numbly, he watched William rise and begin pacing in front of the seaward window, restless fingers twisting a gold signet ring on his left hand. After several passes, the prince paused and gazed out to sea. For several seconds, both of them watched the silent parade of ghost ships gliding out of the mist toward safe harbor between the arms of the breakwater. In the stillness, they could faintly hear the thud of shelling thirty miles away and the occasional closer whoop of a destroyer overtaking slower ships.

"You never told me what the Leo mission was all about," William said after a long silence. "Do you think he'd succeeded before all of this happened?"

Graham tried to make his shrug convincingly noncommittal, for while most of the mission itself could be discussed freely with the prince, some of the methods could not. He also dared not indicate that he knew for certain Michael was still alive— or had been half an hour ago.

"We have good indications that he had."

"And if he doesn't come back?"

Graham sighed. "If he doesn't come back, we'll have to find another suitable agent and start all over again. Some of the information is—very sensitive," he added, wondering where he *would* find another suitable agent to handle some of the material he hoped Michael was carrying.

"Bloody war," the prince said, shaking his head dejectedly as he leaned both hands against the back of his chair. "Didn't you already lose a plane and a crew?"

"And a wireless operator and a courier," Graham added. "They'll all be very difficult to replace."

"To replace? How does one really *replace* human lives? And now Michael. . . ."

The prince sighed as he turned to lean an elbow against the side of a window casement, absently brushing a strand of fair hair off his forehead as he continued to stare out at the ships.

"I'm sorry, Gray. I know you didn't come here to listen to me echoing all your own worry. Maybe he's all right. I'm no good at waiting, though. Waiting isn't standard in a prince's training—unless, of course, he's the Prince of Wales." He glanced at the toes of immaculately polished shoes. "I suppose my brother would have known how to do that, at least."

Graham had no words to answer that, for he knew, perhaps better than anyone else, how the abdication more than three years ago had wounded this youngest royal brother, who would never wear the crown. That crown had its burdens, as the new King was discovering and the former King had realized all too well. What Edward VIII had never grasped was the fulfillment that could also come from exercising a sacred trust and duty whose beginnings stretched back beyond recorded English history. Modern Britain no longer gave more than lip service to the "divine right" of kings, but remnants of that mystical concept remained, nonetheless, in the peculiar reverence and affection in which Britain had almost always held its Royal Family. William, a descendant of that royal line and a student of history, could not but feel the tragedy of his brother's dilemma acutely, as had all of England.

Graham was saved from having to answer by the appearance of Wells in the doorway of the next room, one hand over a telephone receiver.

"Beg pardon, sir," he said as William turned. "I have a call for Colonel Graham, patched through from Operations. It's a Brigadier Ellis."

Instantly, Graham was on his feet and moving to take it, not pausing to ask the prince's permission, even in front of Wells. He could feel his pulse racing as he nearly snatched the phone from the aide and clapped it to his ear. William had been right on his heels, waiting eagerly as Graham spoke.

"Graham here."

"Gray, this is Wesley Ellis," came the familiar voice, couched in an odd combination of formality and casual friendship— doubtless for the benefit of anyone listening in. "I believe I have some information on that landing you wanted."

"I understand, brigadier. Go ahead." Had Audrey picked up some further hint of Michael's whereabouts?

"There's been a change of plan," the brigadier continued in a maddeningly offhand tone. "I think you'll want to meet a minesweeper called the *Lydd*. That's *L-Y-double-D*. Have you got that?"

"*Lydd*. Yes, sir!" Graham grinned and turned toward William, raising one thumb in the classic cockney sign of cheer.

"Jolly good," came the glib reply. "I'm afraid there's been a bit of damage, but nothing that can't be mended. I think you'll find that it meets all your needs—picture perfect, as it were. Was there anything else I can do for you?"

Damage but mendable—and picture perfect. It meant that Michael was not seriously injured and that he had the film. Bless Audrey! She'd done a better job than he had—though he wondered whether she had picked up any of the frightening imagery he'd experienced. To find out, however, he was going to have to own up to having been on the Second Road alone and take hell from Alix. He could hardly do that now, with William waiting at his elbow, but he could at least give Ellis the opening to indicate whether anything else *had* gone amiss.

"I can't think of a thing, brigadier," he replied, still smiling, though not quite so broadly. "I'll get back to you if I do. Everything else is all right, then?"

"Yes, quite," came the slightly puzzled reply.

"That's welcome news—and thank you very much," Graham said, breathing a faint sigh of relief.

"Not at all. Glad to be of service. We old war horses like to keep our hands in, you know. Cheerio."

"Good-bye, sir."

He allowed himself a profound sigh as he cradled the receiver, suddenly very weary, then picked it up and began dialing the operations number.

"The pickup ship is the *Lydd*?" William asked.

"So it would seem."

"How did Ellis find out?"

Graham raised an eyebrow and evaded with the absolute truth.

"I don't ask. Sometimes it's better not to—hello? This is Colonel Graham. Put me through to Commander Collingwood right away, would you?"

Covering the mouthpiece with his hand while he waited, he glanced at the prince again and smiled. "I was about to say that I don't question Wesley's sources of infor—hello, Coll? Graham here. I've just been informed that my chap may be aboard a minesweeper called the *Lydd*. Would you find out when she's due to dock?"

As he spelled the name for Collingwood, he was relieved to see that William seemed to have accepted his explanation.

CHAPTER 4

NEITHER GRAHAM NOR WILLIAM PROVED VERY GOOD at waiting after the first hour, though they made halting stabs at conversation over fresh cups of tea while listening for the telephone. After another half hour, Graham gave up the pretense of sociability and occupied himself for a time with scanning the harbor and its approaches with a pair of field glasses.

It was not only the waiting that made Graham ill at ease. Compounding his uneasiness was the fact that even though no particular physical symptoms remained to remind him of the episode beneath the bridge, the experience had shaken him more than he realized. He still did not know what had happened—except that the terror he had felt was still vivid in his mind. Only questioning Michael would enable him to distinguish fact from fearful fantasy.

He sighed and raised the field glasses to his eyes again. Outside, the intermittent drizzle had mostly ceased since his arrival at the tower, but mist continued to draw a shifting grey curtain over everything but the harbor itself. From the breakwater, nearly two miles out, all the way to the vast, curving Admiralty Pier embracing the southern edge, the four-square-mile basin of Dover's port seethed with ghost-vague vessels of all sorts and sizes, military and civilian. Beyond the breakwater, only sometimes visible, the unflagging procession of ships coming to and from the port moved in a ceaseless, silent ballet. Very low, just at the threshold of hearing, the blasts of the big guns shelling Dunkirk rattled the windows with man-made thunder.

Closer in, pattern and planning became less apparent but no less efficient. Along Admiralty Pier, where Graham could never remember seeing more than six or eight cross-Channel steamers in peacetime, he now counted more than twenty vessels of various kinds, from destroyers and packet steamers to torpedo boats, fishing smacks, and minesweepers like the *Lydd*—some of them tied up two and three abreast when there was no other space. Arriving ships nosed up to the crowded piers only long enough to disgorge antlike masses of soldiers, who swarmed along the docks to be swallowed up by waiting trains and coaches and whisked away to safety. When the ships were empty, tugs nudged them out to an oil tanker moored in the center of the harbor to take on fuel for yet another run.

Collingwood finally rang back around eight to say that the *Lydd* was expected sometime after ten. Graham relaxed a little, and William seemed to take the news with his usual nonchalance.

But by nine, the renewed drizzle beating against the windowpanes became so oppressive that neither of them could bear to wait out the remaining hour there. Soon Wells was driving them down Castle Hill in the rear-seat splendor of the royal Rolls, gliding unchallenged past sentry posts and gradually into the port facility itself. The rumble of trains and the urgent din of the bells on departing ambulances mingled with the whistles and hoots of the tugs and the whooping of incoming destroyers, all of it overlaid by the murmur of massed human voices, surging and receding.

They had to wait for nearly ten minutes while a train laden with troops pulled out of the staging area close by the pier, and another backed into position from a siding. Another time, they gave way to a procession of ambulances. Beyond, a hospital train waited while teams of stretcher-bearers and other medical personnel efficiently guided the wounded and injured aboard at the far end.

Eventually, Wells eased them to within two hundred yards of the landward end of the pier and parked between two ambulances—as close as even a royal duke might get despite the assistance of the regimental sergeant-major of Guards, who had jumped up on their running board for escort when he recognized the car's chief occupant. Graham glanced at the prince with a roguish grin as Denton came to open his door.

"I fear we've brought the wrong car if you wanted to keep a low profile," he said as bystanders began to notice car and escort and cast surreptitious glances into the car's interior. "They aren't fooled by the uniform."

William shrugged and gave a casual wave and a smile to a pretty Red Cross volunteer who had done a startled double-take as she passed.

"Well, it worked better up at HQ, but I daresay you're right. Why don't I play prince for a while and inspire the troops while you and Denny see about the *Lydd*? No sense all four of us traipsing out to the pier, is there? I suspect my presence might be a liability in such close quarters."

With a chuckle, Graham stepped out into the drizzle and slammed the door, buttoning up his mac as he and Denton began making their way through the crowd, heading toward the pier. When he glanced back a minute later, William was shaking hands with an ambulance crew and chatting with the pretty volunteer, Wells at his heels.

Shaking his head, Graham smiled to himself and jogged a few steps to catch up with Denton. A pretty girl and the prince's resigned statement of duty had been convenient excuses, but ignoring his own comfort to mingle with the evacuation personnel and raise morale was quite in character for William. The prince was at his best when he was interacting with people, exercising the qualities of leadership for which he had been bred. It was part of what had made him such a first-rate agent. Wistfully, Graham considered what a king he would have made, had things been different.

But things were not different and not easy. At dock level, the turmoil and sheer scope of the harbor operation became even more apparent than they had been from Castle Hill. Here the sense of dismay was almost overpowering—for though the evacuation from Dunkirk was going very well, it could not alter the fact that the BEF had just suffered a resounding defeat. Only as Graham scanned the faces of the soldiers streaming past him, disembarking from a shell-scarred cruiser tied up at the end of the pier, did he begin to truly understand the enormity of what these men had just survived.

Some still clung to their weapons and other bits of equipment, but more often they appeared fortunate merely to have gotten *off* the distant beach. All of them were battle weary. Most wore looks of stunned resignation. Many were injured.

One man in tattered and salt-stained remnants of a battle-dress collapsed to his hands and knees and kissed the rain-slick boards of the dock before being helped to his feet by a tight-lipped comrade in arms. Another stumbled from the dock clutching a bullet-scarred helmet to his chest, tears streaming down his face.

Two others supported a third between them, who kept raving about bombs and drowning. Medics intercepted them and gently led the distraught man to one side, while his shipmates continued reluctantly toward the waiting train. A small party of fusiliers, identifiable only by the battered insignia on the cap of their sergeant, marched smartly off the pier and toward the waiting train as if they trooped the colours before their King, though only four of the seven still carried weapons, and one very young looking lance corporal appeared ready to burst into tears at any moment.

Men with minor injuries were shunted aside to first-aid stations for evaluation and treatment by Red Cross personnel. Stretcher-bearers and medical teams waited to take off the dead and badly wounded who were still aboard as soon as the ship cleared. Most of the men simply shuffled past in varying attitudes of numbness and fatigue, dejection gradually changing to guarded hope as army and navy personnel and civilian volunteers drew them toward hot tea and sandwiches before putting them on the trains and coaches queued up at the railhead.

Even in the greyed fog and drizzle, a constant bombing threat remained. The plan all along the coast, wherever troops were disembarking, was to disperse them quickly to hidden staging camps deep in England's heartlands, to rest, mend, and be reoutfitted for reorganizing the shattered British Army. Graham knew the theory—he had sat in on enough of the planning sessions—but only now was he seeing the practice firsthand.

Still slightly overwhelmed, he sent Denton on ahead to make inquiries while he continued to watch the disembarking troops. The man was gone quite a long time, but he was smiling when he reappeared at Graham's side.

"*Lydd* rounded the North Goodwin Light almost an hour ago, sir. That makes her less than an hour out if all goes well."

"Well, that's something, anyway," Graham replied. "Did you find out anything else?"

Denton shook his head. "Not much, sir. A communications officer said he thought she had some dead and wounded aboard, but that's all he knew—other than some wild rumor about *Lydd* having sunk one of our own ships."

"I'm afraid that rumor isn't so wild, Denny. I heard the same thing earlier this morning."

They had at least an hour more to wait, so Graham asked Denton to bring tea back to the car for everyone and went to find William. Damp and cold, the prince was quite ready to return to the car. They warmed their hands around cups of strong, bitter-tasting tea that Denton distributed with apologies, but Graham could not bear to sit still for very long. Soon he and Denton left for the sea wall to watch with field glasses again; William remained in the Rolls with his aide. It was well past ten o'clock before the *Lydd* finally made an appearance.

Graham swept the rails repeatedly with the glasses as the battered minesweeper eased through the harbor entrance, but he was not surprised that he could not spot Michael. The rails were jammed with faces, and Michael was but one of many. When the ship finally nosed into her allotted space and berthed, a few eager souls scrambled over the rails and leaped onto the dock without waiting for lines to be made fast and gangplanks set in place, but Michael was not among them. Ellis had said he was injured, so Graham did not expect him to be among the first to disembark.

But one look at the faces of the men now beginning to stream past was sufficient to convince Graham that they were going to have to watch very closely for their quarry. Handing off the glasses to Denton, he motioned him to a position on the opposite side of the pier so that Michael would have to pass between them.

These men were even more distraught than the others. All were weary beyond reckoning, many without sleep or adequate food for days. Exhausted before they even reached Dunkirk, their ordeal had been compounded by the long wait on the beach. The shelling, strafing, and bombing only added to the battle traumas already suffered.

And just when they thought themselves safe, death had sought more of them in the Channel. Many had spent long hours in the water before being picked up, watching their comrades suffering and dying around them. All things considered, Graham doubted there was a man among them fit for duty just then.

Michael certainly was not. When he finally appeared, limping heavily and with a bloodstained bandage around his left upper arm, he was almost unrecognizable. The brown eyes burned like coals in the sunburned face. The flaxen hair, plastered to his head, was stiff with salt, as was his ill-fitting uniform. He wore no unit or rank insignia, and he had somehow lost his boots.

"Michael?" Graham called, grabbing at his elbow as Michael walked right into him.

Staggering, Michael glanced up at him dazedly—at Denton approaching—then gave almost a sob and collapsed against Graham. He was a dead weight for just an instant as Graham tried to hold him, but then he got his feet under him with an effort and managed to stand. As Denton wedged a shoulder under one of his arms and helped support him, Graham withdrew enough to strip off his mac. Michael was shivering with cold as he turned dazed eyes on his chief.

"I don't know when I've ever been so glad to see someone," he whispered, his voice harsh and raw in the drizzle. "Who found me? How'd you know I was on the *Lydd*?"

"How do you think?" Graham muttered under his breath. "Here, have my mac. You're going to be lucky if you don't take pneumonia on top of everything else."

Michael started to protest, but Graham put the damp mac around his shoulders, anyway, as he and Denton began walking the exhausted man slowly back toward the car.

"You're just damned lucky we didn't rely on *my* contact," Graham continued in a low voice. "I'd located you on the *Grafton*, but by the time I got here, she'd been hit. I think it was Audrey who finally found you. Prince William and his aide are with us, by the way, so watch what you say. We've got his Rolls."

The prince and Wells had both gotten out of the car as the three approached. As Wells opened the back door on the left, William pulled off his warm naval greatcoat and put it around Michael, letting Denton take away the soggy mac.

"Don't argue, just get in the car," the prince murmured as Denton tossed the mac in the boot.

Michael obeyed meekly, almost collapsing as he slid across to the center of the back seat and wrapped up in the coat. Graham scrambled in after him, signaling Wells to start the motor as William went around and got in from the other side. The prince's faithful sergeant-major jumped onto the running board again to escort them as Wells backed the car gingerly into the flow of traffic.

"Get some of this in you and then tell me where you're hurt," Graham said, giving Michael the tepid cup of tea that Denton handed over the front seat. "Sorry it isn't very hot."

Michael was shaking as he gulped the first few swallows, eyes almost closed, but then he began to get hold of himself as he clutched the half-empty cup between his hands and his body warmed beneath the royal greatcoat. The car eased past the train, shedding their sergeant-major, then headed north in the direction of Castle Hill.

"I'll be all right," Michael finally said in a still-shaky voice. "I took some shrapnel in the arm—yesterday—I think it was—but it mostly just aches now. God, I'm cold!"

"How about your leg? You were limping rather badly."

"I don't think it's broken. Some wrenched muscles and bruising, maybe. I got it wedged in some debris trying to pull somebody out. He drowned, anyway."

"Has a medic seen you?" William asked.

Michael shook his head and gulped another swallow of tea. "Someone looked at me on the *Lydd*, but I think he was only a corpsman, sir. That's all a little hazy. There were so many others worse off. . . ." He lowered his eyes and stared into the cup dazedly, then whispered, "I think the worst part was the *Comfort*."

"The comfort?" Graham asked.

"A ship. She was one of ours." Michael drew a deep breath, his face mirroring the horror of the memory. "The *Lydd* sank her. They thought she was an E-boat, I suppose—the one that hit the *Grafton*—and they—they—"

He managed to swallow, his throat working painfully, and William rescued the precariously clutched cup and handed it back up to Denton.

"Gray, it was awful," Michael went on in a strained whisper.

"You could hear the men screaming from below decks as she went down. They didn't have a chance. . . ."

"Easy, son." Graham exchanged a glance with William over the bowed head. "There's nothing you could have done. It was their time. You'll feel better when you've rested. In the meantime, do you have something for me?"

With an obvious effort to pull himself together, Michael took a deep breath and nodded, fumbling in the pouch at his belt until he could withdraw three small metal canisters the size of spools of thread. He held them balanced in one palm and stared at them for a moment before tipping them into Graham's waiting hand.

"These cost a lot of lives," he whispered. "I hope they're worth it."

As Graham—all too aware of the cost—closed them in his fist, Michael swallowed noisily and ducked his head, burying his face in his good hand as his shoulders began to heave. Graham slipped an arm around his shoulders in compassion, wondering whether he dared use any of his more unusual techniques to ease him, but he was leery with William sitting on Michael's other side and Wells in the driver's seat.

"Why don't you try to get some sleep?" he suggested, hoping Michael was sufficiently in control to catch a double meaning.

But Michael only shook his head and murmured, "Can't," blindly weaving his head from side to side with eyes unfocused, reliving his own private nightmares of the past week.

As Wells worked their way back up Castle Hill, Graham considered pressing the issue of sleep, knowing he could even force it if he chose. The discipline developed between himself and the others of the Oakwood group could bypass Michael's conscious resistance and send him into pain-free slumber with a touch and a few well-chosen words.

But the effect could be dramatic, especially with Michael as subject, and this was hardly the place or the audience for involved explanations. Though Denton would never bat an eye, Graham would rather not raise possibly awkward questions on William's part; and Wells, less than a year in the prince's employ, was a wholly unknown factor and kept glancing all too unpredictably at their rescued passenger in his rear-view mirror. There remained also the matter of at least beginning a debriefing before Michael was whisked off for obviously much-needed medical attention.

By the time they pulled into the tower car park again, how-ever, a plan had jelled for dealing with all Graham's immediate concerns. Almost as soon as the car had stopped, he had his door open and was drawing Denton aside as Wells and the prince began helping Michael out.

"Denny, I hadn't counted on Michael being quite so bad off," he said in a low voice, pressing the three film canisters into the other's hand. "While I take care of him, I need you to have this film processed and see what we've got. There's a photography section somewhere in the Ops complex, isn't there?"

With a nod, Denton stashed the film in an inside tunic pocket. "Yes, sir, they've set up several temporary darkrooms. Shall I bother with prints for now or not?"

"Not yet. Just process the film and get back to me as soon as you can—and don't let it out of your sight."

"Right, sir."

"And ring London and tell Grumbaugh we may be looking at an all-nighter," Graham added. "If it's what I hope, we're going to be very busy for the next few days."

Denton raised a hand in acknowledgment as he jogged off toward the headquarters complex. Graham, with a sigh, joined Wells and the prince and helped get Michael upstairs. The young agent groaned, half fainting, as Graham and Wells eased him down on a couch. William headed directly for the tele-phone.

"I'll get a surgeon up here right away," the prince said, already dialing as Wells drew a blanket around their patient. "We probably should have let them see him down at the harbor. Do you think he's in shock?"

"Quite probably," Graham replied, sitting beside Michael and feeling for a pulse. "I've got to at least begin his debriefing while you hunt for somebody, though. It may be a while before I get another chance."

As Michael moaned and opened his eyes, tensing with the pain, Graham noticed for the first time that the pupils were pinpoint, though of the same size, and the gaze a little unfo-cused. Not a concussion, then, but a drug—probably mor-phine. That could certainly account for some colorful nightmares, though he doubted it was sufficient to explain what he had experienced on the Second Road.

"Just try to relax, Michael. We'll have a doctor for you soon. Mr. Wells, perhaps you'd be so good as to find us something to eat," he said over his shoulder as he turned Michael's face for a closer look at the eyes. "Tea and sandwiches would be fine, and maybe some hot soup. Michael, did they give you morphine on the ship?"

As Wells withdrew without a word and disappeared, hopefully for some time, Michael winced and turned his face away from the light.

"Sorry. I'm not remembering too clearly. I think they *did*, now that you mention it."

As Michael shifted position and bit back another groan, Graham glanced surreptitiously at the prince. William had withdrawn into the doorway of the next room with the telephone and was safely engaged, at least for the moment, fumbling in his pocket for a cigarette while he talked emphatically to someone. If Graham was going to ask Michael about the vision, it would have to be now.

"About what time do you think that was?" he asked softly. "Do you remember dreaming?"

Michael's eyes met his in dazed question, some of his pain put aside as he tried to read the reason for the query.

"Dreaming?"

"About a roomful of people in black robes," Graham prompted.

Michael's jaw gaped. "But that wasn't—the film! Dieter's film!"

His eyes went wild as his good hand scrabbled in the pouch at his waist and found nothing, and he started to speak. Alarmed lest the commotion draw William, Graham clamped one hand over Michael's mouth and grabbed his wrist with his other.

"It's all right," he murmured. "You already gave me the film. Don't you remember? And what's this about Dieter? I didn't know you'd seen him on this trip."

As he released Michael, the younger man sagged back into the cushions of the couch in relief.

"Dieter helped me get out of Germany after the pickup plane went down," Michael whispered, barely mouthing the words. "I didn't know who else to turn to. One of those rolls of film is from him. It's a negative—already processed. He's infiltrated a black lodge, Gray. He showed me other pictures. I've been having nightmares about them ever since."

"And that's what the morphine triggered?" Graham asked.

Michael nodded, shuddering as he squeezed his eyes shut. "I'll never forget that face as long as I live."

"A heavy-set man wearing black robes and a mask?" Graham ventured, painfully pulling the image from his own memory. "Perhaps with a saber scar on one cheek?"

Michael stared at him aghast. "That's him! How did you know? Did you link up with my nightmare?"

"A bit more than that, I'm afraid," Graham replied uneasily. "Is it possible that this lodge was working last night and that Dieter was with them?"

"Oh, God!" Michael breathed. "Yes. Yes it is." His eyes misted a little, and he blinked back unbidden tears. "He—he's had to do some terrible things to establish his credibility, Gray. They—took pictures. He said he'd put copies of some of them on the film. There's supposed to be a full report, too."

"Well, we'll see about that when Denny gets back with the film," Graham murmured.

He glanced over at William again. The prince was still on the telephone, but he seemed to be winding up his call. There was no time to go into further details with Michael just now—and perhaps the film would clarify the rest. Now Graham knew he had not imagined what he had seen and that the danger was very real. Provided he stayed away from unguarded forays onto the Second Road until he found out what he was up against, however, he should be safe enough. As for *Dieter....*

"You'd better try to get some sleep now," he said soberly, looking down at Michael again. "We'll talk more about this later."

Michael shook his head and struggled to sit, his eyes going wild with fear and pain as he grabbed both of Graham's wrists.

"No! If I sleep, I'll dream about it. Don't make me—please!"

Twisting one hand free, Graham clapped it to Michael's forehead, pressing him back onto the couch with hand and body. He had hoped to put Michael quietly to sleep, but the boy's fear was too wrapped up with exhaustion now, edging on hysteria, near to blurting out things best unsaid with William only yards away.

"Go to sleep, Michael," he commanded softly but with all the power he could summon. "Close your eyes and take a nice, deep breath—and let it out. Don't fight me. Let go of the pain and sleep—now!"

At Graham's very touch, Michael's whole body went rigid. But as Graham spoke, Michael closed trembling eyelids and went completely limp, all in a single, rasping sigh. Another breath and Graham could take his hand away.

But as Graham sat back and allowed himself a cautious sigh, he became aware of William standing directly behind him. It took a great deal of effort not to tense. If William had heard the part about the men in the black robes—

But, no—he could not have heard that and would not have understood it if he had. The most he could have seen and heard was Graham's induction—and that was simply hypnosis, though he must be careful to steer William away from thinking too much about how he and Michael happened to have that kind of bond. Such inquiries could touch all too close to the truth— and the truth, while undoubtedly fascinating to a man like William, was far too controversial for the involvement of royal dukes.

Feigning a lethargy he did not feel at all, Graham rose and stretched, only half covering an elaborate yawn as he turned and apparently noticed William's presence for the first time. The prince wore a puzzled expression, but he did not look apprehensive or hostile. With care, Graham was confident he could turn the inevitable questions in harmless directions.

"Oh, pardon me for yawning," he murmured, shaking his head behind his hand as he yawned again. "It's been a long past few days. Did you find us a surgeon?"

"Yes, I pulled rank and rousted the admiral's man. He should be here in fifteen or twenty minutes." The blue eyes were still faintly puzzled as he took a drag on his cigarette. "I don't suppose you'd care to tell me how you just did that?"

"Did what?"

"With Michael—you know. It looked like you—made him go to sleep."

"Oh, I did." Graham gestured casually toward the table by

the window. "Let's sit, shall we? We won't wake him just by talking."

Set a little off balance by Graham's nonchalance, William let himself be ushered back to their seats of earlier in the morning. Grey light glinted from the signet on his little finger as he flicked ash into the silver ash tray. He drew smoke deeply into his lungs and exhaled before glancing across at Graham again.

"Well?"

Graham gave him a wry smile and settled back in his chair, making a show of casually stretching his long legs out to the side and crossing them at the ankles. He intended to tell William the truth—there was something about the man that made it almost impossible to lie to him—but one could avoid the lie without necessarily volunteering *all* the truth. He wished he had a cigarette or a drink or something to occupy his hands.

"Well, there's nothing really mysterious about it, though I'm sure it looked that way," Graham said easily. "I gave Michael a form of posthypnotic suggestion. Quite useful, especially in situations like this. I use hypnosis with several of my agents."

"You never used it with me."

"No, but you've seen me use it on myself often enough," Graham countered glibly. "Don't you remember how I used to snatch those quick naps in the field and you could never figure out how I managed to go to sleep so fast and wake up precisely on time?"

"I remember."

"Well." He shrugged and smiled again. "This is just an extension of that sort of thing—quite new and unofficial so far as the Service is concerned. I don't usually need to be so forceful, but Michael was on the verge of hysteria. He also happens to be a very responsive subject. I'm sorry if it startled you."

William snorted, then broke into a slow, lazy smile. "I'll say it did. I must say, I'm relieved. For a moment there, I almost fancied you were going to tell me it was magic."

"Magic?"

Damn! Was William's use of the term only a figure of speech, or was he testing a more serious suspicion? Or was

Graham overreacting because *he* knew that his use of hypnosis was primarily tied in with his occult activities?

"Well, you must admit, it certainly could *look* like magic to the layman," William explained. "I've seen stage magicians hypnotize people before, you know—though I'll confess, I didn't know your interests lay in those directions, too. But isn't that what you chaps deal with every day—you and your occult section—magic?"

Relaxing a little, Graham tried to keep his nod carefully noncommittal. "I suppose one could look at it that way, yes."

"Well, I thought perhaps you'd decided to take it up for real," William went on, gesturing with his cigarette. "After all, if you're going to counter the Jerries' so-called magic . . ."

The tone was playful, the blue eyes twinkling merrily as William stubbed out the last of his cigarette. Abruptly, Graham realized that the prince was only jesting and thought he was, too. He did *not* suspect, after all.

"Magic, eh?" With a chuckle, Graham leaned his chair on its back legs, balancing against the table edge with both his hands as he shook his head and grinned. "I see. Next you'll be telling me that *you* believe in such things. It's just my job, William. You should know that."

"Oh, I do, I suppose, but—"

With a weary shrug, William sighed and glanced at the sleeping Michael. After a moment, he returned his gaze to Graham, suddenly very pensive.

"How I do miss working with you, Gray," he said quietly. "Quite apart from the rare pleasure of having someone I could really talk to, without the barriers of rank, I felt like I was doing something useful."

He smiled halfheartedly and began chasing his cigarette butt around the ash tray with one finger, no longer meeting Graham's eyes.

"Do you know what it's like being a fifth prince?" he asked in an even lower voice. "I sometimes think it's rather like being a fifth wheel—utterly useless."

Stunned, Graham let his chair drop on all four legs and reached across to grip the prince's forearm. He had not heard William so despondent in many months—not that the war allowed them to see one another that often, but this was a bad sign.

Not for the first time, he bitterly resented the orders that had removed William from the Intelligence Service, which he loved, and at a time when William was already foundering in the wake of personal tragedy. It had nearly destroyed him then and Graham was not certain the danger was yet past, though William generally made a good outward show of being able to carry on.

"William, I don't ever want to hear you say that again," he said softly. "Put it out of your mind. I don't agree with the decision any more than you do, but it's done. There are many other useful things you can do to help the war effort. You're here, aren't you?"

William snorted. "My brother was being kind. He didn't really need a royal observer here. Anyone could have done what I've been doing."

"*Anyone* couldn't have done what you did this morning," Graham retorted, sitting back in his chair. "I wouldn't have taken *anyone* along to the harbor or allowed *anyone* to be here while I debriefed Michael. Why do you think I sent Wells off for food? It wasn't just because I was hungry, I assure you. Orders or not, I still consider you a part of my team, William."

The prince ducked his head, a faint smile quirking at the corners of his mouth. "Apart from my family, do you know you're the only one who calls me by my Christian name, even in private? I doubt you can even begin to imagine what that means to me."

The tone did not demand an answer, but Graham suddenly felt very awkward. For a few seconds, he feared that the conversation was about to take an even more maudlin turn, but then William drew a deep breath and seemed to pull himself together. When he looked up, the royal mask was back in place, the expression only a little wistful.

"So, since Wells is still gone, what can you tell me about Michael's real mission?" the prince asked, lighting up another cigarette. "I gather that he's brought back important film of—what?"

Graham let himself relax a little, schooling his expression to careful nonchalance. Other than the Dieter photographs, which he would have to screen alone, most of Michael's overt mission was well known to the rest of the team back in London and could certainly be discussed with the prince. What he must conceal from William would be concealed from the rest of the team as well.

"Well, a great deal of it is part of some fairly straightforward propaganda," Graham said easily. "Are you by any chance familiar with the work of Nostradamus, the sixteenth-century French seer?"

"Nostradamus? No. I think I've heard the name, but tell me about him."

"Well, he claimed to be able to predict the future—and apparently did rather well at it. He set his predictions in four-line stanzas called quatrains—all in sixteenth-century French, of course, and filled with double meanings and obscure references. The interesting bit is that many of them do seem to have come true over the years, even in this century. Several even predict the rise of Hitler, by name, and the general progress of the war so far. The Germans love that, of course."

"He could really predict the future?" William asked, amazed.

Graham shrugged noncommittally. "I couldn't say. A lot of people think he could, though. And we recently learned that some of Hitler's minions are working on reinterpretations of later quatrains to make it look like Germany will be the undisputed victor. They plan to print up leaflets and airdrop them over the occupied countries of Western Europe. You can imagine the effect that might have on France in particular, since Nostradamus was one of their own. Why continue to resist, if defeat is a foregone conclusion?"

William nodded, intrigued despite his obvious skepticism about the very notion of predicting the future.

"I see. Then you're trying to stop them from rewriting these predictions?"

"Not at all. Even if we eliminated the man who's doing most of the work—a Swiss astrologer, name of Krafft—they'd just find someone else. At least we know Krafft's work. No, we're trying to find out what *he's* doing so that *our* Nostradamus expert can write counterinterpretations. Then we can drop leaflets of our own."

"Wait just a moment. *Our* Nostradamus expert?"

Graham shrugged apologetically. "Sorry to blast you out of the theoretical, but we have a chap in London working on the same thing as Krafft. He's doing a marvelous job. All a part of psychological warfare, my friend."

"I—see."

William was silent for several seconds, studying Graham through a veil of cigarette smoke. After a moment, his eyes narrowed, and he leaned forward, stabbing toward Graham with his cigarette in an old, familiar gesture.

"You said that this Swiss who's working for the Germans is an astrologer. Do I infer correctly that our man is, too?"

Graham cocked his head, wondering what William was getting at.

"He is."

"Then does astrology figure in all of this?"

"Well, yes—"

"Yes, *but.* Why do you always have to qualify your answers? Tell me this, then. Apart from the psychological-warfare aspect, how real a tool *is* astrology?"

"Well, the Germans think—"

"That isn't what I asked," William interjected. "I know what the Germans think—or at least what our chaps at Whitehall *believe* the Germans think. Everyone knows that Hitler is fascinated with the occult, that he's rumored to have a stable of pet astrologers—and obviously we have some, too, yourself among them. From this I can surmise that both sides are probably trying to figure out what the other side will do next by what the stars tell them—I know all that. I also know that you pass off your own knowledge of astrology and all the rest as part of parlor magic, in the same league as rabbits out of hats and such. The Germans don't, though. They take it very seriously. And somehow, especially after your little hypnosis demonstration, I suddenly have the feeling that you do, too. Am I right, Gray? Do you actually believe in that stuff?"

Too well trained to show any outward sign of his uneasiness, Graham inwardly squirmed. He had been throwing William off this particular scent for years, but he had never known him to be so persistent. Where *was* the prince getting his questions today? It was about time for the cavalry to come to the rescue—though Graham would gladly settle for Wells or the doctor. At least astrology was one of the more innocuous of the occult sciences. Graham could be fairly direct about that.

"I don't know that 'believe' is exactly the right term," he replied carefully. "Part of astrology is a science, with its own laws and procedures. Interpretation is the tricky bit. Some people do seem to have a knack for making meaningful connections."

"Do you?"

"Well, I don't know that I'm the best judge of that," he hedged. "I can cast a chart, but so can anyone who knows how to read an ephemeris and perform a few simple mathematical calculations. It's part of my job."

"I know that. Have you ever cast *my* chart, though?" William persisted.

"What makes you think I have?"

He had tried to keep his tone neutral, but he knew William had seen right through that one. He could see speculation turning to certainty as William stubbed out his cigarette and sat forward eagerly.

"You *have*, haven't you? And I'll bet you can do more than cast a chart, too! Come on, Gray, what did it say?"

Graham had not seen the prince so enthusiastic about anything in so long that he was a little taken aback. He had never intended to broach this subject with William, but now that he was all but committed, he found himself reacting with a strange mixture of caution and pleased anticipation—as if the thought of sharing at least a small part of his other work with William were suddenly not so alien, after all.

Perhaps it came of Graham's new responsibilities—having to take over for Selwyn—and the more intricate and chilling dimensions that had come with Michael's mention of Dieter and black magical connections in Germany. The unexpected glimpse of evil Graham had caught while searching for Michael still haunted him. He dared not tell William about that, but perhaps there were some things they *could* talk about. Like the prince, who was never addressed by first name outside the bosom of his family except by Graham, Graham had never been able to discuss any aspect of his other life with anyone outside the "family" of Oakwood. The idea of taking William inside that circle of confidence, even in a very small way, felt oddly right. He would have to give that further thought.

"Very well, I can do more than cast a chart," he conceded, "and yes, I have cast yours."

"I knew it!"

"Unfortunately, I don't think this is either the time or the place to go into very much detail. Your Mr. Wells or the admiral's good doctor will be arriving any minute."

"Well, tell me in general, then," William begged. "This is fascinating. I'll bet none of my brothers ever had their horoscopes read."

Smiling wanly, Graham sat back in his chair and rested his elbows on the arms, making a steeple of his fingers. If only William knew. The charts of all the Royal Family were nearly as well known to Graham as his own, and he was certain they were known to others as well, on both sides of the Channel.

But no need to alarm the prince about that, since he only half believed in "this stuff," anyway. If William took it in his head to think beyond their immediate conversation and was meant to know, he would draw that conclusion on his own, soon enough.

"Let's see," he said, trying to stall while he decided how much he wanted to tell the prince. "You and John were born on July 12, 1905, at around three in the morning, as I recall—Sandringham, wasn't it?"

"You know it was." William paused a beat. "Did you do John's chart, too?"

Graham nodded. "I remember being intrigued the first time I compared them. I'd never had a chance to look at twins' charts before. It's fascinating how less than an hour's difference in birth times can change the aspects even for twins. Granted, you and John were not identical, but—well, it was fascinating nonetheless."

"That's amazing. When did you first look at them?"

"When you were assigned to me," Graham replied with a smile. "I wanted to see what I was getting. Nor was I disappointed. Both your sun and your ascendant are in the same degree of Cancer, and your moon is in Scorpio. In fact, both our moons are in Scorpio—within eight degrees of one another. More unusual than that, our ascendants are less than a minute apart."

"Is that good?"

"I think so. Actually, I don't know that I'd go so far as to characterize it as good or bad, but it certainly tends to explain why we're alike in so many ways. A Scorpio moon is particularly appropriate to any kind of secret or undercover work—and you have your Mars in Scorpio as well. Such a placement usually indicates a keen desire for knowledge, information, finding out what makes things tick, ferreting out secrets—that sort of thing. I think it certainly applies in your case, but you need to—"

A knock at the door broke into his recitation, and he grinned wickedly and murmured, "Saved!" as William started. The prince scowled as he glanced at the door.

"We'll continue this conversation at a later time," he said under his breath in a tone that left no doubt that they would do just that. "You don't get off that easily. Come in," he called.

Graham rose as the door opened, shifting into the more formal demeanor that he and William had long ago agreed must be their public relationship—former military superior and prince. Wells, carrying a covered tray, ushered in an elderly navy surgeon wearing the triple cuff rings of a full commander.

"Sir, this is Commander Reynolds," Wells said.

The surgeon's orderlies waited downstairs with a gurney, and within a quarter hour, Reynolds had whisked Michael off to surgery for treatment, assuring both Graham and the prince that their patient would be back on limited duty within a week. With Michael safe, Graham and the prince began eating the soup and sandwiches Wells had brought back. All further thought of food vanished, however, when Denton entered with a bulging manila envelope under his arm.

"Anything interesting, Denny?" Graham asked. Pulling out the first fat roll, he lifted a few frames to the light.

"*Very* interesting, sir. You did know that the third roll had already been processed, didn't you?"

Primed by Michael's warning about the Dieter film, Graham only nodded as he pulled a magnifying glass from his pocket and peered more closely at a few selected frames. Only the general forms of the astrological charts were visible to the naked eye, and a few larger words with the glass, but what he could read was sufficient to bring a smile to his lips.

"Yes, Michael mentioned that," he said casually, putting the glass away. "These are excellent. Are the rest more or less like this?"

"There's a bit of variety, sir. I think you'll want oversize prints of everything before we head back."

"I think you're probably right." He let the film roll back on itself and tucked it into the envelope again as he glanced at William with a pleased expression. "He did a good job."

"So I gathered," William said. "What happens now?"

"Back to work, for me and Denny," Graham replied, returning the envelope to Denton. "Once we've run the prints, I can do a preliminary workup on the way back to London. Then it's probably an all-nighter."

William smiled ruefully. "Would you believe me if I told you I even miss the all-nighters?" he said, extending his hand in reluctant farewell. "We do have some unfinished business the next time we see one another, however. I shan't keep you now, but once this immediate crisis is over, why don't you pop up to Windsor for a day or two, at least for an afternoon? We'll ride if it's fine."

Bowing over their joined hands in a slightly more formal gesture, Graham allowed himself a final smile. He had no doubt that the invitation bordered on a royal command, but he was used to that after his years of friendship with the prince. He would have plenty of time to think about his earlier impulse to confide in William and to plan any necessary strategy.

The prince was far from his thoughts half an hour later, however, as he and Denton pulled the first oversized prints out of their bath. The Dieter film was first. As Graham clipped the first print up to dry, eerie in the red light of the darkroom, he had an odd prickle of *déjà vu*.

He hardly looked at the dark, banner-hung room in the background of the first photograph, though that was unsettling enough. Instead, he found himself bending apprehensively over the developing bath where the next print was beginning to appear—almost being drawn into the image as Denton swished the paper back and forth in the solution.

He had seen the face before—on the Second Road. Its memory sent chills of dread along his spine, and the terror he had felt before returned in full force.

CHAPTER 5

THE SCAR, THE GLITTERING EYES—THE FACE GRAHAM had glimpsed on the Second Road. That alone was enough to convince him that these particular photographs should never fall under official scrutiny. He was also willing to bet it was the face of Michael's nightmare.

Grimly, he inspected the remainder of the prints as they came out of the final bath, each one more horrifying than the last. The final shot on the roll was a single page of close-typed text with Dieter's code name at the bottom. As soon as it was dry enough to handle, he left Denton to finish printing and took all the Dieter material into an adjoining office. He leafed through the prints again, feeling a little sick to his stomach as he noticed additional details, then stuffed all but the final page into a manila envelope and sat back to read Dieter's report.

Graham had never really cared for Dieter, though he had worked with the man from time to time because Selwyn asked him to. Dieter was a brilliant occult scholar and ceremonial magician—more than a match for either Selwyn or Graham—but he was also quite amoral. Despite the coolly dispassionate reassurances of the accompanying report, the content of the photographs left some doubt that Dieter's defection was wholly feigned. That he was German also made him suspect in Graham's eyes.

Dieter's connection with the Jordan family had come through a brief marriage to one of Selwyn's older sisters, who had died tragically in the birth of a stillborn child. It was after her death, early in the twenties, that Dieter made his decision to infiltrate and sabotage high-level Nazi occult operations. In the decade that followed, he broke publicly and apparently bitterly with his dead wife's British relations in order to increase his credibility, adopting an increasingly fanatical pro-Nazi stance.

More recently, Dieter had become an instructor at Vogelsang, one of the three great *Ordensburgen*, or castles, of the orders of Naziism, where SS officers and other future leaders of the Third Reich were indoctrinated into the mystical aspects of racist doctrine. The Oakwood group had had little inkling of his occult progress up until now.

But the photographs made it all too clear just how well Dieter's extracurricular affiliations had succeeded—though Graham would have preferred less disturbing confirmation. The banner-hung ritual chamber of Graham's vision existed exactly as he had seen it: a focus of dark, unspeakable power secreted in one of Vogelsang's subterranean vaults. More chilling was the face of the group's leader—always masked across the eyes, but quite definitely the presence Graham had sensed on the Second Road. Dieter identified the man only as Sturm.

Even Dieter knew little about Sturm other than his name and his alignment. He came and went mysteriously, obviously holding a high rank in one or several black-magical traditions. He was not formally associated with Vogelsang, even though he had hand-picked the members of the lodge Dieter had penetrated from among its faculty and used its physical facilities. His patron was believed to be Himmler, the SS Reichsführer, but it was also whispered that Sturm was in the confidence of the Führer himself.

The implications were staggering, but Graham realized that for the present they must take second place to more official concerns. Dieter's material would have to go to the Oakwood group; Michael's was fodder for MI.6. As Denton emerged from the darkroom with the rest of the finished prints, Graham tucked Dieter's report in with its photos and tried to put it out of his mind as well.

Graham skimmed the rest of Michael's material on the way back to London, bouncing observations and speculations off Denton. By the time they reached the office, he had roughed out a preliminary evaluation that created several days' round-the-clock activity on the part of his staff. They finished at about the same time that Dynamo was coming to a close. Some of the information had been available in skeletal form before, but much of it was new and startling. Even without the Dieter complication, a disturbing picture emerged.

At least the Nostradamus material could be largely discounted so far as Graham was concerned. Ernst Krafft's attempt at reinterpretation was more laughable than alarming to anyone who knew Nostradamus well at all, though it still must be refuted, since some people might otherwise believe it. Ashcroft, Graham's Nostradamus expert, agreed. Drafting a memo to that effect, Graham sent the entire Nostradamus package on to MI.6 liaison. Captain de Wohl, who was writing the British counterleaflet, should get a chuckle out of it when he integrated the new information into what he was doing.

But the rest of Michael's material was no laughing matter. Several months before, the agent who gave Michael the second roll of film had penetrated Himmler's Section VII, which was a rough counterpart to Graham's. His first few reports had outlined the expected array of occult and psychic phenomena being investigated by the Third Reich for possible wartime application: the astrological warfare connected with the Nostradamus operation, mental telepathy to influence the enemy, pendulum dowsing over maps to locate enemy shipping. The new material treated even more serious matters.

Himmler's agents had begun a crackdown on occult practitioners who did not put their talents at the disposal of the Third Reich. Any group with a potentially mystical or esoteric orientation was suspect. Former Freemasons, odd religious sects, astrologers not sanctioned by the Nazi party, occult lodges and study groups, gypsies—all fell under the scrutiny of Himmler's black brotherhood. Some of those who agreed to turn their talents to the support of the fatherland were courted and brought into the Nazi fold; but those who would not or who belonged to groups singled out for elimination were ruthlessly rounded up and never seen again. Graham recognized the names of several once-powerful occultists on the list of the missing that Michael's contact provided. It was grim confirmation that the Third Reich took the entire matter of the occult very seriously.

Most disturbing of all were the copies of astrological charts and interpretations that Michael himself had managed to secure.

Many of the highest echelons of the Nazi high command were represented, including the Führer himself, and even a few Allied personalities such as Churchill and the King. These charts showed subtle differences from a similar set smuggled out six months before—an entirely new hand now involved in the interpretations, far more competent and frighteningly more subtle than previously. Two of Graham's analysts independently concurred: if Himmler or even one of the other lesser lights of the Nazi court had engaged an astrologer of this caliber to advise the Führer, it could make a great deal of difference. The man went by the professional name of *der Rote Adler*—the Red Eagle.

"He's good—too *bloody* good, if you ask me," Grumbaugh confided in the privacy of Graham's office, pushing his glasses on top of his balding head as he spread an array of texts before his boss. "What especially worries me is that I'm not certain he's *only* an astrologer."

"Oh?"

Grumbaugh shook his head, scowling. "Something in the back of my mind connects him with those satanist lodges we've been hearing about. If he's that good an astrologer, what if he's also a first-rate black magician? This is just sheerest speculation on my part, but suppose he turned out to be the same masked chap who's been showing up at secret meetings of the Vril and the *Thule Gesellschaft*, fanning up support? Several items in the Section VII material suggest such a connection. Take a look at these passages I've marked."

While Grumbaugh perched on the corner of the desk and paged through the references, pointing out specific items, Graham skimmed them with growing suspicion. The Vril Society and the *Thule Gesellschaft*—German occult orders spawned at the time of the Great War from roots of the old *Germanenorden*—were violently racist and anti-Semitic. The Thule Group had provided all forty of the original members of the New German Workers' Party, which eventually brought Hitler to power, and had been financed in turn by the high command. Hitler was believed to be an initiate of the Thule Group's inner core, whose orientation was markedly satanic. No one knew how far the Thulist web extended.

But as Grumbaugh guided Graham through the evidence, the overwhelming image that kept coming to Graham's mind was the mysterious Sturm. When they had finished, Graham tilted back in his chair thoughtfully.

He had come to trust Grumbaugh's intuitions. The English-born Jew was his most brilliant analyst: a resourceful if little-known Cambridge scholar who spoke half a dozen European languages fluently as well as reading a handful of dead tongues. He was also one of the most brilliant Qabalists Graham had ever met. If Sam Grumbaugh thought that *Rote Adler* might be tied in with a German satanic lodge, then the possibility certainly should be explored further. He wondered whether he should show Grumbaugh at least a few of the Dieter photographs to get his reaction.

"This *Rote Adler*—you think he's Hitler's pet Thulist, then?" Graham asked. "The one who's working a black lodge on his behalf?"

"The name would fit," Grumbaugh replied. He twitched his eyebrows in a characteristic expression that was pure Grumbaugh, letting his glasses slip back into place as he pulled another page out of his stack.

"Listen to this passage. It occurs in one of last month's intercepts and also in the new material: *Our God is the father of battle and his rune is that of the eagle*. That's a Thulist slogan, pure and simple. In the old German solar mythology, the eagle is the symbol of the Aryan race. The Thulists use it as a secondary insignia, along with the swastika traversed by the two lances. It all fits, Gray. I think he's Hitler's black adept."

Graham opened his desk drawer and pulled out just a few of the Dieter photographs, which he tossed on the desk in front of Grumbaugh.

"I wonder if this might be the same man," he said quietly, watching Grumbaugh's expression shift from surprise through shock to grim endurance as he shuffled through the photos. "He goes by the name of Sturm. He operates out of Vogelsang and draws most of the members of his group from its faculty. The photos come from a private source," he added as Grumbaugh glanced up and started to make bitter comment.

Silenced, Grumbaugh leafed through the photographs a second time very slowly, then dropped the stack on Graham's desk and wiped his palms against his thighs in distaste.

"I don't suppose those could have been staged for our benefit?" he asked quietly.

Graham shook his head, remembering his own vision on the Second Road. "I have no reason to doubt their authenticity. The purpose of the photographs apparently was to incriminate the other participants so that there could be no backing out later on. I'd appreciate it if you'd keep the knowledge of these to yourself."

With a shudder, Grumbaugh looked away. "The Thulists' famous 'astrological' magic," he whispered harshly, "which is neither astrological nor magical in any decent sense but an excuse for depraved tortures and murder. And I'd be willing to bet a month's pay that the victims in those pictures were Jews."

"Some were." Briskly, Graham gathered up the photographs and returned them to his desk drawer. "I think we should put out some feelers on this Sturm. Have Basilby get on it right away. In the meantime, I want you to correlate anything that fits linking Sturm, *Rote Adler*, Vogelsang, the Thulists, the Vril—any black-magical connections whatever that may tell us more about this chap. How soon do you think you can have it on my desk?"

Grumbaugh had it for him the next morning before the rest of the team had even finished their tea. His conclusions sent Graham straight to Dover with a copy for the recuperating Michael, though not before he rang Alix to request a meeting at Oakwood the following evening. Michael was devastated.

"I had no idea he was this involved," Michael whispered when he had read both Grumbaugh's and Dieter's reports and stared at the photographs. "When he said he'd infiltrated a black lodge, it never occurred to me that he would have to go along with—with *everything*."

He had been reading the reports from a wheelchair on one of the roof tops of Royal Victoria Hospital, while Denton turned away unwelcome company at the stairwell door, and now he let Graham take the pages and photos from his lap without resistance.

"I'm sorry, Michael. I thought you were prepared," Graham said apologetically. "You told me he'd shown you pictures."

"A few, yes—and those were bad enough. But these—"

As Michael ducked his head and covered his eyes with his

good hand, Graham saw in his own memory the particular photograph that undoubtedly was haunting Michael: Dieter, unmasked, nordically pale and aristocratic in his long black robe, coolly drawing an SS dagger across the throat of a terrified victim lashed to a great black stone; the spurting blood frozen in midspray; the masked Sturm looking on in obvious approval with several other men whose eyes betrayed unbridled evil. Dieter, Michael's favorite uncle, who had been Michael's playmate and battle charger almost before he could walk, who had played hide-and-seek with him and his older brother on summer holidays in Bavaria. Dieter, whom Michael had adored.

Shaking his head to clear the image from his own mind, Graham put the documents away in his attaché case and gave Michael a few minutes to collect himself. From a purely intellectual standpoint, he supposed he understood why Dieter had undertaken the task he had. Dieter would have said that the end justified the means; that it was permissible, under certain circumstances, to do the wrong deed for the right reason; that to battle something monstrous, one must sometimes employ monstrous measures, regardless of the personal cost.

But Graham had never yet met an acceptable justification for cold-blooded murder by torture.

"How do you feel about a possible Sturm-*Rote Adler* connection, then?" he asked after a little while, trying to gently ease Michael away from the horror. "Do you think they could be the same man?"

Michael drew slow, steadying breath, still looking far younger and more vulnerable than his twenty-two years, and managed a brisk nod.

"It's possible. Grumbaugh certainly seems to think so. Did you show him the pictures?"

"A few. Tell me more about Dieter, though. Did he ever mention anything about Sturm having a background in astrology?"

"I don't remember—no. I don't think so." Michael sighed. "I'm sorry if I seem like a basket case, Gray. I guess I'm just— very disappointed. I know he *says* he hasn't gone over to the other side, but I never thought Uncle Dieter would—would—"

"No one did, son," Graham murmured, watching helplessly

as Michael turned his chair and awkwardly wheeled himself a little ways away.

It was time to get Michael out of here, Graham finally decided; time to put him to work at something that would turn his mind away from his disillusionment. He could finish mending at Oakwood better than in any hospital. Graham would take him there tomorrow when he drove down for the meeting with Alix and the others; besides, they should hear some of this directly from Michael's own lips. For tonight, he would take him back to his own flat.

"Michael, I think it's time I sprung you from this place," he said.

Within an hour, Denton was driving both of them back to London. Graham spent the evening coaxing Michael to write up his official report and occasionally picking up the pieces when Michael would succumb to grieving reminiscences about the flawed Uncle Dieter. Neither of them got much sleep. The next morning, Graham reviewed Michael's mission report with Grumbaugh and his other two senior analysts while Michael slept in and by mid afternoon had reassigned agents to deal with the new thrust of their investigations. Before picking up Michael for the drive to Oakwood, he spent a last bleak hour in the wire service room watching the latest news bulletins clatter off the keys.

The news was less than encouraging. Operation Dynamo had ended two days before, with more than a quarter of a million men evacuated—ten times the number expected or even dreamed possible—but the Battle of France was essentially over. Though the French government had not yet formally capitulated, the end clearly was but days away. Churchill had flown back and forth across the Channel at least three times in the past two weeks, trying to inject heart back into Premier Reynaud's tottering regime, but even he was forced to concede reluctantly that this phase of the war was coming to a close.

The phase to come gave cause for even greater concern to the British. For once France fell, the way was clear for Hitler to step up invasion activities. The plan was known as *Seelöwe*— Operation Sealion. Occupied French ports would provide staging areas for the ships and barges necessary to carry out such an enterprise; captured French airfields would become havens for the bombers, fighters, and paratroop support needed to back it up.

The Royal Navy and RAF were strong deterrents to an invasion, for each could support the other to a point. But the British naval presence gradually would be forced from the narrow Channel straits as the Germans shifted their ships southward into their newly captured ports, and the RAF was still pitifully below strength despite the Herculean output of Lord Beaverbrook's aircraft factories.

If Hitler pressed his advantage, eluding British naval and RAF defenders, and struck while the remnants of the BEF were still scattered weaponless all around the countryside, the invasion would have to be repelled by aged Home Guard volunteers and untrained civilians—old men, boys, and women and children battling in the fields and streets of England, where no invader had set foot successfully since 1066. Against such a threat, Graham began to wonder whether he was mad even to dream of stopping it through any of his own puny efforts.

"I'm sure that Dieter undoubtedly has his reasons, difficult as those may be for us to understand," Graham told the rest of them that evening when they had gathered around the library table at Oakwood with after-dinner coffee. "Unfortunately, his actions put us all in a very uncomfortable position. Aside from the question of whether he can do what he's done without absorbing any of the Nazi taint, there's the fact that a continued association with him on our parts could be construed as tacit approval. I certainly hadn't counted on this, and I know Michael hadn't."

Besides Alix and the brigadier, only two others had been able to join Graham and Michael for the impromptu meeting: Richard, who was Graham's son, and Geoffrey, the brigadier's other grandson and Audrey's older brother, both on emergency leave from their flying-boat base near Southampton. All five men wore uniform. Dieter's pictures and copies of the pertinent reports lay strewn across the table.

"The question of taint is a very important one," Alix replied, flipping listlessly through a few of the photographs again. "Dieter is one of the finest ceremonial magicians I've ever met, but he is also one of the most unstable. I was alarmed when he first announced his intentions, and I'm especially alarmed now that he has actually gained entrance and accepted initiation into a black lodge—especially this particular black lodge. Once one has killed in this manner, few barriers remain. Where is the line one has to cross before one actually *becomes* a satanist, as opposed to playing a role? And how much do stated principles count when one is *constantly* playing such a role, in every outward manner?"

"It isn't like that," Michael murmured, biting at his lower lip. "He isn't really a satanist. I *know* he isn't."

"Perhaps not, but he's certainly made some powerful connections with people who are," the brigadier said, gesturing at the photographs with his pipe. "Nor am I terribly reassured that Gray was drawn to their working. If that could happen, what's to prevent the reverse?"

Graham shivered. That fear had already crossed his mind more than once.

"I don't like it any better than you do, Wesley, but I do think it was probably Dieter who drew me—not Sturm," he said carefully. "Granted, I was vulnerable when I shouldn't have been, but I think it was Michael's nightmare that triggered it. When I touched him, he was probably touching on Dieter because of his concern—and since I've worked with Dieter before and Michael was totally out of control and unfocused, I was drawn toward what Dieter was doing. Remember, I never touched Sturm. I merely saw him."

Geoffrey, redheaded and pale in his RAF blue, balanced his chair on its back legs and scowled.

"And it's pretty clear that he saw *you*," he remarked. "How can you be sure that he won't use you to trace back to the rest of us? I certainly don't fancy the likes of him lurking outside one of *our* circles."

Graham shook his head. "If he *had* been able to follow me back, don't you think he would have done it at the time, Geoff? The longer he waits, the more chance there is that I'll tell someone else, as I'm doing now, and get reinforcements. In any case, I haven't given him the opportunity to try again. I haven't been on the Second Road since, and I don't intend to go on it again for at least a few weeks. If things still look shaky by Midsummer, I'll bow out. In any case, my abstinence won't interfere with the Drake working. The next major thing after that is Lammas—and if things aren't resolved by then, I suspect it will be too late, anyway."

Richard, in appearance more like Graham's brother than his son, sullenly rolled a pencil back and forth under his fingers.

"I think we're stupid to have continued our associations
with Dieter in the first place. How can you possibly stay clean
when you infiltrate a group that demands *that* of its initiates?"
He gestured angrily at one of the photographs. "And how the
bloody hell did you even get together with him this trip, Michael?
I don't recall that we even talked about him last time we all
met."

"Well, how else was I supposed to get out of Germany?"
Michael replied a little defensively. "Uncle Dieter was the first
person who came to mind."

"And he just happened to have these lovely pictures and a
report for you to bring back?"

Michael bristled. "Father told me he'd had word that Dieter
had some important information for us and asked me to collect
it if I got the chance."

"Without telling Gray?"

"Christ, Richard, you'd think I *planned* for the pickup plane
to crash! What was I supposed to do?"

"I think that's enough," Graham interjected. "Both of you.
It's done."

"But don't you even *care* that David went over your head?"
Richard insisted. "If he's going to make you acting chief, the
least he can do is tell you when he's done something that could
affect us all!"

"Richard, let it go. This isn't your affair."

"It isn't my affair when my own father is put into even
greater danger because his chief didn't back him? You didn't
know he'd asked Michael to see Dieter, did you?"

Graham sighed and shook his head. "No, but that's between
David and me," he said softly. "Let's please not belabor it any
further, son. It certainly isn't worth bickering among ourselves.
Can't we leave that to other groups?"

At Richard's sullen nod, Graham continued.

"Thank you. Speaking of which, Alix, I suppose the time
has come when I can no longer avoid approaching some of the
leaders of those groups. Before I leave tonight, can you give
me a list of the ones you've talked to so far?"

"Of course."

"You mean you haven't even started yet?" Geoffrey asked.

Graham sighed and leaned his head against the back of his

chair, closing his eyes. The impatience and irritability of all three young men were beginning to get on his nerves.

"I'm doing the best I can, Geoffrey. Please remember that I'm having to deal with setbacks I was never trained to handle. I never asked to be your man in black."

"But David said—"

"David said that Gray must use his own best judgment," Alix interrupted smoothly, laying a hand lightly on the young man's arm as Graham looked up at both of them. "Other than the lone excursion onto the Second Road, I have no quarrel with that judgment. Gray knows what he must do."

It was the first direct reference Alix had made to the bridge incident. Her tone was mild, but Graham detected the edge of steel beneath, catching her minute nod when she glanced in his direction. Chastened far more by that than by any verbal reprimand she might have given, he lowered his gaze again. The problem was that he knew precisely what was expected of him. The weight of the responsibility grew heavier with each passing day.

"We've all allowed ourselves to get a little tense about this," Alix said after a moment, jolting him from his self-recriminations. "Why don't we take five minutes for everyone to relax? After that, we'll talk more. Any objections?"

There were none, of course, for Alix's word was final when it came to arbitration among them. The old clock on the mantel ticked off the seconds. That and the crackle of the fire on the hearth were the only sounds besides the occasional tap of the brigadier's pipe tool and the hiss of pencil on paper as Richard doodled. Geoffrey smoked a cigarette and studied the glowing ash; Michael stared at his hands. Graham closed his eyes and, with a conscious effort, tried to make his mind a clean slate, seeking to regain a little perspective.

At the end of the five minutes, Alix rose and went to a wooden box on the mantel, removing from it a deck of tarot cards wrapped in scarlet silk. Graham opened his eyes and sat forward expectantly.

"I thought we might consult the cards before continuing," Alix said, unwrapping the cards as she sat and riffling through them once. "We need not be bound by their advice, of course, but a little outside input is always helpful." She put the deck on the table in front of Graham.

"If you'll please shuffle, Gray, we'll do a reading on the general outlook for our plans and see whether we can find some more specific guidance for you."

With a sigh, Graham began handling the cards, cutting and shuffling them distractedly as he tried to frame his question and impart some measure of intuition to their ordering. When he had cut the deck, Alix took the lower half and laid the first ten out in a cross-shaped pattern, not yet turning up any of the cards. The others eased closer to the table to watch, all of them now focused on what she was about to do.

"The first card," she said, putting aside the rest of the deck and turning up the center bottom card. "The King of Swords, Reversed." She wrinkled her brow. "This is the card that covers, the factor underlying the overall situation. Before tonight, I would have said that it was Hitler without fail—a man without compassion, cruel, ruthless. That may still be. However, it could also refer to our *Herr Sturm*, who may be the *Rote Adler* of Gray's report. I suppose it could even be Dieter. Whoever he is, he is certainly at the heart of the problem we must solve."

She slid out the card lying perpendicular beneath it and turned it over—smiling.

"Crossing it for good or ill is the Eight of Coins, sometimes called the Craft card. They who toil honestly shall eventually reap their rewards." She flashed a quick look around the table. "This clearly refers to ourselves, working as we must to defeat the King of Swords."

She next turned over the card at the bottom arm of the cross.

"At the root of the situation: the High Priestess. Rather than a particular person, I would say it stands for depth, activity beneath the surface, hidden goings-on. The whole picture cannot be seen at this point. Perhaps it indicates a need for caution, for re-evaluation. It could refer both to our work to date and to our present assessment of the person or persons represented by the King of Swords."

She turned the card at the left arm of the cross and placed it with a snap.

"What is passing: the World, Reversed. Rigidity, an unwillingness to explore new ideas, stagnation." She glanced up with a tiny smile. "I suspect we are all guilty of this in the past. Perhaps a change is in order. There is fear in the World Reversed.

"And at the crown is what could come into being," she said, turning the top card. "The Knight of Wands. A young man demands changes." She looked up at Graham. "It could be you, Gray, though it's usually someone in their twenties or thirties. Perhaps it's one of the leaders you're about to contact. The crux of the meaning has to do with being open to possibilities for the future. Perhaps one of the other cards will expand on this."

She turned the card at the right-hand arm of the cross and gazed at it a moment before laying it flat. Graham caught his breath as he saw its face.

"Death," Alix said at last. "What is coming into being. There is a strong temptation to relate the card to Dieter and the deaths of the victims sacrificed in his black lodge, but we must not forget that we, too, have discussed the remote possibility of a sacrifice—a willing one, I hasten to add. I would prefer to think in terms of more general transition here, however. There are indications of radical changes for the future, Gray, and you must flow with them, let the past go. If you cling to the past, you may miss opportunities for the future. This may have to do with your Knight of Wands." She tapped the card with a fingernail. "I wish I could tell you more."

Graham inhaled deeply and let his breath out with a soft sigh. The Death card had appeared in spreads before, but never in the future. He had a queasy feeling in the pit of his stomach.

"Let's see the rest of them," he whispered.

"Very well."

She turned the card at the top of the four-card run sometimes called the Sceptre, laid out along the right side of the cross.

"Strength, Reversed: our negative feelings about the situation at hand. We must not lose our nerve or give up, or we will fail. Harmony is essential. Reality must be faced—perhaps a very bitter draught, in light of the other cards, I fear." She paused just a beat. "Do you really want me to go on?"

"No, but you might as well."

Her jaw was set in resignation as she turned the next card, but she relaxed a little as she saw its face.

"The Nine of Coins, indicating the environment in which we must work. A sense of incompleteness, that we have not yet stumbled upon the total answer. That seems accurate enough. Perhaps it relates back to the High Priestess and the need for caution and reassessment. And concerning our positive feelings about the situation"—she turned up the next card—"the Three of Wands." She raised an eyebrow. "That's interesting. Someone hitherto uninvolved is willing to offer help. There's the possibility of a partnership or cooperative venture of some kind. Which of our recalcitrant leaders were you planning to talk to first, Gray?"

Graham smiled crookedly. "I hadn't decided, but under the circumstances, I suppose I'd better make sure it's one of the young ones neither of us has approached yet. We need all the cooperation we can get."

"I'll say," Richard muttered.

"And this is the outcome," Alix said, turning the final card. "The Five of Wands, Reversed." She smiled. "That's better. Opposing energies overturned. Harmony and peace prevail. It could mean not only our own situation here, within this group, but the outcome of the war itself—strife overcome." She ran her eyes back over the rest of the spread. "Any questions or discussion?"

It had not been the best of readings, but it did offer some hope. Richard—hands thrust awkwardly into the pockets of his brown Irvin jacket and mouth set in a grim line—lingered to look over Graham's shoulder at the still-spread cards as Alix shepherded the rest out. When Graham glanced up at him, he did not need to ask what was bothering his son.

"It's all right, Richard," he said, laying a hand lightly on the leather sleeve.

"No, it isn't all right. I pushed too hard. I know that, and I'm sorry. I just didn't want to leave without knowing you weren't angry with me."

"Angry? For caring what happens to me?" Graham asked. He pushed back his chair and stood. "Try to remember that this isn't easy for David, either, though. He's been our man in black for a long time. It's hard to step out of the habits of half a lifetime."

"I realize that. But try to remember that I've spent an *entire* lifetime having *you* for my father," Richard said stubbornly. "I've learned to accept the dangers that *you* choose to accept even if it means possibly losing you—but it's very hard to stand by when someone else puts you in additional danger that isn't necessary. David should have told you he was sending Michael to Dieter. Or Michael should have."

Graham shook his head and sighed, trying to manage a smile. "Perhaps they should have. But it isn't their fault I picked up Dieter. Granted, Michael seeing those photographs triggered the nightmare that linked me to Dieter—because I was looking for Michael—but there was no way to predict that. Even if I'd known he was going to see Dieter, I doubt it would have made a difference."

"I suppose you're right," Richard muttered after a few seconds.

"You know I am," Graham replied. "At any rate, no harm's been done. And I certainly can't fault you for your loyalty."

"No, just my stubbornness," Richard said with a rueful smile. "I'm sorry if I made it more difficult for you."

"You did—but you're forgiven," Graham said gently.

"Yes. Well. I suppose I'd better go, then. Geoffrey's waiting, and we have to be back on base by midnight. Good night."

"Good night, son."

Richard started to turn away, hesitant and awkward, but then he came and embraced his father as he had as a boy, neither of them saying a word. He did not look back as he went out the door.

Graham sat down again after Richard left, reluctantly returning his attention to the cards as Alix returned. She said nothing as she sat down beside him; merely laid her hand over his and sighed. After a moment, he let his gaze wander from their joined hands to her face, a strained smile playing at one corner of his mouth.

"Are they all gone?"

"Yes."

"Good. I was about to ask you how reliable the cards really are. Then I remembered William asking me precisely the same silly question about astrology."

"What do *you* think?" she countered. "The stars work for you; the cards seem to work for me. You shuffled. I can't change that."

"I know." He picked up the Death card in his free hand and stared at it for a moment, then let it fall, not daring to lift his eyes to hers.

"You think it *could* be a card of transition and not literal

death? Do you really think I'm going to come out of this alive?"
he asked.

"I don't know," she said softly. "I do know that you won't
have to face whatever you have to do alone. That's part of my
job."

"Only your job?"

"A bit more than that," she conceded.

He lifted her hand to his lips and gently kissed the palm.
She did not reply, but neither did she pull away or drop her
gaze from his. After a few seconds, he released her and leaned
back in his chair, rubbing his eyes with the heels of his hands.

"God, I'm tired, Alix. No matter how much I do, it seems
there's always more."

"Why don't you tell me?" she said, standing behind his
chair and beginning to massage the taut shoulder and neck
muscles. "Go ahead and get it off your chest."

He grimaced as she worked on a particularly tense area at
the back of his neck. but he felt himself relaxing. He had never
figured out how she managed it, but somehow she knew how
to ease him into a very light trance without even going through
a formal induction. Perhaps it was uniquely a woman's magic.
At this moment, he could hardly imagine greater contentment.

"Well, I have nearly a dozen progressed charts to do for
Grumbaugh, to name just a few," he said, closing his eyes
with a sigh. "He wants to compare my versions with the ones
Michael brought." He hesitated for just a moment, then went
on.

"I also promised to tell William about his chart. I'm supposed to go up to Windsor next week. Did I mention that we'd
had a conversation about astrology while we were waiting for
Michael's doctor? He was quite keen."

"I was wondering how he'd come to ask you about it," she
answered.

Graham yawned and smiled. "I was telling him about Louis
de Wohl's work on Nostradamus and how it related to what
Michael had brought back. He made the astrology connection
himself." His face fell. "Incidentally, he saw me work on
Michael."

The fingers paused for just an instant and then resumed.
"Oh?"

Graham drew a deep breath and made himself release tension

as he exhaled. William had accepted his explanation of what had happened. Why should he be nervous about telling Alix?

"It wasn't much," he said. "Just a straight posthypnotic suggestion to put him to sleep and block the pain. I hadn't meant for William to see. Since he did, I thought the truth was preferable to him thinking I was some kind of latter-day Svengali."

"Then what *does* he think you are?"

Graham smiled despite his uneasiness. "I suppose he thinks I'm an intelligence operative who uses hypnosis with some of his agents on an experimental basis. That's what I told him, at any rate. He seemed a little indignant that I'd never used it with him, but I told him it was new, since he'd left the Service. He seemed to buy it."

"What are you leading up to?" Alix asked. "You're obviously telling me this for a reason."

"I am?"

Graham twisted around to look at her. He had not been aware that he was doing anything besides rambling, indulging his slightly guilty conscience at having let something potentially revealing slip in front of William.

Then he flashed on that moment when, just for an instant, it had no longer seemed quite so important that William never know the truth about his hidden life. In fact, he had almost wanted to draw William into it.

"Perhaps I am," he amended, letting his gaze follow her as she came around to sit beside him again. "He's like family, Alix—almost like *this* family, if you want to know the truth. Did you know that other than relatives, I'm the only one who calls him by his Christian name?"

"That's hardly unusual for a member of the Royal Family," Alix observed dryly.

"No, but the fact that he's permitted *me* the privilege says something about our relationship—don't you agree?"

As she nodded tentatively, he went on.

"He's like the younger brother I never had, Alix—or maybe like a son sometimes. Perhaps it's because I'm always aware that he's of the old line, and I feel that affinity—I don't know. I do know that I've never been able to lie to him outright and can't imagine ever doing so. If I couldn't evade, I think I'd simply keep silent."

He sighed. "You have no idea how good it felt even to *think* about leveling with him—not that I would have, of course. I suppose I just—needed to share some of my fears with someone who isn't involved in them. Does that make any sense?" he finished lamely.

She looked away for a moment, then back at him, her gaze stripping away all pretense.

"Gray, I have to ask you this. Is there anything else I should know about your relationship with William?"

He opened his mouth to answer, "No," then froze, a chill going up his spine.

"What are you suggesting?"

"Forgive me, Gray. I'm suggesting nothing. Before we proceed, though, I have to know. Since Caitlin died, there hasn't been—*anyone*, has there?"

He forced down the reflex anger and made himself relax. He supposed he could not blame Alix for asking, but it simply was not true.

"Only you," he replied with a tight, resigned smile, "and you know how far that's gone. I would never do that to David— or to you. And as for W—"

"Hush," she said, laying a finger across his lips. "Forget I mentioned it or even thought it. I'm considering something quite unorthodox, and I had to ask."

"May *I* ask?"

"All in good time."

She was silent for several minutes. Graham eventually shut his eyes against the sight of her face, unreadable and closed. Finally, he was startled to feel her hand on his again, the soft, graceful fingers gently stroking his.

"I'm sorry to put you through this," she whispered as he opened his eyes. "All of this. I know how difficult it would be for me, if David were having to do what you're doing. Sometimes I'm glad he's at sea so he can't. It's selfish, I know, but I'm afraid it's how I feel."

He managed a brief nod, but he did not trust himself to do more. He had no idea what she was leading up to. After several more seconds, she squeezed his hand.

"Gray, would it help if I gave you permission to confide in William?"

He blinked, unable to believe what he had just heard.

"Do you mean that?"

"Yes."

"But—why?"

"Because of what you said before. He's your friend, Gray—something I think even you are only beginning to realize."

"He's also a prince of the blood," Graham whispered.

"And of the old line," Alix agreed. "Maybe that *is* why you feel such an affinity. Your instincts are usually good, though. If it will ease your mind—having someone besides us to share it with—then I think we have to give it serious thought."

Graham found himself staring at her dumbly, hardly able to comprehend what she was offering.

"David and I have burdened you with a heavy responsibility," she went on softly. "It's only fair that you should receive some of the privileges that go along with it. One of those privileges includes exercising your own discretion as to how much is safe to tell an outsider—this outsider, in particular. I'm sure you realize that we don't often do this, but there are occasionally—exceptions."

An enormous weight seemed to lift from his shoulders as he saw her reassuring smile and knew she really meant it. It was only then that he realized he had been contemplating telling William, anyway, with or without Alix's permission.

He had no opportunity to explore his newly granted freedom before he had his first taste of a new kind of frustration. Several days before he was to drive to Windsor for his visit with the prince, he made his first contact with one of the leaders of the groups they were trying to recruit. The experience left him more confused than ever.

He had hoped to approach one of the younger men first, in accordance with what the cards had suggested, but his first subject turned out to be a woman—not a man, and certainly not young. From his research, Graham knew she must be around fifty. She could also sway a sizable number of very able occult practitioners to their side if she chose to cooperate. Alix knew her well and had already spoken to her at least once—with infuriating lack of success.

He caught only her silhouette initially, though that was distinctive enough. He spotted her as he and Denton were driving along Knightsbridge, heading back to the office from

a rather tense but unproductive meeting that had necessitated
wearing full uniform. She had ducked through one of the park
gates and was walking briskly along Rotten Row in Hyde Park.

On impulse, he had Denton circle the park and let him out
on Bayswater Road, setting his hat precisely at prescribed military angle and adjusting the belt over his tunic. Perhaps the
authority of the uniform would lend extra weight to her first
impression of him. Entering the park near the Serpentine, he
soon located his quarry lingering to admire the swans. He
approached slowly, as if he, too, were only out for a casual
stroll, carefully framing his opening words.

He had never met her in person, but he had studied her
photographs and heard her described in detail by both Alix and
Selwyn. She was short and apparently heavy set, but that was
difficult to judge under her sweeping black cloak. Though a
wide-brimmed hat shaded her face, the features matched her
photographs. Her dress flashed brilliant sea blue through the
parting of the cloak as she neared. Something in the spring of
her step and her air of confidence triggered a response in Graham,
and he had no doubt of her identity as he stepped into her path.

"Mrs. Evans, I believe?"

She stopped and looked him up and down, steady eyes
appraising him in question and confirmation, then nodded and
took the hand he offered.

"I don't believe we've met before, colonel—"

"Graham. Sir John Graham," Graham supplied. "I'm a friend
of Lord and Lady Selwyn."

As he spoke their names, he used his free hand to trace a
symbol on the back of the one he held. It would not have been
known to Alix or even to Selwyn, but it was known to his
companion. He felt her give a slight start, quickly masked,
then respond with a peculiar pressure of her thumb and a touch
of her other hand. Giving him a curt little smile, she firmly
withdrew her hand from his.

"Yes, Sir John, I believe you are," she said softly, "though
you are both more and less than they, I see. To what do I owe
this chance meeting?"

He returned her smile, well aware that she knew the meeting
was not chance at all, then gestured toward a lesser-used path
that would take them toward one of the north gates. So long

as they remained in the open, they were quite safe from being overheard.

"Shall we walk?" he replied. "I know that Lady Selwyn has already approached you on a matter of some delicacy, but perhaps she did not make herself clear. May I be candid?"

"Please do."

"Thank you. In short, I assume that she made you aware of what some of us are planning for Lammas night. Am I correct?"

She gave a brief nod, not looking at him directly as they moved slowly along the path.

"You are."

"Yet you haven't agreed to help us."

"Nor do I intend to. Surely you're aware, Sir John, that my people do not work with other groups and traditions. We will not oppose you, and we certainly do not disagree with what you are trying to do, but we do not recognize the authority of either you or Lord and Lady Selwyn to call for this kind of direct action. We prefer to handle things in our own fashion."

Graham sighed. Alix had warned him to expect this kind of reaction. He had hoped she was mistaken.

"May one inquire why you believe it impossible to handle the matter in your own fashion and also in concert with others of like intent?" Graham asked.

She smiled sweetly. "I could give you several reasons, Sir John, but I fear none of them would satisfy you. Please believe that I bear you no personal emnity and that I would never do anything to hinder you in your plans—but it is not my way, and it is not the way of my students and colleagues. You must do what you feel to be your duty, and we must do ours. There is really nothing more to be said."

"I see."

They had reached the Marlborough Gate, and he followed her a few steps west along Bayswater Road before accepting that it was a lost cause. She stopped when he did, pivoting to glance at him sympathetically.

"They've given you an awesome task, haven't they, Sir John? Not that there's any way to avoid it, I suppose—someone must do it, with Lord Selwyn at sea—but I don't envy you. Alix told me a little of why they chose you."

"She did?"

"My dear, I've known Alix Jordan for many years," she said, touching his arm lightly. "Just because we don't agree on this particular matter doesn't change our friendship. Please greet her for me when next you see her. Good-bye."

She clasped his hand again and smiled, then turned and walked away. He watched her for nearly a block, until the Bentley pulled up beside him and Denton reached across to open the passenger door.

"Sir, you look like a man who's just been jilted," Denton quipped as Graham got in and pulled the door shut. When Graham did not respond, Denton returned to his driving and said no more.

What an extraordinary woman! was all Graham could think as he reviewed their conversation. It was some minutes later before it registered that she had, indeed, refused him flatly.

CHAPTER 6

THE HYDE PARK SETBACK CAUSED GRAHAM TO POST-
pone any attempt at further contacts until he could rethink his
methods. Even more upsetting, he lost an agent that weekend—
one of those only recently reassigned to the *Rote Adler* investigation. The man's control did not know precisely what happened—only that his charge finally turned up in a Frankfurt
alley with his throat slit.

Both incidents were still troubling Graham by the Monday
he planned to visit William, but he tried to put them out of
mind in light of the more immediate considerations regarding
the prince. He spent the morning drawing up a simplified version of William's astrological chart, but by early afternoon, as
he guided the Bentley into the lower ward of Windsor Castle,
he was still undecided as to how much he wanted to say.

William, at least, was in fine humor. The day was fine, so
the prince had horses saddled and waiting at the Royal Mews
as he had promised. Soon he and Graham were cantering easily
beside the Long Walk toward Royal Lodge, laughing and enjoying the weather, the company, and the feel of fine animals
beneath them. At the Copper Horse, they slowed to a walk to
let the horses blow. Graham could sense the question coming
before the first words were out of William's mouth.

"So, is this the proper time and place to tell me more about
my horoscope?" William asked, glancing aside at Graham as
he patted his bay's neck. "No one can overhear us out here—

though I warn you, you won't be rescued by Wells or some admiral's surgeon this time!"

Graham allowed himself a sparse chuckle and relaxed a little, withdrawing a single folded sheet from an inside pocket.

"If I thought I'd need rescuing, do you suppose I'd have let myself be maneuvered into this position? Here. I brought you a copy of your chart."

William grinned delightedly as Graham handed across the paper, but after only a glance at its contents, his face fell.

"Very funny, Gray. Now translate it. You know I haven't a clue what all these numbers and odd squiggles mean."

"Very well. Where would you like me to begin?"

"You mean I shan't have to browbeat you for a direct answer?"

Graham only shook his head and smiled.

"Marvelous!" William considered for only an instant. "That day in Dover, you started to mention something about Mars and—Scorpio, I think it was. How about starting there?—unless something else is customary, of course."

"No, that should do well enough. Let's see. There's the symbol for Mars," he said, leaning across to point it out, "and that's the house of Scorpio. Your Mars is at slightly more than twelve degrees Scorpio. As I think I mentioned before, this placement, in addition to the Scorpio moon, bodes well for success in undercover-type activities—which we know is certainly true, judging by your past performance. Mars is also squared by Mercury."

"Squared?"

"That simply refers to a relationship between the positions of the two planets," Graham replied, trying to keep it as simple as possible. "Mercury square Mars can be the signature of a very bright mind, which it certainly is in your case, but it also has its touchy, even irritable aspect—which can be an attribute of a Cancer sun as well. It can also be very impatient. I don't suppose that sounds like anyone you know?"

William drew rein and stared at Graham in amazement. "You can tell all of that just from a few symbols and numbers?"

Graham returned a sheepish smile. "I told you in Dover that it was an art."

"I dare say. I do dare say." William was quite frankly staring. "And if the astrology is an art, one has to wonder how much of the rest goes beyond theory, too. It isn't all just counterpropaganda, is it, Gray? You really do believe in it."

It was the perfect lead-in if William continued to be receptive. As they walked their horses toward Great Meadow Pond, Graham briefly related what had surfaced as a result of Michael's film: the mysterious *Rote Adler*, who seemed to have connections with satanic lodges in Germany; the even more sinister Sturm—who might be *Rote Adler* himself; and Grumbaugh's suspicion that *Rote Adler* was Hitler's new master adept, working black magic to help win the war for the Germans. He also mentioned the murdered agent in Frankfurt. When the prince did not seem too taken aback by his matter-of-fact discussion of occult activities in Germany, Graham confided his fear that *Rote Adler* or Sturm or whoever was working magic in Hitler's behalf might interfere with the occult measures that were being taken in Britain to prevent an invasion.

"Are you telling me *we* have people who are doing that kind of thing?" William asked incredulously.

"Well, not in the same manner, I should hope, but—yes, there are those who are trying to stop the invasion."

"With *magic*?"

"There's ample precedent in English history," Graham hedged as they let their horses stand knee deep in the pond to drink. "Some of the people you'd least expect have been involved. One of the most solid examples has to do with Sir Francis Drake and the sinking of the Spanish Armada. Did you know that he was reputed to be a master magician?"

William made a face. "You've been reading too much folklore, Gray. Drake was a minister's son."

"True. However, according to legend, Drake stopped the Armada by calling a grand coven to raise a Channel storm."

"A coven? As in witches?"

"Not—necessarily," Graham said carefully. "Coven originally meant any group of twelve plus a leader: Charlemagne and his twelve peers, Arthur and his original twelve Knights of the Round Table—even Jesus and his disciples, for that matter. The King and his council of twelve ministers could also be said to constitute a coven in the general sense."

"Still sounds like witches to me," William retorted with a grin. "What's a *grand* coven, then?"

"Only a gathering of a number of covens," Graham said

easily, "though I'll concede that in this case, they were groups of—well, let's just call them occultists. Some of them would have called themselves magicians, sorcerers, cunning folk— or witches. The point is, they were all adept at redirecting the forces of nature—using magic, if you will—and they all rec- ognized Drake's authority to call them together to work for a common goal: to protect their country from invasion by raising a storm to wreck the invasion fleet."

"Humph. We could use one of those now," William said with a snort. "But I still say it sounds like a delightful but improbable folk tale. God knows, England abounds in them. You don't really believe it happened that way, do you?"

Restraining a smile, Graham glanced down at the reins threaded loosely through his gloved fingers, the ripple of mus- cle under the chestnut coat as his horse raised its head. Wil- liam's comments had been glib, quite casual, but Graham thought he detected a note of more intense interest. He would see what happened if he offered the prince a few more tidbits to spark his speculation.

"I don't know," he said. "Whatever you and I believe, a storm *did* blow up, and the Spanish fleet *was* scattered and wrecked. It was a decisive naval victory, as you know, and some say it hadn't only to do with Drake's seamanship. You've surely heard the famous story about him playing bowls on Plymouth Hoe with his captains when word came that the Spanish fleet had been sighted off the Lizard?"

William nodded. "First-year naval history classes. He said something about having time to finish his game *and* defeat the Spanish." He raised one eyebrow. "*We* were always taught that he was simply waiting for the tide to turn so he could sail."

"Perhaps," Graham agreed. "Another interpretation would have it that he could afford to be blasé because he knew meas- ures had already been set in motion to ensure his victory by other means—and that version doesn't even necessitate refut- ing the theory about the tide."

William gave a nervous chuckle. "You're implying that magic is real. Don't you think that's reaching a bit?"

Graham managed a nonchalant shrug, but inside he was churning. William continued to sniff at the bait; time now to give him something more substantial to chew on.

"You tell me," he returned. "What would you say if I told

you that similar measures were taken to stop Napoleon from invading—that Drake's drum is said to have been heard all along the coast at the height of the French threat? Supposedly, Drake swore on his death bed that if his drum were beaten in England's hour of need, he'd come back. Some say he has, Nelson and Blake being two of the more prominent of his reincarnations. For that matter, there are men alive today who will swear that they heard ghostly drumming at Scapa Flow in this century when the Germans were preparing to scuttle their fleet at the end of the Great War."

As he glanced aside, William was shaking his head.

"This is all too incredible. It's like saying that—that King Arthur really *is* asleep in Avalon and that he'll come to save England when she's in need, as the legends promise. I haven't seen *him* lately—and God knows, we're certainly in need!"

"Does the fact that you haven't seen him mean he isn't here?" Graham asked innocently. "Would you know him if you saw him?"

"What?"

"Here's something else of interest," Graham continued with a tiny grin. "Do you happen to remember what kind of engines we use in our Spitfires and Hurricanes?"

The prince looked at him blankly.

"They're Rolls-Royce *Merlin* engines, William. Defending England. Think about it."

William stared at him in something approaching shock for several seconds, then rolled his eyes and broke into a chuckle.

"You're too much! You nearly had me believing you for just a minute there."

But his mirth did not last. When Graham did not join in, William's face fell, and he glanced away in confusion, nervously backing his horse a few steps in the shallows. There was a kind of desperate apprehension in his eyes as he turned to Graham once more.

"Come on, I'll race you to the tower!" he cried, touching spurs to his mount and taking off in a shower of spray, not waiting to hear whether Graham agreed.

Graham held back, letting him have several seconds' head start, then followed at a more leisurely canter, though his horse wanted badly to go with the other. It was clear that William needed a chance to think.

He watched the prince take his bay over a fence beside the open Forest Gate, then veer right and disappear into a copse of trees near the tower. Graham continued following at his same easy pace, going through the gate instead of over the fence, slowing to a trot and then a walk as he, too, entered the trees. A few dozen yards in, he found the prince sitting on a fallen log in a clearing, smoking a cigarette as his horse busily cropped grass. The reins were looped over the handle of the riding crop in his other hand. No hint of emotion could be read on the finely chiseled face.

"It took you long enough," William said, flicking ash against the log as Graham drew rein.

Graham remained in the saddle, though he let the horse drop its head to graze.

"Call it a hunch. I thought you might need a few minutes to collect your thoughts."

"Good hunch." William tapped the log beside him with his crop. "Sit if you wish."

Swinging down easily, Graham pulled the reins over his horse's head and led it a little nearer the other before sitting next to William. The prince slid over to make more room, turning his attention to a mud smear on one boot and scraping at it idly with the end of his crop. He would not look at Graham.

They sat that way for several minutes—William smoking, Graham waiting, neither of them speaking. Graham let himself drift with the silence for a while—the bird and insect sounds, the soft snuffling of the horses searching for greenery among the leaves, the whisper of William's breathing beside him— but though he kept hoping William would be the one to resume conversation, he soon realized that was not to be. William had outwaited him too many times in the past when some sensitive topic waited to be discussed.

With a sigh, Graham flipped a leaf across William's boot with the end of his crop, trying a tentative smile as William glanced his way.

"This place has quite an interesting magical history; did you know that?"

William snorted: an expression of somewhat uncertain bravado.

"So we're back to that, are we? All right, I'll play along.

They say that some of my royal ancestors are supposed to haunt various parts of the castle. I suppose you believe that, too."

"I couldn't say," Graham replied, ignoring the implied challenge. "Actually, I was referring to this part of the park. They say that when calamity threatens England or the Royal Family, Herne leads the wild hunt through these woods astride a fire-breathing black horse. He wears a stag-skull helmet with the antlers still attached, deerskin clothes, and red-eyed hounds run with him. Some say he pursues a mystical white stag. That's also been seen around these parts from time to time, though the old oak it used to fancy was destroyed almost a century ago."

"I've read about Herne," William said uneasily. "He's just another ghost. They say he was warden of the forest to Henry VIII—"

"And that he committed suicide after being accused of witchcraft," Graham finished smoothly. "Actually, he probably goes back to Cernunnos, the Celtic god of the underworld, or perhaps Odin, who rode the wind on eight-legged Sleipnir—remember your Norse mythology? There may also be connections with other ancient gods of forests and hunts and the sun."

William sighed and glanced away, troubled, finally dropping his cigarette and grinding it out with a booted heel. When he raised his eyes to Graham again, he looked scared.

"Gray, I—Christ, I feel silly asking this, but somehow I— you're not a—a *warlock*, are you?"

"The word would be *witch* for either sex," Graham said carefully, "but as Shakespeare said, 'What's in a name?' That particular one has picked up all kinds of negative associations over the years. Try another."

"A—a magician, then," William whispered after a stunned pause.

"Better, but still smacking of charlatanism to some. How about 'occultist'? That takes in a lot of territory without being overly judgmental."

"Without being—bloody hell!"

William stood so explosively that his horse shied, snorting and backing, spooking Graham's in turn. Both men had their hands full for the next few seconds.

When order was restored and the horses grazed peacefully once more, Graham gingerly resumed his seat on the log, not

daring to speak. William remained by his horse for a while
longer, his back to Graham and one arm draped over the saddle
while he continued to stroke the animal's neck, fiddling with
a strand of mane. Finally, he half turned to glance uncertainly
at Graham.

"You know, every time I think I understand you, you come
up with something I hadn't counted on," he said. "This one
takes the prize. God knows I trust you, Gray, but—did I
misunderstand? Do you really, *seriously* mean to imply that
you practice witchcraft? Don't fog the issue with technicalities
of language. Do you or don't you?"

Graham inclined his head minutely. "That would be one
way of putting it—yes."

He heard William swallow, the sound very loud in the silence of the clearing, and watched the fear flicker across the
otherwise controlled face.

"But isn't that the same as—as black magic and—and devil
worship?"

Graham smiled and shook his head. "None of those three
is equivalent, William," he said softly. "For one thing, magic
isn't black or white; it's power, which is neutral. Like anything,
it can be used or abused by good or evil men. Witchcraft does
use what you'd call magic—causing changes in conformity
with will is how one man once defined it—but it really has to
do with reverencing the old gods of Britain and harmony with
nature."

"What about devil worship?"

Graham shrugged. "That's a Christian concept. No self-
respecting witch would worship a Christian god of evil."

"But I thought that was the main accusation in the old witch
trials!" William protested, crossing the distance between them
in three long strides and sinking down gingerly on the log beside
him again. "Didn't they hang and burn witches for worshiping
the devil?"

"That was the allegation," Graham replied. "But *devil* was
the inquisitors' name for any god who wasn't Jehovah, the
Lord of Hosts. The witches called their gods by other names,
so naturally they were devil worshippers in the eyes of the
Christian authorities." He lowered his eyes, thinking of his
own function at Oakwood and in other places and traditions in
the past.

"Actually, each coven did have a man in black, who was sometimes mistakenly called a devil by outsiders. He was merely the priest who represented the god in rituals and led their meetings. He certainly wasn't the same as Satan, the embodiment of evil. Unfortunately, there are and always have been some people who are seduced by a fascination with evil and wanton destruction. They're satanists, however, like Sturm and the Thulists, perhaps. They have nothing to do with the old faith."

William mulled that for some time, though much of the tension seemed to have gone out of him with the last exchange. He lit another cigarette—murmuring his thanks when Graham cupped his hands around the flame to block the breeze—then smoked it nearly all the way through before turning to look at Graham again. Graham met his gaze openly, trying to project as much confidence, reassurance, and trust as he could. After a few seconds, a ghost of a nervous smile twitched at William's mouth.

"You know, it's just occurred to me that the old laws against magic and witchcraft are still on the books. But I suppose you're aware of that."

"All too well."

"Yet you've just told me that you're a w—an occultist," William amended, "which makes this conversation a very dangerous one for you, doesn't it? You didn't have to tell me—God knows, you've gone all these years without telling me before—yet you've told me now." He paused to swallow. "Are you in trouble because of it, Gray? Have you come to me for help?"

With a sigh, Graham shook his head. "Not—directly. I—Christ, you must think I'm totally mad, Will—though you've certainly taken it far better than I feared you might." He sighed again and gazed up at the leafy canopy above their heads.

"No, I suppose I really told you because I needed to talk to someone I could trust—someone who isn't involved in the actual problem." He glanced at the prince. "You've sworn oaths as a Freemason, William, so you'll understand that I'm bound by similar oaths not to divulge certain things, but I'm—feeling very alone right now. I've been asked under oath to do something for which I'm not really trained, and I'm not doing a very good job of it so far. There's nothing you can do about that, of course, but it helps to be able to talk about it, anyway. You don't mind, do you?"

"Mind? After all the times you've had to sit and listen to me? Don't be daft!" William paused. "What is it that you're supposed to do, that you're not trained for?" he asked. "Are you allowed to tell me?"

"I could tell you in general, I suppose, but I'm not sure you're ready for that much at once," Graham murmured, suddenly getting cold feet. "Besides, I'm not even sure it's fair of me to ask you to share the burden. You shouldn't be involved at all. It could be dangerous."

"Because of who *I* am or who *you* are?"

"Perhaps a bit of both. I haven't given you a great deal of choice about whether you even want to be involved, either. I fear I've presumed a great deal on our friendship."

"Let me be the judge of that," William replied. "I don't suppose it's even occurred to you that I might welcome someone presuming on a friendship for a change. And you've certainly given me the means to retaliate, if I were truly offended."

Graham averted his eyes. "A measure of my desperation, I suppose. I still shouldn't have gambled with our friendship. I apologize for that."

"No need. I'm honored that you would trust me with something like this."

"I don't know that it's an honor," Graham answered with a shrug. "More of a burden, I should think. In any case, I'd rather you didn't make any final decisions until you've had a chance to digest some of what we've been discussing. Take a few days or a week to think about it. Then, if you're still willing to take on the job of father confessor, we'll talk again."

"You promise?"

Graham sighed wistfully. "Do I have a choice? I mean, if you want to talk about it again, I suspect we're bloody well going to talk about it again. I've hardly put myself in a position to say no, now have I?"

At Graham's tentative smile, William snorted and got to his feet, dusting leaves and bits of tree bark from the seat of his breeches.

"Why do I have this feeling that your argument wouldn't hold up right now regardless of whether or not I wanted to continue?" he said, watching as Graham also stood. "Don't answer that. Allow me *some* illusions about the might of my rank."

"You know me better than you think," Graham replied. "However, I think it's better if you do take the time to let it all gel. I've given you a great deal to swallow."

"I shan't argue with that," William agreed. His face brightened as he glanced at his watch. "Speaking of swallowing, shall we head back and see what's on for tea? We're late, but with any luck, my nieces will have left a biscuit or two. I'll bet you didn't realize that even royals are on rationing these days."

"And here I thought I'd escape all that by hobnobbing with a prince," Graham quipped as they caught their horses and mounted up. "Do you mean to tell me you're eating Spam and dried eggs at the Palace, too?"

"Come dine with me next week and you'll see," William grinned. "I have no idea what cook will manage in the way of food, but at least the cognac is still supurb."

They continued to discuss the annoyance of rationing as they started back at an easy pace. Perhaps a third of the way back, they spied an open Daimler heading toward them at speed from the direction of Royal Lodge. Wells stood on the passenger side, waving urgently with one hand as the driver blared on the horn to attract their attention. The horses laid back their ears and fidgeted as the car kicked up gravel coming to a stop.

"Sir, we've been looking everywhere for you," Wells said, jumping down to take the horses' bridles. "There's terrible news. Italy has declared war. Colonel Graham, you're wanted at Whitehall right away for a meeting."

The meeting, which lasted well into the evening, proved to be only the first in a series of events that made the following week even more difficult than Graham had anticipated. Italy's entry into the war sparked a new flurry of intelligence activity that extended through arms of all three services. Directives given at the Whitehall meeting—and others that followed in the days thereafter—kept Graham and his staff busy well into the following weekend.

Much of Graham's work involved routine coordination with other intelligence sections, expanding all of their operations into the Italian sector, but high on their list of priorities was a stepped-up attempt to positively identify *Rote Adler*. Graham's superiors were aware of the political influence of the Thulists and the Vril; if *Rote Adler* could be connected with either or both of them, they would gain greater insight into the thinking of the German high command. But Graham's section made no major breakthroughs that week, though at least they lost no more agents.

Nor did more wide-sweeping efforts on the part of His Majesty's Government have much effect on the outcome of the battle still winding toward its inevitable conclusion in France. Despite repeated trips back and forth across the Channel by Churchill and others, the faltering French leadership proclaimed Paris a free city two days after the Italian declaration and abandoned her to her fate. Two days later, on the fourteenth of June, the victorious army of the Third Reich entered Paris in a display of force calculated to demonstrate the utter folly of continued resistance to the invincible German war machine.

The French government had already fled, first to Tours and then to Bordeaux. Now, on the sixteenth, an embittered Paul Reynaud resigned as French premier, unable to persuade the frightened French cabinet to let him carry on the war from North Africa or some other French possession and unwilling to be the one to surrender. The new premier, Marshal Petain, sued for an armistice with Germany on the following day.

That evening, Winston Churchill addressed the British people and told them the fate of their former ally. The following night, he reiterated his report to the House of Commons in a speech also broadcast by the BBC. Graham and William heard the speech from William's sitting room in his suite at Buckingham Palace. Their after-dinner brandy was all but forgotten as the famous voice reverberated from the wireless.

"What General Weygand called the Battle of France is over," Churchill told them gravely. "I expect that the Battle of Britain is about to begin. Upon this battle depends the survival of Christian civilization. Upon it depends our own British life, and the long continuity of our institutions and our Empire. The whole fury and might of the enemy must very soon be turned on us. Hitler knows that he will have to break us in this Island or lose the war. If we can stand up to him, all Europe may be free and the life of the world may move forward into broad, sunlit uplands. But if we fail, then the whole world, including the United States, including all that we have known and cared for, will sink in the abyss of a new Dark Age, made more sinister, and perhaps more protracted, by the lights of perverted science. Let us therefore brace ourselves to our duties, and so bear ourselves that, if the British Empire and its Commonwealth last for a thousand years, men will still say: 'This was their finest hour.'"

As the broadcast concluded, the measured phrases of the prime minister giving way to applause and then the voice of a BBC commentator, Graham rose to turn off the wireless as the prince lit a cigarette from an inlaid box at his elbow. The luxury of the royal sitting room seemed quite isolated from the bleak predictions the prime minister had just outlined. Furthermore, the two men had dressed formally for dinner that evening, even though mess dress was almost never worn in wartime. William enjoyed wearing the stars and ribands of his orders and was always amused when the opportunity arose to bully Graham into wearing his, for he knew how Graham disliked formality.

Now Graham unhooked the collar of his tunic and eased his neck with an audible sigh of relief as he returned to his chair, ignoring William's bemused smile. The prince raised his glass in informal salute as Graham sat back down. All evening, the company had been as mellow as the vintage cognac.

"So, I'll wager that Winston's speech will soon be quoted by every bloke in Britain," William said. "'Their finest hour.' He does know how to turn a phrase, doesn't he?"

Watching the light flash fire from the facets of the glass in his hand, Graham nodded absent-mindedly. "That's so. He sounds the pulse beat of the British people like a well-tuned drum. Sometimes a bit difficult to work for, I grant you," he added, gesturing with his glass, "but geniuses were always thus. He certainly knows his business. I don't envy him a bit."

"Nor I."

Both men sat quietly for several minutes, each absorbed in his own thoughts, until William glanced at Graham again, breathing smoke lethargically upward through his nostrils.

"Did you mention drums deliberately to remind me of Drake?" he asked softly. "We can't be overheard in here," he added, following Graham's glance toward the closed doors, "and no one would dream of entering without knocking."

"Suppose we turn on the Victrola, just for added insurance?"

Graham countered with a faint smile, rising to do it. "Ah, 'Egmont.' Beethoven makes marvelous background for a discussion of the esoteric."

As he adjusted the volume and resumed his seat, William watched with an air of vague puzzlement, gesturing with his cigarette as Graham took up his glass again.

"Esoteric? I thought that had to do with philosophy—intellectual matters."

"In general, I suppose it does," Graham agreed. "But in the literal sense, it means hidden, secret, something taught only to a select few. You're a Freemason, aren't you?"

"You know I am."

"Well, Freemasons follow an esoteric tradition of sorts, though most of its real power has been somewhat diluted over the centuries so that it's largely a philosophy today. A more practical consideration, however—and one of the reasons Hitler is suppressing your brethren in Germany—is that they're more or less secret and their members are usually known to one another. The perfect nucleus for forming a resistance movement." He paused a beat. "There are many, many esoteric traditions, including Christianity. I work in several of them."

"I see." William thought a moment, frowning. "But haven't you implied that magic is a part of most—ah—esoteric traditions?"

"In a general sense, yes."

"Even Christianity?"

"Yes."

William looked dubious and a little shocked but not overly alarmed. Still Graham realized he was going to have to handle the next few minutes very delicately. William was not avidly religious, but his very blood and breeding dictated a certain outward conformity with custom and observance. His brother was head of the Church of England, Defender of the Faith. Members of the Royal Family were expected to attend services on Sundays as a family and to set a pious example. William had always followed that aspect of his role without question.

"Let me put it to you this way," Graham said slowly, thinking each point through. "What single aim would you say that all religions, all ethical philosophies, have in common?"

"Well, I suppose it would be perfection of the human spirit, salvation of the—"

"No, something more fundamental than that," Graham broke in, shaking his head. "I'll save you the guessing. It's a closer understanding and interaction with the creative force—call it what you will: God, Buddha, Allah, Great Zeus, Mithras. All the great religions and philosophies have headed toward it in their different ways—trying to know the godhead and to somehow emulate it, control it, make it work for them. And how do we do that? Some people would call it prayer: an attempt to communicate with God and persuade Him to do what we ask. Isn't that exactly what was happening when we had that national day of prayer a few weeks ago, during Dunkirk?"

"Well, I think prayer is more than—"

"No, I know that isn't *all* prayer is, but let me finish. When the King declared a national day of prayer during Dunkirk, what were we trying to do? We were asking God to stop the Germans and save our soldiers. And since we managed to get something like ten times the number of men out of Dunkirk than we dreamed possible, some folk are calling it a miracle. Nothing so dramatic as changing water into wine or multiplying loaves and fishes, I suppose—or was it? 'With God's help,' we managed to save a quarter of a million men we thought were lost. I'd call that a miracle, by the classical definition. I could also call it the result of magic—and I'd be right about that, too."

"But we're talking about two different things," William protested.

"Are we? You'd call it a miracle when you pour your heart and your fondest wishes into a petition to God and your prayer is answered. We'd do much the same thing and achieve approximately the same result, but we'd call it by another name."

"Magic?"

"Magic."

William had several drags on his cigarette while he thought about that, not looking at Graham but not avoiding him, either. He sipped at his cognac again.

"You've spent a great deal of time, both tonight and last time, trying to convince me that magic is real and that it somehow ties in with something mysterious that you're doing," he said slowly. "I've done a bit of reading since we last talked, too." He looked directly at Graham. "Are you trying to duplicate what Drake did?"

Graham fingered the glass in his hands and drew a deep breath, let it out slowly. They were into it now.

"You do believe in getting right to the heart of a matter, don't you?" he murmured.

"That isn't an answer. Besides, I learned it from you. *Are* you trying to work some kind of magic to stop Hitler? I mean you, personally."

Without speaking, Graham gave a slight nod. William stared at him, glass poised midway to his mouth, then took a slow, deliberate sip and rested the glass carefully on the chair arm as he took his time swallowing.

"I didn't really expect such a direct answer," he said after a moment. "And you said before that we have people who are—no, it can't be anything official. MI.6 does odd things, but—it *isn't* official, is it?"

"Not in any technical sense, no."

"But there *are* individuals?" William guessed. "At least a few. Like Michael."

Graham shrugged noncommittally.

"They're outside MI.6, then?"

Graham gave another nod.

"And you're their—their man in black?" William ventured, stumbling a little over the unfamiliar term.

"For now. Our real leader is serving with the Forces, as one might expect, though he comes back when he can. That's part of what I was talking about when I told you I was having to do a job for which I wasn't really trained. I'm not *un*-trained," he added, "but these are hardly ordinary times. I think even— the *real* one would be hard pressed under the circumstances."

William blinked and suddenly seemed to remember he had a drink at hand. He took a distracted swallow, coughing a little when it did not go down quite smoothly, then looked up carefully at Graham again.

"What—what are you supposed to do?" he asked.

"Let me see if I can explain it in terms you'll understand," Graham said slowly. "We *are* trying to stop Hitler by magic, the way Drake did, but obviously a mere storm won't be sufficient. So we raise a cone of power—a visualization of mental energy, I suppose you could call it, or a telepathic thought wave—and we direct it toward Hitler. We try to put the idea in his mind that he shouldn't even *attempt* an invasion—that if he does, he'll fail. We've done this once already—last month, on the Eve of May—and we'll try it again this Friday, which is the Summer Solstice. A third working is planned for Lammas, the first of August. That's where Drake comes in—and my problem."

"The thing you aren't trained for?"

Graham nodded. "It's traditional for these things to be done in threes, with the third usually being the most powerful. My superiors have decided that the Lammas working should involve a grand coven, to boost our power and increase the chance of actually getting through to Hitler. Everybody doesn't have to be in the same place for the actual working, but we do need to get the key leaders of the various groups to agree to do basically the same kind of thing at the same time."

"I shouldn't think that would be too difficult," William said.

"More difficult than one might think. I've been ordered to convene the grand coven, but the various leaders are very jealous of their own traditions and authority and see no reason why they should cooperate with someone else's man in black. Drake knew how to get around this problem. Unfortunately, I don't."

William had been listening so raptly that the cigarette in his fingers had burned down almost to his knuckles. With an exclamation, he stubbed it out in the nearby ash tray and rubbed his fingers briskly. As he settled back in his chair and picked up his brandy again, he was very thoughtful.

"There's something that doesn't make sense here," he said after a moment. "If it's actually possible to—to raise this kind of power—if magic really works—why not just kill Hitler and be done with it? Save everyone the trouble. Aren't witches supposed to be able to kill people?"

Graham winced, almost instinctively glancing around the room.

"I was afraid you'd ask that. Actually, I won't say it's impossible under the right circumstances, but the price can be dreadfully high, and one never knows whether such an act is in keeping with the overall plan. Direct murder is rarely a solution. It's—a little complicated to go into the ethics of the thing right now. Let's just say that changing someone's mind, their inclination, is generally easier and far safer than trying to change something in their body or environment to kill them.

Besides, we know he has black adepts working to protect him
from such direct attacks, like the fellow Sturm I told you about.
What we're planning is indirect and may not be detected as a
threat. That makes it far more likely to succeed."

"I see. Or actually, I don't see," William replied. "My mind
tells me you're speaking English, but I'm not certain I've understood more than two words you just said. But put that by the
way for a moment. Back to Britain." He gestured with his
glass. "If everybody is so keen to stop the invasion, why
won't these chaps you've been approaching cooperate? I would
assume, from what you've said, that they all do some form
of—'white magic.' If I understand *that* correctly, then they
should be in favor of anything which would stop a chaotic force
like Hitler."

"So one would think," Graham agreed. "Unfortunately,
they're frightened."

"Frightened? Of what? Hitler's chaps? Do they think this
Sturm fellow will strike back at them with his black magic?"

Graham shook his head. "I doubt that even crosses their
minds. Most of them don't even know he exists. Besides, as
powerful as we suspect Sturm to be, even he would find it
difficult to retaliate against individuals if they were all working
toward a common goal.

"No, fear of persecution is the key here, I think. They're
afraid someone outside of their group will talk and their activities will become known. I know the thought has crossed *my*
mind."

William's jaw dropped.

"But it isn't as if they *burn* witches and magicians anymore,
Gray. This is the twentieth century."

"Yes, and the stake is not the only place where one may
burn," Graham returned a little sharply. "Under the best of
circumstances, a modern occultist will probably be branded as
an eccentric, if not a charlatan. The latter is what the law would
say. Not everyone has as good a cover as I do. For most people,
the reality is that discovery of one's occult connections can
spell the end of one's social standing and even one's job.
Remember what we discussed at Windsor? You had and still
have the power to utterly destroy me, at least career-wise, even
if you weren't who you are. Can you imagine Whitehall's
reaction, for example, if you were to go to them with what

I've just been telling you? Some of the others have as much or more to lose."

"I hadn't thought of that," William said after a moment. "Back to this grand coven, though. What will happen if you can't get them to cooperate?"

Graham shrugged and sighed. "We'll do the best we can, I suppose. There's a woman down in Hampshire who's been backing us all along. She has a large group, and they'll work with us. There are a few others we can count on. In the meantime, we're also working on a direct link to the Drake incident, to try to find out how *he* convened a grand coven. He must have had some way of ensuring that they would come, some way of putting out the call with sufficient authority."

"That sounds promising. How can you find *that* out?"

Graham hesitated. William's questions were getting a little too specific. Though he still seemed honestly receptive and not at all frightened or hostile, too much information would serve neither his nor Graham's best interests.

"Well, that's the tricky bit," Graham said slowly. "I—seem to have an affinity with Drake. Maybe I'm his reincarnation in this century, like Blake and Nelson before. In any case, I'll be doing a—it's rather like a hypnotic age regression, really. If it works, maybe I'll learn what Drake did. It wouldn't hurt to learn a little about his weather magic, either," he added with a grin, hoping to defuse some of the impact of what he had just said. "Bad weather, on top of everything else, could foul the most astute German invasion plans. You saw what the right weather did for Dunkirk."

"Dunkirk?" William raised an astonished eyebrow. "You don't mean to say—"

"Good heavens, no!" Graham laughed, grateful for the diversion. "I wish we did know such things. Our people have been accused of 'whistling up the wind' for centuries, but I suspect that actually they were just good at reading the early signs of already extant storms and such. It would have seemed like cause and effect to people who were already prepared to believe it could be done. Drake *does* seem to have done it, but I tend to believe he was an exception. I don't really expect anything to come of that part of my inquiry."

William continued to look just a little dubious.

"What—kinds of things are involved in finding out about the other?" he asked hesitantly. "If you can tell me, that is."

"Well, we'll want—to collect some items that belonged to Drake, for their association value—things like that. With any luck, we'll be doing the actual working at Buckland Abbey, down in Devonshire. That was Drake's estate, you know." Graham lowered his eyes, running a fingertip idly along the rim of his glass. "This must all seem very strange to you. You must think I've gone quite mad."

"No. I only wish I knew how to help you."

"Just listening helps," Graham replied with a smile. "Thank you."

With a wistful shrug, William unstoppered the brandy decanter and poured them each another cognac, a wordless operation that yet carried a measure of thoughtful camaraderie. When he had finished, he sat back in his chair with a heavy sigh and gazed at the fireplace over the rim of his glass.

"Is anything wrong?" Graham asked after a moment when William did not speak.

William shrugged. "Nothing that hasn't been for some time. I envy you, Gray. You're doing something useful, both in the Service and in this other—thing." He gestured with his glass. "And what do I do? The fifth wheel spins and does nothing. The extra prince smiles, shakes hands, inspects factories and troops, and makes the same dreary little speeches over and over. And none of it means a bloody damn!"

He quickly drained his glass and poured another without looking at Graham, his face set in bleak isolation. Graham was stunned. Of all the reactions he had prepared for, he had not even dreamed of this one. William was slipping into one of his despondent moods again, unconvinced of his own worth and unaware how his mere existence made a difference—and not only to Graham.

Could he not see that the inspection tours, the speeches, were just as important a part of the war effort as anything Graham was doing? Had he forgotten his actions at Dover? The people loved and revered their Royal Family with a fierce devotion that had not diminished over the centuries, even if most of them, including that family, did not remember the sacred ties with the past. William was a prince of the blood and a part of all that even if he did not know it. But how to convince *him* of that?

"You don't see the meaning, do you?" he said quietly. "You really don't see how it all connects, even with what I'm doing."

"Don't humor me," William muttered. "I'm not a child. You don't have to pretend. Spare me that, at least."

"By God, I won't spare you!" Graham said softly, his eyes going cold as William looked up in surprise. "I'm tired of hearing you sell yourself short."

William scowled and glanced away. "Now you *are* presuming on our friendship."

"Indulge me, then. God knows, I don't ask that very often. You really don't think any of this touches you?"

The prince shrugged and lit up another cigarette, a sullen expression making his face a mask. As Graham's eyes swept the stiff, immaculate figure, abruptly he knew the approach to take.

"Very well," he said after a moment. "Tell me about that star you're wearing tonight—the one that doesn't match mine."

William glanced down at his chest in automatic response, a look of confusion cracking the mask.

"You mean my Garter star?"

As Graham nodded, the prince sat back and peered at him oddly, already off balance.

"Now you *have* gone daft."

"Perhaps. Perhaps not. How much do you remember about the founding of the order?"

William grimaced and rolled his eyes ceilingward. "Is this to be another of your improbable history lessons?"

"If you don't wish to find out what I have to say, you have only to say so."

When Graham said nothing more, William put aside his glass with an impatient sigh and made an elaborate show of tapping ash from his cigarette. When a response still was not forthcoming, he sighed again and inclined his head.

"Very well. What about the order?"

"Thank you," Graham said with a slight dip of his chin and the ghost of a smile. "Suppose you first give me a historical setting in which to place my tale. Tell me about the institution of the Order of the Garter."

William took a deep drag on his cigarette and folded his

arms across his chest as he glanced idly at the ceiling. "The order was founded by King Edward III in the mid fourteenth century after a lady dropped her garter at a court ball," he said as if reciting from rote. "To save her reputation, the King is supposed to have buckled it around his own leg and said, '*Honi soit qui mal y pense*'—dishonoured be he who thinks evil of it—and that became the motto of the order which Edward formed shortly after that."

He looked at Graham at last. "Why are you asking me this? You're surely not going to try to tell me there's something— what was your word?—*esoteric* about the Order of the Garter, are you?"

"No, I just thought I'd ramble on about a totally unrelated subject." Graham relaxed a little and had another sip of cognac. "Are you aware, William, that a blue or a green garter was anciently the sign of leadership in the witch cult?"

At the prince's surprised intake of breath, Graham continued smoothly. "I thought not. England was not Christianized as quickly or as completely as orthodox historians would have one think, you know. That's hardly surprising when one recalls that most literate men of those days were of the Christian clergy. It stands to reason that written history would have a decidedly Christian bias.

"The matter of historical accuracy is not confined to religious matters, however," Graham went on. "The winners— the people in power—write the histories or have them written. Look at your much-maligned ancestor Richard III as just one example. If he'd won at Bosworth Field, I dare say the chronicles of his reign would have presented him in quite a different light. But since he lost to Henry Tudor, we have only the Tudortold tales of what a terrible king he had been—the horrible hunchback uncle who murdered the little princes in the tower and all. If Thomas More and Shakespeare had been writing for Plantagenet patrons instead of Tudors . . ."

William, who had been listening in astonishment as Graham spoke, recovered his previous skepticism with a blink and flicked ash from his cigarette with a sly grin.

"You're digressing, Gray. Get back to the garters and the witches. This is very entertaining, but I don't think you can bring this one back on the track and make me believe it."

"No? Let me tell you a little about the witch cult in England, then. You said you'd done some reading in the past week, but you obviously didn't do enough. In the Middle Ages, the old religion—paganism, if you will—was still flourishing among both the common people and certain of the nobility. The real cult, involving worship of the ancient gods and goddesses of Britain, had little to do with what later became the subject of the so-called witch hunts. A great deal of what came to be believed about the witches derived from the same sort of mentality that produced the Inquisition and the crusades against other kinds of heretics on the Continent: Cathars and Albigensians and even some remnants of Templar belief. As a Freemason, you're aware of that aspect of my story, I'm sure."

"You're saying that Jacques de Molay and Geoffroi de Charney were witches." William said indulgently. "Do go on. This gets more fantastic by the second."

Graham sighed patiently. "You're not listening, William. In France as well as in England, the ecclesiastical hierarchy was aware that the conversion to Christianity was incomplete, that paganism was flourishing side by side with orthodox Christianity. Officially, they did their best to discourage it.

"But even the priests often managed to meld the two traditions into an acceptable blend without qualms. Many pagan customs were simply assimilated wholesale into Christianity. That same kind of synthesis was involved in the formation of the Order of the Garter."

"Strange, I always thought it had been modeled on the court of King Arthur and his knights," William said archly.

"That was one of the outward justifications," Graham agreed. "But let's look at the lost garter incident more closely. You didn't say whose garter it was, but that isn't particularly important, anyway—only that the lady was of very high rank at court. It could have been Philippa, Edward's queen, or the Countess of Salisbury. Or even the King's own cousin, Joan the Fair Maid of Kent, who later became Countess of Salisbury herself—and Princess of Wales after that, as wife to the Black Prince. I tend to suspect it was Joan."

"Go on, go on," William urged, gesturing with his hand.

"I am. In any case, when as important a lady as any of those lost the garter of her pagan rank at a court function before the King and probably assorted ecclesiastical authorities, things could have gone very badly for her," Graham continued. "When

Edward picked up that garter and buckled it around his leg with the immortal words, at very *least* he was taking her under his protection. He's also said to have mentioned something about making it 'the most honourable garter that ever was worn, e'er long'—though Edward may already have been aware of its significance, since he later asked his private secretary to look into the 'background and traditions of the Order of St. George and the Garter.' It makes little sense to have inquired about this unless there *was* an earlier significance to the garter, and Edward knew of it."

William frowned. "You seem to know quite a lot about an order to which you don't even belong."

"It's my business to know," Graham returned softly. "I told you I wasn't totally untrained. I've given you the more conservative interpretation of Edward's actions in picking up the lady's garter. Shall I suggest a broader one?"

"Why not?" William smiled ruefully. "I don't believe a word of this, anyway."

"I know you don't. Humor me just a little longer. If Edward *was* aware of the esoteric meaning of the garter, we might construe that, by his action, he was essentially acknowledging his own support of and possibly membership in the very cult signified by the garter—maybe even taking on the position of an incarnate god for his subjects who still followed the path of the divine king. He would have been neither the first nor the last of your illustrious ancestors to assume that role."

"The divine king?" William interrupted. "Wait a moment. Are you saying that the idea of divine right came from—"

"The very thing. Anciently—and by that I mean from the earliest tribal times—the king was the embodiment of the land and life-giving forces. As such, he had to remain strong and vigorous if the land was to prosper. It followed that as his strength waned—as he got old—it became necessary to replace the aging king with a new, younger vessel to carry the strength of the land.

"So the king was sacrificed, his blood spilled on the earth, and a new king crowned, usually on a seven-year cycle. Later, kings were no longer sacrificed every seven years, but a substitute was slain, as long as the king was strong. The idea of the king's divinity persisted in our notion of rule by divine right. There may even have been instances of the divine sacrifice in historical times. The death of your distant ancestor, William Rufus, was almost certainly a sacrificial slaying. There were undoubtedly others later on. But I didn't mean to digress too far from old Edward Three and the Garter."

William shook his head bewilderedly. "You're more than a little wonky, Gray. A garter *can* just be something to hold up a stocking, you know. It doesn't have to be some magical—"

"Still not convinced, eh? What did I tell you about covens the last time we talked?"

"The idea of twelve plus one?"

"Um-hum."

"What about it?"

"Think about the organization of the order: twelve knights for the King and twelve for the Prince of Wales. That's twenty-six: two covens. There are also twenty-six poor knights and thirteen canons, making a total of five covens in all. I'd guess that to be more than coincidence."

"But it's a *Christian* order, founded on classic *Christian* principles."

Graham smiled and shook his head. "The principles are universal at their heart, William. In the beginning, the reverence of the Garter Knights for the sovereign of their order put even God in second place. Read the order's original statutes of institution sometime. For the first century or so after the founding, the knights entering the St. George Chapel at Windsor for meetings of their order would make their obeisance *first* to the sovereign or his stall and *then* to the presence signified at the altar. They believed that the God Incarnate was among them in the person of their king. This kind of reverence for the monarch, to one degree or another, extended at least into the reign of James I."

William shook his head. "Why am I even listening to you? This is utter rubbish!"

"Is it? What else was Christ's crucifixion but a sacrifice of the divine king?" Graham retorted, determined not to let up. "King of the Jews and Son of God—God Incarnate. And I could name you dozens of other divine king sacrifices from the traditions of other religions—Osiris, Tammuz, Mithras. . . . If one believes in any of those, including Christianity, how is that so different from believing that the king assumed the godhead at his anointing and then stood in the stead of the god during his reign? It all goes back to the times when the king was priest as well as ruler, making sacrifices on his people's behalf—and the sacrifice was not always just incense and sheep."

"But that was *then*."

"Yes, but we certainly do retain elements of the old priestly ordination in our present coronation ceremony—the anointing, the vesting with priest-like clothing. It's still sometimes referred to as the sacring of the king. Perhaps it's even significant that to this day, only Knights of the Garter are permitted to hold the canopy over the king during his anointing. Think back to your brother's coronation—or your father's, if you can remember it. An interesting custom, don't you think?"

William had actually stopped breathing as Graham hammered home his final points, and now he let out his pent-up breath in an audible sigh as he sank back in his chair. All the fight was gone out of him. After a moment, he remembered the cigarette between his fingers and stubbed it out distractedly, but Graham could see him eyeing his Garter star from quite a new perspective as he pushed his glass aside.

"Oddly enough, it does make a certain kind of sense," William murmured when he glanced up at Graham again.

"It also carries the potential for a great deal of controversy and scandal, were your knowledge to become known," Graham said quietly. "That's why I've never told you any of this before." He sighed. "On the other hand, it does seem somehow right that you should finally know. Maybe I've realized that from the beginning. Perhaps that's why I fought so hard to force you into being what I knew you could be when that spoiled, arrogant young Lieutenant Victor first came under my command," he continued with a wan smile. "Perhaps we even knew one another in some previous life and unconsciously I recognized the bond."

William smiled self-consciously, still a little nervous but obviously pleased at the idea.

"Do you really think so?"

"It's possible." Graham flashed on a mental image of William's horoscope, suddenly making a previously unnoticed connection with an aspect of his own. "Now that I think about it, our charts do tend to confirm that. My south node falls in your first house. It's a little wide, but it certainly fits. Odd that I never noticed it before."

"What are you talking about? Noticed what?"

Graham shook his head and grinned. "Sorry. I keep forgetting that such things mean nothing to you. Such a configuration is often a sign of a karmic tie—some connection from previous lives. I'll bring both charts and show you next time we meet. On the other hand"—he shrugged—"perhaps it doesn't mean a thing. Astrology is no more infallible than any other science."

"Or art?" William returned with a tiny smile.

"Or art," Graham agreed, though suddenly he felt uneasy.

Apparently restless, William rose and moved nearer the fireplace to stare unseeing at the bric-a-brac there, one hand in a pocket and the other rubbing the back of his neck in an awkward, nervous gesture. After a moment, he half turned to Graham again.

"This—tie of the Royal Family to the—the old faith. Do you think it still exists today?"

"Not consciously, for the most part, especially for the royals themselves," Graham answered, wondering what he might unwittingly have said to elicit William's growing restlessness. "I think it persists for the people in the mystique of royalty, however. That's why your appearances and speeches are so important, even though they may not seem that way, compared to more dramatic action. You're a part of the same royal line which anciently gave us sacred kings. In that sense, they become very much your people, and you their prince."

"But it's my brother who's king, not I."

"Yes, but blood is blood regardless of the order of birth. That makes you rather special."

"Then you think—"

A discreet rap at the door cut William off in mid-sentence, and he mouthed a single-word expletive under his breath before clearing his throat with a nervous cough.

"Yes?"

It was Wells, who inclined his head apologetically.

"I beg your pardon, sir. There's a Mr. Grumbaugh on the line for Colonel Graham." He shifted his glance to Graham. "He says you're to pick up a message at the Admiralty straightaway, colonel."

Graham rose at once. "Tell him I'm on my way, please, Mr. Wells. And have my driver bring the car around, if you will."

As Wells withdrew and Graham tossed off the last of his cognac, the prince drifted a little closer.

"What's on, then? Is Grumbaugh a part of your—Drake thing, after all?"

Graham nearly choked on his drink. "Good heavens, no! It's probably some ciphers we're expecting. Ultra—you know. They won't release them to anyone but me." He set down his glass and began struggling with the collar of his tunic. "Grumbaugh's working the late shift tonight. I told him to ring me if the word came through. He's the only one who knew where I was dining this evening, and I told him any interruption had better be urgent—so I suppose it is."

"Well, I suppose you'd better see about it, then, hadn't you?" The prince stuck out his hand. "At any rate, I'm glad we had a chance to talk—even if we were interrupted. Incidentally, may I ask a favor?" he added as Graham's hand touched his.

Graham, his one hand clasped between the prince's two, had a sudden premonition of impending crisis.

"What favor is that?"

"I'd like to be with you when you do that Drake thing you talked about."

CHAPTER 7

FOR AN INTERMINABLE INSTANT, GRAHAM COULD ONLY stare at William in dumb disbelief. Suddenly, he was all too aware of the feudal symbolism of his hand between the prince's and the obedience the implied relationship suggested. He realized, too, that William had very likely intended the connection, rightly anticipating that what he asked would put Graham on the spot.

But why had William asked such a thing and with the weight of such compulsion? Graham had not even been sure the prince believed most of what they had been dicussing.

No formal oath of feudal allegiance bound the two of them, prince and man, as it might have done in medieval times. Graham was not William's vassal in any technical sense. But Graham now realized that a hint of such a link had been building between them for some time—perhaps even from the beginning. The mystique of the royal was far more than the coolly reasoned historical theory he had voiced so glibly not minutes before. William *was* his prince, in the fullest sense of the feudal relationship expressed in their clasped hands.

Yet there were other obligations that must take precedence even over the wishes of a prince. William had asked the impossible. If it was Graham's duty to serve this man, it was also his duty to protect him. A magical operation was no place for the uninitiated, especially a royal duke. Besides, Graham was

111

not alone in what was planned. He had others to protect as well, who stood in similar relationship to *him*.

"Sir, I—can't allow that," he whispered formally. "You're putting me in an extremely awkward position by even asking. It isn't entirely up to me, in any case. There are others to be considered."

"Your—superiors will be there?" William murmured.

Graham nodded, not wanting to even imagine what Alix— or David!—would say. But the blue eyes did not waver, and the royal hands slackened their grip not at all.

"Gray, I'm sorry. I know it isn't fair of me to ask. It isn't just a passing fancy, though. I couldn't begin to tell you why, but it's—important that I be there."

"William, I—"

"Will you *listen*?" William hissed under his breath, his eyes oddly desperate. "I promise I won't interfere. And you know I'll be discreet."

As Graham continued shaking his head, searching for words to persuade William that it simply was not possible, Wells appeared at the door again, Graham's coat and hat in hand.

"Colonel, your car is ready."

"Gray, please!" the prince repeated. "At least promise that you'll think about it, that you'll ask the others. That's all I ask."

"All right, I'll think about it," Graham returned in a low voice, though he knew he had no intention of relenting even if the others agreed.

"Thank you," the prince murmured under his breath, then continued in a slightly louder than normal voice as he gripped Graham's hand in an ordinary handshake and released it.

"Good night, then. A pity we've had to cut our evening short, but duty calls and all that. Do ring me next week, when you get the chance. I hope they let you get some sleep tonight."

As Graham shrugged into his coat, he wondered how he *would* sleep even if he had the time. Of all the possible outcomes of this evening's dinner, this was one he had not expected.

To cap his evening, there were no ciphers awaiting hi.n at the Admiralty. The summons turned out to be a ruse. A young subaltern led him to the door of an obscure office on the second floor and then left him despite his low-voiced protests and demands for an explanation. When he entered the office, he understood why.

He knew whose aide the attractive WRNS rating was and also her real function as resident clairvoyant to the powerful man she served. He followed her into the next room without question and sat down to wait, taut with expectation when she left him. He tried not to think about William.

The distinguished-looking naval officer who shortly entered wore a captain's four cuff rings on his uniform sleeve and a gold staff aiguillette on his shoulder, but it was not that which brought Graham to his feet at once. The two of them held equal military rank and were almost of an age, but they generally moved in quite different circles. The man noted Graham's mess dress with a raised eyebrow and a bemused lift to one corner of his mouth, too tired to really smile. He gestured with the manila envelope he took from under his arm as he perched on the corner of the bare desk top.

"So, I hear it took a royal duke to get you out of battle-dress. Have a nice dinner, did you, colonel?"

Graham took the man's measure with faint amusement, catching the slight twinkle of response in the light eyes.

"So, it must have been *your* aide who put Grumbaugh on the panic to get me here, sir," he replied, warming to the other man's charisma. "I assume it was important enough to interrupt a glass of very fine cognac."

"Well, now, Gray, if you don't want to know what I've arranged about Buckland—"

Graham held up both hands in surrender and shook his head, grinning broadly. "I yield to your lordship's impeccable sense of priorities. Were you able to get permission?"

"I was." The man pulled a sheaf of forms from the envelope and fanned through them as Graham moved closer to look on. "You should find all the authorizations in order. I had to pull a few strings, but most of them are quite untraceable. It's set for the fifth of July, as you requested."

"Perfect. I do appreciate it, sir."

"Not at all. You were quite right about parts of the estate being used as a storehouse for naval supplies, by the way. That made things considerably easier. If explanations are necessary, I shall say it's for a top-level meeting of some of your agents—

which is true, in a sense, I suppose—though if anyone asks why you picked the middle of a God-forsaken moor, I don't know what I'll tell them. I shan't inquire why you really want it, though I can guess."

Graham replaced the forms in the envelope and slipped the lot inside his coat with a smile. "I'm sure your guess is at least close to the truth, sir. And I do appreciate everything you're doing to help. This may make the difference, come August first. Thank you."

The man shrugged, but he also smiled. "All a part of the service, old man." He glanced at his watch. "Well, I must go. Some engineers are supposed to tell me whether my poor old ship can be refitted by the end of the year. I suppose you heard about the beating she took."

"Some rumors about a stubborn captain did cross my desk," Graham replied with a congratulatory nod. "You're back to sea, then?"

"On one ship or another, probably for the duration—at least that's what I hope for. I'll be doing convoy duty for a while. Anyway, good luck."

He stuck out his hand, somewhat to Graham's surprise, and Graham clasped it with a slight bow before leaving the office. As he made his way back to his car, he found himself comparing the man he had just left with William. Somehow the similarity disturbed him. It was one thing for this man to be an aware scion of the old line; it was quite another for a prince of the blood to be wanting the same kind of knowledge and beginning to use the weight of his rank to get it.

"I told you, I don't *know* why he wants to be there," Graham said wearily as he and the others relaxed in the library at Oakwood three days later, after their Midsummer working. "As far as I can tell, it came right out of the blue. I think even he was surprised. Looking back, I probably shouldn't have mentioned it in the first place, but at the time, it seemed quite logical."

David Jordan, Lord Selwyn, the master of the house, moved into the pool of moonlight streaming through the closed French doors and gazed into the summer night. Beyond him, the precisely trimmed hedges of the garden's boxwood maze stood out in bright-honed planes of silver and inky shadows. In the center of that maze, though only the roof top could be seen from anywhere on the grounds, lay the place where they had worked: by day, a trellis-sided gazebo twined with roses and ivy; by night, some nights, their temple and magical working place.

When Selwyn did not speak, Graham rose and joined him. Behind them in the room, the two women poured tea and arranged sandwiches and biscuits by candlelight; the three younger men, Richard, Geoffrey, and Michael, divided their attention between the coming food and the conversation in progress between their elders. The brigadier leaned casually against the wall beside the doorway, watching and listening to Graham and Selwyn but saying nothing, pipe smoke curling lazily in a slight draft that managed to sneak past the door frame.

"You mentioned congruencies in your two charts," Selwyn said after a moment. "What in particular?"

Graham sighed and rubbed at a dull throbbing behind his eyes. He had participated in the working this evening, but the tension of being constantly on guard against a contact from Sturm had left him far more exhausted than usual.

"Well, just for openers, we both have the same ascending degree and sign: nineteen degrees Cancer rising—less than half a minute apart, in fact—and we both have Scorpio moons in our fifth houses, also very close."

"How close?"

"About eight degrees. We also both have angular suns in water signs, and we both have Pisces in the midheaven, less than two degrees apart, with our suns strongly aspecting it. The thing I flashed on while I was talking to him and which I'd never noticed before was my south-node placement in his first house—a possible karmic link. We also have Pluto and Neptune in our twelfth houses, referring to occult matters." He paused a beat. "Maybe he *should* be allowed to come."

"Would it be physically safe for him in terms of the military situation?" the brigadier asked. "I've heard rumor of something big brewing at Plymouth."

Graham smiled wanly. "I wish I knew where you get your intelligence, Wesley. You're quite correct, however. Right now, a sizable chunk of the French fleet is anchored at Plymouth and wondering what the bloody hell it's going to do once the armistice is signed." He glanced at the others and lowered his voice so only Selwyn and the brigadier could hear. "I assume you know what's being considered, David. Your ship was mentioned in some of the dispatches."

Selwyn propped himself wearily against the door frame and closed his eyes. "I'm to pick up a shipload of Royal Marines next week and stand by for orders to proceed to Plymouth and seize the ships by whatever force is necessary to keep them from surrendering to the Germans." He looked up at the moon. "Bloody war! Since when are we supposed to fight our allies?"

"It's going to be even worse in the Mediterranean," Graham murmured. "Did you know Peter's ship is going to Oran?"

"*Bloody* war!" Selwyn repeated bitterly.

After a moment, the brigadier gestured with his pipe. "Let's get back to the duke," he said softly. "You've confirmed my fears about the situation in Plymouth, Gray. If you did want him to come, would it be possible for him to bypass Plymouth?"

"Certainly. But Plymouth should be resolved by the fifth. I'm simply trying to anticipate potential problems in advance." Graham glanced at Selwyn. "I'm not sure I have the authority to make a final decision, anyway. I'm only the acting chief. If David says no, then it's no."

Selwyn turned slightly in the moonlight, silver gleaming in the once-dark hair. He had been their chief for nearly fifteen years, since the death of his father after the Great War. With Alix, he had led them with careful wisdom, not objecting or resisting as Graham's emerging talents gradually equaled and even surpassed his own in some instances, though leadership had remained firmly in his hands until a year ago. When, at the beginning of the war, it became clear that Selwyn himself would be at sea much of the time, Graham had been the logical choice to assume the leader's role for the duration, especially in light of the need for the Lammas coordination. The brigadier judged himself too old, and the other men were far too young and inexperienced.

But the habits of fifteen years could not be put aside as easily as the mere words were spoken, by either Selwyn or Graham. They had already discussed the Dieter affair, and Selwyn had apologized for encroaching on Graham's still-hesitant supervision. The matter of William was an altogether different proposition, for immediately it touched on everyone who would be present at the Drake working, not to mention the more far-reaching implications for William's future involvement. Even if the decision were put in Graham's hands, the others must also agree, especially Selwyn.

"It will have to be your decision," Selwyn finally said. "I told you before that I'd try to avoid stepping on your toes again. Right now, however, I'm thinking about the security of this group. His Royal Highness doesn't know me in this context, and I'd really rather he never did. But you need me at Buckland, Gray—and if he's there, my cover is blown. And frankly, besides yourself, I probably have the most to lose of any of us if he were to go sour."

"He wouldn't go sour," Graham muttered, half turning away, hands jammed in the pockets of his black wool robe. "I'd stake my life on it."

"You may be doing just that."

"Well, it wouldn't be the first time," Graham retorted. "Look, David, I haven't any proof, but I think he may see his participation as a way to do something positive for the war effort—something besides making speeches and doing all the other dreary things so often expected of royals. Maybe I overdid it when I was trying to convince him he was useful, but he'd gone off on that old fifth-wheel argument again." He sighed. "I have to consider the charts, too. Something's at work here besides coincidence. I've also been thinking about the tarot reading Alix did. What if *William* is the Knight of Wands, who's supposed to offer help?"

"She told me about the reading," Selwyn said, "but I'm not sure we want his kind of help. The *last* thing we need is to get a member of the Royal Family overtly involved with the old ways."

"Don't be too sure," the brigadier said, chomping on his pipe. "There's a heavy weight of tradition in the old line regardless of the fact that the present-day incumbents aren't consciously aware of it." He blew smoke toward the ceiling, letting his pale eyes follow its drift. "They seem to come along when they are needed, and when they do, they seem to know what's to be done." He shifted his glance directly to Graham, the old eyes strangely piercing. "Do you want him there when you scry for Drake, Gray? You sound as if you're half convinced he should be there."

Graham bowed his head. "I don't know. But if the logistics are possible, I'd like to have that option. I *can* say that my misgivings have nothing to do with whether or not I trust him. It's whether I could put his presence sufficiently out of mind to work effectively. I wouldn't want him frightened. And I certainly wouldn't want him hurt because he got frightened for *me* and tried to interfere."

"Yes, but will he accept your discipline if you tell him that?" Selwyn asked.

"I think so."

"You have to *know*."

"Come and have some tea while it's still hot," Alix said, pushing between them and drawing the blackout curtains back into place. "You men are all alike: grouchy as bears until you've had something to eat. Afterward, I'll read the cards again if you like, David, but Gray just may be right. Anyway, I don't think any of us need to make up our minds on empty stomachs."

As she hooked an arm in the arm of each of the two men and Audrey turned up the lights, Graham glanced across at his chief. The Earl of Selwyn wore a look of resignation.

Alix got out the cards after they had eaten. After Selwyn shuffled the deck, she laid the cards in the old, familiar pattern and began. The first card up was the Knight of Wands.

"Well, fancy that," she murmured as she glanced at her stunned husband and the equally aghast Graham. "I'm sorry, David, but you shuffled them. I can't help how they fall."

Selwyn only shook his head resignedly as she turned her gaze back to the cards.

"At the heart of the matter lies the Knight of Wands. He offers new ideas which may be advantageous."

She pulled the next card and turned it, laying it across the first with a faint snap.

"Crossing it for better or worse is the Nine of Wands." She paused a beat. "Discretion is in order, protection of one's own interests, but obstinacy could be a problem. The basis of the situation"—she turned the third card and raised an eyebrow as she laid it on the table—"is the Ten of Wands. Tremendous responsibilities, perhaps oppressively so. David, this seems to be focusing on you as well as Gray."

As her husband frowned and eased his chair a little closer, she turned the next card.

Selwyn was less skeptical when they had finished. By the time they had reviewed the reading and compared it to the previous one, discussed William's potential involvement further, and outlined the measures that would have to be taken to accommodate the presence of an outsider, even Selwyn had to admit that the duke's attendance might be safe enough if Graham still wanted him to attend.

"I suppose we can hardly just cut him off after you've told him as much as you have," he said to Graham, tilting his empty teacup to glance idly at the leaves in the bottom. "Other than us, he isn't going to see a great deal—as long as you don't produce any pyrotechnics in the mirror, of course."

"Pyrotechnics?" Graham grinned weakly. "Not bloody likely, thank you. Wrong element. Drake worked with air, if you'll recall—storms and such. Besides"—his face assumed a more sober and troubled expression—"I'm not yet sure *I* want him there."

Moré than a week later, Graham still had not made up his mind. Nor had his official duties allowed him time to dwell on the matter. William rang almost daily at first and left openings each time for an obviously wished-for response, but he made no overt reference to their last meeting. Then he was gone on an inspection tour to Scotland for nearly a week, which made it easier for Graham to delay reaching a decision.

By the third of July, two days before the scheduled Buckland working and a fortnight since his last real contact with the prince, Graham was still undecided. He *had* been watching developments at Plymouth more closely than he might have, just to keep his options open. He had even investigated ways of getting William safely to the vicinity of Plymouth without arousing any undue curiosity. That part, unlike the ultimate decision, had been easy.

It now appeared that the seizure of the French fleet would be quite resolved by the fifth, thereby eliminating any potential danger to William's physical safety. A boot-legged copy of Selwyn's sailing orders had crossed Graham's desk over the weekend directing the earl to bring in his shipload of men the night of the second. If all went smoothly—if all *had* gone smoothly, for it was now nearing noon of the third—the exercise would provide an ideal excuse for H.R.H. The Duke of

Clarence to make a surprise inspection visit to Plymouth to
view the aftermath and bolster morale among the French crews.
Selwyn would have to make the final decision on whether that
part of the potential plan was feasible, based on his assessment
of what was now occurring.

After that, however, it was Graham's decision again. By
calling in a series of favors owed by an air commodore at
Southampton, he had been able to get Richard and Geoffrey
placed on standby for a flight to Plymouth on the fifth, but
that part was still quite flexible. So were tentative arrangements
for housing and for getting William to Buckland. Now he was
awaiting the go-ahead from Selwyn, still undecided.

With a sigh, Graham returned his attention to the transcript
he had been working on all morning, checking the translation
of an unusual phrase against the original and making a marginal
note for someone to check a possible quirk of wording against
their files. He had been reminding himself for hours that the
Drake operation must be kept in its proper perspective. Magic
was a very good thing, and powerful if appropriately employed,
but it was an adjunct, not a substitute, for hard, honest work
of the more usual sort. The latter was what Graham's superiors
must always see. They could understand an astrologer called
Rote Adler, who appeared to be advising the Third Reich.

To a dull background chatter of teleprinters in the next room,
Graham immersed himself for the next several hours roughing
out a synopsis of everything they now knew about *Rote Adler*,
for sufficient data now existed to begin realistic counter measures. They had received confirmation the previous week that
Sturm and *Rote Adler* were one and the same—from an agent
in Berlin, who nearly paid for the information with his life.
An unsolicited follow-up report from Dieter had provided additional biographical material that validated the first report.

The Oakwood reaction to Dieter's report had been resound-
ingly negative, even from Michael, despite its strategic value.
Useful though Dieter's insights on Sturm might be, the taint
of the satanic connection made them all very uncomfortable.
Far too much was at stake in the weeks ahead to risk a betrayal.
In fact, it made Graham uneasy that Dieter knew as much about
their plans as he did.

Considering Dieter, Sturm, and *Rote Adler*, Graham succeeded in putting William out of his mind for a while, but

shortly after two, the racket of the teleprinters intruded briefly as the connecting door between his office and the next opened and closed. The sight of Denton approaching with a yellow signal flimsy snapped him instantly back into his previous concerns.

"Is that what I hope it is?"

"Lord Selwyn's signal? Yes, sir. I don't know if it's the answer you're wanting, though," he added, handing it across the desk.

"You read me too well, Denny," Graham replied, running his eyes quickly over the few lines.

OBJECTIVE SECURED STOP IF STILL DESIRED CAN
ARRANGE MATTER WE DISCUSSED FOR FRIDAY FIFTH
JULY STOP RSVP STOP SELWYN ENDS

He could feel Denton watching him expectantly, but he only nodded and laid the signal aside before gathering up the notes he had been making.

"Thank you, Denny. I'll handle it from here. Would you please give these to Grumbaugh and ask him to follow up as I've indicated?"

As the chatter of the teleprinters receded once more with Denton's departure, Graham moved the signal back to the center of his blotter and stared at it unseeing.

He could say yes now, if he wanted to. He had only to open his desk drawer and take out the timetable he had constructed in the preceding week and pick up the phone. As his hand came to rest on the cool bakelite of the receiver, he realized he *did* want William at Buckland. Nor was there now any physical excuse of danger to prevent it, any logistical reason to refuse.

Still, there were other dangers, not the least of which was not knowing where things might lead next if William came and saw and was not satisfied with that. Nearly all his life, Graham had been trained to protect and shield the Royal Family from harm. To let William become involved with the occult, even if only as an observer, was to open the possibility for terrible scandal and controversy. Graham was not sure he was ready to shoulder that kind of responsibility merely to satisfy a royal whim and ease his own sense of isolation.

Annoyed with his continuing vacillation, he closed his eyes and nudged his body into a light hypnotic trance to relax for a few minutes while he set his mind to correlating everything one last time. He even let himself cling to the possibility that William might have changed his mind, that he might not be so keen after further consideration in the stark reality of the passing days. It *might* be true. . . .

Rousing himself, Graham pulled the single sheet from his desk drawer and scanned its well-known contents slowly, aware that he was but stalling, then picked up the phone and resolutely dialed William's London number. The prince was not there, so he tried Windsor. He got through after only two intermediaries. He kept his voice carefully formal as he tried to frame his words just so.

"Good afternoon, sir. John Graham here. Sorry to be so long getting back to you."

"Gray? Delighted! How did you know where to find me?"

Graham allowed himself a grim smile, glad that the prince could not see his face.

"Why, this is MI.6, sir," he said lightly. "We make it our business to know everything." He drew a deep breath. "Are you by any chance still serious about that request you made over the after-dinner drinks the other week, or were we both just a bit in our cups?"

There was a quick intake of breath at the other end and then dead silence for several heartbeats. Graham had given the prince an easy way out if he wanted it. As he held his breath in anticipation, he could sense that William was framing his words just as carefully as he, as aware as Graham that this was not a secure line.

"Yes, I am, Gray. I'm quite serious. Is it on, then?"

To his immense relief, Graham felt no twinge of apprehension or regret once the words had been spoken. The real venture into the unknown was only now beginning, but his anxiety seemed to have vanished with William's confirmation. Perhaps it was going to be all right.

"It's on," he replied, forcing his hand to release its death grip on the phone as he began breathing again. "Perhaps I can tell you more about it when I see you. That isn't why I rang, though," he continued, shifting into the transition speech he had rehearsed so many times in his mind. "I don't know whether

you'd heard—probably not, since it's such a new develop-
ment—but the French fleet at Plymouth and Portsmouth are
now secure. Royal Marines seized the ships early this morning.
Word just came in."

"That's fine news," the prince replied with an expectant lift
to the end of his statement.

Graham picked up a pencil and began drawing little circles
on the edge of his notes. "Yes. Our chaps apparently did a
first-rate job. In fact, the admiral commanding, Plymouth,
wondered whether you might possibly come down and make
an impromptu inspection, perhaps on Friday. I know it's rather
short notice, but the combined fleet will be sailing fairly soon.
He thought a royal visit might be good for morale, theirs as
well as ours."

"Yes, I think it might at that," William replied. "Wells,
bring my calendar, would you?"

Other voices in the background became more distinct—
William evidently had been working in his office—and his
tone was more certain as he continued. It was obvious he had
made the proper connection immediately: a visit to Plymouth
only coincidentally had to do with what had just occurred in
the historic harbor.

"We're checking my schedule now, Gray. Yes. I've got
something on tomorrow, but Friday would be fine. What arrangements have been made?"

"I have a flying boat standing by at Southampton," Graham
said. "They can fly you over Portsmouth Harbor for an aerial
look at that half of the operation, then have you in Plymouth
for luncheon with the admiral and his flag officers and a tour
of inspection in the afternoon. Overnight in Plymouth and return on Saturday at your leisure. Can you get a train out of
Victoria early Friday morning, or would you rather come as
far as Southampton tomorrow evening?"

"Hold on. We're checking."

He listened to more murmuring, the crackle of timetables
being opened and refolded, the hollow, muffled change of
sound as William apparently put his hand over the receiver.

"How about an 0847 arrival at the Southampton Terminus
on Friday morning?"

"It couldn't be better," Graham replied, making a note of
the time on his own schedule. "How many shall I tell them to

expect in your party? I'd suggest as few as possible, since we're operating on such short notice."

"Let's see: Wells and Griffin, my valet, I suppose," came the tentative response. "I don't think I can do with any less if it's overnight."

Graham smiled grimly to himself and made another note. He did not know whether William had yet thought about what his staff would do while he and Graham went traipsing off to Buckland, but Graham had decided days ago that he did not want to have to deal with alibis that might later be questioned. Two men could be incapacitated with relative ease, however, and never suspect a thing amiss the next morning. He would have to enlist William's cooperation in that, but the prince had done such things before when he worked for Graham; Denton would be available to watch-dog the two while Graham and William were gone.

"We can manage that, I think," he said confidently. "I'll have a driver collect you at the Terminus Station at 0847. Your flight shouldn't take more than three-quarters of an hour."

When he and the prince had exchanged a few more pleasantries, Graham rang off. He sat and shivered in afterreaction for several minutes, breathing deeply. Then he quickly encoded two brief messages and took them to the signal room: one to a ship at anchor in Plymouth Harbor and another to an air crew at RAF Calshot, near Southampton.

CHAPTER 8

TWO DAYS LATER, AS WILLIAM, DUKE OF CLARENCE stepped onto the dock at RAF Calshot, returning the duty officer's salute, he wondered whether he really knew what he was doing. Ahead, Griffin and a pair of airmen were loading their few pieces of luggage into the motor launch that was to take them to their flying boat, but William's mind was already in Plymouth—though the city in his imagination bore little resemblance to the one he was about to visit.

He had never been to Plymouth, though he had spent much of the past two weeks engaged in careful research on the city and its most famous son. Unfortunately, he had found little to reassure him about the aspect of the place that was most on his mind. The supernatural game into which he had invited himself so casually did not seem to have any written rules—or if it did, he had not found them. All he had really managed to do was to confuse and frighten himself quite thoroughly.

He wondered what the day—and night—would bring. As he climbed aboard the launch and took a seat in the stern beside his aide, glancing up at his personal standard snapping in the breeze, he also wondered what he might unwittingly have gotten his staff into. Gray had not said it in so many words, but it was clear to William that the two would have to be put out of commission at least for the evening. He hoped he would be given some indication as to how Gray wanted him to handle

that, though he was prepared to deal with the situation himself
if no instructions came.

At least the day was fine for flying: a little foggy but bright.
The fog would burn off before another hour passed—perhaps
even by the time they were airborne. As the motor launch
headed out toward the moored flying boat, hull spanking smartly
against a light chop, William breathed the sea air deeply and
told himself to stop worrying.

The day itself was quite predictable. Nothing mysterious or
mystical about that at all. There would be the usual renderings
of royal and military honors by innumerable smartly turned out
naval officers and enlisted men, with uncountable ships to
survey approvingly, salutes to return, hands to shake, and the
obligatory little speeches all along the way that the British
expected of their royalty. He had done it so often before, he
was certain he could do it in his sleep—boring, especially in
light of the night to come, but at least it would help keep his
mind occupied.

Nor was his transportation even unusual. He had flown in
Sunderlands many times before, even from this very base, and
had often piloted them himself. The huge flying boat they were
approaching floated ponderously on the water before them like
some green-dappled aquatic bird, sleek and familiar. Nothing
new here, either.

But as they came under the port wing toward the bow, he
was astonished to see a familiar face waiting in the doorway
to greet him: Richard Graham, Gray's son. Abruptly, a new
piece clicked into place in the puzzle, this one oddly reassuring.
He wondered why he had never made the connection before,
at least in the past few weeks. Was it possible that Richard
was one of the others Gray had to consult before consenting
to William's presence? Would Richard perhaps be present there
tonight?

"Good morning, Mr. Graham," he called, rising to return
Richard's brisk salute as a seaman heaved a line up to the rigger
in the flying boat's bow. "Gray didn't mention you'd been
given your own boat now."

Richard had been on several air crews that had flown for
the prince before, and he grinned amiably as the launch was
drawn closer and the line made fast.

"I received my own command about four months ago, sir.

We're honored to have you flying with us today. Come up and meet the rest of our crew."

Richard offered him a hand as he scrambled aboard, both of them ducking to ease' back through the doorway. Beyond young Graham were two more air-crew officers and a second flight lieutenant with red hair whose name escaped William for the moment but who looked very familiar. The rest of the crew were sergeants of various trades, none of them past their mid twenties as far as he could see. He felt almost old as he shook hands all around. He would be thirty-five in exactly a week.

"You're related to Brigadier Sir Wesley Ellis, aren't you?" he recalled when Geoffrey had been introduced, suddenly making a connection with Dover and Gray's call.

"Yes, sir, his grandson. It's kind of you to remember," Geoffrey answered with a smile that seemed to confirm William's suspicions. "Welcome aboard."

"Yes. Thank you."

For the next few minutes, William merely tried to stay out of the way of Wells, Griffin, and the rest of the crew while they stowed the luggage and secured the boat for flight, wondering exactly how Richard and Geoffrey fit into the picture. One of the sergeants showed him and his staff to seats in the wardroom for takeoff, but as soon as they were airborne, he was invited up to the flight deck, where, to his pleasant surprise, Geoffrey vacated the second pilot's chair for him and relieved the navigator. Below them, the docks of Southampton were receding under their right wing, Southampton Water gleaming in the morning sun as they headed toward the Solent. The headphones in the leather flying helmet William pulled on helped muffle the growl of the four Bristol Pegasus engines.

"Jonesie, stand by to send the 'friendly' signal and fire the colors of the day as we come up on Pompey," Richard was saying as William plugged into the intercom and got himself settled. "With luck, sir, they'll remember we're due to fly over, and they won't open fire," Richard continued aside to the prince as he scanned the horizon warily. "It's said the Portsmouth barrage puts up such thick flak, one can walk on it."

William nodded knowingly, confident that no real danger threatened if Gray had arranged things.

"I'll trust that our chaps know we're up here," he said. "They do have some important targets to protect, however."

"You'll get no argument on *that*, sir," Richard conceded, glancing at the prince with a droll smile. "May I assume that someone briefed you on what happened here on Wednesday?"

"I have a general idea. Actually, I was more interested in Plymouth, since that's where we're headed, but wasn't there something about one of the French submarines putting up a fight here in Portsmouth?"

Richard nodded as he adjusted a throttle. "More of a skirmish, actually, sir. It was the *Surcouf*, one of their larger subs. Apparently, her crew weren't certain they wanted to surrender to our chaps. Both sides lost a man before it was over."

William shook his head and grimaced as Richard continued.

"Other than that, the French crews came ashore quite willingly," Richard said. "A lot of them have even signed on to fight under Admiralty orders for the duration. Look up ahead, sir. There's the harbor."

As Richard dipped the right wing and made a wide turn out over the harbor basin, William braced himself and peered down. They were over the Gosport peninsula now, approaching from north and west of the naval base. Just ahead and to their right, the anchorage glittered like a sheet of speckled glass. While they circled above the British fleet, Richard pointed out several of the captured French destroyers and light cruisers as well as scores of smaller minesweeping and antisubmarine craft and a few submarines, the *Surcouf* among them. The seizure of the French fleet had been to no one's liking, but William was well aware of the danger, had the ships fallen into German hands.

He was silent as they left Portsmouth behind and headed west along the Solent, his thoughts gradually returning to Plymouth, his earlier apprehensions, and curiosity about Richard's part in all of this. Richard cast several glances in the prince's direction that might have spoken apprehensions of his own, but before William could decide how to sound him out, the boat's rigger poked his head through the hatch between them to inquire about tea preferences. As soon as the tea was distributed and the hatch closed,

Richard reached into a pocket of his Irvin jacket and pulled out a small yellow envelope, flashing a warning with his eyes as he passed it across to William.

> *Administer 2100–2130*
> *Will collect you 2200*

Gray's instructions scrawled on the outside of the envelope were succinct, the yellow capsules inside familiar. As William pocketed the envelope and glanced at Richard, the young pilot reached pointedly to the volume control of the intercom and pretended to adjust it. William nodded and sat back, silent.

At least the intended disposition of Wells and Griffin for the night was no longer a question. William longed to pump Richard for further details, but anything said over the intercom would be heard by the rest of the crew, and to try to shout above the rumble of the engines, while possible, was to risk that the flight-deck crew might overhear. While William brooded on this frustration and sipped at his tea, acutely aware of the capsules in his pocket, Richard made a thorough check of his instruments and then glanced casually at the prince.

"Care to take over for a while, sir?" he asked, his expectant smile very reminiscent of his father.

"I was beginning to think you'd never ask," William replied, grinning as he settled his feet into position and took the controls.

For the next half hour, under Richard's relaxed supervision, William lost himself in flying the Sunderland, the Portland Naval Base and Lyme Bay gradually slipping under their wings. They made landfall again over Start Point, continuing westward along the coast until Plymouth Breakwater and Sound came into sight. Richard took back control for the landing, but he let the prince stay in the second pilot's chair instead of returning below. Soon the flying boat set down smoothly in the roads at Plymouth.

The flying had taken William's mind off other matters for a while, but as they taxied the mile or so to RAF Mountbatten, east of the sound, wallowing a little in a choppy sea, his earlier apprehensions came flooding back. He thought about the envelope in his pocket and where Richard and Geoffrey fit into all of this—and the rest of the crew, who seemed not to be in on things, but one could never tell.

Was Richard a witch, or whatever Gray was, like father like son? And if Geoffrey was, what about the brigadier? Who else might be involved whose connection had not even crossed his mind?

Fortunately, he was not given over long to think about it, for as they approached the "trots" where their boat was to moor, he could see the admiral's barge heading out to meet them, white ensign fluttering at the stern. It was time to don his princely demeanor.

With a sigh, he went below to let Griffin tidy his uniform and get him ready to disembark.

Graham arrived at the prince's quarters that night on schedule, he and Denton both in heavy, knee-length duffle coats with hoods drawn up, for the weather had turned filthy with the dusk. In the obscuring rain, they slipped easily from car park to entrance, passing the Royal Marines on duty without challenge, for these particular men had worked for Graham before. It was precisely ten when Denton knocked at William's door.

William himself admitted them, as Graham had hoped he would. The prince's set expression confirmed the events of the past half hour. As Graham and Denton followed him into the sitting room, they were met with the unaccustomed sight of Griffin the valet sprawled asleep in an easy chair by the electric fire, feet propped up and an empty glass on the side table at his elbow. Wells was nowhere to be seen.

"Where's Wells?" Graham asked in a low voice.

"Asleep, through there." William's gesture faltered just a little as Graham stripped off his coat to reveal a shoulder holster nestled in his armpit and a bulky lump of folded fabric around his waist. "Incidentally, I gave them each a tot of whiskey with their tea—remembered it was compatible with your capsules. Lord Selwyn gave me a vintage bottle aboard his ship this afternoon when the weather started to change. I don't suppose you know anything about that? It's just occurred to me that he's Michael's father."

As Graham removed and unfolded the waist bundle, it became a black polo sweater and dark fatigue trousers such as he himself wore. He had suspected that William would make the connection about Selwyn, but he was not going to rise to the bait and confirm it. The prince would see for himself soon enough. Shaking his head to forestall further questions, he held a finger to his lips and handed the clothing to the prince.

"Put these on and keep your voice down until we're secure," he whispered, already moving back to the chair where Griffin slept.

Denton had pushed back the man's left sleeve and was tying the arm above the elbow with a length of rubber tubing. A small bottle of alcohol and a tuft of cotton lay on the table beside the empty glass. As William peered over his shoulder, Graham opened a case from his pocket and took out a loaded syringe.

"What are you doing?" William whispered.

"Just get changed. I don't want anybody waking up while we're gone. What do you make him, Denny, about thirteen stone?"

Denton nodded, swabbing the man's wrist where he had pushed back a chrome wrist watch. "Close enough, sir. Let's stick him right here, where the edge of the tattoo runs over the vein. If he notices anything tomorrow, he'll think his watch band pinched him."

As expected, William moved off to dress as Graham bent to the job at hand. The prince had never allowed squeamishness to interfere with his work, but Graham knew he had had enough of needles as a sickly child to last him a lifetime. When Graham and Denton had finished with Griffin, they went into the next room and repeated the process with Wells. The aide stirred a little as they tied his arm, and looked like he might wake when the cold swab touched his skin; but once the drug was in him, they could see him sink visibly into a deeper sleep.

After that, Graham helped carry the unconscious Griffin to the other bed in the room, where Denton could watch both men at once. When he returned to the sitting room, the prince was buckling his belt, the handsome face very sober above the black polo sweater.

"Hardly standard issue, that," William said in a low voice, jutting his chin toward Graham's holster as he pulled on Denton's duffle coat and covered his bright hair with its hood. "You're not expecting trouble, are you?"

Graham shrugged into his own coat and moved with William toward the door.

"No, but we'll be ready if there is," he said. "Shall we?"

"Go."

Graham's commandeered staff car was soon purring north along the Tavistock Road, its shielded headlights thrusting only narrow slits of light into the moonless night. The rain cut their visibility further, but Graham knew the road and was able to make good time. As they neared the turnoff toward Milton Combe, he glanced at the silent silhouette beside him. William had spoken hardly two words since they left Plymouth—common enough behavior when they were working on an assignment but a little unexpected under the circumstances.

"It's a little like the old days, isn't it?" Graham said after a few more seconds. "May I ask what you're thinking about?"

In the dim glow of the instrument panel, he could see the flash of William's tentative smile.

"That's the stupidest thing you've ever asked me. I've been sitting here scaring myself, of course."

"Scaring yourself? Whatever for?"

"What do you think? I thought I'd try to prepare a little for tonight, so I made the mistake of reading up on Drake and his legends. I suppose you know that his ghost is said to drive a black coach along this road, pulled by headless black horses?"

Graham had to chuckle. "Ah, yes, that legend. Let's see. He supposedly was condemned to this rather pointless fate because he consorted with the devil to build quick additions to the abbey where we're going—the abbey he ruthlessly stole from the poor monks who had built it. The fact that the abbey had been secularized long before and that Drake bought it from the previous owner is rarely mentioned. Three days it was supposed to have taken, wasn't it? And headless hounds follow the coach?"

William snorted. "We must have read the same book." He paused. "Seriously, Gray, what else should I know about tonight? I'm the first to admit that I may not have realized what I was getting myself into. Don't get me wrong. I trust you, and I'm not trying to back out. And you've made enough of an impression on me that I don't suppose I really believe Drake consorted with the devil, but I—don't want to make a fool of myself or put you at risk."

"Your timing is impeccable," Graham replied, slowing for the turn toward Milton Combe. "I was about to broach the subject myself. Incidentally, you can stop worrying about the headless horses and hounds. We just turned off the Tavistock Road."

"How reassuring you are. I was hoping you'd tell me there's no such thing."

"Ah, but what fun would *that* be?"

As William's head swiveled to stare at him, Graham restrained a smile and peered more intently into the rain to negotiate another tricky set of curves, though he kept the prince in his side vision. So far, their tone had been light, but Graham was glad to note a sober undercurrent as well. Even after giving permission for William to attend, a faint fear had lingered that the prince might not take the night's work seriously. His reaction so far was reassuring.

"Quite frankly, the most important thing for you to remember is to do exactly as you're told and not interfere," Graham finally said. "Whatever you may see or hear or even feel, you must stay where I tell you to and say and do nothing. Is there any question in your mind what that means?"

He heard William's soft intake of breath.

"Now I *am* nervous. I thought you said it would be like a— a hypnotic regression. Why do I have the distinct impression that something else may happen?"

"I won't lie to you," Graham said. "Something else *may*. I doubt you'll be aware of it if it does, but if you are, do nothing. I mean that, William," he added as he sensed a beginning protest. "Let the others handle it. They know how, and you don't."

"But—"

"Please don't argue with me, William. The others still have some misgivings about you even being present, but they've deferred to my judgment. I'd like to have you there, but don't make me regret my decision."

"Very well."

Graham glanced aside sharply before easing through another turn, then allowed himself a sigh.

"I'm sorry. I didn't mean that as harshly as it may have sounded. I'm under a little strain myself tonight."

"You don't have to apologize," came the low-voiced response. "I've intruded myself on this operation. I should have enough sense to shut up and follow orders. I've got out of the habit lately."

"You're doing fine."

"I'm not doing fine—I'm a nervous wreck. And every time I think about it more, I scare myself worse. Why couldn't there have been a moon tonight?"

Graham had to smile despite William's obvious apprehension.

"I suppose I ought to explain about lunar cycles," he said. "It has to do with mimicry."

"Mimicry?"

"Yes, just like in astrology: *As above, so below*. The idea in this case is to begin new endeavors when the moon is waxing, as it is tonight: to harness that propensity to grow, to increase in brightness, and to apply it to the matter at hand."

"But the moon doesn't really grow," William protested. "The earth's shadow gets smaller."

"Of course—and we know that now. But our ancestors didn't up until a few hundred years ago, and our racial memory still regards the moon as growing and shrinking, regardless of what astronomers tell us." He glanced aside at William. "It's the symbolism that's important, Will. Everything that you'll see tonight is tied in with symbols which key the mind to move in certain directions. That's what ritual is all about. You've seen it work in church or in your Masonic lodge."

"I suppose that makes sense when you put it that way," William agreed, though his tone was still a little doubtful.

Graham chuckled again, though not unkindly. William was actually taking this far better than he'd dared to hope.

"Just keep your eyes and your mind open and you may be amazed at what you learn," he said. "In any case, what can you expect tonight? Let's see. For one thing, I'll not formally introduce you to anyone. They all know who you are, of course, and you may well recognize some of them, but they would like to retain the illusion of anonymity as much as possible. I'm sure you understand. Working in front of an outsider is a very big step for all of us. If it weren't for the unique nature of what we're doing tonight, you simply wouldn't have been allowed at all."

"I understand that, and I'm grateful."

"Good, because quite frankly, it's all on me, since I'll be the primary—ah—operative tonight. By the way, I'm not being deliberately evasive when I hesitate over a word like that. I'm simply trying not to confuse you any more than you already are, or will be. I'll try to answer specific questions on the way back."

He heard William's controlled sigh, obviously little reassured, and then a weak "Thank you." They were within a mile of the abbey gate now, and Graham realized he was going to have to hurry if he hoped to finish his briefing before they arrived.

"It's not quite as solemn as all that," he said gently. "It *is* serious business, though. Let's see. Once we get there, certain—ah—preparations will already have been made that needn't concern you. Basically, they have to do with—let's call it a psychic cleansing of the room, like the censing and sprinkling with holy water that one sees in a church, and with approximately the same effect."

"I can't see that?"

"Afraid not—for the same reason you wouldn't allow an outsider to witness a high-grade Masonic ritual unless he'd been properly prepared. There's nothing ominous involved; it simply isn't done. That part has nothing to do with what I'll be doing, anyway. The purpose is to neutralize any random influences which might intrude on Drake. He's our only real target for tonight."

"That makes sense, I suppose," William said. "What will *you* be doing, then, that I'm allowed to see?"

"Well, I told you it was like a hypnotic regression, but it's sometimes also called scrying. After everyone is settled, I'll sit in Drake's chair, in his drawing room, and try to look back on him in a blackened mirror."

"Not a crystal ball?" William asked, a trace of humor returning to his voice.

"Ah, then you've heard of scrying." Graham smiled. "No, the mirror is better in this case. I'll use a candle as a focus for going into a kind of trance, but my eyes may stay open, and I may speak. That's perfectly normal if it happens, so don't be alarmed."

"*Normal*, he says!"

Graham had to force himself not to laugh, William sounded so apprehensive.

"I assure you, it is. I've arranged for you to be sitting behind and slightly to one side of me so you can watch my face in the mirror. That's really far less ominous than it sounds, since most of what happens will be going on in my mind, anyway."

"Then you don't think there'll be much to see?"

"Not with your eyes, but—"

He found himself about to go into a discourse on psychic *senses and bit off the rest of his statement with a shake of his head. He was not sure whether William was ready to handle something like that or not, but William took the speculation out of his hands.

"But what?" the prince asked. "Are you implying some kind of mental perception? From me?"

"It's—possible," Graham conceded, fearing that the possibility was quite real. "You're of the old line, as we call it— the royal and sacred lineage of England—and your ancestors trod the ancient ways until quite recently. But there's no way to predict ahead of time, just as I don't know for certain how I'll react. Until and unless something happens, there's just no way to know. In any case, it isn't something to be frightened of," he added, reaching under the seat to pull out a black-knit Balaclava helmet, which he handed off to the prince. "You'll want to put this on now and pull it well down over your face. Don't take it off until we're safely upstairs. We don't want you recognized."

As William obeyed, they turned right and stopped beneath an arched stone gatehouse, deep in shadow. When Graham lowered the window, a darker shadow materialized beside the driver's door, and a dim red light was shone in both their faces. He felt William stiffen next to him at the soft, deadly snick of a rifle being cocked farther back in the darkness.

"Colonel John Graham," he said in a low voice.

The light was switched off.

"Pass, sir. The rest of your party are all here."

As Graham drove on, riding the brakes as he eased the car down a shallow hill, he could hear the rustle of the prince turning to glance back at the receding gate. Of the sentry, there was now no sign.

"One of yours?" William asked.

"Not in the sense we've been talking about," Graham said with a low chuckle. "He works for me, though. I'll bet you didn't know that this is a top-secret meeting of some of my deep-cover agents tonight, did you? It's true, by the way. Did you also know that Sir Francis Walsingham, the founder of the British Secret Service, is said to have used witches as his first information-gathering network?"

The prince's muffled "humph" was still a little nervous but no longer disbelieving as they pulled around the last long curve and into the yard by the west entrance.

A battle-dressed soldier with a black-smeared face met them just inside the darkened entryway with rifle readied, but he slipped past them to take up a post outside as soon as he recognized Graham. Briskly, Graham led his charge down the corridor and into an oak-lined stairwell, guiding him up by the light of a single candle on the first landing.

Another candle, shielded in red glass, glowed by a door at the end of a long gallery leading back in the direction they had come. As they approached it, a dark shape in RAF uniform detached itself from the shadows and fused into the form of Richard. Graham, one hand on the prince's elbow, felt his start of surprise as Geoffrey silently appeared on his other side.

"You can take off the mask now," Graham said, shucking his coat and weapon and exchanging them for a long black robe that Geoffrey laid over his arm. "And I believe you already know these two gentlemen. Richard, have we got a spare robe for our guest? I think he'll feel more comfortable if he looks like everybody else."

As the two younger men helped William from his coat, Graham withdrew a few yards and donned his own robe, though unlike William, he did not retain his clothing underneath. Since the room in which they would work was unheated and un-heatable, the robe was sturdy wool, but more important, it did not bind or constrict; comfort was critical. The cut was also enough like a conventional monk's robe or choir surplice to be reassuringly familiar to their apprehensive royal visitor.

Graham set his boots and socks aside, flinching a little at the first shock of cold wood against bare feet, then rejoined the others as Richard was knotting a black cincture around the prince's waist. William's face was very white above the black of the monk's cowl, but he made a halfhearted attempt at a smile as he looked up at Graham.

"I shouldn't want to be misunderstood when I say I've got cold feet," he whispered, "but is there some esoteric reason for this of which I'm not aware?"

Graham glanced at the royal feet, then back at William.

"It's akin to taking off one's shoes on holy ground. Does that make you uncomfortable?"

"No, just cold."

Graham smiled. "Good. Just to reassure you, I think they've put a cushion down for your feet. If you're ready, then . . ."

As William nodded, nervously smoothing his fair hair into place, the two younger men vanished into the shadows again. Even though they had spoken no word, Graham sensed a warmth that had been comforting to William, and he was grateful. With a little bow that somehow seemed quite natural, he led the prince to the door and knocked, waiting until he felt the latch move under his other hand.

The candlelight inside seemed bright after the red-lit hall, but it was created by only a single taper in the center of the long table. Four more red votive lights, like the one outside, were set around the perimeter of the room. A breath of incense and a hint of lemon oil and old wood hung on the air.

Alix moved to the left of the door as they entered, her blonde hair hanging loose almost to her hips, folds of her robe obscuring the blade Graham knew she held in her right hand. The brigadier waited behind the table, and before it a man Graham knew the prince would instantly recognize, as soon as he got a good look at him.

Selwyn nodded stiffly as William's jaw dropped, but the interchange covered Alix's brief bending to draw her blade across the threshold of the door she had just closed behind them. She caught Graham's free hand and drew him with her as she returned to her place by Selwyn's side, leaving William standing a few paces behind. Graham kissed her hand as she slipped her other arm around her husband's waist and simultaneously laid her blade on the table behind them. William did not seem to have heard the faint scape of metal on wood as she sealed the door. Now he would see only a staghorn-handled letter opener when they moved aside, and possibly wonder what it was for.

"Good evening, David," Graham said softly, clasping Selwyn's hand and nodding reassurance. "I'm pleased to report that your whiskey was a great success. No problems at this end, I take it?"

"We're ready," Selwyn murmured.

"So are we. Shall we get started, then?"

The room was as he remembered it from his several other visits over the past few weeks. The deep window recesses were covered with double layers of blackout curtain, but otherwise he was sure it looked much the same as it had in Drake's time. The Drake armchair was set at the head of the table, and beyond it, just to the right of the fireplace in the north wall, was a splendidly carved settle, wide enough for three people. William would watch from there. A court cupboard and an ancient garment press were pushed against the eastern wall beneath the famous portrait of Queen Elizabeth—all vintage of the years when Drake had lived here. Several other dark-toned paintings hung on other walls, including one of the great captain himself.

Graham gazed at the likeness of Drake for a moment as the others set about their final preparations, aware of William easing closer to his back, but then his attention was caught by Selwyn pulling something bulky from underneath the table, its shape obscured by a black cloth. As Selwyn lifted the object to the table, the cloth fell away, and Graham almost gasped. It was Drake's drum.

He nearly forgot William. He nearly forgot everything else in the room. He had never seen the drum except behind glass. The difference was breathtaking.

Nearly three feet high, almost too large for a man to grasp around its circumference, the drum's sides were painted with Drake's arms and crest on one half and decorated with a pattern of small metal studs on a crimson background on the other. The rims at top and bottom were also crimson, the drumhead a yellowed, ripply vellum. He could feel the drum drawing him already, from clear across the table, and it was all he could do not to reach out and touch it right then.

All at once, Alix was moving between him and the drum with a bowl of water, and the compulsion was broken. Averting his gaze, Graham dipped his hands and dried them on the towel across her arm, then gestured minutely toward William with his eyes. The prince dipped his fingers as he had seen Graham do and returned the towel to Alix with a shy nod. As she took the bowl away, Graham laid one hand on William's sleeve and guided him to the fireplace settle.

"Well done. Now, this is your place until either I or the lady tell you otherwise. Her command supersedes even my own. Do you understand?"

At William's solemn nod, he returned to stand at the east of the table and drew up the hood of his robe, his attention drawn ever more intently to the waiting drum.

CHAPTER 9

WILLIAM SHIVERED A LITTLE AS HE SLID BACK ON THE carved settle and tried to make himself disappear against the wood, relieved no longer to be under Graham's scrutiny—or the others'. He watched Gray pull up his hood, the rest following suit, and surreptitiously he did the same. Huddling in the shadow of the hood eased his nervousness somewhat.

He had been a little dubious about the robe they had put on him, but he was glad for it now. The others wore the same kind of garment, though the cords around their waists were red, not black. He also did not think they were wearing anything underneath, despite the chill of the room. He had seen Gray strip by casual stages while he thought William was distracted with his own robing. He wondered whether they would have worn anything at all, had he not been here. He had read that in the old days the witches sometimes marked their revels in the nude.

He shuddered at the thought—not the nudity but the unknown rites the old tales implied—and told himself sternly that if he kept this up, he was only going to scare himself again. The people in this room bore little resemblance to the folk of the old accounts. Three of the four were his friends or acquaintances, even if he had not guessed the extent of their occult interests before.

Brigadier Ellis's involvement certainly came as no great surprise, for William remembered the telephone call at Dover

141

and then Geoffrey's presence on the plane and outside. Ellis was Gray's father-in-law, too. The one who surprised him was the Earl of Selwyn, despite his own earlier, jesting quip about Selwyn's whiskey back at Plymouth.

Yet Selwyn *was* Michael's father, as William himself had observed, and a long-time friend of Gray's. He should have foreseen. Selwyn also had to be the group's man in black, who had stepped aside in favor of Gray because of the war.

And the woman, to whom all of them seemed to defer— he had a feeling she was Lady Selwyn, though he had never met the earl's wife. She and Selwyn seemed to be in charge of things tonight—though exactly where that put Gray, he didn't know. Gray obviously carried a great deal of weight despite Selwyn's presence, or else it would not have been his decision as to whether William might attend. But Gray himself had stressed that the lady—he had seemed to capitalize the title by his very tone—was ultimately in charge.

The four of them were consulting quietly, the countess— for so he persisted in thinking of her—doing most of the talking while the three men listened, Gray looking vaguely distracted. William could not hear what they were saying, so he turned his attention cautiously to the rest of his surroundings to keep his mind from going off in frightening directions again. The room, at least, was real. Now that he was here, he was not as sure about the other.

He inspected the paneling, burrowing his toes more snugly into the cushion they had provided to keep his feet warm. The oak—said to have been installed at the order of Drake himself—was still magnificent. In the past few days, he had taken in so much about the great Elizabethan captain that he could almost picture Sir Francis striding boldly into the room with his charts under his arm, spreading them on this very table under the portrait of his Queen and benefactress on the east wall.

And the drum—that conjured more mystical images: the drum, whose beat would summon the spirit of Drake to save England from her enemies threatening by sea. He had seen Gray's reaction when Selwyn first brought it up on the table and uncovered it. It had seemed to pull him like a magnet. William wondered whether there really was something to this business of reincarnation that Gray had mentioned so casually.

The chair had been Drake's, too. What would happen when Gray sat down in that, if the mere sight of Drake's drum evoked such a reaction? Suddenly, he was very uneasy for his friend.

Relax, William, he told himself sternly. *He knows what he's doing.*

He shifted uncomfortably on the hard seat and withdrew further into his hood like a turtle in its shell, unable to prevent another apprehensive shiver. This was ridiculous! He had never had reason to doubt his courage before. He had faced danger often enough—far more often than most people suspected. Besides, Gray had assured him that there was no danger here so long as he did as he was told.

Why, then, was he trembling? What was it about the thought of a few people pottering about in an ancient room and creepy robes that set the hackles rising at the back of his neck? Was it the suspicion that they really were engaged in magic?

Magic, indeed! Now he was beginning to believe what Gray had been telling him.

And yet if he did not believe it at least a little, why had he almost insisted on coming? He had not been able to explain it at the time, and he had no better answer now. If he did not believe, why was he sitting here in this silly robe and expecting something to happen when Gray sat down in that chair a few yards away?

Nor was there any doubt in his mind that something would happen. Already, something ancient and powerful, alien and yet vaguely familiar, seemed to be stirring in the room. He could feel it prickling along his spine, in the pit of his stomach, making his pulse quicken in anticipation. Was it all imagination, born of Gray's casual references to the old line and his own yearning to *do* something that would make a difference, or was it real? Did he even want to know?

Movement caught William's eye, and he looked up with a start. The countess had finished her briefing. As she and the brigadier removed velvet wrappings from a heavy, gilt-framed mirror and set it upright at the end of the table, Gray pushed back his hood and slipped into the Drake chair, pulling a tartan lap rug around his legs and lower body. He and Selwyn spent several minutes adjusting the angle of the mirror and trying different placements of the candle the countess brought closer; then Gray glanced over his shoulder at William with a reas-

suring quirk of a smile before settling back in the chair. Selwyn
lowered the drum to a cushion on the floor close by Gray's
right and sat on a stool with it braced between his knees, hands
resting on the rim. The countess and the brigadier withdrew to
stools on Gray's left and facing him. After that, no one moved.

Not a sound broached the silence. William sat a little straighter and watched the candlelight flicker and crawl along the
carving of the gilt mirror frame like something alive. Gray's
image shone darkly in the blackened glass, the hazel eyes hardly
blinking, the face stilled and devoid of emotion, perhaps already in trance. William tried to imagine what Gray might be
seeing. . . .

Breathing out in a faint sigh, Graham let his body relax and
settle and began to put the others out of mind, gradually shut-
tering off outside distractions. He could see his face in the
mirror, smell the incense lingering on the air, sense the others
watching, but he paid them less and less attention, even William. Stilled, he let his mind begin to drift with the candle
flicker, gradually detaching himself from the eyes that gazed
back at him. Almost, he could touch that Other, waiting to
pull him into the past. Joining it was now only a matter of
time.

Resolutely, he settled down to the business of bringing it
through. He drew a slow, deep breath and let it out with a
conscious effort to clear his lungs of all of it; drew another
like it, and another, until he felt the beginning tingle of over-
breathing in lips and fingertips. His trance was deepening steadily, his vision taking on that curious tunnel aspect that was a
sure sign of stilling and readiness—passive, receptive—and
he let the breathing shift back to a shallow, easy rhythm, dismissing further consciousness of any of his bodily processes
as a factor for concern. He lingered there at the balance point
for an endless several seconds, neither willing nor desiring
anything further, until he felt Alix touch his wrist in old signal.

That started him back along the road of time and memory
and past lives. This, too, was familiar, though he had never
done it before with such specific intent. To his right, Selwyn
began to tap softly on the drum—slow, slow, soon catching
and holding the rhythm of his heartbeat in a cadence ancient
before the Romans came to Britain—expectant, compelling.
As the complexity of the drumming increased, though not the

volume, Graham sensed himself sliding into even greater depths of trance, relaxing, centering, balancing.

His right hand began to twitch then, to lift, and he knew immediately where it would go. A part of him watched quite dispassionately as it rose from the chair arm and drifted jerkily to the side, so separate from his conscious control that it might not have been his hand at all, guided by something deep beyond his consciousness. Unerringly, it sank toward the drum, his conscious will receding as the distance closed. The touch of the vellum and the smooth wood of the rim was an almost electrical tingle shoving him deeper, a catapult flinging him back in time as the drumbeat went on, answering his rising pulse beat.

He gasped, his head jerking against the chair back as his eyes half closed, for the speed was dizzying, disorienting, and he could not seem to focus. After an eternity bound up in a heartbeat, the backward flight slowed, and so did the drumbeat. As he gazed into the mirror again, images began to materialize from mist and fog that only he could see: vague, hazy at first, taunting, teasing—something about the mirror, which for an instant was not the one that physically stood before him.

Then, in a blink, all was changed.

He was Drake, and exultant. The drum was under his hands, throbbing and potent, as he drummed out the ancient rhythms and the dancers whirled. On a moon-drenched hilltop he sat with the drum braced between his knees, wind whipping his hair and mantle around him in growing frenzy. The very ground reverberated with the power being raised, the energies pulsing with his heartbeat and shuddering through his body in an ecstasy that was part pleasure and part pain. Around him, the dancers leaped and twisted as the bonfire surged and receded—nearly a hundred dark shapes circling the round of which he was the center, raising the righteous power to rend the Spanish fleet.

He was their chief, at least for this night—their man in black, their leader—he who publicly had been recognized as such a seven-year ago, in praeternatural anticipation of their need, this fateful year of 1588. He had summoned the grand coven, and they had come from the far corners of England in answer to his lawful call—the Wicca, the wise, they whose ancestors had long kept the old faith, which reverenced the land and the power that made it fruitful, and danced the sacred rounds with their lord and lady to mark the wheel of the changing seasons.

The old faith had been, long before the Christians' narrow view of God. The Sacrificed One in his White Christ aspect was but another incarnation of that vast creative Whole so often made manifest in human form, in different times and different places. Jesus himself had danced the sacred dance with his disciples in that other coven, twelve plus one.

> *I would pipe: dance ye, all. . . . Eight singeth praise with us. . . . Twelve danceth on High. . . . The Whole on High hath part in our dancing. . . . Whoso danceth not, knoweth not what cometh to pass. . . . Now, as thou respondeth to my dancing, behold thyself in me even, as I speak, and seeing what I do, keep thou silence on my Mysteries. Only thou that danceth may perceive what I do: for thine is this passion of the Humanity which I undergo. . . . If thou wouldst know concerning Who I Am: know that with a word I danced all things and I was in no wise shamed. . . . I leaped and danced, that thou shalt understand the Whole. . . .*

Yes, the White Christ had known—and many of his priests knew, too—that the dance was a great sorcery, yet another means of reaching toward the Source. The blind forbade it, fearful of the power that came of surrendering mind and will to the sensual movements of the body, seeing it as a triumph of flesh over spirit, of Devil over Christ; but the Wicca knew otherwise, and some of the White Christ's priests danced with them here tonight. Those who understood the Whole still shepherded their flocks along the Path, keeping the old worships alongside the new, from lowly peasant lad and lass to highborn lord. Even kings kept counsel with the Whole, marking the seasons and the seven-years. Not even a king would deny it—or a queen!

The chanting surged and rose and fell with Drake's ever more insistent drumming: ancient words to summon ancient powers. Faster now the dancers whirled, weaving the spell, binding it to will, stamping out the steps and the patterns that could make even winds obey. He could feel the power growing, could almost see it as a faintly glowing cone towering above the circle like a beacon as the dancers danced—a tight-wound living spiral, surging like the lunar tides, winding up the energies, sending forth their will to spare the land—and he laughed with the joy of it!

Flashes of the future, then, though he knew he drummed yet on that Plymouth hill. The routed Armada fleeing with shortened sail before unprecedented August gales—in August, one of the sacred months of sacrifice! The vast superiority of Spanish numbers, Spanish guns—the scudding thunderheads, grounded ships breaking up, the wind ever shifting to the English advantage.

While the English fleet found sheltered harbor in Kent and other ports along the Channel and rejoiced at their deliverance, the storms drove the Armada north and west to shatter on the Scottish coast or be driven ashore on Ireland as they tried to round the isles and get back home. Not before or since had a fleet been chastened thus.

A beat, a ripple in the mind-flow, a shift to an older time and place. Suddenly, Graham was no longer on the hilltop above Plymouth, drumming up the Spanish defeat. He was still Drake as he blinked, hand twitching on the drum, but instead of the hill's fair moonglow, he was plunged into sunlight so bright he had to squint. He almost raised his hand to shield his eyes, a minute part of him wondering why the others did not shrink from it.

The chair commanded now, not the drum, though the drum was not far away. The chair was made from timbers of his ship, the *Golden Hind*, and he stood on her quarterdeck at a dock at Deptford, on the Thames, waiting for his queen. It was the fourth of April, 1581, and he was just six months' returned from circumnavigating the globe.

He did not know what the royal visit would bring, though he thought the Queen was pleased. On his return, before the year turned, he had spent six long hours alone with her at Richmond and still was not certain where she stood. Up until that meeting, he had thought her relatively unsympathetic to the old ways, though her court had always abounded with men steeped in the Art—Dee, Walsingham, Sidney, and others, too highly placed to name. Only recently had he learned that she, too, knew the secret connections of that great order of knighthood in which she was sovereign—knew the power there that even she would not deny, else deny her royal blood.

They had spoken of the Spanish invasion threat, increasingly real since the time of her father, and she had told him she feared the inevitability of war with Spain. Doctor Dee had read it in the stars, she said—Dee, who had also chosen the most auspicious moment for her coronation nearly thirty years before. She had asked of the things he had found on his voyage, and he had brought her gold and silver and emeralds the size of a man's finger and set in a crown that she wore at New Year's court.

She said the Spanish ambassador called him freebooter, corsair, and even outright pirate; that the King of Spain demanded his head for the raids he had carried out so successfully on Spanish ships and storehouses along the South American coast. What did he think of *that*?

He had told her he was no pirate, but privateer, and the Queen's good servant. She had laughed delightedly and sent him back to Plymouth to tally up the booty.

Now he paced back and forth on the deck of his gallant little ship, men and vessel alike all set in order for the royal visit—flags and pennons lifting on the spice-laden breeze, crew drawn up in proud salute. Trumpets blared their greeting, strident in the morning sun, as the royal party approached. Drums beat out a brisk tattoo.

He met her at the rail and bowed her aboard. The royal standard was broken, leopards and lilies snapping brightly defiant against the London sky. As he knelt to kiss the slender white hand and raised his eyes to hers, he thought he read approval and a sly amusement, but her words conjured quite another impression.

"So, Captain Drake. The Spanish king demands that we send him your head," she said loudly, pivoting so that all might hear. "What think you of that?"

As Drake remained on one knee, believing her goodwill of earlier on yet fearing her caprice, she cocked her red-wigged head at one of the men who had accompanied her. He was the emissary of the French king's brother, who sought her hand. He was also Spain's enemy.

"How say you, my lord of France?" she asked him pointedly. "Shall we give our Spanish cousin what he demands?"

As the French ambassador demurred, Elizabeth laughed.

"I see I shall have to take matters into my own hands, shan't I?" She extended an imperious, ring-bedecked hand toward her captain of the guard, suddenly solemn. "Give us a sword, Sir Christopher, and it mind you, see that it is sharp!"

A hush descended on the ship, Drake's officers and crew stiffening, though no one dared lift a hand to interfere. The Spanish observers in the Queen's party craned their necks for a better view. The Queen's captain, Sir Christopher Hatton, moved forward obediently, though he was Drake's friend and patron and had helped to finance the maritime venture. The very ship on which they stood had been named in his honor, for the great stag in Hatton's family crest. Hatton had shared in the spoils when Drake returned—as had the Queen.

But Hatton's patronage could not save Drake now, if the Queen meant to slay him. As the sword hissed from its scabbard, gilded hilt shimmering in the sun, blade aflame, Drake knew a queasy moment of dread—though he was quite prepared to die if it was to be at *her* hand. He had died for kings before. . . .

The Queen took the weapon and hefted it experimentally, letting the moment gather full effect as Drake's heart pounded. Then she flashed a crafty smile and gave it over to the Frenchman, hilt first.

"Nay, his head is precious to us, my lords. We could not give it up to Spain. Sir Ambassador, would you assist us? For it is our intention to knight Captain Drake in token that he hath opened up bold new horizons to our English seafaring!"

As she put the hilt in the astonished Frenchman's hand and laid her own atop it, the ship's company and assembled crowd went wild with joy. Drake gasped.

His vision blurred momentarily, and he hardly felt the blade touch his shoulders, or heard her words, "Arise, Sir Francis," or the renewed cheers as the Queen raised him up and led him slowly around the crowded deck to show him off. They paused once when she stumbled, his arm supporting her while she rubbed at her ankle and said that it was nothing. As they moved on, however, something glittered on the deck where she had stopped. Silence fell as she turned in apparent amazement.

It was one of the royal garters—purple, not blue as the Garter Knights wore, but the gold of its embroidery was very

like theirs, and the buckle nearly identical. The resemblance
could hardly be coincidental—or the losing of it.

Leicester and Howard, and Burghley, the Queen's secretary—Garter Knights all—bristled defensively and eased their
way closer to their royal mistress to watch intently. The Frenchman started to pounce on the garter, for he had sent similar
prizes to his royal master in the past as tokens of the Queen's
esteem, but something in her look and in the faces of the Garter
Knights stopped him in confusion. Smiling, the Queen turned
her glance to Drake in pointed favor.

Her meaning could not have been clearer. With a bow,
Drake knelt and picked it up, touching it reverently to his lips
before offering it back into her keeping. She took it and allowed
him to kiss her hand again. As he rose, Burghley and then the
other two favored him with stiff little bows. The royal mandate
was confirmed. Those with eyes to see could not miss the
implication.

The trumpets sounded a new fanfare, and the drums struck
up a flourish to cover the moment—Hatton's sense of show-
manship to the rescue—but the beat of *the* drum came through
above the others, yanking Graham away before he could puzzle
out what it all meant—out of Deptford and even out of Drake.

Before he could even draw confused breath, foundering in
a between-time during which he was—*other*—he was slammed
backward in time again—this time to other lives, other roles.
The flashes were so rapid, one after the other, that he could
only grab onto the arms of the chair and try to ride it out, eyes
screwed tightly shut against the images that came cascading
into consciousness, intense and often terrifying.

*Blood. Blades flashing by light of sun or moon or fire. Deeds
done by stealth or, more often, in full view of witnesses. Judicial
murders—or sacrifices....*

Sometimes he was the slayer, sometimes the slain—but
always, what he did was in the service of the Whole. Whether
the king must die, or sacred substitute, it was meet that consecrated blood should spill upon the land from time to time.
The living god must die for the good of the people; he who
struck the sacred blow was as much a part of the plan as the
divine victim himself. Sometimes he was the friend of the
victim and knew with his friend that the time for sacrifice had
come....

*A forest . . . summer . . . fitting bolt to crossbow as a king
turned to his fate and smiled, ready target, red hair bright
against the shadowed trees. The bright blood soaked the spongy
forest floor as the King pitched forward and fell on the bolt,
ensuring a mortal wound. . . . And Graham—though that had
not been his name then—gathering the dead King briefly in
his arms to weep before the lonely flight to France. . . .*

A name came to Graham then—*Tyrrel*—and Graham, too,
wept at Buckland, in a body far removed from that other man
mourning in the August stillness of the New Forest. . . .

Other names had he borne, too, in other lives: a knight
named FitzUrse in a darkening Kent cathedral; a monk named
John at a place called Swineshead Abbey, set to slay a namesake
king with poison of a toad; a knight named Wallace; a prince
named George; Drake, of course, and others, closer to the
present—though more recent memory seemed to elude him.

At all times and in all those places, he had carried out his
appointed destiny, keeping the cycles of sevens, when kings
or their substitutes must die for the good of the land. The best
ones went willingly to their deaths, some of them even joyful,
well aware for what purpose they died.

The land must be renewed, the virility of the sacred king
ensured. In its time and season, it was a right and proper thing
for the anointed king or his surrogate—the man made God—
to die for the common good. Even the White Christ had said
it: *Greater love hath no man. . . .*

He felt a touch on his shoulder, as though from far, far
away, and the vision rippled, wavered. His body cringed from
the contact, but his mind reached out to it.

He had not sought these other lives; he had intended only
to seek out Drake, for very specific information. He must
abandon these other disturbing memories and get back.

He felt the touch again, solid, more insistent, and he reached
out with one blind hand, grasping for its source and finding a
woman's softness. He fastened on her hand and crushed it to
his lips, a living lifeline helping to warp him back. Another
hand gripped his from the other side—strong, sure—a hand
he had known before in many lives. Between the two, he clung
like a drowning man, forcing his way back across the centuries
to finally surface with a gasp.

He heard Alix's relieved sigh as he turned his head and

brought her into focus. With a sigh of his own, he raised his other hand to brush her cheek tremblingly and confirm that she was real. Selwyn's explosive snort at his right was one of relief and disapproval mixed. Graham tried not to look as shaken as he felt as Selwyn moved the candle closer and turned him toward its light.

"Are you sure you're back?" his chief asked, looking closely at his eyes and waving a hand across his vision close on. "Let me see you blink, Gray. Focus on my hand."

As Selwyn snapped his fingers, Graham blinked several times and gave a cautious nod, still disoriented from settling into his own memories so quickly. The mirror caught his eyes and started to pull him back, and he blinked again.

The mirror. What was there about the mirror, another mirror?

"Was that Drake's, by any chance?" he breathed, staring as if he had never seen it before. "I remember something about a mirror, right at the beginning."

"What do you remember?" Alix asked.

He squeezed his eyes shut for a moment, trying to capture the memory, then looked into the mirror again.

"I think I had one on my ship," he whispered, halfway back in Drake. "I could see the movements of the enemy ships and hear their captains' orders. I—"

He raised a hand to his forehead and shook his head, the memory lost. Alix turned and motioned for the brigadier to cover the mirror and take it away. The movement brought Graham back with a snap, the final link at last severed. He managed a wan smile as his glance flicked over their worried faces: Alix, Selwyn, the brigadier. . . .

"William?"

He wrenched around. The prince was poised on the edge of his seat as if he were about to explode, hands gripped tightly along the seat edge to either side. By the look on his face, Graham wondered what had kept him there.

"It's all right," Graham blurted. *"I'm* all right."

He took a deep breath and let it out, willing his momentary apprehension for William to recede. He did not want the prince to see him this way.

"Wesley, why don't you take our guest outside while I debrief?" he murmured. "He can wait with Richard and Geoffrey if you need to go. William, I'll be with you in a few minutes. We'll talk on the way back."

"What about the mirror?" William whispered, not moving from the settle. "*Was* it Drake's?"

"I don't know." He glanced at Alix. "Was it?"

She shook her head. "Not this one, though he *was* reputed to have a magic mirror aboard his flagship which worked as you described. Had you read about it?"

"Not that I recall. Besides, we've used this mirror before, haven't we?"

"Yes. However, before we continue this discussion..."

She let her voice trail off as she gazed past him at the prince, and Graham nodded.

"You're right. William, if you'll excuse us, please."

He tried to stand as the prince rose, but it was too soon for that. Selwyn caught him under one arm as he reeled, and William grabbed his other, but for a moment he feared he might pass out. The episode and his embarrassment were real enough, but they were also convenient. While he supported himself against the edge of the table, only half feigning further dizziness to keep William's attention, the brigadier took care of the door.

"Sorry. I shouldn't have stood so soon after coming out of deep trance," Graham said apologetically. "It was just a little dizziness. I'm really all right."

William eyed him somewhat dubiously as he was ushered out, but Graham raised a hand in reassurance and somehow mustered a smile. He managed to maintain it until Richard had brought in his clothes and gone out again. Only when the door had closed did he allow himself to slump bonelessly back into the chair, closing his eyes. He heard Selwyn sit down with an indignant snort.

"All right, what the bloody hell were you trying to do?" his chief said, drumming fingers on the table in annoyance. "Alix, does he do this sort of thing often when I'm away?"

"No, and I don't know what happened," she replied, pulling up another stool. "We'd only planned to scry for Drake—I thought. Where *did* you go, Gray?"

Graham rubbed his face with hands that felt like they belonged to someone else. "I wish to hell I knew. The Drake part was fine. There at the end, though, I seemed to be killing kings—and being killed sometimes. Can someone get me a

pencil and paper? I want to write down some names before
they slip away."

He tried not to think until he had scribbled out the list. That
part of his trance was hazy, and he wasn't sure he didn't want
it to stay that way. When the others had read what he wrote,
Alix looked up at him wistfully. Selwyn's expression was unreadable.

"Well, what did I snare?" Graham asked softly. "Was it a
series of dreams or past-life memories or what?"

"The second, I think," Alix replied. "Look at your list again.
Do any of the names mean anything to you now?"

"Nothing in particular. I suppose I've read about most of
them at one time or another, but . . ."

As he leaned forward lethargically to pull at the pile of his
clothes, Selwyn thrust a restraining hand across his chest.

"Are you sure you ought to dress yet? You may not be quite
settled."

Graham managed a weak grin as he shook out his trousers
and began pulling them on. Both took a lot of effort.

"I'll be all right. Doing something ordinary helps me ground
myself."

He stood long enough to zip his trousers and pull the robe
off over his head, but the exertion seemed to drain him of what
little energy he had regained. White-faced, he collapsed back
into the chair, the sweater crumpled in his lap.

"Gray, I've never seen you this disoriented," Alix murmured. "Talk to us! Get yourself focused. Tell us more about
the names."

He blinked and sighed again, then began wearily pulling on
the sweater, his voice coming muffled through the wool.

"Ah, FitzUrse, right off. He was one of the knights who
killed Becket, wasn't he?"

"Yes. Who else?"

"Ah—William Wallace? That doesn't make sense. He was
a Scot."

"Executed by Edward I, however," Selwyn said. "That may
be the connection. An interesting pairing, though: FitzUrse and
Wallace, a murderer and a victim."

"No, slayer and slain," Graham corrected without even
thinking. *"Slayer of kings and slain for kings am I. . . ."*

Alix looked at him sharply. "What was that?"

"Sl—" Graham stopped in confusion. "What did I say?"

"Slayer of kings and slain by kings am I," she repeated. "It sounded like you were quoting."

He shook his head, seized by the words again. "No, not slain *by* kings; slain *for* kings. *Necator regum sum, et pro regibus necor*. A big difference."

He blinked, then buried his face in his hands and tried to sort it out.

"God, where did I get all that?" he murmured, suddenly a little scared. "What the bloody hell was I, Alix? Some kind of karmic executioner?"

"Perhaps, in a sense," Selwyn replied slowly, "but more likely a great deal more than that. It sounds like you've been part of the sacred king cycle: FitzUrse killing Becket for Henry II; Wallace *being* killed for—Edward?" He cleared his throat nervously. "However, if you've also been Drake and some of the others who have followed after him, then you've been a defender as well." He paused just a beat. "I would think that's your function in *this* life, based on what we're trying to do."

"It sounds like you're trying to reassure me that we haven't been talking about a repeat sacrifice this time around," Graham said quietly. "Do you think the memories may be meant to prepare me for that possibility?"

Selwyn looked very uncomfortable. "We knew that was a remote possibility when we started. I don't see that anything has changed as a result of tonight's working."

"Let's go on from here," Alix said, circling several names. "I don't see that it serves any purpose to speculate further about Gray's role right now. Gray, you have Tyrrel on your list. Was that Walter Tyrrel, who was connected with William Rufus?"

"Rufus? Of course!" Graham sat back in his chair, suddenly remembering the redheaded king of his vision. "That's who it was. For some reason, that one had details."

When he closed his eyes, the scene came crisp and clear, though this time he was remembering, not reliving it.

"We were hunting. It was the day after Lammas, in a year sacred for him and the land; he was forty-two, and it was a new century. He turned and smiled at me as I wound the bolt into my crossbow. He knew. We'd talked about it. He gave me the bolts." His eyes popped open, but he was still seeing it for a moment.

"I shot him. He fell on the bolt. He was dead before I could reach his side. I remember I wept. . . ."

"You wept here, too," Alix said, gently laying a hand on his as his voice quivered at the ending. "Anything else you can remember about it?"

He shook his head and began pulling on socks and boots, wanting to give his hands something to do.

"Nothing else about him," he murmured. "I'd certainly like to know what triggered all the bits that hadn't to do with Drake, though. All these memories about sacrifices—"

"Let's forget about sacrifices for the moment," Selwyn said gruffly. "What about Drake? Did you get what you went for?"

Graham sat back with a sigh and rubbed absently at the space between his eyes. If the possibility of sacrifice made *him* uneasy, then it must be doubly distressing to Selwyn, who had all but drafted Graham to take his place as man in black—and as sacrifice, if it came to that. For all their sakes, best to get on with Drake, who had merely been a defender. At least the Drake memories were not so threatening.

"I don't know that I got exactly what we were looking for, but I certainly made a contact," Graham said, forcing himself to put the other out of mind. "I *was* Drake, by the way—I didn't just pick up information about him. For the first part of it, I was sitting on a hilltop above Plymouth Sound and drumming while the grand coven danced around me and raised the power for the Armada storm. You and the drum were ideal background for that part of it, David. The drum provided the thread which drew the whole first part together." He shivered. "It was even more mystical and powerful than the old tales let on."

Selwyn smiled for the first time since the scrying ended. "Was Drake the local man in black, then? Is that how he convened the grand coven?"

"I'm not sure. I *think* so. I'm going to have to do some more thinking about that. As nearly as I can tell, he appears to have received some kind of mandate directly from Elizabeth. Do either of you happen to know whether she dropped a garter while she was knighting Drake?"

"A garter? As in Knights of, or witches?" Alix asked.

Graham shook his head, remembering the purple velvet. "I don't know. Close enough not to make a difference, I suspect. I had the distinct impression he found her far more sympathetic and knowledgeable about the old ways than history paints her. There's some kind of Garter connection, though. Several Garter Knights were in attendance, and the incident seemed to mean something to them. She had Drake pick up the dropped garter, and he kissed it before he gave it back. After that, the Garter Knights saluted him."

"That's curious," Selwyn said, retrieving Graham's pencil. "Do you remember which Garter Knights? That's easy enough to check."

Graham closed his eyes, picturing the three men. "Ah— Leicester, Burghley, and Howard. That's Charles Howard of Effingham. I had the feeling that I knew him well."

"Not surprising. He was lord high admiral by the time of the Armada, and probably your boss," Selwyn said. "What you've described seems odd, though. Drake was never a Knight of the Garter."

"It doesn't sound as if he *had* to be," Alix said with a raised eyebrow. "Gray, can you give us any other names that could be verified historically?"

Graham nodded. "Sir Christopher Hatton. He was captain of the Queen's guard. She used his sword. And the French ambassador did the actual knighting. I can't remember his name, but Drake may not have known, either."

"All right, I can check that, too," Alix replied, chewing on her pencil. "Anyone else?"

"Not just now." He dropped his head into both hands. "Jesus, my head hurts! It's really just started to hit me."

"You've been a busy boy," Selwyn muttered, rising to begin massaging the back of Graham's neck and shoulders with both hands. "Come back and sleep aboard my ship tonight and we'll talk more when you've slept. Do you think you're fit to drive?"

"I'll ask William. I don't think he'll mind."

"William? My dear chap, colonels don't ask—"

"This one does," Graham replied, rising shakily and smiling to disarm Selwyn's surprise. "Really, David. It's all right. He used to do it all the time. Besides, it will help take his mind off some of what happened tonight. If I'd known how it was going to go, I'm not sure I would have let him come. We've probably scared him witless."

"Don't be too sure about that," Alix said, walking with him to the door. "He may surprise you. Ask him about it. I have a feeling he may sense more than meets the eye."

He wondered what she meant by that, but there was no time for further speculation. Outside the room, he put on a reassuring face for Richard and Geoffrey as he shrugged into the duffle coat his son held, noting vaguely that William was already back in Balaclava helmet and coat, waiting attentively.

He knew he was preoccupied as he led William back down the stairs and to the car, but somehow he was reluctant to break the silence and sensed the same reluctance in William. Even when the prince had pulled the car back onto the paved road and settled in for the drive back to Plymouth, neither of them said a word.

CHAPTER 10

THEY DROVE IN SILENCE FOR THE FIRST QUARTER HOUR, William at the wheel and Graham with his head tilted back against the seat, eyes closed, bracing himself for a barrage of questions that did not come.

He wondered why. Though William had always been close-mouthed while actually working on an assignment, it was not like him to keep silent once a tight spot was past and questions could be asked. Certainly Graham did not expect silence after their conversation on the trip out. As he watched William light his second cigarette since their departure, the brief flare of the match illuminated unexpected nervousness and even apprehension. That surprised him even more. As far as he was concerned, the worst of the night was over. Why, then, was William still so edgy?

"Are you all right?" he finally asked in a low voice. "Is something bothering you about what happened back there?"

William drew smoke deep into his lungs and exhaled it briskly over his right shoulder, where it dissipated through the partially open window.

"I could ask you the same question."

"But you haven't. Why not?"

"Because I've been waiting for you to jump all over me for not following your orders!" came the terse reply. "Go ahead and get on with it. I deserve it. I was wrong. I admit it."

Graham quickly skimmed back over the past three hours in

his mind and was still puzzled. What was William talking about?

"I must be too exhausted to follow you. What orders do you mean?"

"What other orders did you give?" William snapped. "You told me not to move from where you put me. I moved. Selwyn and the lady seemed not to mind," he added defensively.

Instantly, Graham flashed on the hands drawing him away from the abyss as he fought his way forward from the memory regression: Alix and Dav—bloody damn! So that was it.

He had assumed the man's hand was David's, but in fact it must have been William's. Yet the feel of it, psychically, had been so solid, so familiar. . . . Was it possible that he really *had* known William in another life? Their charts had hinted at it, but he had all but dismissed that before as wishful thinking.

He remembered glancing back at William on the settle, and the look on his face, and wondering what had kept him there. Now it was clear: nothing had. William must have recognized his distress and rushed to grab his hand before Selwyn could, somehow knowing instinctively how to help Alix pull him back. Why hadn't Alix said something?

He pressed the heels of both hands over his eyes and tried to think. She had, of course. Her words simply had not penetrated his fatigue. Something about William probably sensing more than meets the eye. . . .

Well, William had done that, all right—and bloody well, too. A breach of orders, yes, but hardly one to which Graham could take violent exception under the circumstances.

He glanced at William again, suddenly remembering that he had not yet answered the prince's taut self-accusation. The fine hands were clenched white-knuckled on the steering wheel, only barely discernible in the faint illumination from the instrument panel, the tension in the face more sensed than seen. Berating himself for the inexcusable delay, Graham shook his head and reached across to touch the prince's arm in reassurance. William flinched.

"Jesus, Will, don't jump out of your skin!" Graham breathed. "I'm sorry. I just *now* realized that it was your hand and not Selwyn's—which should tell you something important about whether it seemed right at the time or not." He shifted his gaze out to the darkness ahead of them, watching the narrow head-light beams sweep the road as they went around a curve.

"Frankly, I'd have to say that you probably did exactly the right thing," he admitted, "though I'd rather not even think about the headache I'd probably have if it *hadn't* been all right. So I suppose I'll have to forgive you for not following orders *this* time—but don't let it happen again."

The falling tension was almost tangible. With an enormous sigh, the prince pulled over and stopped, shoulders slumping in relief as he leaned his forehead against the steering wheel between his hands and took a deep breath.

"Please don't ever do that to me again, Gray," he whispered, raising his head. "When you didn't say anything for so long, I didn't know what to think. God knows, you'd made a big enough issue about not interfering. I wouldn't blame you if you were sorry you ever let me come."

"No, I'm not sorry," Graham replied, suddenly aware that it was true. "Are you?"

"Good God, no! I'm totally confused, of course—though that can hardly come as a surprise. What happened? I got the impression that things didn't go exactly as planned."

Graham snorted at the eagerness in the voice. "I'll say one thing in your behalf: you've a bloody marvelous gift for un-derstatement. We'd better keep driving, though, if you feel up to it. To tell the truth, I'm not exactly sure what *did* happen."

"Well, did you find out about Drake?"

"Drake? Yes, indeed. Damned if I can figure out what it all means, however. Part of it had to do with Queen Elizabeth."

"Good Queen Bess, eh?" William had eased the car back onto the road, and now he glanced at Graham as he increased speed. "What did you see? Maybe I can help."

"With respect, I doubt it. If Selwyn and the others haven't been able to crack it yet—"

"With respect, maybe a fresh point of view is exactly what you need," William replied, almost a little archly. "I do have some insight into the thinking patterns of monarchs, after all. In any case, it can't hurt, can it?"

Graham supposed it couldn't, so as they drove, he briefly outlined what he had told the others about the scene on the *Golden Hind*. William asked a few questions during the reci-tation, but he was silent after Graham had finished. Graham began to wonder whether it had been a waste of time until William cleared his throat and glanced his way again, a dark shadow against the darker shapes of fleeing countryside.

"You may be right," the prince admitted. "Perhaps I need some time to digest the bits about Drake and old Bess like the rest of you. I have a feeling I'm going to be doing a lot of that in the next few days—maybe with some mental indigestion, too."

Graham chuckled, but his amusement was quickly dampened as William went on.

"Let's talk about that final part for a moment, though, if you don't mind. What happened then? Your hands were gripping the chair arms so hard, I really wondered whether the oak could take it. And your face—Jesus, Gray, your face! I think that's the only time I was really scared."

Graham drew a deep breath, suddenly cautious. He had not been going to tell William anything about the unplanned memory excursions. *Slayer of kings and slain for kings*—he was not sure the prince was ready to handle that. For that matter, Graham was not sure he was ready to handle it himself.

He could safely talk about past lives in general, however, perhaps even mentioning a few names. He would bypass the talk of slaying and slain.

"I went into a series of flashbacks to other lives besides Drake's," Graham said carefully. "I'm not sure why, and I don't remember much about them other than very brief images, but those were what caused the reaction you saw. It isn't that uncommon, though the intensity was a little more than I would have expected. Actually, one rarely knows what one is going to get in the usual run of past-life regressions."

William seemed to be turning that over in his mind as he negotiated a narrow turn. Then he said, "These other lives— were you able to identify any of them?"

"A few. The clearest one was an ancestor of yours: old William Rufus. I think I was one of his retainers."

"Rufus? Really? I seem to recall he's buried at Winchester."

At Graham's grunt of agreement, William went on.

"As a matter of fact, you've mentioned him before, haven't you? Something about his death being some sort of pagan sacrifice, wasn't it?"

Graham smiled, though a vague foreboding was stirring at

the back of his mind. Why had he even bothered to censor his account?

"Something like that. You know, you're getting quite a knack for pulling odd bits together. Why the great interest in old Rufus?"

William chuckled. "He's another William, of course. When John and I were small, we spent a lot of time indoors because John was sick so much. Nanny used to read to us about our ancestors. I can tell you all about Williams I and III also, if you like. Ask me anything."

The prince's voice was jovial, almost inviting a response, but Graham resisted the temptation. He was too tired for mental sparring and definitely reluctant to explore the other past life material with William until he'd had a chance to think about it more on his own. The unsought recall made him very uneasy, and somehow the uneasiness had to do with William as well as himself.

"Not tonight, I think. You're entirely too cocky not to be telling the truth." He paused. "On a more serious note, however, we'll be arriving back at your quarters very shortly, and there may not be an opportunity to talk privately again for some time. Was there anything else you wanted to ask about tonight?"

William drew a deep breath and let it out audibly.

"Boldly into the breach. Yes. The woman who seemed to be in charge—is she Selwyn's wife?"

"She is. But remember what I told you about letting on that you know in the future."

"I'll remember. Ah—what did she do behind us, just after we went in?"

Graham glanced at the prince in mild astonishment. He had been almost sure William hadn't noticed.

"I told you before that the room would be prepared before we arrived," he said truthfully. "Cleansed of negative elements and sealed off so that no distractions could enter while we worked. She was closing the gate she'd opened before we came in."

"I see. That's why we had to wait outside for a moment after you'd knocked. And the brigadier was opening it up again before he took me out?"

"You really don't miss a thing, do you?" Graham replied,

verbalizing what he had only thought before. "Anything else you'd like to know? State secrets, perhaps?"

"Well, you asked whether I had any questions." William took another deep breath. "This gate—if it hadn't been opened, could we have entered the room, anyway?"

"I wouldn't have wanted to try," Graham said. "Would you?"

"Ah—pass on that one for now. That's really out of my depth."

"Well, at least you're beginning to realize that some things are."

"Now who's being cocky?" William returned. "Another question: how did you go into trance like that? I've read more about hypnosis since we last talked about it, and the countess— what was her name, if I may ask?"

"Alix. You'd find out, anyway—damned MI.6 smart aleck!"

"Why, thank you. You did train me, after all. At any rate, I was wondering how you went into such a deep trance without her saying anything. I remember you spoke to Michael that day in Dover—and I would assume that you're both experienced subjects."

Graham let himself relax a little. They were almost back. If he could stay on this relatively safe topic long enough, there would be no more heart-stopping questions about matters arcane until he could think things through. Surely things would look better after a good night's sleep.

"We *are* experienced subjects, but there are a lot of factors that can influence response. Pain, for example, can make it very difficult to concentrate on a purely mental process. That's why I talked Michael into a trance, even though ordinarily he could go quite deep with a touch or any of a variety of other nonverbal signals—which is what Alix did with me. Going into trance is easy. Using it for something definite can be quite another story. There's nothing magical about a trance per se."

"Indeed. Do you suppose I could be hypnotized?"

"Surely. It isn't a parlor trick, however. I thought I'd made that clear."

"You did. I still might like to try it some time, though. Who knows? Maybe I've even had some of these past lives you keep talking about."

William chuckled at that, and Graham laughed with him,

but as they threaded their way through the wet, silent Plymouth streets, Graham wondered whether the prince realized how close to the truth his speculation might be. William's intervention and the rightness of it at the time pointed to some kind of connection that could quite well involve past lives, some of them undoubtedly touching Graham's. Nor could Graham deny the rush of warmth from the thought.

But the intervention raised other questions—immediate questions that almost invariably led to an even greater involvement on William's part.

Was William, the Knight of Wands of Alix's reading, destined to play a part in what was unfolding? Or had Graham merely seen William in the cards because he was looking for justification for his own actions and wanted the card to be William?

And if the Knight of Wands *was* William, how far dared they let him go? Did they even have any control over it anymore, or must they simply stand by and accept things as they came, trusting that some provident fate would keep the prince from getting in over his head?

Above all, if Graham and William had known one another in some previous life and Graham had been slayer and slain, then who had William been?

William's flight back to Southampton the next morning was uneventful but not uninteresting. The Sunderland took off shortly before noon into a sky washed bright blue and pristine from the night's rain. William watched Plymouth and Lord Selwyn's warship grow smaller and smaller as they climbed for altitude and headed east, but his thoughts invariably ranged back to the night before and all that he had seen and heard.

At least a night's sleep, however truncated, had taken the edge off his confusion. He felt far more confident now that he was in a familiar environment again, heading back to London. Griffin was a little stiff this morning—Denton had put him back in his chair to sleep off the night's "drink" when William and Graham returned—and Wells mentioned a slight headache at breakfast, but neither man seemed any the worse for wear or found anything particularly amiss. Denton apparently had done his job well.

William felt a little initial awkwardness with Richard and

Geoffrey when he first returned to the flying boat, but that
soon evaporated in the face of the two younger men's good
spirits and obvious warmth toward him. He could not put a
finger on the reason for it, but he decided not to question it.
Somehow he felt far less the outsider among them today, though
they still deferred to his rank with respect and careful courtesy.

As soon as they were airborne, he was again invited forward
to occupy the second pilot's chair for the duration of the flight.
To his unexpected pleasure, they spent the next half hour in
good-natured bantering, as if the night before had not occurred—or perhaps because it had, he later realized. When,
just before landing, Geoffrey hesitantly invited him to join them
for lunch at their officers' mess, he never even thought of
declining.

After lunch, the two took him on an informal tour of their
base—an activity for which he ordinarily would not have been
able to muster much enthusiasm, seeing more than his fill of
such tours in the course of his more usual duties—but somehow
this was different. Wherever he went, his presence seemed not
only well received but actively appreciated by officers and men
alike. He stayed far later than he had planned, but he found
he was oddly reluctant to leave these men who were so inti-
mately connected with the world he had glimpsed the night
before—though neither of them spoke a word about it.

He thought more about the previous night on the way to the
train station, and on a whim asked Wells to check the departure
schedule from Winchester, twelve miles farther north on the
line. When he found that it was possible to connect with a
London train at seven, he asked their driver to take them there
instead. He had never seen the cathedral, and it seemed a shame
not to stop, since they were so close and had the time. His
own staff seemed a little surprised, but their plucky WRNS
driver headed north without a word of comment.

Dusk was falling and Evensong halfway done by the time
they reached the cathedral. He left Griffin with the car and
driver—and would have left Wells, except that the aide would
have been scandalized at the thought of his royal master entering
so public a place unattended—then slipped quietly through a
side door and along the dim south aisle. The choir was singing
the Creed.

A verger started to intercept them, for visitors were discouraged from wandering about the cathedral during services, but when the man saw Wells's staff aiguillette and got a closer look at William, he bowed and quietly ushered them to seats in the back of the south choir stalls. William and his aide were not the only men in uniform in the rows behind the choir boys, so they were able to blend into the shadows without arousing undue interest as the sung *Amen* faded away in the stillness and everyone knelt for the Lord's Prayer. William bowed his head and half covered his eyes with one hand as he slipped to his knees, glad for the dimness and the anonymity it afforded. After a few seconds, he was not even as keenly aware of Wells kneeling in the stall beside him.

He was not sure why he had decided to come. It was true that he had never been to Winchester before, but that never would have mattered in the past. Though he regarded himself as a reasonably religious man, he had never thought of cathedrals as being much different from one another except in architectural terms. Winchester's difference lay in the fact that William Rufus was buried here. He had known that before, but somehow it was a more important consideration after last night's conversation with Gray.

It was not so much what Gray had said but what he had not said that sparked William's interest. William had the distinct impression that Gray had been evasive, that he had not told all he had seen of the redheaded Norman king. Gray had wept while in his trance—something William had never seen him do even when his wife died. It was so astonishing that William had not even dared to ask about it.

Had he wept for Rufus? Had he perhaps *been* Rufus and seen and experienced his own death in that New Forest hunting mishap? William was not at all sure he believed that Rufus had been some sort of pagan sacrifice, but the death certainly had occurred. Could Gray have seen a glimpse of that?

The officiating minister stood, and all eyes turned toward him as he sang alone, only his face and hands illuminated by the dim reading lamp on the prayer desk before him.

"O Lord, shew thy mercy upon us."

"And grant us thy salvation," the choir answered.

"O Lord, save the King."

"And mercifully hear us when we call upon thee."

The litany continued, sung back and forth between minister

and choir, and William let his thoughts wander again, eyes searching the cathedral.

The cathedral was beautiful. The graceful sweeps of carved wood and stone gave his heart joy. He liked the very feel of the place—the smells, the spaciousness of soaring arches, the lush resonance of voices raised in prayer as they had been for at least a thousand years.

He studied the play of lamplight on the tracery of choir stalls, screen, and pulpit while a part of him listened. Turning his gaze upward, he drank in the colonnades and fan vaulting, though the great windows were boarded up because of the blackout and the glass removed to preserve it. Color remained in the choristers' cassocks and surplices, however: subdued splashes of crimson and white against the age-worn patina of the stalls, and the glow of the reading lamps reflecting off snowy linen and polished brass fittings.

"Lighten our darkness, we beseech thee, O Lord," the minister intoned, "and by thy great mercy defend us from all perils and dangers of this night. For the love of thy only Son, our Saviour Jesus Christ. Amen."

The people sat. The choir stood to sing the evening's anthem. William listened attentively for the first few bars, easing to one side in his seat so that the deep framing of the stall kept his face in shadow, but the young voices gradually encouraged his thoughts to wander again, lulling him into some other dimension.

Just ahead of him, down at the level of the choir floor, his eyes came to rest on a scarred black tomb slab, slightly peaked along its length and resting on a base of creamish stone like that of the floor paving. It looked very old, and he wondered idly whether it might be William Rufus's resting place. High on the stone screens farther to his right, he could just make out several painted mortuary chests, but he thought they were from an earlier time. He remembered reading once that they contained the bones of early Saxon kings and queens and bishops.

He wondered who they were and whether all of them had followed the Christian faith—what it might have been like to be alive in a time when the two faiths had walked side by side. Was it really possible that they still did?

He was jarred back to the order of the service by the minister's call for prayer for the King's Majesty, and he slid dutifully back to his knees.

"With thy favour to behold our most gracious Sovereign Lord, King George," the minister recited, "and so replenish him with the grace of the Holy Spirit that he may always incline to thy will, and walk in thy way. Endue him plenteously with heavenly gifts. Grant him in health and wealth long to live. Strengthen him that he may vanquish and overcome all his enemies, and finally after this life he may attain everlasting joy and felicity. Through Jesus Christ our Lord. Amen."

William lost the thread of the set prayers for the rest of the Royal Family and clergy even though he knew he was included in them, if not by name. Now he was remembering his family in his own way: proud Mama, alone now, with Papa gone; Bertie and his beloved Elizabeth and the two adored nieces, Lilibet and Margaret Rose; his sister Mary and her husband and sons, and Harry and Georgie and all their families—and his brother John, who had died when they were thirteen; and especially the exiled David, who had been so kind to him as a boy, and given up his crown, and might as well be dead. . . .

By the time he had prayed for them all, the service was ending. The choir and ministers filed out through the choir doorway, followed by a more random trickle of laymen and women who had attended the service, civilian and Forces. William remained kneeling, his face partially covered with one hand in hopes that no one would disturb him, but after a moment, the verger appeared in the choir doorway with an older man he thought was the minister who had led the service.

William sighed and stood as the two men hesitantly started toward him, putting on one of his more approachable demeanors. If he could manage it without seeming too awkward, he wanted a few minutes alone with Rufus's tomb before he left— though at this point, he was not even certain he had identified it correctly.

"Sir, would you rather be left alone?" Wells murmured, rising to stand beside him.

"No, it's all right."

William moved down into the choir and nodded toward the two clergymen, inviting their further approach with a smile.

"Your Royal Highness?" the verger said tentatively.

"Good evening. I hope I haven't intruded."

"Certainly not, sir. It's an honor to have you here. May I present Canon Thompson, our minister this evening, who wished to pay his respects?"

"Your Royal Highness. We are most honored by your visit. May I or one of the vergers show you anything of particular interest?"

"Thank you, no. I see that you're about to lock up for the night, so I shan't keep you. I was on my way back to London, and it occurred to me that I had never visited your beautiful cathedral. I believe that some of my more remote ancestors are buried here, are they not?"

The verger basked in the royal interest.

"Indeed, they are, sir. Up there on the choir screens, you can see funerary chests containing the bones of many of the Saxon kings and queens: Canute and Emma, Kynewald, Kenulph; Matilda, the queen of Henry I. And of course, Henry's elder brother, William Rufus, is there under the tower."

"Indeed? That one over there?"

"Why, yes, sir." The man raised a well-bred eyebrow as he nodded toward the tomb slab that William had already suspected. "I suspect you know, of course, that it's said Rufus was not a true Christian. When the entire tower fell a few years after he was buried here, some attributed it to divine outrage that such a man should be buried in consecrated ground. It all had to be rebuilt," he ended wistfully.

"Not that he was a bad king," Thompson hastened to add, lest the prince infer some criticism of the current royal line. "Times were different then, and we must not judge his morals too harshly by our own standards."

William chuckled and held up a hand in amused protest. "You needn't defend him to me, gentlemen," he said. "He's but a distant and collateral ancestor. All we share is a name."

As the others joined his amusement with obvious relief, William realized that if he were going to have his moment alone with Rufus, it would have to be soon. Quiet descended even more heavily as the last of the people filtered out through the rear doors. Wistfully, he allowed his gaze to sweep around the choir and sanctuary as he sighed.

"What a beautiful place, and how peaceful. Do you suppose I might have a few minutes alone here, canon, before you lock up? I've seen so much of war in the past few days. It would be a welcome interlude, and deeply appreciated."

Phrased thus, his request could hardly be refused. Assuring him that his tarrying would not at all inconvenience them, the two clergymen took their leave and bowed themselves out of the choir. William sent Wells after them to wait at the car, then sat in the closest stall and listened for the last footsteps to recede down the nave. Only then did he rise and move silently to the black tomb slab. He stood at its head and let one hand rest on it casually, just in case anyone should come upon him, then allowed his eyes to sweep its length. The stone was unadorned with cross or script or any other decoration, but its stark simplicity was the more compelling for that.

So, William Rufus, he thought, wondering whether the living Rufus had ever stood where he now stood. *What were you really? What were you to Gray, in that vast other time, that he should have wept for you? Were you really a pagan, slain for your gods? What does that mean exactly?*

He glanced at the sanctuary and altar screen beyond, at the carved Christus on its cross, at the figures of the saints grouped around it in dignified attendance, then returned his attention to the king whose mortal remains lay under the stone beneath his hand.

Gray says that all the gods are One—that Jesus, up on that cross, was but one of many great men made gods incarnate to teach us how to love. An interesting theory, and not what I was taught—and yet it doesn't seem wrong somehow—only different.

What kind of force is Gray meddling with, though? I believe him when he says it isn't evil, that Drake had nothing to do with the Devil—with Satan, rather—but they used to hang and burn people for what Gray and his friends are doing, even though he does claim it's for the good of England.

He glanced furtively at the crucifix on the altar screen, then shook his head and smiled at himself—feeling guilty for talking to a long-dead king!

Now I am overreacting! But you know all that, don't you, old boy? And you probably know about Drake, too, don't you? If you were of the old faith, then perhaps you already understand this link that Gray hasn't been able to forge yet: the secret of how to get the magical folk of today to work together.

It has to do with garters, doesn't it? That's why he remembered that scene on the Golden Hind.

He thought about the Garter star he would have worn on his breast in peacetime and then about the Garter itself. Garters. And Queen Elizabeth—another monarch who, like Rufus, had left no offspring. Could there be some vague connection there, perhaps? Was that why Gray had seen Rufus unexpectedly, after seeing Elizabeth?

With a shake of his head, William allowed himself an exasperated sigh. Even if this was the right line of reasoning, he was not going to follow it out here. If he lingered much longer, Wells would begin fretting and come to look for him—though what danger Wells might see in his solitary meditation in a deserted cathedral was beyond William's fathoming. Wells sometimes took his bodyguarding duties far too seriously.

He sighed and ran his hand along the length of the tomb slab as he moved a few steps closer to the altar, then bowed his head and said another prayer for his brother's health and strength. Gray had said that prayers were a form of magic. If so, then it was not inappropriate that William offer up such magic here, with his hand still on the tomb of one who was said to have lived by it.

When he had finished, he nodded respect to the altar and went back along the tomb, stroking the age-scarred stone a final time. Then he strode out through the choir door and down the nave, ready to face the final farewells of the verger, canon, and other officials who undoubtedly would have assembled by now. Such was expected of royals, part of the job. He did not really mind.

CHAPTER 11

GRAHAM SLEPT ABOARD LORD SELWYN'S SHIP AFTER he collected Denton and left the prince and did not stir until nearly dusk the next evening, when the brigadier came aboard. Later, the three men dined privately in Selwyn's cabin and rehashed the previous night's work. After the earl broke out another bottle from his private stock, the discussion settled down in earnest.

"I'd say the Queen definitely meant to give him some kind of magical acknowledgment," the brigadier finally said when Graham had reiterated his Drake recall twice, in trance the second time to enhance his memory. "But if you're to be a modern-day parallel, I don't see how we're going to manage that for you. One can hardly walk up to the King of England in this day and age and say, 'Your Majesty, we need a grand coven, and we'd like you to publicly acknowledge Sir John Graham as your man in black. Could you put it on the BBC tonight, please?'"

Selwyn snorted, and even Graham chuckled at the lunacy of that, but the mood lightened considerably as they continued their discussion.

"What about those Garter Knights?" the brigadier asked when they seemed to have exhausted their speculation on the Queen.

"Leicester, Howard, and Burghley," Selwyn said, leaning back in his chair to pluck a thick volume from one of the shelves behind him. "I did a little reading while you were asleep, Gray. You came up with some interesting correspondences, for a man who supposedly has little background in this period."

As Graham shifted uneasily, Selwyn opened the book to a place marked by a folded sheet of ship's stationery and opened the sheet, holding it at arm's length until he could find his reading glasses.

"Let's see. We know quite a lot about Leicester, of course: Sir Robert Dudley, the Queen's favorite of long standing. He was admitted to the Garter in 1559, the year after Elizabeth became Queen. I believe they were less than a year apart in age. Created Earl of Leicester in 1564, died in 1588, within a month of the Armada victory. He was known to move in court circles that included a number of persons with occult interests: John Dee; Sir Francis Walsingham, of course; ah, the poet Edward Dyer, a known student of the occult; and Sir Philip Sidney, whose father was also KG. Philip was a follower of Dee, by the way."

He looked up over the top of his glasses. "Any of that suggest anything to either of you?"

"Perhaps," Graham said thoughtfully. "Interesting that Leicester should die so soon after the Armada. How old was he?"

"Well, he wasn't young, at least for that time," Selwyn replied, making a rapid calculation. "Fifty-five, or in his fifty-sixth year. So was Elizabeth."

Graham raised an eyebrow. "That's also interesting. Eight-sevens. It could fit a regnal cycle. That year was certainly critical for Elizabeth in other respects."

"It was also seven years after Drake's knighting," the brigadier offered. "Just for curiosity's sake, when did Drake die?"

Selwyn smiled. "Seven years after that, in January of 1596."

The brigadier puffed several times on his pipe and nodded. "Go ahead. Let's hear about the others."

"Very well. Charles, second Lord Howard of Effingham. He was admitted to the Garter in 1575 and later created Earl of Nottingham; lord high admiral and technically in command at Cadiz and in the sea defense against the Armada, though Drake was his second and probably actually ran the show. By the way, his father, William, the first Lord Howard, was also lord high admiral and KG; and his wife was the daughter of Lord Hunsdon, another KG, who was also the Queen's nephew."

As Graham whistled low under his breath, the brigadier snorted.

"A close-knit lot, weren't they?"

"So it would seem," Selwyn agreed. "And all of them were very close to the Queen. Burghley—William Cecil—was her principal minister for more than forty years; admitted to the Garter in 1572. Incidentally, you mentioned Sir Christopher Hatton as being present, Gray. He wasn't KG at the time of Drake's knighting, of course, but he *would* have been by the time of the Armada."

"You're joking!"

"No, admitted to the order in 1588. He was already Chancellor of England by then. If we assume that he was installed at St. George's-tide, as was usually the case, then by the summer of 1588, we have at least four Garter Knights who witnessed Drake's knighting and possible reception of a mandate which went with the retrieval of the Queen's garter. Hatton was another favorite of the Queen, by the way, and another gentleman with known interests in the occult."

After a moment, Graham tilted his chair on its back legs and gazed abstractedly at the ceiling. "Leicester, Howard, Burghley—and Hatton. Are any of their descendants KG today?"

"There are two with the Cecil surname, but I'd have to check with Black Rod to be certain of the exact connection," Selwyn replied. "The Marquess of Salisbury might be a direct descendant, but he's also nearly eighty years old. I don't know about the Marquess of Exeter. I've never heard anything to link either man with the old faith, however."

"Then that's probably because there *isn't* anything," Graham said with a sigh.

"Perhaps. Anyway, I've made you lists of both the Elizabethan and present-day holders just in case they might be useful. You might as well take them."

"Let's get back to the Queen and her very interesting garter, then," the brigadier said as Graham slipped the lists into his pocket. "Is it possible that she let Drake keep it? Could he have shown it as the sign of his authority when he summoned the grand coven seven years later?"

"No, later in the day she gave it to the Frenchman to send to the Duc d'Alencon," Selwyn said emphatically. "All the accounts agree on that. Incidentally, the presence of our four KG's isn't noted specifically in any of the accounts I had at hand, but that doesn't mean they weren't there. Given their relationships with the Queen and the importance of Drake's exploits, it's quite probable that they would have attended her that day to see what was going to happen to him. Burghley was her chief minister and would have been concerned about offending the Spanish and starting a war prematurely, since Drake had been privateering against Spanish ships and ports. Leicester and Hatton were her favorites and very jealous of the Frenchman's suit on behalf of d'Alencon as well as being jealous of one another. In addition, Hatton was Drake's friend and patron; therefore, he had a personal interest in Drake's fate. Howard was lord chamberlain of the royal household, as well as a man with long-standing ties to the sea. In fact, I can't conceive of them *not* being there under the circumstances."

"What about the other details?" Graham asked. "Was I fairly close on those?"

"Damned close. I even rang up a few experts to be certain. The few discrepancies are mostly sequential, and fall well within the realm of different historical interpretation. The fact that the lost garter was reported at all makes it a significant point, and very likely more than meets the eye."

"Which means I couldn't just have dreamed it up," Graham said, his sigh conveying relief and uncertainty.

Selwyn took off his glasses and laid them precisely on the table before him, gazing across at Graham with an expression of pride and just a little awe.

"Gray, did you ever seriously think you had?"

They worked on into Saturday night, but mostly they went in circles after that. All of them were convinced that the sequence Graham recalled from the *Golden Hind* was significant for their purposes, but a useful coordination continued to elude them. Graham left them on Sunday at midday after too little sleep and spent the rest of the day in travel.

Monday morning was booked solid with appointments, including a last-minute request from his immediate superior to attend an eleven o'clock meeting at Whitehall in his behalf.

Muttering under his breath, Graham put on a proper uniform and had Denton drive him over. He hoped for time to call Alix and check on her progress with his list of king-slayers, but he never had the chance.

Nor did he ever discover precisely why his presence had been so urgently required at the meeting. He recognized colleagues from naval intelligence and the Air Ministry, but the topics discussed never touched even remotely on an area of Graham's particular expertise or his boss's. The meeting was mostly a rehash of things he already knew. To amuse himself, he studied the others present and tried to decide how seriously they were taking it, a detached part of him jotting down salient points of the proceedings. The dual function helped to take his mind off the fact that his tie was slowly strangling him.

One man, a major's crowns on his shoulder straps, caught Graham's attention fairly early on. His precise military function was as nebulous to Graham as that of most of the other men in the room, for that was the nature of gatherings of combined intelligence services; but outside the military, Graham knew very well what Thomas Collier did. Collier was the grand master of an old and well-established occult fraternity whose aid Alix had tried to recruit, without success, not two weeks ago for the Lammas working. Graham knew him only slightly from meetings of this sort and nods in the halls, but he knew the man's magical tradition very well and was himself a high-grade initiate, though no longer affiliated with any of the group's lodges in England. Collier had no idea of Graham's connection with Alix or the occult world.

The man's presence rankled Graham all through the meeting, though neither of them said a word. Awareness of Collier's refusal to cooperate became increasingly irritating. Graham had gained no new insights into leverage since his Hyde Park failure, but by the time the meeting was over, he had decided to go ahead and approach Collier if he could manage it at all discreetly. He must face the possibility that the Drake mandate might *never* be understood—and Collier *might* respond to Graham where Alix had failed. Even if Collier refused again, Graham was reasonably certain he would keep silent, if only for the sake of the oaths they had both sworn in times past.

When the meeting broke up shortly after one, Graham contrived to leave at the same time as his quarry, nodding amiably as they rode up in the lift together with several other officers and staying near him as they approached the main doors. Outside, the sky was looking sufficiently ominous that Graham was glad to see Denton waiting by the Bentley at the curb. A glance at Collier confirmed his hope that the major had not thought to have himself driven.

"Well, if it isn't Germans, it's rain, eh, major?" he said genially, glancing up at the clouds and then at Collier with a friendly smile. "I hope your driver didn't go far."

Collier shrugged. "I'm afraid I walked, colonel. The weather looked fine when I left."

"Yes, it *will* do that, this time of year. Rotten luck. May I offer you a ride, then?" Graham said, gesturing toward his car, where Denton was already opening the door. "You're just over at Wellington Barracks, aren't you?"

"Why, yes, thank you very much. Are you sure it won't be any trouble?"

"Not in the least," Graham said as he slid in beside Collier. "Denny, the major is going to Wellington Barracks."

"Right, sir."

They settled into the Bentley's comfortable back seat, and Denton eased them into traffic headed south along Whitehall. After a few seconds, Graham turned casually to his companion.

"I'm given to understand we have a mutual acquaintance, major," he said in a conversational tone, watching sidelong as Collier turned unsuspecting eyes in his direction.

"Oh? And who is that, sir?"

"The Countess of Selwyn. I believe she called on you at your home a few weeks ago."

Collier stiffened just a little, though he covered his uneasiness well.

"Lady Selwyn? Why, I know her slightly, colonel, but I can't imagine what she could have told you about me."

"Can't you?" Graham leaned forward and touched Denton on the shoulder. "Take the long way around, please, Denny."

As they circled Parliament Square, heading into Broad Sanctuary and Victoria Street, Graham cranked up the glass partition, closing them off from Denton. Collier was definitely pale now, hands white-knuckled on the edge of his attaché case.

"I don't understand, colonel," the man whispered in a last,

desperate attempt to evade. "If this is some kind of security ploy to test my loyalty—"

"You know it isn't, major—at least not an official one," Graham replied softly. "Surely you realize that I'm putting myself in a far more precarious position than yourself, by revealing myself to you."

Collier looked at him with a start. "You?"

"We share a common oath—*Frater Augustus*, isn't it?"

At Collier's gasp, Graham reached across and traced a sign on the back of the man's hand with his fingertip. Collier bowed his head and squeezed his eyes shut in denial, but Graham knew his sign had been recognized and accepted.

"So you do understand what I'm talking about," Graham continued. "You should also know that I was very distressed to learn of your decision not to cooperate with Lady Selwyn. It's one of the most important things that people like us can do to help win the war, *frater*. The threat of invasion is no less serious today than it has been in other times when our ancestors and predecessors did their parts. Why did you refuse?"

Collier swallowed hard and opened his eyes to stare at the attaché case on his lap, shoulders slumping dejectedly.

"Those were different times, colonel. It's too dangerous now. If you know that recognition sign, you should understand that."

"I know many signs," Graham countered, though he did not raise his voice. "And I am more aware of the danger than you can even begin to guess. However, I ask you to consider the possible alternative if nothing is done. Concerted action is our very best hope: unanimity of will to break Hitler's nerve and put a stop to his threats of invasion once and for all. This island must *not* be conquered!"

"No one could argue with that," Collier muttered. "Your motives are sound. But the implications of a joint enterprise— I simply cannot ask my people to do it. You're talking about a grand—you *know* what you're talking about!" he said a little belligerently, with a glance at the apparently oblivious Denton. "How dare you even ask it? You haven't the authority. You know as well as—who the bloody hell do you think you are?"

Graham sighed. By *who*, Collier actually meant *what*—and that, Graham could not tell him because he did not yet know himself. Nor dared he insist further, else he might undermine whatever slender vestige of authority Collier did feel he had, forever destroying the possibility of future concord.

They were headed up Buckingham Gate now, so he leaned forward and tapped on the glass in signal to proceed to their original destination, resigning himself to yet another defeat.

"Never mind, then, major," he said in a low voice. "I'm sorry if I wasted your time or gave you cause for alarm. I understand your fear. Perhaps I had simply hoped for a little more courage."

"It takes more than courage, colonel," Collier said as the car pulled up in front of Wellington Barracks. "I have to say that I admire yours, but it takes more than that. Don't bother your driver to let me out. I can manage. Thank you for the lift."

As the door slammed, Graham leaned back in the seat and sighed.

"And that, I suppose, is that," he said to no one in particular. He lowered the partition once again. "Might as well take me back to the office, Denny. Maybe I can get something done this afternoon. I certainly didn't just now."

His office was to prove no refuge, however. He found Prince William sitting behind his desk waiting for him when he returned, immaculately polished shoes resting casually across one corner and elbows propped on the chair arms. As was typical of late, when he wished not to draw attention to himself, the prince wore the plain service uniform of a naval captain, without decorations. He smiled good-naturedly at Graham's expression of unabashed surprise and swung down his feet.

"Hello, Gray. Your chaps in the next room said you'd probably be back from your meeting soon, so I decided to wait."

Graham tossed his hat on the coat tree and yanked his tie loose, trying not to look as unsettled as he felt. The last person he wanted to see today was the prince, especially when he had so much to do. All he needed was a mental sparring match with him, on top of Collier's refusal and the pressure of trying to crack the Drake connection. Nor could he read any hint of the reason for the royal visit on William's face.

"I must say, you've caught me at rather a busy time," he said quite frankly. "I've been running all morning, I haven't had a thing to eat, and I don't know when I'll be finished tonight. I don't mean to be rude, but was there something in particular you needed me for?"

William raised both eyebrows. "Why, what a warm greeting for an old friend," he said mildly. "You might have said, 'How nice to see you, William,' or 'I trust your trip back from Plymouth was pleasant, sir,' or even murmured low under your breath, 'Your Royal Highness,' and rendered a smart salute in appropriate military greeting. I don't demand a great deal of formality from my friends, as you know very well, Gray, but I do expect simple courtesy and would demand it of anyone else but you. Do you think I'd intrude like this, without even ringing in advance, if I didn't feel it was important?"

With a sigh, Graham leaned both hands heavily against the edge of the desk and bowed his head. He had almost presumed too far, even allowing their friendship.

"Please accept my apology, sir," he murmured contritely. "William, I'm sorry. I've just had rather a large setback that I can't really talk about here. I didn't mean to be short with you or to show disrespect."

"That's better." William stood and picked up his hat. "As a matter of fact, I'd come to collect you for a drive. Don't take off your coat. I shan't take no for an answer. I found I hadn't any engagements for today, so I gave my staff a well-deserved day off and drove myself over. I've even brought along a lunch of sorts. Don't argue. Just come along."

"A lunch?" Graham watched incredulously as William set his hat jauntily in place and came around the desk, good humor apparently restored. "Where?"

"I haven't decided yet. Right now, I have this yen to look at some docks."

"Docks?"

"You heard me. Come along now. Don't be cross. We'll take my car. As you can imagine, I've been doing a great deal of thinking since we last talked."

"I'll bet you have," Graham muttered under his breath as he grabbed his hat and straightened his tie. "Will you *please* tell me where we're going so I can at least give Denny some idea where to find me in an emergency?"

"Deptford" was all the prince would say.

He was more talkative once they were in his car and on their way, heading out the Old Kent Road. He told Graham

briefly about his morning and slipping away alone, then asked
Graham about his. Graham told him, without mentioning names.
When he had finished, William was aghast.

"You mean this chap just refused, flat out?"

Graham shrugged. "He was very polite about it, almost to
the end, but yes, I would have to say it was a flat refusal. He
was a frightened man."

"How frightened?" William asked. "I mean, now that he
knows what you are, you don't think he'd expose you, do
you?"

As they turned more easterly toward Greenwich, Graham
shook his head. "No. He was upset but not *that* upset. And he
doesn't know entirely what I am. He simply didn't accept my
authority to ask what I was asking. I don't suppose one should
blame him. He did acknowledge my recognition sign, however.
Years ago, I worked in his tradition, as I've worked in several
others in addition to my own. His order is—similar to Freemasonry in its degree system."

"You don't follow it anymore, then?"

"Not actively, no, though I still respect its tenets. And oaths
such as he and I swore are binding for life, as you know. I
don't believe he'll break his."

William snorted. "Not if the penalties are anything like the
ones for the oaths I took. My brother George is grand master
now, you know. He succeeded Great-uncle Arthur last year.
You aren't really a Christian, are you?"

Graham had been half expecting the question for some weeks,
but its context now, when finally asked, brought a smile to his
lips despite the awkwardness of the subject matter. There had
been hardly a pause between Great-uncle Arthur and the fatal
query.

"Your leaps of unabashed logic never fail to amaze me.
How detailed an answer would you like?"

"I didn't think I'd get a simple yea or nay, knowing you,"
William replied. "Keep it fairly short. We're nearly there."

"Very well. In the most orthodox sense, no, I'm not, though
there are aspects of that particular faith which I admire quite
a lot. The old and new religions have coexisted for a very long
time. It's unfortunate that so many people have been tortured
and killed for the narrowness of other people's religions instead

of rejoicing in the common fullnesses. No one has a monopoly on truth, I think."

"I can't argue with that, I suppose," William said. "But don't you believe in Christ and the Trinity and all that? I've seen you in church before. You didn't seem uncomfortable."

Graham chuckled, his own good humor completely restored by the prince's directness.

"Part of it is protective coloration—church attendance, I mean—but why should I have been uncomfortable? Do you think it matters where or how one bows one's head to truth? The creative force wears so many forms and guises—why should anyone be forced to honour only one?"

William was silent after that, though obviously thinking. Very soon, he parked the Rolls behind the Royal Naval College and led Graham around to the river embankment, Graham toting the paper sack that the prince had produced from the back seat. After a short stroll along the promenade, they found an empty bench set back from the pavement and sat down to eat. A metal guard rail partially obscured their view of the Thames itself, but hardly half a mile farther up river to the left lay the Deptford dock area. William did not mention it as they ate their meat pies and chips.

Because of the threatening sky, only a few of the other benches were occupied. Pedestrians along the promenade were also scant. Still, enough other servicemen were about that Graham and the prince could pretend to be just two more men in uniform, enjoying a quick lunch in the out-of-doors—though the oak leaves on their cap peaks did command the occasional closer look from passers-by. The attention was always discreet, however, and reminded William of his experience at the bake shop where he had bought their lunch.

"It's always the same," he murmured, drawing the peak of his cap closer over his eyes as an old pensioner on crutches took a sharp look at him and then continued on by as if he hadn't seen him, after all. "They knew it looked like me, but they decided it couldn't possibly *be* me—all by myself, buying Cornish pasties like anybody else—so they pretended not to notice. Sorry there's nothing to drink."

Graham chuckled companionably and said it didn't matter, feeling far more mellow with food in his stomach, and both

of them drank from a public water fountain after they tossed
their luncheon debris into a wire dustbin.

"As you may imagine, I've given a great deal of thought
to what we discussed the other night," William said a short
time later as the two of them continued walking slowly westward along the promenade. "Some of it is just plain incom-
prehensible, quite frankly, but I did check on a number of the
historical details. Did you know, for example, that shortly after
Drake's knighting, the *Golden Hind* was permanently laid up
in dock at Deptford as a sort of Elizabethan tourist attraction?"

Graham flashed an incredulous grin. "Was she really?"

"She was. She was starting to rot away by 1600. A Swiss
traveler reported taking a piece back home with him for a
souvenir. I suppose the chairs must have been made shortly
after that. There are four, by the way. I didn't have a great
deal of luck locating the exact position of the dock, but it was
probably somewhere along there."

He gestured toward the vista of the river before them, where
the banks of the Thames curved away to the right, then shoved
his hands into his pockets and was silent as they continued
walking. Graham wondered where all of this was supposed to
lead—the prince was on to something, or thought he was—
but he tried to curb his impatience as he waited for the next
link in the chain of logic. This could be no easier for William
right now than it was for him.

"Did you really have to bring me here to tell me that?" he
asked lightly after a considered pause.

A sheepish smile tugged at the corners of William's mouth.
"Well, you said that places can hold associations, didn't you?
If that weren't true, why did we go all the way to Buckland?"

"Well, I asked for that," Graham retorted, though he smiled
as he said it. He thought further about the implications of what
William had just said, then continued. "Are you suggesting
that being here might make it easier for me to remember more?"

"I thought it might. Why don't you tell me again what
happened when the Queen lost her garter?"

Graham stopped and stared at him. "You really *do* believe
me, don't you?"

William shrugged, but his attempt at casual nonchalance
did not quite succeed.

"I'm not completely gullible. I did some checking." He pulled a slip of paper from his pocket and unfolded it.

"I was looking for some evidence that Elizabeth herself felt there had been some kind of supernatural intervention in the Armada victory. If what you've been saying is true, it wouldn't have been overt, of course, but—well, there were several medals struck to commemorate the event. "*Afflavit Deus et dissipati sunt,*" he read from his paper. "That's what it said on one of them. 'God blew and they were scattered.' This drawing was on the reverse of the medal. Is it a magical symbol of some sort?"

The sketch the prince handed Graham had been hurriedly done, but the intended meaning was clear enough to make him raise one eyebrow in surprise. He did not answer just then, for they were coming abreast of an old man feeding pigeons from a wheelchair. The pigeons parted as the two of them strode through the flock, re-forming behind them as the old man stared. When they were well past, Graham handed the paper back.

"It's a sort of magical protection—a circle warding. Probably Dee's work."

"I thought it might be, if the rest was true," William replied. "Mind you, I'm not saying I believe everything you've said, but I do believe something extraordinary happened Friday night. I can't explain it—but I thought we might see what happened if we tried to use the information as if it *were* true. Does that sound at all useful?"

Graham gave a wry smile. "That sounds pretty qualified to me—but go on, I'm listening."

"No, it's my turn to listen, your turn to tell me."

They had reached an observation platform jutting out from the river bank, a little more secluded from the traffic of people going back and forth along the promenade. Gesturing for them to go out on it, William stuffed his paper back in his pocket. Only an occasional gull winged in low to investigate the possibility of a handout.

"Let's go back to the beginning," William said. "Tell me again what happened when the Queen lost her garter."

Graham rested his forearms across the rail and interlaced his fingers, gazing down into the water. He supposed it was worth a try.

"Everyone got very quiet," he said softly, letting himself begin to see the images again on the eddies and currents below. "There were three Garter Knights in her party—Leicester, Howard, and Burghley—and they went absolutely wooden. No one wanted to move except the Frenchman. He would have run and picked up the garter, but the Queen's glance froze him on the spot."

"Then what happened?" William urged.

"Then she looked at me. Something seemed to pass between us—an electricity, almost. She looked very pointedly at the garter. There was no question in my mind that she meant me to pick it up."

He swallowed, aware that he was being drawn even deeper into the memory, and his voice dropped in volume and pitch, less like his own.

"I moved to obey her. I couldn't have helped myself if I had wanted to—and I didn't want to. No one made a sound as I picked it up. Somehow I knew that it was far more than just a garter. That was why I kissed it before I gave it back to her. It might have been a holy relic. My kissing of her hand, then, was an act of profound homage, not only as her new-made knight. And when those three men bowed to me, I marked them for the future: Leicester, Howard—"

He gasped and blinked, then shut his eyes and let himself go deeper into trance, for a new set of images was forming. A part of him was aware of William watching expectantly, even a little anxiously, but another part trusted that the prince understood enough of what was happening not to be afraid or interfere.

Assured at that, he put William out of mind and turned his attention wholly inward, shakily drawing a slow, steadying breath. As he let it out, he was plummeted back to that dark hilltop above Plymouth Harbor, in the midst of the grand coven.

He was not alone before them this time. Though he stood there as *her* man in black tonight, there were two others with him—*Garter Knights*, dark mantles almost black in the firelight, the garters around their knees unmistakable, though their faces were masked!

They had helped to call the covens here, lending their weight to that which *she* had already granted him against this time. The masks were a formality, almost a ritual accoutrement, for nearly everyone in England knew the two knights by name, if not by sight. Howard was the Queen's great-uncle once removed, married to the daughter of Lord Hunsdon, who was nephew (and some said half brother) to the Queen through Mary Boleyn. Hatton was lord chancellor now, and himself only just gartered a few months before as a fresh reminder to the people of his favor with the Queen—and he, too, had been present seven years before. No wonder the grand coven had come!

The two clasped hands with him wrist to wrist, one after the other, then backed into the shadows, their point made. Now Drake was alone before them, raising his arms to enjoin their attention. As he opened his mouth to speak, Graham felt the image waver and let it go. When he opened his eyes, he was back beside the Thames, with William looking at him in elation.

"You *did* see something else! I knew I was right to bring you here! Are you all right? What did you see?"

Slowly, Graham nodded, disentangling his fingers and flexing them several times as he shook free of the final vestiges of *other*.

"I made another connection," he said carefully. "It may even mean something for our present dilemma. Somehow, the Garter Knights *are* the key. Look."

From his breast pocket, he drew out the two lists Selwyn had made: Elizabeth's Knights of the Garter and those alive today. On the Elizabethan list, he pointed out four names with circles around them.

"Now here are the men who saw the incident on the *Golden Hind*: Leicester, Howard, and Burghley. And here's Hatton. Hatton wasn't a Garter Knight at the time, but he was by 1588. He was present with Drake when the grand coven was convened, and so was Howard. Howard was related to the Queen by blood and by marriage with blood as well as being Drake's superior as lord high admiral. With them at his side and seven years for stories of the incident aboard the *Golden Hind* to have spread, how could anyone have refused if asked to come and help?"

William had been watching him avidly, his own expression stilled and unreadable, but now he turned toward the river again. A faint foreboding began to grow in Graham's mind until William glanced back at him.

"How many years has it been since you were knighted?" William asked softly.

Graham blinked, his mouth going dry. He thought he already knew where William was heading.

"Seven. Why?"

"That's what I thought: the same as Drake. It would certainly seem that he had a mandate, wouldn't it? A royal mandate and Garter Knights to back him up. May I see your lists?"

Graham handed them over without daring to ask why, watching as the prince scanned first the Elizabethan and then the modern one. After a moment, William pulled a pencil from an inside pocket and began writing.

"Your newer list is incomplete," the prince said, scrawling five more names at the bottom and underlining the last. "You've counted the regular Garter Knights, but you've forgotten those related to the King."

As Graham took back the amended list, he could feel his pulse pounding in his temples. William's list was by ducal title, but Graham knew them all: Connaught, the King's great-uncle; Windsor, the former King; and the three remaining royal brothers, Gloucester, Kent, and Clarence. Before he could even open his mouth to deny the implication of the underlined final name, the prince was reaching into an inner pocket once more to withdraw a flat leather-bound jeweler's box. He handed it to Graham with a pleased smile and took the lists, slipping them into his coat pocket.

"Tell me if you think that might be of any use in what you're trying to do," he said softly.

With a sinking feeling in the pit of his stomach, Graham eased open the spring lid far enough to peek inside, closed it abruptly, then opened it again to stare in disbelief.

Inside lay William's Garter star, red cross of St. George surrounded by the blue-enamel garter: *Honi soit qui mal y pense.*

CHAPTER 12

THE GARTER STAR SEEMED TO PULSATE AGAINST ITS BED of dark-blue velvet. The bright enamel and cut metal rays shimmered in the fitful sunlight.

"I suppose the Garter itself would have been a more appropriate symbol for what I'm trying to say," the prince remarked as Graham began shaking his head. "However, its box was a little long and narrow for concealing on one's person. I rather thought our discussion might come to this. Now don't keep shaking your head at me, Gray. It's all perfectly logical. Drake had his royally connected Garter Knights, and you must have yours. I'm only one, but I fancy I'm closer to the crown than Howard or Hatton were. I think I'd do well enough."

"William—"

"Please let me finish. Naturally, we can't send my star or garter 'round to summon these chaps you seem to think you need, but I don't see why I can't use whatever clout I have to get them all together for you. We don't have to tell them what it's all about ahead of time. Then you and Lady Selwyn come out and tell them the real reason for the meeting."

Graham continued to shake his head, too stunned to even close the box and give it back.

"Sir, I can't let you do it."

"Please don't 'sir' me at a time like this," William said softly. "And why can't you let me do it?"

Graham closed the box with a snap and thrust it back into

189

the prince's hands. "You don't know what you're offering. You haven't thought out the full implications. You don't understand how it could be taken if you were seen at my side while I asked those people to do what I have to ask them. You're a royal duke, William. Your brother is the King of England, head of the Church of England, Defender of the Faith. If one, even *one*, of those people opened their mouths afterward, where would you be? Where would your brother be?"

"My brother need never know."

"But *they'll* know! Don't you understand? If you were to function as you've just outlined, you'd be seen doing it in his behalf. You'd imply his sanction even if it weren't true."

"Why couldn't it be true, then?" William asked. "Why not ask his sanction, at least unofficially? He's the anointed King. You said that the sacred king stands in the place of God in these matters. Maybe he *should* know about it. Or does he already?"

Graham shook his head sharply. "He doesn't know. No one in the immediate Royal Family knows anymore besides yourself. It's said that they never know unless the need is acute. Oh, there are relatives whose names you'd recognize if I were permitted to tell you, but no one in the close succession. And it must stay that way."

"But why?"

Graham leaned both elbows against the rail and massaged his temples with his thumbs. How to make him understand?

"Look, William. There isn't much holding this country together right now. We're a little better off in some ways than we were a month ago—at least we got most of the BEF out of France—but it's going to get worse before it gets better. You heard what Churchill said: 'The Battle of Britain is about to begin.' Well, it began some time ago."

"I'm aware of that."

"Well, are you aware what we have to fight that battle with? I don't think you are. Not enough planes, not enough pilots, not enough armed forces or materiel to equip them—we haven't recovered the Dunkirk losses yet, you know."

"Do you really think I don't know that?" came the angry retort. "What do you take me for?"

Graham looked away painfully. "I take you for a man who loves his country more than even *he* knows and wants desperately to help save her," he said quietly. "But I don't think this is the way. You don't yet perceive the delicate balance we're walking. Right now, there are only about two factors holding us together in addition to the monumental war effort of the British people and sheer, unadulterated luck: Mr. Churchill's unconquerable optimism and the incredible personal courage and example of the King. We must do nothing to jeopardize your brother's position."

"But how would—"

"No, this time you let *me* finish. Don't you see? Everything else is upside-down except the Crown. The King and Queen are the single most potent symbol of stability and faith that can get this country through the war. The people need that stability. They're afraid, and for good reasons—and they could be made even more afraid if you or any other member of the Royal Family became involved in something controversial, especially something as far outside the familiar bounds of their faith as magic."

"But I thought you said a lot of people still keep the old ways alongside the new, and they still believe."

"A lot of them do," Graham agreed, glancing furtively over his shoulder to make certain they were not being overheard. "But many of them don't. Some that do are not consciously aware that they still do. The great majority would be positively scandalized if they thought witchcraft were rampant in the royal house. Remember, that's tantamount to satanism and devil worship in the popular view—and enough laws are still on the books to make things very messy for a prince who got his hands dirty. Don't think you'd be immune because of your rank. Remember the uproar less than four years ago simply because a king wanted to marry a divorced woman. What do you think the press would do with a prince who got involved in witchcraft?"

The prince slipped the box back in his pocket and bowed his head, but the action was not one of surrender, only re-grouping. Graham watched him closely, still a little stunned at the combined audacity and brilliance of the offer, but he could read no hint of the next argument in eyes or set of hands or jaw.

After a few moments, William glanced at him again and Graham braced himself.

"Will you at least concede that my analysis of the Drake situation was a sound one?" William asked.

Graham nodded warily.

"And will you also agree that the modern analogy is sound, at least in theory? That you need a KG to vouch for you, if you're to invoke the same kind of authority that Drake did?"

"Perhaps. But you can't be that KG. We'll find another way."

"What other way? Listen, let me approach it from another angle. How many people are we talking about?"

"Perhaps twenty or so. No more than thirty. That isn't the point."

"I never said it was. Let me finish," William said, almost a little irritated. "I set up a—a social event—a reception, or something like that. No one declines a royal duke's invitation. That gets them all in the same place at the same time. After that, it's up to you."

"That sounds intriguing except for one small detail," Graham countered. "Other than a few rare exceptions, you do not know any of these people, and it's unlikely that you would have become aware of them through normal channels. What makes you think even a royal duke could single them out without arousing some kind of suspicion?"

"Suspicion of what?" William returned. "It's you and Lady Selwyn who've been approaching them so far. No one could have any notion of my connection with you in that context. I could say that I wish to recognize some of the small, generally unnoticed contributions that people are making to the war effort. Everyone is doing something, after all. You could vet them in advance and come up with a legitimate justification for each of them. For that matter, I could do several of these gatherings as blinds, before the real one, just to further confuse the issue—intimate little gatherings of patriotic people under royal patronage. Now what is dangerous or suspicious about that?"

"Nothing so far. Go on."

"Very well. Once they're there, I tell them that I've been asked to gather them on a matter of national security—and if a threatened invasion isn't that, I certainly don't know what is. I then state that I have been told that this is a matter of extreme delicacy, that even I do not know what is going to be said. That I have been advised not even to be present because of the sensitivity of my position near the Throne. I then turn them over to you and Lady Selwyn and leave the room. By the way, I wear my full Garter accoutrements to greet them, so that that part of the significance can't possibly be lost on them. Now why won't that work?"

Graham shook his head. "Because I won't let you do it, for starters. The beginning part is fine—brilliant, in fact. But you'd still be involved up to your royal eyebrows, and you're still the King's brother even if you try to function in a private capacity. Everything I said before still holds. To reiterate just one of the more obvious dangers, suppose someone talked afterwards?"

The prince drew a deep breath and let it out with a sigh, temporarily stymied, then stared out across the river for rather a long time. By the look on his face, Graham knew he still had not given up.

"You said twenty to thirty people could be involved," William said, glancing at him again. "How many groups do they represent?"

Graham did a quick mental count. "Perhaps fifteen or so. I'm allowing two representatives per group, but they wouldn't necessarily all send two."

"Hmmm. I should think it might be cut to one per group. These groups—they're all—esoteric fraternities of some sort, like this chap you talked with this morning?"

"More or less, I suppose, but—"

"Like Freemasons? I mean, do they swear oaths of secrecy?"

"Well, yes, but—"

"Suppose you were to bind them all by a common oath, then?—not to speak of what they saw and heard once they left the room."

"They wouldn't—"

"*Will* you let me finish? It isn't as if we'd be asking them to violate previous oaths. They'd be free to tell their own people what they need to know to get the job done. But you and I, for example, are in sensitive positions. They'd understand that our identities must remain confidential. I'll bet that Howard and Hatton even wore masks."

Graham's head shot around to stare at the prince. How had he known that? Graham was sure he had not mentioned it.

"As for the others," William went blithely on, "well, it isn't as if we're asking them to do anything they wouldn't do, anyway, are we, for God's sake? All we're asking is that they do whatever they do all at the same time. What's so awful about that?"

"Put that way, you make it sound so simple," Graham murmured, wishing that it were.

"Implying that it isn't?"

"Unfortunately, no." Graham sighed. "Listen, you've made a most generous offer, and I shouldn't want you to think I'm not grateful. But I simply can't let you get involved any further. You already know more than you should. When I think of the danger I've exposed you to—"

"Now wait just a moment! You didn't exactly force me into anything," William snapped. "As I recall, I've resorted to some rather compelling coercion along the way."

"Yes, and I should have been more firm about saying no despite that. I won't be a party to that happening again. Whatever arguments you care to offer, it's too dangerous. You can't do it."

"Can you, without me?"

Graham had no ready answer for that, though he continued to protest. They argued more in the car when it began to rain. The argument continued all the way back to St. James' Park, ceasing only for their passage through the carpeted corridors. When they gained the relative privacy of Graham's office, William would have started in again, but Graham flatly forbade it. In desperation, Graham rang Alix and asked if he might bring the prince to her. Perhaps it was his turn to pull rank and resort to compelling coercion.

A few hours later, the three of them were sitting around the library table at Oakwood, making a civilized pretense of afternoon tea while Graham outlined the prince's offer fairly but in tones that left no doubt of his disapproval. William stubbornly insisted that they could not succeed without him. Alix appeared to be maintaining a neutral stance, though her glance at Graham when they first arrived spoke volumes about what she thought of his bringing the prince to her home on such short notice.

"You do realize, I hope, that you've put us in a very awkward position, sir," she said, lacing her fingers together on the polished oak. "You've presented us with the first possibly workable plan I've heard to accomplish what we need to accomplish. Unfortunately, because of who you are, it would be almost impossible to use what you've presented."

William had been toying with a silver teaspoon while Graham concluded his synopsis and Alix spoke, but now he set it aside and folded his hands to match hers. By the look on his face, Graham suspected he was still a bit in awe of Alix— which was exactly what Graham had hoped for. If William thought Graham could be inflexible or stubborn, he had yet to see how resolute a woman like Alix could be, functioning in her official capacity as she was now.

"I decline to accept what you've just said, for two reasons," William finally said, obviously choosing his words carefully. "First of all, you've admitted that it's a possibly workable plan and that you haven't any other. Second, you've said that it would be *almost* impossible to use me. You're far too careful a woman to use that word unless it's precisely what you meant— which at very least means that you haven't made up your mind yet. What else can I say to convince you?"

Graham glanced at Alix in question. Was that what William had read from her words? Oddly enough, she did not seem to be denying what had just been said. She eyed the prince coolly, taking his measure just as surely as if she had laid the scarlet cords against his body in sacred ritual. To Graham's surprise, William did not back down from her gaze. After a moment, Alix lowered her eyes under demure lashes.

"The plan is basically sound," she conceded. "What concerns me most at this point is how to protect your public image—and, by association, that of the King. Gray is perfectly correct to fear for your reputation."

"I agree. That is the weakest link," William replied.

"Good. We have at least one point of accord, then," she said. "Another possibility has also just occurred to me. You mentioned the taking of a common oath of secrecy. They would never accept that suggestion if it came from Gray or even from me, but they might accept it from someone else among them. I have in mind Dame Emma, Gray. She's respected by everyone, even if some of them fear her."

"Who's Dame Emma?" William asked.

Graham poured himself another cup of tea. "I mentioned her before, though not by name. She's the lady in Hampshire who's promised her help. She commands six other groups besides her own, and more will come if she asks."

"I do recall, now that you mention it," William murmured. "Will she do it, though?"

"Ask the oath?" Alix nodded. "I think so. Her tradition and ours have close ties. As I said, she has already agreed to help as best she can, even if the others won't."

"Then you can let me help, too," William said, a faint grin lifting his mouth. "There's no reason you can't."

Alix pushed her teacup slightly to one side and returned his gaze evenly.

"There is at least one that I can think of immediately, which has not been mentioned so far," she said. "If we were to agree to this—and I stress the word *if*—if we were to agree to this, you would have to accept certain ground rules from the very beginning."

"Name them."

"Number one—and I will be blunt. Though it is the man in black who provides the public face, it is the priestess who ultimately commands. I am she. If you truly wish to be a part of our endeavor, it must be on my terms. I am not arbitrary, but the final responsibility is mine, and so, therefore, must be the final decisions. Are you willing to abide by that?"

His lips parted as if to raise a question, but then he ducked his head in a nod.

"I accept it."

"But?"

"It was not a reservation, my lady," he replied, meeting her eyes less confidently. "Some of your—terminology is unfamiliar. The crux of the matter is that you are in charge. Gray told me that before Buckland. I would not contest it."

She inclined her head regally, more like a queen receiving a subject than a countess acknowledging a prince's acquiescence. Graham watched William take it without a flicker of resentment. Perhaps Alix was right. Perhaps the prince did belong among them. Graham's heart had told him that almost from the beginning, though his head had a dozen valid reasons why it should not be.

"Second," Alix went on. "After myself, my husband and Gray hold authority, in that order, and then the brigadier. I would expect directions from any of them to be taken as if coming from me."

"I do not question that," William said. "However, may I assume that, wherever possible, decisions regarding myself would be made by joint consensus—that I would be allowed to give my opinion before a decision is made? In support of this, I point out that if I had not argued with Gray, we would not now be having this discussion, since neither of us would have reached this conclusion on our own."

"A point well taken," Alix agreed. "However, I reserve the right to be arbitrary if I feel the occasion warrants it. I would expect, for example, that if you have been told to sit still and do and say nothing, you would do precisely that. I would *not* expect another repeat of Buckland."

"No harm was done—"

"*Fortunately* not," Alix said firmly. "However, that result can hardly be attributed to anything but fool's luck. You know very little as yet. You—or Gray—might not be so lucky next time. It could have been very dangerous."

William bowed his head, but Graham could sense the thin edge of resistance in the set of his hands on the chair arms.

"I apologize—to both of you. It will not happen again."

"Very well." She glanced at Graham, then returned her attention to the prince. "There is one other thing of which you should be aware before you make any further commitment. I doubt that even Gray has told you this."

The prince's eyes flicked to Graham in question, but Graham only shrugged.

"Your offer of assistance has come as no great surprise, at least to me, even though none of us knew the form it would take. It has been foretold in the cards for several weeks now. I suspect that may have been at least one factor in Gray's decision to let you come to Buckland with him. Am I right, Gray?"

Graham sighed and gave a curt nod.

"Your precise role has not been clear," Alix went on, "and still is not, but there is little doubt that you are fated to be involved in what is unfolding. The question now is to what extent?"

With a nervous gesture, William reached into his coat for a cigarette, glancing at Graham.

"You never said anything about cards, Gray. What is she talking about?"

"The tarot cards," Graham replied. "An ancient form of divination. Modern playing cards derive from them. One asks a question while shuffling the deck, then lays out a certain number of cards in one of several patterns. Different positions represent different aspects of the answer—time factors, persons involved, strong and weak points. . . ."

While he explained, Alix had brought out her deck and fanned it face up, selecting some of the cards that had appeared in previous readings. When he had finished, she reviewed a few of their names and meanings. William studied the Knight of Wands the longest, shaking his head as she buried it in the deck and began gathering them up.

"I'm sorry if I appear skeptical," he said, flicking ash into an ash tray, "but—fortune telling, for God's sake! It just seems so—so medieval!"

"With respect, sir, your very title is medieval," Alix purred. "Does that make it suspect?"

Graham suppressed a grimace, half expecting a royal explosion, but to his surprise, William merely grinned.

"*Touché*, madame. But really—"

As he gestured with his cigarette, Alix slapped the deck down in front of him with a smile that cut him off in midsentence. Graham knew the expression well and almost pitied William for his naïveté. Alix would pull no tricks out of hats or cards out of packs, but the challenge had been offered. Graham had no doubt the cards would respond.

"Go ahead and shuffle them," Alix said, watching the prince with faint amusement. "I'll never touch them, nor will Gray. I think the question in all of our minds is clear enough, but concentrate on it, anyway, as you handle the cards. Gray, may I see you a moment?"

While William shuffled the cards, she drew Graham off to one side, her eyes never leaving the prince.

"He has pluck, you must admit," she murmured. "I suspected, after Buckland, but this is rare."

"Yes, and he could get himself and all the rest of us into very rare trouble," Graham replied.

"I can't argue that. Something about it feels all right, however. Probably akin to the feeling you had when you agreed to let him watch you scry. Let's see how he responds to a card reading—and what the cards say. If you're still adamantly against it afterwards, I'll say no, but there's a reason he's been led to make the offer he has. I think he understands the risks, and I think they may be acceptable."

Graham shook his head. "As you said, Alix, it's your decision. The very thought scares me silly—for the King's sake, if not any of our own—but if you think it's worth the risk—"

"It *may* be," she said, leading him back to the table. "That's all I've said so far."

William was still shuffling the cards, though his eyes had never left the two of them while they whispered together. As Alix sat, he placed the shuffled deck precisely in front of her. His glance at Graham, settling on his other side, was unreadable.

"So," said Alix, "are you satisfied that the cards have in no way been manipulated?"

"Yes."

"Bearing in mind that there are seventy-eight cards in this deck, would you agree that the chances are very slim that any of the cards I pointed out before would show up in the first ten cards after a random cut?—the Knight of Wands, for example, since we've identified that as your card in previous readings."

William smiled nervously and nodded. "That sounds fairly remote."

"Let me ask you this, then," she continued. "I have no more idea than you just what cards are going to come up for us this afternoon, but are you willing to at least listen to my interpretation even if it seems medieval? Keep in mind that Gray knows the cards, even though you do not, and will try to see them in their most unconvincing light, since he does not want to believe that you should become more fully involved."

The prince glanced at Graham. "Is this true?"

At Graham's nod, William allowed himself a reluctant shrug.

"Such enthusiasm," Alix murmured. "But no matter. The cards don't mind whether you believe in them or not. Would you cut the deck, please?"

With a puff on his cigarette, William reached across and picked up half the deck, which he set to one side.

"Thank you. Now, without turning the cards over, I'd like you to lay out the first ten in the pattern I'll show you. I won't touch them, because I want you to be certain that I've not influenced the outcome in any way. Do you understand?"

"I understand."

As William began laying out the cards, Graham rubbed both hands across his face and tried to clear his mind. He was not really certain he wanted to see what the cards had in store for him and William this time, but Alix was giving neither of them any choice. When William had finished the spread and laid the rest of the cards aside, Alix pointed at the traditional first card, lying in the center of the cross-design and underneath another.

"The first card represents the underlying factor of the situation—what covers it, as we say. Would you turn it up, please?—from the side, so that you don't affect the orientation of the card."

As William obeyed and Graham saw the card's face, he could only sigh and rest his head on his hands. How had she done that? It was the Knight of Wands.

William's jaw dropped in amazement.

"Isn't that—?"

Alix nodded matter-of-factly. "The Knight of Wands: a young man offering assistance. Even more apt now, in light of your Garter proposition. *You* are the underlying factor in the question you have asked, to no one's great surprise, I think—though Gray is clearly dismayed that this same card has shown up in all three readings—aren't you, Gray?"

Graham only shook his head. "I'm not going to fight it anymore, Alix. Do you want me to concede now or later?"

As she smiled in answer, William eyed the other cards a little suspiciously.

"What else?"

"Turn the next card and see," Alix said, pointing to the one lying perpendicular to the upturned knight.

He did.

"Crossing for better or worse, the King of Wands," Alix said. "Excellent leadership possibilities. It appears the knight may be due for a promotion. Here I would say it refers to your prospective role as a representative of the King, as Howard and Hatton were. Whether or not this is a good thing remains to be seen from the rest of the cards. Turn the one at the lower arm of the cross next, please."

"You go ahead," William said uneasily. "I'll concede that you couldn't have done anything to the cards. I don't think I want to touch them anymore."

"Very well." She turned the next card with a smile. "At the root of the situation is the Two of Wands. It is a card of endeavor and partnership—perhaps a bit more formal a partnership than that indicated by the Three of Wands, which Gray and I have seen before, concerning the Knight of Wands. In this case, it is probably your actual offer of assistance, as opposed to the potential, which we saw before.

"At the left arm of the cross, what is passing." She turned the card. "The Two of Coins. Trying to cope with two situations and still maintain harmony. To be involved or not to be involved. We have all had questions on that score in the past, but this is passing away."

Graham saw her glance at the prince as she turned the next card, but William did not seem to notice. His eyes were riveted on the cards, intrigued.

"At the crown: the Tower, Reversed—what could come into being. The process of change has begun, though it is still within your power to stop it. Here I would say it represents your tentative commitment to us. You have started changing, accepting that something is happening beyond your present understanding, but we have not yet given our consent for this to go on."

She turned the next card. "What is coming into being—the Three of Cups. This is generally a hospitality card, a sign of congeniality. It also indicates metaphysical interests and things lying beneath the surface. Under the circumstances, I would say it probably refers to the gathering you propose. If so, I would say it could have a favorable outcome. Gray, do you agree?"

Graham nodded sullenly. As before, if he had not known better, he would have had to say that Alix had rigged the cards; and as before, he knew there was no way she could have done so.

"Top card in the sceptre," she said. "Judgment, Reversed. This position represents negative feelings about the prospect at hand: an uneasiness about some aspects of what you are getting into, a fear that you may, indeed, be judged harshly for becoming involved with forces outside your understanding—the niggling fear that *we* may not be as we have said. But in your environment"—she turned the next card with a coy smile—"is the Magus, the Magician. In this position, I believe it speaks for itself. You are surrounded by magi, and will be, increasingly, if you continue on your present course."

"You and Gray?" the prince asked.

"And others, met and unmet," Alix answered with a smile. She turned the next card and froze for just an instant. It was nothing William noticed, but Graham saw it and peered at the card more closely as Alix continued to speak. It was only the Six of Cups—a good card as far as he knew.

"The Six of Cups," Alix said. "The position indicates positive influences." She pursed her lips. "The Six of Cups usually represents happiness coming from the past, sometimes an inheritance. In your case, I would say it probably has to do with the ties you are discovering with the old ways—perhaps the ancient Garter connections. And finally"—she turned the last card—"what will come: the Hanged Man."

She paused just a beat, and Graham was sure something was wrong.

"The Hanged Man is a card of psychic awareness, of new and innovative ideas, of getting in touch with higher wisdom," she said neutrally—which Graham knew was true, but the card could be read with far more negative connections as well. "I'd say you're already getting a taste of all of that—and will get more, if you help us gather the grand coven. You do seem to be involved with us."

She scanned the overall spread a final time, nodding to herself, then scooped up the cards and returned them to the rest of the deck, making a show of jogging the edges against the table top. She did not look at Graham. William appeared to be bewildered.

"Well, Gray?" Alix asked.

CHAPTER 13

GRAHAM RUBBED AT A FAINT STUBBLE OF BEARD WITH one hand and tried to read more meaning behind Alix's reaction. She had cut the reading short. Though she had given William a positive interpretation of the final card, she had seen something else as well; Graham preferred not to ask in front of William. He was not certain whether it had to do with the question at hand or something else, and she was giving him no clues.

"I suppose it could work," he said tentatively.

"And?"

He shrugged, resentful that she would not give him more to go on. "You've talked to more of our reluctant magi than I have. Do you think the risk is acceptable?"

"Yes."

The monosyllable was as neutral as he had ever heard, and conveyed so little of her inner state that he still was not certain how she felt about the question. He assumed that she was basically in favor of taking William into their confidence and accepting his help; otherwise, she would not have admonished him as she had or allowed the circumstances to be explored further. But in case he might have misinterpreted, he tried to offer her a last, graceful way out, if she wanted it.

"I won't oppose it, then. Don't you think you ought to check with Dame Emma before giving a final answer, though?"

"I'll call on her later in the week. She isn't on the telephone, so I can't ring her. I doubt she'll have any objections, however, if that's what you want."

Again, the neutral answer, putting the responsibility squarely back on him. But even if he agreed, that would not close the option of having Dame Emma back out, he suddenly realized. She had given *him* an out as well. With that meager reassurance, he glanced at the prince and nodded.

"Very well. You've heard the discussion. You can't say you haven't been adequately warned. Provided Dame Emma agrees and you still want to do it after all of this, you're on. Are you satisfied now?"

As he leaned back and crossed his arms in disapproval, William managed a weak smile.

"As someone said a short while ago, 'Such enthusiasm.' However, if the two of you were trying to frighten me off, you haven't succeeded. I know it's dangerous. I never pretended otherwise. But since we've all finally admitted that, I think it's time we settled down and did some serious planning. Now: whom did you want invited to my little soirées?"

Their main list presented no difficulty, Alix had put it together weeks before. It needed only a plausible set of war activities appended to provide cover justifications if anyone should ask. Two more lists took rather more time to compile, but they were done with the same meticulous attention to detail. Site and time determinations were hashed out over sandwiches and tea as the evening wore on. They also spent nearly an hour on the wording of the invitations that would go out under the arms of H.R.H. The Duke of Clarence. A hall clock struck eleven as they finished up.

"I should think that ought to do it for now," Alix said, delicately covering a yawn and stretching stiffly. "I do need to check with Dame Emma before the invitations are sent out. Also, I'd like to cover a few more things with Gray in private tonight. Do you mind staying over, sir?" she asked William. "It's dreadfully late to be starting back for London. I've already had rooms made up."

William stubbed out the last of his current cigarette and glanced at his watch, shaking his head as he blew out smoke.

"I shouldn't, really. I have an early engagement tomorrow."

"How early?" Graham asked.

"Ten o'clock, as I recall. At least it's in London, not out

in the country somewhere. However, I'd have to drop you off and stop at the Palace to change and collect my aide by eight at the latest. It would mean an awfully early start. Still, I shouldn't want to leave you stranded if you and Lady Selwyn have further business."

Graham shot a quick look at Alix. She had given no further indication of undue concern while they plotted their strategy, but nor was eleven o'clock an hour to be beginning a casual chat, especially with William in the house. What was it she wanted? Something about the cards, perhaps?

As his eyes flicked minutely from her face to the deck still lying by her elbow, then back again, she nodded casually. It might only have been agreement with the prince's last words.

"I'll ask cook to do breakfast at six," she said, rising to press a call button beside the fireplace. "If you leave by seven, you should easily be able to meet a ten o'clock appointment. David has made the run in far less time, and there's very little traffic with the war on."

William shrugged, apparently unconcerned after her reassurance.

"Very well, then. Thank you. I'll need to ring London and tell them not to expect me, however. Where is the telephone?"

"Jennings will show you," she replied as a knock at the door heralded the appearance of the butler. "Jennings, His Royal Highness is staying the night. Please take him to the telephone and then show him to his room and see to whatever he needs. You may retire after that. I shan't need you anymore tonight."

"Very good, my lady. This way, sir, if you please."

With murmured good nights all around, William went out with Jennings. As soon as the door closed behind them, Alix breathed a long sigh. Graham gazed across at her in annoyance.

"Will you please tell me what's going on? First you hedge the end of a reading in ways that make no sense to me; then you let me tell him that we'll use his plan even though we all know how dangerous it is. Then you practically shanghai him into staying the night. Is something very wrong or very right?"

She took a cigarette from a box on the mantel and lit it with a hand that shook slightly. She almost never smoked.

"I don't know yet," she said, sitting again. "I can't put my finger on it. That's why I asked you to stay."

"*Was* there something negative in the reading, then?"

"It could be read that way. I'd rather not say just yet. Are you too tired to do some trance work?"

"No. Why?"

"I don't know that, either. Not exactly, anyway. I did some digging on those other names you gave us at Buckland, and there are several points that aren't clear. I have this nagging suspicion that it all ties in, that there's something we're overlooking."

Graham frowned. "Important enough that we need to look for it tonight?"

"I think so. I know it's awkward." She blew out smoke in a nervous gesture. "I have to ask you to do something even more awkward, too."

"Oh?"

She would not look at him.

"I need to work with you in trance. I don't want to have to worry about *him*."

"William? But he's already gone to bed."

"I want to be certain he stays there."

"That he stays there?" He looked at her in surprise. "What makes you think he wouldn't?"

"I simply don't want us interrupted."

"Well, do you want me to post a guard or just lock him in?" Graham retorted.

"Neither."

"What, then?"

"You managed to deal with his aide and valet at Plymouth, I believe."

With a queasy little turning in the pit of his stomach, Graham slumped back in his chair. He could hardly believe what he was hearing.

"Alix, I can't drug a royal duke."

"Can't you? I'll do it myself, if you can't."

"You know it isn't that," he whispered, troubled. "Is it really necessary, though?"

"I would not ask if I didn't think so. Surely you realize that."

He swallowed with difficulty, still searching for a way out.

"I—don't think I can do it without telling him," he said. "He trusts me."

"That is your decision," she said in a low voice. "The deed is not."

He sat unmoving for several seconds, still rebellious, then rose wearily, head bowed.

"Very well. He won't like it, though."

"You're damned right I don't like it!" William snapped, glaring at Graham twenty minutes later from his bed, where he sat with the bedclothes pulled up to his waist and his arms folded stubbornly across his bare chest.

Graham sighed and set the offending glass of milk on the bedside table. He had told William exactly what was in it and sketched the reason as best he could. The prince was not convinced.

"Look, William, I don't like it any better than you do, but I don't think you realize how complex all of this is. Alix and I are working on a number of different levels, some of them very delicately balanced. If it will reassure her to know that you're asleep and can't intrude on what she needs to work out with my help, then it seems like you could go along. You said you'd accept her authority. If you're to be a part of this team, that means abiding by that, as you promised."

"Why can't I just promise to stay here? If you'd waited half an hour, I really would have been asleep. Isn't my word good enough?"

"That isn't the point. Now either drink the milk or let's forget the whole thing. I'll tell her you've changed your mind, and we'll go back to London tonight, if that's what you want. I didn't have to tell you what it was, you know. I could have just had Jennings bring you your usual nightcap, and you never would have known, any more than Wells and Griffin did."

"Well, why didn't you?"

"Because that isn't the way to build trust, dammit! Because there may be other times when I *have* to ask you to do something without being able to tell you why. I want the rest to be as honest as I can make it. That's the only reason. If we don't trust one another, we might as well forget the whole thing. It's one of the tenets of the game—perfect trust."

"Is it perfect trust to be so afraid I won't keep *my* word and stay here, that you have to drug me?" William retorted. "You can't have it both ways, Gray!"

Graham sighed. He had not wanted to go into the whole rationale he suspected behind Alix's order, but he supposed there was no choice now.

"I don't see it as a matter of not trusting you," he said slowly. "There are many factors that can influence—what she wants to do with me when I go back downstairs. We already know that there's some kind of psychic link between you and me. You saw it at work at Buckland when I was coming out of trance, even though you weren't aware what you were doing at the time, and still aren't. I think that's what worries her— the unpredictability. She's probably afraid you might do the same kind of thing again—psychically, not physically, and certainly not deliberately, but it would increase the danger to both of us, nonetheless. She's only trying to protect us, William. That's her job. Why won't you let her do it?"

William thought about that for a moment, then cast a resentful look at the glass.

"It ordinarily comes in a lovely yellow capsule, as I recall," he murmured sullenly. "Did you really have to put it in the milk?"

"You might have palmed the capsule. I taught you how."

William smiled in spite of himself—a quick, ironic grin— then picked up the glass and held it to the light.

"Well, I suppose I can look forward to a terrific head in the morning, like poor old Wells. Do I get the needle, too?"

"I don't think that will be necessary," Graham replied as William sipped cautiously and then began drinking it down. "In fact, that's probably what gave Wells his headache—not what you just drank."

He smiled sympathetically as William made a face and handed back the empty glass.

"I know there isn't any taste—it's the idea," William muttered, sliding further under the blankets and lying back on his pillow.

Graham watched him settle, then went into the adjoining bath and rinsed out the glass. When he came back, the prince's eyes were already dilating slightly, though he resolutely refused to close them.

"Will you stop fighting it?" Graham said, sitting companionably on the edge of the bed. "It's done. You're going to go to sleep in a few minutes now, whether you want to or not. Meanwhile, I can't leave until you're out."

"Well, you can jolly well wait another few minutes until I *am* out," the prince replied. "I want it noted for the record that I resent this like hell—and you can tell your Lady Selwyn that I said so, too. I don't know where you people get off being so high and mighty. One would think you're the only ones taking any risks. I'm in this now, too, you know."

"I could hardly forget that," Graham said, noting the beginning slur in William's voice. "But right now, this is your part in the battle plan. Hasn't anyone ever told you? They also serve who only lie and sleep?"

"I think I'm being poked fun at," the prince grumbled around a yawn. "It isn't fair. You wouldn't laugh at Michael or one of the others if they were in this predicament."

"If Michael or one of the others were in this predicament, they wouldn't be fighting the inevitable. They'd be cooperating. Now take a nice deep breath and go to sleep."

As he said it, Graham reached out offhandedly and touched the prince's forehead lightly, just as he would have done for Michael or any of the others under the circumstances, not thinking how it might be taken. To his surprise, the blue eyes rolled up under trembling lids and then closed as the prince breathed out in a little sigh—a textbook response to a post-hypnotic trigger. Was it possible that William had just gone into a trance?

"That's right," he breathed, watching in amazement as all the classic signs came across the relaxing face. "Deep asleep. . . ."

And William was, and not entirely from the sedative he had just taken.

This was totally unexpected. He and William had spoken of trust, but Graham had not dreamed that the prince would give him such a graphic demonstration of it. Shaken, he stood and gently drew aside the blankets far enough to expose a bare right arm and raise it in the air. However he moved it, it hung suspended in perfect catalepsy—a response that was surely beyond William's ability to fake. Graham straightened the arm and ran his hand along it several times, with the whispered suggestion that it was becoming rigid—and it would not bend.

Still hardly able to believe what he was seeing, Graham canceled the suggestion and returned the arm to the prince's

side, then pulled the bedclothes back into place. He had no
sure way of knowing how much of what he was seeing was
drug induced and how much was genuine trance, but he decided
to proceed as if William still could hear him.

"Deeply relaxed, William," he said in a low voice as he sat
on the edge of the bed again. "You've achieved a very good,
deep trance, but we haven't much time before your sedative
puts you to sleep for real. Before it does, I want you to examine
very carefully how it feels to be deep in trance, the way you
are now, and remember it.

"Not consciously. In fact, for now I want you to forget
everything that's happened in this room tonight. I promise you,
there's nothing sinister behind it. I simply don't want you to
have to be anxious about it. Remember only that I brought you
an ordinary glass of milk before you went to sleep. Wake up
refreshed and confident in the morning, with no adverse effects
from your medication. Do you understand?"

He heard the prince's faint "yes" and was still surprised.
He had not realized that William would be such a good subject,
though the sedative certainly had taken the edge off any normal
first-time resistance.

"Thank you," Graham whispered. "Now, in case you and
I should want to work together with a trance state in the future,
as I sometimes do with Michael and the others, I want to give
you a posthypnotic trigger. Do you remember the way Michael
went into trance for me at Dover?"

"Yes. . . ."

"Fine." He touched his finger tips lightly to William's forehead the way he had before. "In fact, you've already used that
trigger once. Remember how it worked then, and this signal,
and what it feels like now. And know that you and I can
duplicate this state whenever there's need, and you can go even
deeper as I guide you. Is that all right?"

"Yes," came the reply, though dragged from greater depths
this time.

"Good. Go even deeper now and let go. Your sedative is
taking over, so just let it happen. Don't fight it. Go to sleep—
and forget all this."

He withdrew and watched for several minutes, checking the
pulse in the side of William's neck and the pupils under slack

eyelids, then stood and shook his head. He was still shaking it as he rejoined Alix in the library.

"Is everything all right?" she asked as he closed the door and locked it.

A smile quirked at one corner of his mouth, but it was as much a sign of nervous reassurance to himself as an expression of amusement.

"You tell me," he said, settling bonelessly into an easy chair. "After some rather animated discussion in which we touched on the subject of perfect trust—and much against his preference, mind you—he took the sedative. That was only the beginning. He then went into a spontaneous trance—a rather good one, too."

"He *what*?"

"You heard me." He leaned his head against the back of the chair and closed his eyes. "I can't think of a single more poignant way he could have chosen to demonstrate his trust of me. It made me feel like a first-class cad. I suppose Michael and I must have made much more of an impression than I thought."

"Michael? Whatever are you talking about?"

"At Dover. Remember I told you he'd watched me put Michael under?" he asked, opening his eyes as she moved a straight chair closer and nodded. "Well, I don't know what possessed me to treat him like Michael, but I did. He was getting drowsy from the drug, and fighting it. He said something about me not treating Michael or the rest of you this way. I told him that Michael wouldn't be fighting the inevitable, and to take a nice deep breath and go to sleep. Then I touched his forehead, just as we usually key one another. He must have remembered that same sequence with Michael, at least on an unconscious level, because the next thing I knew, he was under. I could hardly believe my eyes."

Alix was shaking her head by the time he finished. "Are you sure he was in trance and not just asleep?"

"Are you doubting my ability to tell the difference?"

"No, but—"

"He doesn't know enough to have been faking, Alix—and certainly not with the drug in him. I ran several tests, and he passed them all." He paused. "I suppose the true test will be in the morning. I told him to forget the whole sequence of the sedation and trance. I also set up our standard posthypnotic trigger. It seemed a shame to waste the opportunity—and one never knows when one will need such a thing."

She shook her head, looking not at all reassured. "I hope you know what you're doing. Has he asked you about hypnosis before, other than the time he saw you and Michael?"

"Yes, on the way back from Buckland. He wanted to know how I'd gone into trance without words being spoken. He understood my explanation. He also expressed an interest in past-life regression. You can bet I put him off on that one."

"Well, you may want to continue putting him off on that," she murmured, still oddly ill at ease, Graham thought. "Have you given any more thought to your own regressions?"

"Only the ones about Drake," he replied, pulling a footstool closer and propping up his feet. "I was hoping you'd managed to come up with something further on those, and that was why you wanted to work with me tonight."

"It was. Now I'm not so sure. This whole thing with William bothers me."

"Then why did you let me agree to have him become further involved? And what about those last two cards?"

"I'd rather get back to your regressions first," she replied, collecting several closely typed sheets of foolscap from a drawer and returning to sit by his chair.

He reached for them, but she shook her head.

"No, I don't want you to read this yet. I'd like you to go into trance and see what further you can recall, now that you've made the initial contacts. David rang me about your hits on Drake and Elizabeth, and you've told me what you and William uncovered. Let's see what you'll come up with on the others without prompting. I have some background for guiding you now—and asking the right questions."

"All right," he agreed, removing his already loosened tie and draping it over the chair arm. "At least this isn't as emotionally loaded as the other. Any special approach you'd like me to use, or shall I just settle in and wait for instructions?"

"Go ahead and get comfortable. I want to scan my notes one more time," she said.

With the ease of the well-trained subject, Graham closed his eyes and went into trance, feeling the familiar, fluttery sensation, over an immeasurable instant, that signaled its deepening to a normal working level. He paid brief attention to his body, making certain it was comfortable, letting his breathing settle into the slow, shallow pattern that would sustain him while he turned to other considerations. Then he simply let himself drift in anticipation.

"Take another deep breath and let go," came her voice as her hand finally touched his forehead in familiar cue.

He obeyed and felt himself settling into yet a deeper level, lethargy stealing across his limbs and further cushioning him from outside distractions as he focused on her touch and waited. The touch disappeared, to become discernible again on his left wrist. He could feel her fingertips resting lightly over the pulse point. Concentrating on the strong, steady beat took him deeper yet.

"That's fine," he heard her say. "Find a depth where you can still hear and speak to me. Are you there?"

"Yes."

He breathed the answer almost inaudibly, all his awareness concentrated in her voice and the touch of her hand on his wrist.

"Good. Now, in a few seconds, I want you to begin casting back in time as you've done before. Then I'm going to read you the list of names you gave us after your last regression. I want you to flow back with those names and try to focus in on one of them. Are you ready?"

"Yes."

"All right. Begin going back now. Back to your childhood and beyond...your birth...and before that. Go back to Drake...and keep going. Someone named George...and Sir William Wallace...a monk named John...Sir Reginald FitzUrse...Sir Walter Tyrrel...."

He could feel himself hurtling back past the years in response, each name conjuring brief, bright memories that flashed and lingered only in after image by the time he could try to focus on them. Some were evoked by the names he heard, others admitted of no naming he could recall, yet he knew that all of them were a part of him.

He let them flow, not even trying to hold to any one of them, until he sensed a slowing. Abruptly, with an almost physical jolt, he was in another awareness, another body, another set of memories.

CHAPTER 14

HE WORE MAIL AND LEATHER. HIS MAILED FIST WAS
wrapped around the hilt of a sheathed sword, ready, as he and
the others stepped through the narrow transept door. Spurs
jangled against the threshold, and steel-shod boots echoed against
the grey stone floor.

Incense hung heavy on the air, along with the scent of candle
wax and the musty pungence of damp vaults and moldering
tombs. He could feel the pulse beat throbbing in his temples—
and at his wrist, where a human touch kept some part of him
anchored other-when—but he was not Graham any longer. He
was Sir Reginald FitzUrse, the King's man and bearer of a
sacred obligation.

Keen in the dimness, he looked out past the nasal of his
Norman helm and waited for his eyes to adjust to the inner
twilight, every sense straining against the silence, against the
anticipation. Grey against the greyer walls, he could make out
arches springing from a clerestory level and the paler jewel-
gleam of windows high over his left shoulder. Ahead, candlelight played on column, wall, and a chapel beyond. A voice
niggled at the edges of his consciousness, wanting words from
him, but he was too deeply involved to pay it mind or describe
what he saw to the disembodied presence that somehow was
with him, yet not with him. It was sunset—the appointed hour.
It was time to move.

He glided forward like a beast of prey unshackled. Two

others flanked him, one to either side, and a third lingered at the door behind them to guard against intruders. Ahead, beside the great support pillar of the north transept, the sacred victim emerged from shadow, a young monk at his side bearing the heavy processional cross as if it were some great knight's standard. Clearly, the monk had not the eyes to see what was about to happen.

"Hold!" the monk cried, darting in front of the victim to bar their way with his cross. "This is the house of God! For the love of God, this is your archbishop! Forbear!"

"We know the man," FitzUrse said, drawing steel.

The blade hissed from its scabbard with a sound like a serpent stirred, cold and deadly in the nearly darkened cathedral. It was echoed in the slithering sound of Tracy and le Breton drawing theirs. Behind them, Morville's weapon was already in his hands. FitzUrse heard it clash against stone as Morville secured the transept door and moved to guard the nave approach, for there were archbishop's men in the back of the church who must not interrupt the ritual. The pulse beat in FitzUrse's temples quickened.

The archbishop stood his ground as they moved yet closer. He knew why they had come. All of them were dancers in the sacred round, playing out their designated parts. FitzUrse would make the pretense of negotiation, as agreed, but the outcome had been decided long ago—sealed by a king's words and the crowning of a young king and the will of the victim himself. It was the sacred year, the sacred hour. The sacred substitute must die, lest the land be afflicted.

"Do not try to escape, archbishop," FitzUrse called, knowing he would not. "Will you raise the anathema you pronounced on the King's men or no?"

The victim shook his head, following the pattern.

"I may not, for the sake of my office."

"Do not provoke us, Thomas of London!" Tracy retorted. "You force us to drastic measures by your stubbornness."

"Here am I, the priest of God. Do what you must. I will not be moved," the victim said.

The tableau seemed to freeze for just an instant, then started again in slow motion. The victim turned insolently as if to walk away toward a downward passage. As FitzUrse lunged forward to seize the archbishop's pallium and pull him back, intending

to create just enough of an uproar to justify the greater force
of swords, Tracy and le Breton joined in the scuffle and also
laid hands on him, swords already poised to deal the fatal
blows.

The victim—no stranger to warrior ways—twisted in their
grip to fend them off, his eyes hot with anger at their presumption. As his gaze met FitzUrse's in that first instant of
protest, FitzUrse feared the man had lost his nerve.

"No!" the victim shouted. "Reginald, you are my man!"

The others faltered, well aware that their colleague had been
vassal to this man—and that to lay hands on him thus was
against all the laws of chivalry—but FitzUrse caught the double
meaning and yanked the victim closer, raising his sword. The
victim had not quailed but had singled him out to strike the
first blow.

"FitzUrse, you pander! I am your liege!" the victim cried,
in unmistakable confirmation of FitzUrse's action. "Remember
your duty!"

At the same time, the flashing eyes were averted to permit—
yea, to *will*—the sacrifice.

"Take him!" FitzUrse shouted, jerking the man around with
such force that his skullcap went flying, leaving the tonsure
bare. "In the King's name, strike!"

The victim's one free hand flew to his eyes to block the
sight as the sword descended, lips moving in final prayer. The
monk would have interposed himself between victim and
blade—still unaware of the true nature of what was happening—but le Breton caught him in a glancing blow that skittered
down the shaft of the processional cross and wounded the man's
shoulder even as FitzUrse's blade descended true.

Blood burst from a hand-sized gash across the victim's tonsure and crown as FitzUrse's blow connected, with Tracy's
stroke but a heartbeat behind, cleaving the skull. The victim
gasped and staggered to his knees, already dying as le Breton
also struck, blade shattering against the stones. Morville joined
to strike the fourth and final blow. The victim toppled slowly
northward, as was seemly, life already fled. So quickly, the
deed was done. . . .

Breathing hard, FitzUrse leaned on his sword and tried to
catch his breath, almost sick at the exertion and the emotion.
At their feet, the sacred blood pooled and seeped into the stones,

struck from the crown that had borne the victim's anointing as archbishop seven years before. There was blood on FitzUrse's blade, and he wiped it shakily on an edge of the victim's sacredotal robe.

The sacred victim was slain, his sacred blood spilled upon the ground. With his sacrifice, he sanctified the young king's life and ensured the prosperity of the land for at least another seven years. FitzUrse played out his part of that pageant and would live out his life in honor for having slain the sacred king's surrogate, though he would endure the form of royal displeasure for a little while.

But as he bowed his head in homage to the God lately housed in the cooling body at his feet, his moment of meditation was shattered by a stranger scampering out of the shadows to ghoulishly scrabble his sword point in the shattered brains. It was all FitzUrse could do to force down the gorge rising in his throat.

"Stop it!" he hissed, flat blading the man away from the body. "Enough of this. We must all away."

Then, in a ringing voice, he called toward the rear of the nave, where some of the archbiship's men and a few laymen from the town still cowered—ritual words to those with ears to hear and hearts to understand.

"Mark well! He wished to be king, and more than king— let him then *be* king!"

Then, to murmurs of consternation and affirmation, both, he led the others toward the transept door and into the outer darkness, not looking back. . . .

Color rippled and swirled behind Graham's eyelids—an interlude of rainbow maelstrom just distinct enough for him to realize he was no longer the Norman knight FitzUrse. Then he was plummeting backward again in time and into another life. He sensed an in-between time in passing that was not limbo but something far more reasoned and orderly—distinct and purposeful, if only he could have lingered to remember—but then he was in a familiar scene and body again, again with a sacred mission. He rode once more in the New Forest, ten seven-years before the death of Thomas Becket, and he knew well the Red King who rode at his side.

The King was dressed for hunting, rich russets and browns of leather and homespun dark against his pale-grey steed, the heavy face florid as usual, topped by the shock of red-blond hair peculiar to the offspring of the Conqueror. It was Tyrrel—who was Graham—who wore blood red today. The fine cross-bow given him by the King was strapped to the saddle by his knee, the sharp steel quarrels in a quiver at the other side. The shadows were lengthening, for the hunt had not even started out until midafternoon.

"It is the morrow of Lammas, Wat," the King said, drawing rein to gaze across at him in compassion. "Now is the appointed day and the proper hour. Be merry, for thou art much blessed to be the instrument of the God."

Tyrrel bowed his head and tried not to see the crossbow with its tight-stretched string.

"You honor me, my liege. And yet I wish that it were some other man you had chosen for the deed."

"And doubt that the deed was done in love?" The King swung down from his grey with a smile and came around to hold Tyrrel's bridle, stroking the neck of the bay distractedly. "Nay, friend, thou knowest the terms of the sacrifice. 'Tis not the slaying but the laying down of life for the land, the spilling of the sacred blood—yet, the dying is better if it be at the hand of one who loves the victim." He laid a gloved hand on Tyrrel's boot. "Dost love me, Wat?"

Tyrrel closed his eyes and nodded, blinking back tears of grief.

"Lord, you know I do!"

"Then come and perform this last act of love in my service, sweet friend," the King whispered. "Come. I am not afraid. It is my destiny. For this was I born."

Not looking at the King, Tyrrel swung down and began unstrapping the crossbow from its place. The straps in the buckles were stiff beneath his fingers, and he could not reach the quarrels from where he stood. As he went numbly to the horse's other side, the King turned and began strolling slowly away from him, boots turning up dead leaves and moss on the forest floor, making a soft, rustling sound like a deer.

Tyrrel fitted a bolt to the weapon. Each click of the ratchet, as he cocked it, seemed to echo through the forest like a new doom. He raised it far enough to ensure that all was in order, then held the readied weapon close along his thigh as he moved away from the horses. No need to show the King his death before he must.

The King's back was to him, perhaps a dozen steps away. Tyrrel could hardly miss at this range, and he an expert shot, but he moved yet nearer to pause beneath a sacred elder tree. If the deed must be done, it must be quick and sure. Sacrifice demanded that the sacred blood be spilled upon the ground, but it did not require that the victim suffer. As Tyrrel raised his weapon, the King stopped beside a giant oak and turned slightly, one gloved hand resting against the trunk.

"'Twill be a beautiful sunset, Wat," he said softly, not seeming to see the weapon as he turned full body toward Tyrrel and met his eyes, then raised his own to the sunlight slanting through the leaves as his face went set. "Shoot, in the God's name, or it will be the worse for thee!"

Tyrrel felt his vision blurring as he shouldered the weapon and sighted, but he did not falter. Only as his finger tightened on the trigger did he see the King's eyes drop to his again for just an instant. In that fraction of hesitation, he fired and the bolt went just a little wide, glancing off the tree trunk before burying itself in the King's breast.

"Sweet face of Lucca!" the King gasped, one hand catching himself against the tree as the other clutched involuntarily at the barbed death in his chest.

The crossbow fell from Tyrrel's numbed fingers as he stared in horror. "William, my God!"

"Not thy fault, Wat. Stay back!" the King murmured through clenched teeth as he sank to his knees. "Hard enough for thee. I distracted—Finish it . . . myself. . . ."

With that, he pitched forward on his face, driving the bolt out through his back and dying instantly.

Tyrrel ran to him then and caught up the King in his arms, but it was over. Like Ishtar weeping for her son-lover Tammuz or Isis for Osiris or the Marys for the White Christ, he held the still-warm body close and let the tears stream down his cheeks—tears of grief and thanksgiving. As he laid the body back upon the earth and rose to leave, his destiny fulfilled, Graham was once more able to draw himself apart.

"Gray . . ."

He could hear Alix's voice coming from far away, but a part of him still did not want to listen to her.

"Gray, you're too deep. Come up a little, so you can talk to me," the far-off voice insisted. "Look at the lives and tell me what you see. Tyrrel . . . FitzUrse . . . Wallace . . . George . . . the monk named John. . . ."

He managed to fasten on the final name, and an image formed behind his eyelids of a man riding into a monastic courtyard with a handful of ragged men-at-arms. Somehow he knew that he was a brother of that community and that the new arrival was the King. Unlike the FitzUrse and Tyrrel memories, however, a part of him now knew he was but observer, even though he saw through other eyes.

"He has not done well by the land," he murmured aloud, seeming to watch the King from some vantage point outside the refectory door, where the royal party entered to dine. "His barons are in revolt. Even as he joins us, he flees from them. They say he has lost the royal treasure in the Wash."

"What is the year?" a woman's voice asked softly. "What is your name?"

"'Tis the seventeenth year in the reign of King John," Graham replied. "I am Brother John, a monk of Swineshead Abbey."

"What are your orders, brother?" the voice asked. "Have you been told to kill the King?"

He swallowed and saw himself in memory, preparing the cup.

"It is known what must be done. The King himself has said that if he lives another six-month, there will be famine in the land."

"Why is that?"

"He is forty-nine and has found no substitute to die for him," Graham replied. "Even though his heir be not of age, the land cannot stand another seven-year without the blood."

"Do you kill him, then?"

He nodded, a curt, nervous gesture, for he sensed the chill of his own approaching death, but there was resignation in his voice as he replied.

"I am infirmarian here at Swineshead. We have the knowledge to extract the poison of a toad, to distill it into the very metal of the cup," he said softly. "The King will drink, and it will soon be over. He is one of us. He will know his fate and accept it when it is upon him."

"But if the King dies by poison, how can his blood be spilled upon the land?" the question came. "Is this not required?"

He smiled—a patient, secret smile. "Those who prepare the body know their duty, lady. When he is boweled, they will see that the blood goes where it ought. It is ever thus when a king dies that his parts be buried throughout the land and the blood spilled to lend their blessing."

"Was this done?"

"I know not, lady."

"But he *does* die in that year," she said. "Does he drink the cup, or is it other death? Go forward in time and tell me what you see."

Graham turned his head against the chair back, not wanting to go on, yet compelled by the voice.

"He drinks, but I must drink before him," he said uncomfortably, grimacing as a ghost of remembered cramping in his gut started to double him over with very real pain.

"Enough. Do not relive your own dying," she commanded. "Let go of this life and move on. Go forward in time and tell me what you see."

He sighed and released it, grateful for the respite, and merely drifted for several heartbeats. Then, with a wrench, he was else-when again—sitting a horse behind his Scottish schiltrons on a slope east of Falkirk and waiting for an English charge.

"Who are you?" the woman's voice came to him softly, intruding on his concentration as he examined the scene behind trembling eyelids. "What do you see?"

He shook his head, seeing the faces of his Scots spearmen turned trustingly to him for words of cheer and knowing there were none to offer. They faced a far superior force.

"I have brought you to the ring, lads. Dance if you can!" he cried aloud.

Even as they cheered him, loyal to the last, he was plunged into the midst of battle: leading their charge against the heavily armored English knights, watching his men fall before Edward's Welsh bowmen.

"What is your name?" the woman's voice persisted. "Stand back and observe. Tell me what you see."

He moaned as the scene of carnage rippled away, then stiffened as later memories of the same life intervened.

Betrayal and capture. English knights taking their prize back to London. And *he* was that prize.

"*Who are you*?" the outside voice insisted.

"Oh, God!" he sobbed, still far too deep to respond to anything but the terror of sudden comprehending. "They mean to slay me for another land, another king! I would gladly die for my own lord—but for this English usurper?"

He was gasping for breath, his head rolling from side to side, but the grasp on his wrist began to pull him out a little and calm him as the woman's voice soothed.

"Detach yourself!" the voice demanded. "Do not feel it. Tell me only what you see and hear. Are you Wallace?"

Shuddering, he gave a curt nod—felt her hand tighten on his wrist to keep him from slipping deep again.

"Good. Tell me what you see, then. You were captured by the English at Glasgow after being betrayed by your own. Tell me of your trial. *Remember* it—do not relive it."

He drew a deep breath and felt a part of him relax, watching as the scene took shape before him.

"Westminster Hall. It is the sacrificial month. They say I have forsworn my oath of fealty to their English king and set myself as king in my own land. They crown me with laurel to mock me."

"Yes, go on. . . ."

"They—seat me in their great hall facing north, with the laurel on my head, and the travesty of trial proceeds. But they know, as well as I, what they really do. It is not the King they mean me to die for but the Lord Edward, who is twenty-one and needs a life."

"Do you offer a defense?"

He shrugged and gave a weary smile. "To what purpose? The English know my innocence. I never gave my oath to any English king. But the English prince must have his sacrifice, and they have chosen me."

"You know this to be true?"

"Of course. It is plain for anyone with eyes to see. My life must end before the month is out."

"You need not relive that."

Despite her words, he sensed the further memory welling up to consciousness, though this time he felt nothing. He was totally detached from what the eyes of the doomed Wallace saw.

"They name it traitor's death," he murmured, "but the form of execution is time hallowed. They drag me on a hurdle to a place called Smithfield. The ground is sanctified by other sacred blood. A peacefulness surrounds me as they walk me to a copse of elms where a noose awaits—and other things."

"Do not go on," the voice said sternly. "You need not live this death."

But he paid her no mind. He was victim this time, not the instrument of sacrifice. His body would be slain and might cry out in its weakness, but the sacrifice was all a part of the pattern. He found himself fascinated by the different perspective.

"The rope is rough around my neck, but there is no pain as they hoist me off the scaffold," he whispered. "Darkness encrouching on my sight, and then a great jolt as they cut me down still living—a burning in my belly—"

"Gray, don't!"

He could feel her nails digging into his wrist, but he shook his head and almost smiled. There was no cause for fear.

"I am apart from the pain," he assured her. "My dying eyes behold my blood streaming from the wounds they have given me. I watch it soak into the earth. I retreat to the Second Road as I have been taught to do. I look down at what they do to my body, beyond their pain, and it occurs to me that it does not even matter that I am dying for a foreign prince.

"Only the land matters—*all* the Isle of Britain—not just Scotland, England, or Wales. Thus have died the long line of sacred sacrifices through the eons, to fecundate the land and make it fruitful. The Lord Edward knows it. I think he even sees me as I drift above my body and gently loose the silver cord. . . ."

Graham slipped into gentle darkness then, losing the thread of Wallace until the voice called him back. Again, he swooped into another set of memories, though these were more of knowledge than participation. He could sense a rough impatience in that part of him, mirroring the cunning and ruthlessness of the man whose identity he now assumed.

"Who are you?" the voice demanded.

He was far enough apart to know that it was Alix asking, though a part of him lodged in yet another life.

"George Plantagenet, brother to the King," he replied briskly.

"Which King?"

"Why, Edward, of course—the fourth of that name."

"I see. And what year do you die?"

"In 1479, in the sacred month of February. The King is thirty-five."

"You are a sacrifice, then?"

"Yes."

"And how do you die?"

He smiled—a taut, crafty grimace with no warmth whatever—seeing it all from a point somewhere above the body of the doomed George.

"A dagger thrust up under the ribs to the heart," he said clinically. "It is very well done. There is little pain, but the blood flows."

"A dagger thrust?" the voice murmured. "But if you are—tradition has it that you were drowned in a butt of Malmsey."

"Has it? I know nothing of that."

"Well, perhaps tradition is wrong," he heard her murmur. "Are you content to die as sacrifice, then?"

Graham shrugged. "I would rather die as king than as substitute, but the end is the same. It is necessary."

"I see. Go forward, then. Who else have you been?"

He was out of George Plantagenet in an instant, but somehow he could find no other name until he reached Drake. Yet there was something in that intervening time...

"What after that?" Alix urged.

"Others played their roles," he found himself saying. "I was called to—other tasks."

"What other tasks?"

Stillness. A closed door. Somehow he knew he was not allowed to answer.

"Can you tell me more of those tasks?" she repeated.

He found himself shaking his head.

"Very well. Is there anything else we should explore?"

He drew a deep breath and rolled his head several times from side to side, not in negation but in a gesture of futility at trying to dredge forth something that would not quite come. There was something....

"Something—yes. Can't...quite...remember. Something about—Tyrrel...and FitzUrse. Mustn't forget...."

"What mustn't you forget?" she urged. "Go deeper, Gray. Focus on it and bring it to the surface. Read its meaning."

He shook his head again. "Can't. Not time yet.... William...important....No more...."

The concentration set things spinning. Hands clamped to his temples, he groaned aloud with a physical vertigo as well as a psychic one and tried to pull out. Her touch on his forehead eased the discomfort a little, drawing him nearer to his own body and memories, but he opened his eyes too soon. Disorientation throbbed behind his eyeballs even worse than at Buckland.

Wincing, he dropped his head into his hands and shuddered, almost sick to his stomach.

"Jesus, Alix, I think a bomb went off inside my head! What did you do to me?"

"Go back under and let's try coming out again," she said, moving to the chair arm and putting her thumbs to his temples. "Relax and take a deep breath...."

He let his hands fall to his lap and obeyed, retreating immediately to the comfort of trance. After a few minutes of concentrating on her words and the light pressure of her thumbs along the sides of his head, the pain subsided, and he let himself gradually come out again. A shadow of dull ache persisted behind the bridge of his nose as he cautiously opened his eyes, but it could almost be a mere lack of sleep. Nothing compared to what he'd felt a few minutes before.

"Better?"

"Much." He sighed as she took away her hands and sat back cautiously. "I *will* tell you this: I can do without another session like that for a long time. If this is what it takes to be an adept, I'm not sure I want the job."

"I'm not entirely certain you have any other options," she replied, leaning back to retrieve her notes from the chair. "I could do without the side-effects, however, and I'm sure you could. You went really deep again, especially there at the beginning. Who were you?"

"FitzUrse again, in detail this time—and Tyrrel, also in detail. I would have given you a running comentary if I'd been able, but—"

As he shrugged, Alix handed him the typewritten pages.

"You don't have to apologize. Before you bother to say

much more, I think you'd better read this. I don't know whether it will reassure you or scare the hell out of you."

He sighed. "Why do I have the feeling I was dead right about a lot of details I have no business knowing?"

"You may wish you'd rephrased that part about being dead-right, but go ahead and read," she replied, quirking a nervous grin at him before going to light another cigarette. "I need a few minutes to think some things through."

He read what she had written. After the Tyrrel and FitzUrse accounts, he thought he was prepared for the rest. The Swineshead material tallied reasonably well, though there was less to go on, and the death of William Wallace seemed fairly straightforward—though Wallace's mystical observations at the moment of death obviously could not be substantiated.

What brought him up short were the few paragraphs on George Plantagenet. He had not known, and had not even remembered it in trance, but George Plantagenet had also been a Duke of Clarence.

He shivered and looked up to see Alix sitting in the chair in front of him again, holding two tarot cards. He could only see their backs, but he had no doubt they were the same two she had refused to read earlier for another Duke of Clarence.

"What cards?" he asked in a dead voice.

She dropped them face up in her lap and turned somber eyes to his. "Six of Cups and Hanged Man—though I think you knew that."

He closed his eyes briefly, inexplicably chilled, then rose and began pacing restlessly, tossing the notes on the table in distaste, not meeting her eyes.

"You got to the part about the other Duke of Clarence, didn't you?" she said.

He paused by the fireplace and leaned his elbows on the mantel. Clasping his hands before his chin, he stared sightlessly at the stonework a few inches away and thought about the man asleep upstairs.

"Are you implying that there's a connection between the two?" he said after a moment. "That something from a past life of William's may account for his being thrust into our work just now? Is that what the Six of Cups means?"

"It's a sobering coincidence of names, you must admit," she replied, not answering his question. "As a matter of fact, it's a rather ill-fated title. Only one Duke of Clarence has died in his bed, at a ripe old age. That was William IV."

"And what about our William?"

She shrugged. "Well, we know that at least one of his past lives has touched you in this life or you wouldn't have mistaken him for David that night at Buckland. That same night, he asked you about hypnotic regression and expressed an interest in finding out more about his own past lives—and tonight he set himself up to do just that, though I doubt he's aware of any of this on any conscious level."

"Well, at least he can't have been that other Clarence, because *I* was," Graham said, looking back at her in faint challenge.

"No, but perhaps he *was* one of Drake's Garter Knights, and that's what has led him to offer his assistance the way he has," she replied thoughtfully. "That one incarnation could account for everything we've mentioned. There—*is* another possibility, however," she added, glancing down at the cards.

Graham blinked, his throat suddenly going very dry.

"What—other possibility?" he managed to ask.

"Well, the Six of Cups could mean a great many things, many of them quite benign," she said reluctantly. "It could refer to the Garter connection I mentioned in front of William, but it's also a card of inheritance and lineage. He *is* of the old line, after all; the line of the sacred kings. When you add to that the Hanged Man—" She picked up the card and gestured toward him with it.

"The Hanged Man *is* all those lovely, physically awakening things I said when he was here, Gray, and I'm sure they all apply—but look at the literal meaning of the card. The Hanged Man is a *sacrifice*—and that was William's outcome card."

Graham was hardly aware of crossing the space between them or snatching the card from her hand, though the chill of growing dread sat on his chest like an evil spectre.

"Do you know what you're saying?" he gasped, staring at the card in trembling fingers. "Do you realize what you've just suggested?"

"I'm saying," she said softly, "that I want to know where that puts our present-day Duke of Clarence in relationship to what you've just been reading. I especially want to know where

he fits into the rest of what you've been starting to remember—
the recalls *besides* Drake."

Numb with the implications, Graham felt his way to the
edge of his chair and sat, weak-kneed.

"You think he might have been one of my victims?" he
asked.

"I think we must consider that possibility—yes," she replied.

"No. I won't accept that." He tossed the card back in her
lap angrily, eyes defiant. "Even if it were true in the past, it
isn't now. Why couldn't *I* be the Hanged Man? It's only natural
that I'd show up in his reading. I've been the catalyst for
everything he's done so far. I think it's fair to say that he
wouldn't have become involved in *any* of this if I hadn't stupidly given him the opportunity."

"That's true."

"Besides, you and I have talked before about the remote
possibility of a sacrifice being necessary to seal the Lammas
working," he continued desperately. "If there has to be one,
I'm it. I accepted that role when I agreed to act for David.
Obviously, it wouldn't be the first time I've functioned in that
capacity."

"All that you've said is true," Alix said. "Are you suggesting
that William might be *your* slayer, then?"

"I'm not suggesting he has a part in *anything* to do with
that," Graham returned hotly. "But better that than for me to
be his. That's one thing I won't do, Alix, no matter *who* orders
it."

Alix sighed and shrugged. "Well, with any luck, neither
you nor he will ever have to make such a decision," she said.
"Perhaps we're both overreacting. Perhaps I saw more in the
cards than is really there. We *do* need his help for the gathering
of the grand coven leaders, though, If he hadn't offered, we'd
still be wondering how to do it."

"We haven't done it yet," Graham muttered.

"No, but I think we will now. If Emma agrees to her part—
and I have no reason to suspect that she won't—there's really
very little room for things to go wrong." She laid a hand on
his arm in comfort.

"Try to forget I even mentioned the other, Gray. We've
probably been worrying for nothing. Besides," she added with

a sly little grin, "we need not be compelled by the past any more than we let ourselves be ruled by my cards—or your stars."

He had to smile at that. He told himself that she was likely right. He wanted to believe it. But as he made his way up to his room a little later, he found himself remembering Tyrrel and FitzUrse. He tried not to think about the men they had slain in the names of the sacred kings.

CHAPTER 15

AT BREAKFAST THE NEXT MORNING, A BRIGHT AND cheerful William gave no sign that he remembered anything unusual about the night before. Nor did he mention it when he and Graham drove back to London. They chatted about logistical details for the three receptions, and William inquired casually how Graham's session with Alix had gone, but he accepted Graham's vague reassurances at face value and did not press for details. He dropped Graham at the office near St. James' Park in plenty of time to make his own engagement and put Wells to work on the invitations that afternoon, since the first of the receptions was only a week away.

The go-ahead from Alix came through the following day, and the invitations went out. Graham did not hear from the prince for several days after that, for William left on Thursday for a long birthday weekend at Windsor with the rest of the royal family, inspecting military units in London with the King's party on Saturday and attending Sunday services at the Royal Chapel, in Windsor Great Park. Given their previous discussions, Graham suspected that the prince would somehow find the time to visit the Garter Chapel in the course of the weekend. His suspicion was confirmed when William returned on Monday to dine with him, Michael, and the brigadier in a belated birthday celebration. Later that evening, Graham and the prince began to go over the background William would need to set

230

the stage for him and Alix at the final reception. The first one was to take place the following evening.

All three receptions were held at Laurelgrove, the brigadier's country house near Eynsford. The brigadier hosted the first two at the prince's side, as would have been expected, but the other attendees were never aware that Graham and Alix were also present. Hidden behind the one-way mirror installed for the occasion between drawing room and parlor, they observed William's handling of the first two groups of guests and afterward offered critiques. William needed no coaching on his actual handling of people, for he had long ago excelled at going out and mingling, but by the third night, they had helped him establish a smooth and predictable pattern of timing.

Timing was important for several reasons. One of the most important was the problem of Wells, William's aide. As was appropriate, he was at William's side for the first two meetings. He had seen to the preparation of the invitations, was aware of the official reasons for the composition of the guest lists, and could hardly be excluded without arousing unwanted curiosity.

But nor could they allow him to be present for at least the heart of the third meeting—and slipping him a doctored drink was too risky to try a second time so soon. A ruse would be necessary to draw him away for a few hours. They decided it would take the form of a call from the Admiralty at the appropriate moment, requiring some trustworthy agent of the prince to pick up a confidential dispatch at once. Since William was planning to stay the night at the brigadier's rather than drive back under blackout conditions after the reception, the message could not await William's return. It made perfect sense to send Wells on the errand.

Thus, while William and the brigadier mingled with their guests as they had the previous two nights and waited for the call, the unsuspecting Wells was never far away. Because it was wartime, William had opted for naval dress uniform rather than civilian evening attire, wearing with it a gold staff aiguillette, as one of the King's personal aides, and the riband and star of the Garter. He would add the Garter collar after Wells had gone. Several of his guests, male and female, had chosen military garb as well, and the room glittered with the various orders, medals, and decorations to which they were entitled.

From the other side of the one-way mirror, Graham, like the prince, also waited for the call that would lure Wells away. He was restless by the time the brigadier left William and joined him. They had decided to underline his role as man in black, so rather than a uniform, he wore his usual black polo sweater with a black jacket and trousers—an image that would register with most, though not all, of the evening's guests. He gave Ellis a bleak look but said nothing.

After a few more minutes, Alix came in and slipped an arm around each man's waist. Her gown was the exact shade of William's blue Garter riband, the long, pale hair braided and coiled around the top of her head like a tiara, adding inches to her height and an even greater command to her presence. She smiled reassuringly as she gazed up at Graham, the brown eyes coolly appraising.

"My, but you do look wonderfully powerful and persuasive in all that black, doesn't he, Wesley?" she said.

As the brigadier snorted approvingly, Graham grinned, completely destroying the somber image.

"The butterflies in my stomach needed that," he said. "Has the call come in yet?"

"No, but it shouldn't be long now. How is our royal host doing?"

"His usual, charming self," Ellis replied. "Everyone always says that Kent is the most outgoing and personable of the brothers, but I don't see it. They haven't watched Clarence in action. He has them eating out of his hand."

"Let's just hope they keep eating," Alix muttered, surveying them briefly. "He does have that charisma, though. How about our guests? Any fireworks yet?"

Graham shook his head. "Not that I've noticed. Oh, a few of them have recognized one another. Those who are rivals have managed to gracefully move on to more congenial company, but it doesn't seem to have occurred to any of them that H.R.H. could be in on a deliberate gathering like this. They think it *has* to be coincidence."

"We'll see how much they still believe in coincidence when they see the two of us," Alix said dryly. "If they don't become hysterical in the first thirty seconds, we may actually have a chance of getting them to talk about something besides the weather, the war, and how utterly too-too it is to be recognized by a royal duke."

"I shouldn't hold my breath if I were you," Graham said, peering more intently through the glass as a footman entered and spoke with the equerry in attendance at the far door.

"A-ha! That will be our phone call. Our good Mr. Flynn tells His Royal Highness—and H.R.H. feigns surprise and excuses himself as planned, leaving his ever-faithful but over curious aide to attend to his guests."

They watched William disappear through the door nearest them, and very shortly, Flynn was sent to fetch Wells. Soon after that, William joined them in the parlor, worrying at the knot of his tie with a nervous gesture.

"Well, he's off to London," the prince said, peering through the mirror with them. "Gray, are you sure we've got the right list tonight? They all seem so—normal."

Graham could not help a grin. "I hope you weren't expecting tails and cloven hooves after all we've told you. The vicar over there would be absolutely scandalized."

William bit back a smile as he followed Graham's gaze to a man in clerical collar talking animatedly with Dame Emma.

"Hmmm, I daresay you're right. I gather he doesn't know about Dame Emma's—ah—religious preferences?"

At Alix's muffled snicker, the prince shrugged. "Well, I didn't think so, but frankly, I wouldn't be surprised at much of anything tonight. Someone tell me again about that portly chap talking to Sir Robert."

"Avery," the brigadier said. "He's high up in one of the Rosicrucian orders. And don't be deceived by his looks. Beneath that teddy bear exterior is a first-rate ceremonial magician. He also wields a great deal of civic authority. I believe he plans to stand for election next year, as a matter of fact. He'll probably win, too."

Alix brought over the prince's Garter collar and laid it around his shoulders, securing it under his epaulettes as they continued reviewing the guests. They had tried to think of a way for him to wear the Garter itself, but the formality required would have been out of keeping with the occasion. William, like the King, had a distinct aversion to lapses of protocol, especially wrongly worn orders. Even the wearing of the collar was not the usual practice outside ceremonies of the Garter, and he adjusted the pendant "George" with a distracted grimace as Alix fussed over him.

"I'm just trying to get them all straight in my mind, now that I've seen the real people instead of pictures," William said, glancing out at the room again. "Which are the two bearded chaps again, please?"

"Conwy and Carey," Graham replied. "The taller one is Carey. He's—"

"No, don't tell me—the Qabalist. I remember that," William supplied.

"Very good. How about Conwy, then?"

"Ah, Welsh nationalist and practicing Druid," William replied with a reckless smile. "And the woman next to him is Mrs. Murphy, from the Cotswolds—a witch, as I recall. How am I doing, chief?"

Graham stiffened in automatic response. He wished William had not said that.

"Other than being a bit too specific with your terminology, you'll pass," he managed to reply.

"What do you mean? Calling her a witch?"

"No, calling me chief." He forced himself to relax a little. "That title has a rather definite connotation for us," he explained. "It goes with this"—he stabbed with his thumb at the black he wore—"and it describes the relationship of the rest of us to Lord Selwyn, and temporarily to me, but it doesn't describe *your* relationship to *any* of us. Even if it did, that's the last thing you'd want to intimate to our guests out there. You *must* remain aloof from any sectarianism, William. Your brother is Defender of the Faith."

"Do you really think I could forget that?" William muttered, much taken aback.

"I'm sorry." Graham sighed. "I didn't mean to be short. It was an automatic reaction to protect you."

A short but awkward silence fell upon them, followed by William's visible regathering of his composure.

"Well, let's get on with it, then," he said bravely. "Are you ready?"

With a shrug and what he hoped was his most confident smile, Graham extended his hand, which William clasped.

"I think I'd almost rather face a firing squad—and might, before this is all over—but, yes, I'm ready. I'd say, 'Give 'em hell,' but under the circumstances, I fear that might be in poor taste."

That brought a smile back to William's lips along with a nod of agreement as he released Graham's hand.

"I dare say, you're probably right, but I'll do the best I can. Stand by, then, and wish me luck."

William left them with a briskness to his step that gave lie to the apprehension he felt. He waited until he was clear of the room before giving in to the nervous impulse to clasp the George on his collar like a protective talisman, wishing Gray had not made the allusion to hell. As long as he did not freeze up, the rest of the evening should go as smoothly as the first part. He kept reminding himself of that as he paused outside the door that led back to his guests. Peering through the peep-hole set at eye level, he could see that they were almost ready for him.

The footmen were withdrawing with their trays. At the far end of the room, Michael had replaced one of the equerries previously on duty and was now assisting with the placement of chairs in a double semicircle, facing a larger chair whose resemblance to a throne was not at all coincidental. When the chairs were arranged and the last of the servants had withdrawn, saving Michael and Flynn, Michael closed the double doors and took up a post with his back to the doorknobs. William knew that another of Gray's men was guarding the other side of the doors to forestall interruptions and that Denton prowled the halls. The guests were still milling quietly, unaware that anything had changed.

The stage was set, wanting only William's signal for the play to begin. Before, he had keyed his formal remarks to his guests along the lines of congratulations for jobs well done; he would begin the same way tonight. With his hand on the door-knob, William leaned his forehead briefly against the door and prayed for guidance, wondering whether the God of his child-hood would listen in such a cause. Then he gave the knob a turn. Through the peephole, he saw Flynn draw himself to attention in acknowledgment of the royal signal.

"Ladies and gentlemen, His Royal Highness The Duke of Clarence, KG," the man's voice announced with all the pre-cision of a proper herald.

The door opened, and William stepped through. Eleven

pairs of eyes turned to him as he entered, eleven heads bowing in respect as he paused before his chair. Insanely, he found himself wondering whether Flynn, the extra equerry, might be lured into royal service. Good aides were so hard to find, especially in wartime, and he could use another.

He forced himself to put the thought out of mind as he scanned the faces, giving them one of his most disarming smiles.

"A formal good evening to you, one and all, ladies and gentlemen," he said genially, sitting and gesturing for them to take their seats. "Please make yourselves comfortable. We have come now to what could be construed as the official part of our evening, though I hope to avert any stuffiness which the word 'official' might suggest. This will be akin to what I believe the American president calls his 'fireside chats.'"

They chuckled a little in response to that, settling into the chairs amid some good-natured murmuring and side chatter as William watched the battle lines take shape. Sir Robert, his Masonic brother, was in the front at the far left, with Dame Emma, the vicar, the Rosicrucian, and the two greybeards ranged across the row from left to right. Behind them, at dead center, Gray's stubborn Major Collier seemed to be a line of demarcation between two ceremonial magicians, male and female, and a man and woman of the Wicca. What seemed odd to William was that the polarizations had been almost entirely unconscious on the parts of the participants. No one yet seemed to have drawn the proper conclusion.

"Well, then," he said easily when he had their attention again, "I'm sure you are all aware of at least one of the reasons I've asked you here this evening. All of you, in your various ways, have been contributing greatly to the war effort, whether it is through your actual military service or that of your loved ones, your civic support, or your volunteer work on the home front—making things easier for our Forces when they come home. While it is not in my power to make official recognition of these contributions, I wanted you to know that on a private level, your efforts have not gone unnoticed or unappreciated. England needs the support of all her people in these troubled times, in all the myriad ways in which they can assist, however small. And so, from the bottom of my heart, I wish to thank you for what you have done."

As he watched them drink in his praise and mentally preen

themselves, he paused to draw a deep breath, leaning his elbows on the chair arms and making a steeple of his fingertips. So far, they still suspected nothing. It was going to be fascinating to see how much more he could tell them before they caught on.

"There are other aspects of the war effort which I wish to discuss with you this evening, however, and chief among them is the ever-increasing threat of invasion," he continued. "As no one can fail to be aware, what Mr. Churchill has dubbed the Battle of Britain has already begun. Every day, Fighter Command repels increasingly vicious bombing attacks on our shipping and in our forward coastal areas, at a terrible cost to men and machines. In addition, I am informed that two days ago, Adolf Hitler issued a document known as Directive No. 16 in which he has the audacity to set his official timetable for the invasion of Britain. I say he must be stopped, just as Napoleon and the Spanish Armada were stopped."

They were definitely listening now, unsure whether to be more horrified by the news of Hitler's intentions or appalled by the implication some of them thought they read regarding the previously thwarted invasions. Alix, in her previous approaches to all of them, had given each the background on the Armada and Napoleonic victories and their parallels with the present situation. A few cast furtive glances at their neighbors, but only one or two seemed to show that they had made the connection, and even those guests were unsure.

"Now, before I go on, allow me to assure you that my own involvement in what I am about to say is of only recent occurrence and at a very low level compared to all of you," William said carefully, watching their expressions. "As the King's brother, I am well aware of the delicacy of my position and its historical vulnerability. You will understand this statement more fully when I tell you that I have been made aware of each of your various—ah—esoteric interests. Indeed, that is the second reason you have been asked here tonight."

A deathly stillness suddenly descended on the room, the upturned faces stiffening to tight-drawn masks, some of the eyes blazing in mute outrage, flicking toward the doors. William paused only for breath, fearful that if he stopped, he might not be able to regain his momentum.

"Now, before anyone becomes unduly alarmed, allow me

to reassure you, on my personal word of honor, that so far
as I am concerned, nothing said in this room tonight will go
outside these doors—*including* these other aspects of your private identities. In that regard, suffice it to say that I am told
you represent a cross-section of the faiths and philosophies of
Britain and that all of your services and skills are needed jointly
if we are to survive these days ahead. That includes Freemasons
like myself and Sir Robert there—who, incidentally, knew
nothing beforehand of my intentions for this evening—Rosicrucians, Gnostic Christians, Qabalists, Druids, ceremonial
magicians of various persuasions and orientations, and even
witches—who, I'm told, are not the same as devil worshipers
or satanists, for those of you who may still be thinking in
medieval terms. I leave it to each of you to decide who is who,
if you don't already know, though I suspect all of you know
far more than you let on."

He scanned them evenly, still holding them with his eyes.
"You have different ways of looking at things, ways of doing
things, ways of causing things—and don't look so shocked
that I'm aware of this, Robert," he interjected, glancing sharply
at his Masonic colleague in the first row, "—but in this instance, we all have a common goal: that is the stopping of
Hitler.

"Now, as some of you know, some things are already being
done along more conventional lines," he continued in a milder
vein. "In addition to the expected military preparations, the
King has declared several national days of prayer—and there
will be more, I assure you. The Catholic bishops ended a week
of special prayer just last Sunday. The World Evangelical Alliance urges all of us to pray at noon. All of these are good
things. I should like to suggest, however, that some of your
methods may be even more effective than military activity or
common prayer. Unfortunately, though I am reliably informed
that all of you have been approached and asked to do whatever
you do in concert with others, most of you apparently have
found what you consider to be good and prudent reasons to
decline. I should like to know why."

Consternation finally rumbled audibly among his listeners,
ending as Carey, the Qabalist, slowly stood.

"Sir, with respect, you place us in a very difficult position.
All of us have sworn oaths which—"

"Which, in addition to requiring secrecy, also demand responsible use of whatever influence one may gain by the practice of one's particular discipline. Am I correct?" William asked pointedly, though he did not pause to give Carey time to reply. "Without being inappropriately specific, I can tell you that my Masonic oaths were so slanted. Does a Qabalist have a lesser duty? Is the working of the paths of the tree of life, the seeking of alchemical purity, a lesser quest than that of the perfect ashlar?"

With raised eyebrows, Carey gave a slight inclination of his head and sat down to whispered comments. Collier, who had been looking increasingly uneasy, shot to his feet.

"Sir, I must protest. I do not pretend to understand Your Royal Highness's involvement in all of this. I am not certain I want to know, for reasons which you have already hinted. But if you have been approached by the same sources who approached me, I must tell you that there were, indeed, good reasons why we could not agree to what was proposed. Frankly, sir, I am appalled to hear a prince of the blood speaking in this manner."

"And I am appalled to learn that there are those among my brother's subjects who are unwilling to give the full measure of their support to this war effort!" William snapped. "Of what use is greater knowledge if it is not used for greater aid? Is it worthy to garner this knowledge only for the increase of one's own pride?"

"Sir!"

"Please sit down, major. I have more to say."

Collier's jaw dropped, but he sat. Not a word was spoken as William scanned their stunned faces. For the first time since he had entered, he remembered that Gray and Alix and the brigadier were listening. He hoped he was doing all right.

"Very well, then. We all have our jobs to do, and mine tonight is to tell you a story, in hopes that at least some of you will reconsider your previous decisions." He sat back in his chair more casually.

"In 1581, my many-times-removed ancestress Queen Elizabeth came aboard a gallant little ship called the *Golden Hind* to knight one Francis Drake, who had just circumnavigated the globe. She lost a garter on Drake's quarterdeck that day, just as another royal lady lost a garter at a ball during the reign of

Edward III. For some of you, it will be significant when I tell you that Drake, in the presence of several Knights of the Garter, picked up that garter at the Queen's behest and returned it to her."

He glanced down at his own Garter riband and star before continuing.

"I am inclined to speculate that this action by the Queen constituted a mandate to Drake: a royal recognition, in as specific terms as were consistent with the Queen's official position, of Drake's potential authority in the times to come—seven years later, to be precise. Because in 1588, at Plymouth, Sir Francis Drake is said to have convened—to keep the terminology as neutral as possible—the *occultists* of England to perform a magical working against the Spanish Armada. Specifically, they worked to raise a storm."

A muttering started to ripple among them, but William cut it off with a curtly raised hand.

"Please! Now, those of you who remember your history will recall that, in fact, a storm did come, and the Armada was defeated against fearsome odds. It was regarded as a miracle, even at the time. Whether Drake's action had any effect on that outcome, I leave to you to decide. I have postulated, however, that the reason Drake could command this gathering of magical practitioners was that he had the royal mandate in the form of the Garter Knights who had witnessed his knighting and the subsequent retrieval of the Queen's garter. Seven years later, I believe it was they who stood by Drake to give legitimacy to his coordination effort when he put out his call."

Most of them were eying his Garter accoutrements by now, suddenly aware of the collar, which had not been there earlier in the evening. From the expressions, William saw that he was leading them down precisely the path he had planned. He hoped Gray and Alix were ready to make their entrance, for it was getting very close to time.

"I believe we have a close parallel to Elizabethan times today," William went on. "Again, England faces invasion. Again, there is a man who can be construed to hold the royal mandate—whose knighting seven years ago was witnessed by myself, a Knight of the Garter, and other Garter Knights. Again, the Sovereign can have no active part in all of this—perhaps even less in these times than was possible three and a half centuries ago—but a representative of the Sovereign is aware of the need. At least one of the Garter Knights who supported Drake's leadership for the Armada working was related by blood to the Queen; I think that my relationship to the King goes without saying. I should probably add here that His Majesty knows nothing of what is occurring here tonight."

He took a deep breath, hoping Gray was ready. "I take this role of royal and Garter patron upon myself, then," he said solemnly, "well aware of the personal risks I incur by doing so. The need is very great. Now I wish to present to you a man who, I believe, can function as our modern-day Drake—not to command you, as I do not command you, but to help direct the combining of your many and varied abilities to repel this new would-be invader. Sir John Graham."

As Flynn opened the door, the presence of Alix at Graham's side elicited several gasps of surprise and more than one set of raised eyebrows, but no one dared voice an objection. If there had been any lingering doubt before, William's intentions now became perfectly clear. His masterful handling of the first part of the evening had also been sufficiently impressive that Graham no longer had any qualms about William remaining in the room for the rest of the meeting; they had argued about that in the week just past. Now Graham only wondered whether he could sustain the mood William had created.

No one moved as Graham and Alix entered, paused to make sparse bows before the prince, and took their places to either side of him. Alix sat in a chair to his right, and Graham stood on the left with one hand resting on the finial of the chair back. The symbolism of the physical link to the royal patron was not lost on those who watched.

"Good evening, ladies and gentlemen," Graham said quietly. "First of all, I must apologize for the manner in which this meeting had to be arranged. It was never my intention to involve His Royal Highness in this, but under the circumstances, his kind offer could hardly be declined. I believe that at least several people in this room know firsthand that I tried, as did Lady Selwyn, to do it more conventionally. I hope that all of you will appreciate the risks His Royal Highness has taken to arrange this meeting for us."

In the back row, Mrs. Evans lowered her eyes uneasily, and

Collier's face took on a more stubborn set, but Graham went on without pause.

"What is important is not the past, however, but the future. You have all been approached by Lady Selwyn and given the basic premise of what we propose. It is basically the same as Drake's grand coven. We ask that each of you convene your respective groups, and any groups over which you have influence, for a joint working on Lammas night. I stress that the actual method of working is up to you.

"Naturally, the more people who can work together in one place, the better. We realize, however, that a true grand coven is neither practical nor possible among so many divergent traditions as you represent, spread over so wide a geographic area. Merely to have all of you working by your own methods at the same time toward a common goal should give us far more power to send against Hitler than even Drake was able to raise against the Armada."

A man in the second row stood, arms folded belligerently across his chest—another man in black, master of many groups and individuals working in a tradition founded in Elizabethan times.

"Would you have us wish destruction upon Hitler, then, Sir John, and incur the wrath of the fates upon ourselves for daring to judge another? Would you put yourself above the lords of karma?"

Graham shook his head as the man sat down. "No, sir, I would not. However deserving of destruction we might feel Hitler to be, that is not our place to judge. I am suggesting that we concentrate our efforts on the invasion itself—not to stop it once it starts, by storm or other calamity, but to prevent even the attempt to invade. By this, I mean that we work on Hitler's mind. We whittle away at his confidence so that he comes to doubt he can succeed even if he tries. It doesn't matter what we call our methods—prayer, ceremonial magic, Masonic ritual, witchcraft. The point is that we raise energy in whatever way is appropriate to our own traditions and then send our reinforced wills toward him with a single intent: *you cannot come, unable to come*—words to that effect.

"Nothing more overt, for Hitler himself is a black adept, highly trained, and might detect an open psychic attack. We feel that this more subtle approach of undermining his nerve is the safest and least arguable course overall."

The vicar had gone a little pale, obviously distressed, and Graham nodded in his direction.

"Did you have a question, vicar?"

The man cleared his throat nervously. "Are you saying that Hitler is a black magician?"

"I am. Specific facts are difficult to confirm, but we believe him to be an initiate of long standing in a group called the *Thule Gesellschaft*, within the old *Germanenorden*. These orders spawned many of the mystical elements of Nazism, including the theory of an Aryan master race and hatred of the Jews. Certain evidence suggests that the Thule Group is also a front for a network of other groups of equally dubious motive, most of them political in nature and many of them definitely slanted toward the blacker aspects of ritual magic. There's no doubt that the Thulists are black."

"Come now, colonel, isn't that what any occult fraternity always says about the opposition?" Collier challenged. "That *they* practice black magic, while *we* obviously practice white?"

Graham shrugged and put his hands in his pockets. It was a valid question despite Collier's way of putting it.

"You be the judge, major. I don't want to alarm our more conservative colleagues by going into needlessly gruesome detail, but I will say that an inner core of the *Thule Gesellschaft* is known to be openly satanist in all its nastiest connotations. Reliable evidence indicates that ritual torture and murder are used routinely as a means of raising power and consciousness. This is in addition to the warped sexual practices and other forms of sadism and human degradation which are part of the satanist's stock in trade. Such operations may, indeed, raise power, but what kind and at what cost to the operator?"

William's brother Freemason, Sir Robert, shifted uneasily, white-faced at Graham's account. Like the vicar, he definitely fell into Graham's category of a more conservative member of their gathering.

"Sir John, I'm finding all of this very hard to believe. To a certain extent, I must agree with Major Collier. What you've told us sounds almost too evil, too perverted—the kind of propaganda that one's own side always tells about the enemy to make them into boogeymen and goblins. Next you'd be having us believe that the Nazis slaughter babies and eat them."

"I have no need to exaggerate," Graham said quietly. "The facts speak for themselves. These are no usual wartime atrocities, magnified to make the enemy look worse. What I have told you has been going on for some years. No, this is symptomatic of a far more deeply seated wrongness—one with which, unfortunately, we have to deal. We must be careful that we don't become tainted in the process, pulled down to their level. That is why the indirect approach has been suggested to prevent the invasion, rather than a direct attack on Hitler."

The other man in black nodded agreement. "You've answered my objection on that count, then."

"But you have other objections," Graham supplied.

The man shrugged but said nothing.

"Very well. What other questions may I answer for you?" Graham asked. "Vicar, have I alleviated your fears?"

The vicar fidgeted in his chair, still looking vaguely uncomfortable.

"What about the date? May I ask about the significance?"

"Of course. You're surely aware that in the Christian calendar, Lammas is a festival of first fruits. The name comes from the Anglo-Saxon meaning 'loaf mass' and refers to the bread made from the first wheat or corn which is offered to God at the beginning of the harvest season. As Lugnasad, Lammas is also the festival of the Celtic sun god Lugh. Either way, Lammas marks the first signs of waning solar influence— a singularly appropriate time to work against Hitler, since he has adopted a corrupted sun symbol in his swastika. By concentrating our work between the hours of ten and midnight on Lammas, we feel that we can maximize our effect on Hitler. Of course, those of you who need or wish longer workings may certainly extend in either or both directions, as seems appropriate."

"You keep referring to *we* and *us*, colonel," Collier muttered, fidgeting in his chair. "Just who are these people who have been making decisions about how the rest of us should conduct ourselves? What makes you such a bloody expert?"

Graham sighed. "It should be obvious that Lord and Lady Selwyn are my immediate superiors, major—and you should know better than to ask beyond that. As for my expertise, which aspect do you question? Militarily, I can tell you that RAF reconnaissance only last night observed stepped-up *Seelöwe* activity in several of the occupied Channel ports. We know that the Germans are massing barges and other materiel for the planned invasion.

"Nor is that the whole of it," he continued patiently. "Occultly speaking, the situation is no less grave. Even were it not for what I have already told you about Hitler and the Thulists, I can assure you that esoteric disciplines such as astrology and divination have been and are now being used against us by the German high command. Hitler makes very few important moves wtihout consulting his astrological advisers. An entire section of German intelligence in Berlin is devoted to harnessing the occult sciences for wartime use. One of the more insidious examples involves the use of dowsers and pendulum practitioners to determine the location of our convoys and major troop concentrations. I'm not saying that they are having any great success at this—for which we must be grateful—but the fact remains that they are making the attempt. All of what I have just told you is fact, not conjecture, gleaned from documentable military intelligence which crosses my desk daily."

There were gasps, murmurs, and a few knowing nods around the room. Graham waited for the reaction to play itself out.

"Are there any other questions?"

There were many, but they grew increasingly less hostile as Graham managed to field each one with satisfactory answers and reassurances. Alix said little during the exchange, and William nothing at all, though the prince followed all the comments attentively. When, after half an hour or so, things seemed to be winding down, with all in varying if sometimes grudging agreement that a joint effort was not only possible but desirable, Graham held up a hand to curtail further discussion. He hoped Dame Emma was ready for her cue.

"Very well, ladies and gentlemen. I think we've said all that is really necessary. For security reasons, I'd rather this discussion did not go on much longer. There are servants in the rest of the house who cannot be diverted indefinitely without arousing their curiosity, and all of you must return to your respective homes. We don't want trouble with the authorities because of blackout or curfew violations. So if we are all in agreement at last . . ."

After a brief, tentative pause, Dame Emma slowly stood, nervously fingering a strand of exquisite pearls.

"There is one thing more, Sir John," she said, apparently searching for just the right words, though they had gone over this several times beforehand. "Please don't misunderstand. I certainly have no quarrel with what has been decided here tonight. Whatever the outcome of this meeting, I would have led my people to the sea on Lammas to raise the cone of power. We have done it twice already and will continue to do so periodically until the need is past.

"I *am* concerned, however, that you should have put your reputation so solidly on the line for us by coming here tonight and sharing what must surely be classified information. A careless word from any of us could do you great harm."

There was a soft murmur of agreement from several of them, but Graham only gave a deprecating shrug.

"I worry even more about His Royal Highness," Dame Emma continued. "He has put himself in an even less enviable position by his mere presence here tonight. Of the many traditions represented among us, there are several which would cause no flicker of scandal if it were learned that a prince of the blood had associations with them. Indeed, His Royal Highness has freely acknowledged that he is a Freemason, as are most of the men of the Royal Family. The vicar, and possibly a few of the rest of you fine people, would raise no eyebrows as royal acquaintances.

"My group, however—" She flashed a nervous smile. "Well, really, what *would* Buck House say about the King's brother consorting with witches?"

That evoked a titter of nervous laughter from several of the guests, but it died quickly. After an awkward silence, the woman in the back row beside the other man in black cleared her throat.

"Just what are you suggesting, Dame Emma? Surely you don't mean to imply that one of us would betray His Royal Highness."

Emma shrugged. "My faith is built on perfect love and perfect trust, just as yours is, my dear. I would hope that those principles mean something to all of us even if they are not stated in so many words. However, we are going to have to go back to our respective groups and repeat a certain amount of what has been said here. What I am suggesting is nothing beyond what any esoteric fraternity or association requires of its members, and that is an oath of secrecy—that the names of His Royal Highness and Sir John go no farther than this room, under any circumstances, and that the rest of what we have discussed is repeated solely as necessary to accomplish our stated goal."

Several nodded enthusiastically, but there were still some murmurs of dissent.

"I should like to know by what higher authority you propose such an oath might be sworn," the other man in black asked. "As has been amply pointed out, our traditions and even our faiths are different. There is no common ground for that."

"I agree," the vicar said. "I and mine are willing to work as equals in this particular instance because the need is great, but we are still separate. We cannot swear by any pagan god."

As the company erupted in renewed controversy, most of them on their feet, Graham glanced down at William uneasily, wondering whether he or William should try to intervene. The prince had not moved from his chair—still sat with elbows propped on chair arms, hands clasped before him, legs elegantly crossed in his immaculate naval uniform. Graham tried to catch his eye, but the prince was intent on the arguments. Before Graham could decide what to do next, William had uncoiled from his chair and risen, one hand smoothing his Garter riband. The argument died down almost immediately, as his audience was reminded of his presence.

"Sit down, all of you."

William did not raise his voice, but the tone demanded instant obedience. All of them sat, even Graham surreptitiously pulling an extra chair closer to perch gingerly on the edge of its seat. The matter had now been taken out of his hands. He hoped the prince was not about to make a colossal blunder.

"I—am—appalled!" William said at last, almost spitting out the words, when he had their undivided if wary attention. "I have been sitting here for nearly an hour now, listening to people who supposedly love their country quibble about tiny, insignificant differences of method while, a few hundred miles away, a monstrous man plots their country's ruin! Do you suppose that I came here for *my* health tonight, ladies and gentlemen? I assure you, I did not. I came for England's!"

Somewhere in their midst, a woman gasped. One of the

men in the back row opened his mouth and started to answer but then thought better of it and subsided when he saw William's eyes. William's jaw tightened and then relaxed a little as he continued on a milder note.

"It may interest you to learn that there are surprisingly few things a prince can do for his country in time of war," he said with a slightly bitter note. "We visit military installations and factories behind our own lines, and we make encouraging little speeches. We show the royal colours. We're not permitted to go out on the front and fight with the rest of our people. We're told, 'What if you should be captured, sir?' Not *killed—captured*! We are not even given the privilege of dying for our country, like other folk!"

"Sir, with respect—" Avery began.

"Be quiet, sir! I'm not finished. And that wasn't with respect, and you know it. You, at least, have been presented with an option which may do something to help—which is more choice than I have, for all my rank and royal birth. Yet you—all of you—persist in this pointless, petty bickering! Is it only an empty phrase, this 'perfect trust' you seem to value so?"

"No, sir, but—"

"I don't want your equivocations! You either trust or you do not. If you do, then it seems to me that the least you can do is to give one another a simple reassurance that you mean to follow through with what you say you agree upon. Swear by England if you must have a common object of the oath. Are we not *all* bound unto her cause?"

A sickly, stunned silence stretched on for several long seconds. Graham was afraid to even breathe for fear of disrupting the fine balance. William stood there glaring at them like some absolute prince of long ago, sparing no one, marking them all with his cold blue gaze, daring them to dispute him.

Finally, Dylan Conwy rose and came slowly forward, his bearded face set in an odd, almost hopeful expression.

"Sir, I will swear such an oath to England—through you."

As whispers of reaction spread among them, with several emphatic nods of agreement, Graham chanced a quick glance at Alix, not certain he had understood correctly. But Alix stood as Conwy approached, nodding almost imperceptibly as the older man came before William and stopped. Graham stood too, suddenly very uneasy.

Conwy stared into the prince's eyes for a timeless instant, Graham unable to tell who was measuring whom. Then, as Graham held his breath, the old man inclined his head in a dignified bow.

"Sir, in my religion, we do not kneel to any man, but I will kneel to you and place my hands between yours as a token of my obedience to what has been asked," he said, suiting action to words and looking up into William's eyes. "I swear that I shall keep silent regarding what I have seen and heard here tonight, saving only what must be revealed to those similarly sworn so that your wishes may be carried out. May all my powers fail me and my weapons turn against me if I break this, my solemn oath."

As Graham looked on in amazement, wondering whether William had caught the multiple levels of meaning in Conwy's words, the prince glanced out at the others and then back to the Druid leader, his hands still clasped around the old man's.

"This I have heard and receive for the sake of England," he said steadily. "God grant that I may be worthy of the trust you have shown me by the giving of this oath, and may He bless you in whatever form you may acknowledge Him."

Conwy nodded, touching his forehead to the clasped hands, and then William raised him up, guiding him to Alix's side, for Sir Robert had moved into place behind as William finished speaking. Now William's Masonic brother bent his knee, also offering his joined hands in homage.

"Sir, by the oaths which we have sworn together, I pledge you my obedience in what you have asked—so help me God."

"By the oaths which we have sworn together, I pledge you my support," William replied, murmuring something else that Graham could not quite catch.

After he raised him up, Dame Emma approached and swore.

"May all in accord with this oath swear likewise, with their hands between the hands of this puissant prince," she said as she rose and moved aside.

Gradually, the others came, even Collier finally bending knee with the others, until all had sworn save Graham and Alix. Not a word was spoken as the last of them returned to their seats and remained standing, all eyes still fastened on the prince.

William ducked his head briefly, only Graham able to see the start of tears, which the prince quickly blinked back. When William looked up at them again, his eyes were still bright with emotion.

"I think we all, perhaps, have learnt a lesson in humility tonight, my friends," he said softly. "I hardly know how to thank you for the trust you have placed in me. You have also given me something I feared never to have: an opportunity to serve in a very special way, to unite you in a common cause for our beloved land. Whatever the outcome of your effort, I shall always cherish this night in my heart, knowing that perhaps I was instrumental in some small way. I have only my prayers to offer on Lammas night, for I have no esoteric training beyond my Masonic indoctrination and my childhood faith—despite what some of you may have thought because of my association with these brave folk." He gestured toward Graham and Alix. "But I assure you that I shall spend the hours of your working alone in prayer. Perhaps that will help in its small fashion. God bless you all and give you safe journey home."

"God save England!" Conwy spoke up, glancing around at the others encouragingly. "And God save the King!"

The call was traditional at the end of patriotic gatherings and was picked up and repeated with varying degrees of enthusiasm as William inclined his head in acknowledgment. But Graham felt another twinge of uneasiness as he followed William and Alix out of the room. He could hear the others beginning to talk among themselves as he closed the door behind them, and he was shaking his head as William turned to glance at him.

"What is it?" William asked, dropping back beside him as Alix led the way toward the parlor. "Did I say something wrong?"

Graham gave a perplexed grimace. "I'm not sure. It's just that you may unwittingly ha—"

He broke off as Alix stepped through the parlor doorway and stopped stock-still, so suddenly that Graham and then William collided with her. Beyond, an angry-looking Denton was crouched over the supine and motionless body of Wells, binding the man's hands tightly in front of him with a scarlet cord—

the aiguillette from Denton's own uniform. The brigadier stood over both of them with a silenced automatic pistol trained on Wells's midsection.

"Damn and bloody damn!" Graham swore under his breath, pushing Alix and William the rest of the way into the room and pulling shut the door. "What happened, Denny?"

"Sorry about this, sir, but I think we have ourselves a spy. I caught him listening at the drawing-room door."

CHAPTER 16

THE BETRAYAL TOOK ONLY AN INSTANT TO REGISTER. Suddenly, the reticence Graham had always felt around Wells made sense.

"All right, we've got to get to the bottom of this," he said briskly, propelling Alix toward the door. "Alix, go find Michael and ask him to bring the kit from my car. He'll know what I mean. Wesley, is there a secure room on this floor where we can take our friend without being seen? If we have fireworks when he comes to, I want more than a slab of glass between him and our departing guests."

"Let's take him to my study—two doors down the hall on the left," Ellis said, already beginning to urge the prince in that direction as Graham and Denton hoisted the unconscious Wells between them.

They reached the study without incident and dumped Wells unceremoniously in a wooden swivel chair. Denton untied his hands only long enough to strip off his coat and resecure Wells to the chair arms. As Alix returned, beckoned to their new location by William, Graham checked their prisoner's pulse and looked under his eyelids.

"He'll be coming around in a minute or two. Better give me details quickly, Denny."

Shaking his head, Denton pulled up a straight-backed chair and sat back on Wells's left, one hand gripped firmly along the man's wrist to catch the first sign of returning consciousness.

"I don't know where he came from, sir. I saw him leave like he was supposed to, but he must have suspected something and doubled back. He could have been outside that door for ten seconds or as long as ten or fifteen minutes."

"Where were you?"

"Mostly around the other side, sir, where the other servants were likely to come. We never dreamed he'd come back. He must have entered through a rear window. It can't have been accidental."

"He couldn't have gone to London and back in this time, either," the brigadier offered. "I'm afraid we have a serious problem, Gray."

"Alix, watch the door for Michael, please. William, did you have any inkling that he'd become suspicious?"

"None. He's always been the ideal aide: efficient, discreet— I find this very hard to believe. What possible motive could he have?"

"He's coming around," Denton murmured, turning the prisoner's face full on by the chin as the eyelids fluttered. "Come on, mate, we know you're awake. No use trying to fake it."

Wells moaned as he came to, apparently too dazed initially to fake anything. The sight of the four of them staring down at him sobered him fast, especially the brigadier with his weapon. He turned wide, frightened eyes on William in appeal, but his employer was not receptive.

"I should like to believe this is all part of some ghastly mistake, Mr. Wells, but somehow I fear the mistake was yours," William said. "Do you want to tell me your version of what happened?"

Wells grimaced and stretched his neck from side to side several times, apparently still disoriented, testing his bonds.

"Someone hit me from behind, sir," he whispered almost reproachfully.

"That occasionally happens to people who go snooping where they have no business," Graham said. "You realize, of course, that Sergeant Denton or the brigadier would have been perfectly within their rights to shoot you instead of just knocking you out?"

The prisoner's head jerked up in response. "For looking in

on a reception? Come off it, colonel! I was trying to see whether I was needed inside again. I didn't want to disturb something."

"Indeed?" William said. "I thought I ordered you to London. Do you have the dispatch you were sent for?"

Wells lowered his eyes. "No, sir."

"Why not?"

When Wells did not answer or look up, Graham shook his head and turned away. So much for the hope that this might be easy. Michael joined them and handed over a black medical bag, which Graham passed on to Denton. The sergeant withdrew to the desk a few feet behind Wells and began selecting items from the bag.

"Very well, let's start with a simpler question," Graham said, returning to their prisoner as the brigadier settled in a nearby easy chair where he could keep the man covered. "Where is His Royal Highness's car? You hid it in a nearby lane so you could sneak back here, didn't you?"

"I have nothing to say."

"That attitude isn't going to help your case," William said. "You're going to have to talk eventually. You know that."

Silence. After an extended pause, Graham glanced at Michael.

"Did you notice the car outside?"

"No, sir."

"All right, it can't be far away. Alix, go with him, please. You don't need to be here for this."

He went with them to the door, closing it behind them, then beckoned for William to join him. Across the room, Denton was rolling up Well's left shirt-sleeve while the brigadier looked on, the automatic now stuck in his belt. Wells, tight-lipped and almost grey with fear, had turned his head away and closed his eyes. Graham stared intently past the prince at Wells for several seconds, then flicked his glance to William.

"Do you think he's innocent?"

William shook his head, looking at the floor.

"He can't be." He paused a beat. "We're going to have to kill him, aren't we?"

"Sooner or later, I expect so. A lot depends on what answers we can get out of him. Denny is giving him something to loosen his tongue, but if he *was* outside the door long enough to figure out what was going on—well, how do you lock up a former royal aide with information like this? All he has to do is open his mouth once and you and we have had it. If you can think of another solution, I'm willing to listen, but I'm afraid it doesn't look good for old Wells."

William shoved his hands in his pockets, still not looking up.

"I hate this kind of thing. It's bad enough to have to kill a man in self-defense before he kills you. . . .' "

"That's exactly what this is," Graham murmured. "*Exactly*. In any case, you won't have to do it. *If* we decide it's necessary, Denny or I will give him an overdose at the end. He won't feel a thing. Then we'll—arrange for an auto accident on the London road: your car, a ruptured petrol tank and explosion, with lots of fire. . . . There won't be any question. He's overdue at the Admiralty al—"

"Get him under fast!" the brigadier gasped as the other side of the room erupted in a scuffle and assortment of grunts and muffled exclamations.

Wells was struggling to escape from his chair, head whipping frantically from side to side and unbound legs flailing. The brigadier fought to apply a choke hold around his neck, and Denton tried to immobilize his arm long enough to get a needle in it. As the chair went over with a clatter, Graham launched himself across the room and sat astride the squirming Wells, helping Denton pin the arm while William tackled the scrabbling legs. At that moment, the brigadier found his pressure points and clamped down hard, holding doggedly until Wells twitched and went limp. Denton slid his needle home in the same instant, simultaneously loosing the rubber tourniquet and injecting Wells with several cc.'s of the drug.

When no one moved for several seconds, including Wells, Denton sighed heavily and straightened, holding the syringe steady until the other three could ease the chair and its unconscious occupant back to an upright position. As Graham helped Denton tape the syringe in place, William indignantly brushed dust from his uniform and glared at all of them.

"Will someone please tell me what that was all about?" he muttered. "I thought you two had things under control."

Ellis, his hands still resting cautiously on Wells's shoulders from behind, shook his head and let out a relieved sigh.

"Sorry, sir. Gray, you're not going to believe this, but I think he's one of us. I saw his aura shift."

"You what?"

Graham left Denton to finish up and moved with Ellis a little apart from their prisoner. A thoroughly bewildered William watched both men mutely.

"I think he was trying to go into some kind of trance," Ellis said, retrieving his automatic from where it had fallen in the scuffle. "I was watching his aura, and it started the same kind of compacting and shifting that yours does when you're going on the Second Road. You don't suppose he belongs to one of our guests, do you?"

"That would be *too* much coincidence," Graham replied. "But if he isn't one of ours..."

As his voice trailed off in speculation, William pulled at his sleeve.

"What do you mean, 'If he isn't one of ours,' and 'watching his aura'? What are you two talking about?"

Graham sighed. "It appears your Lieutenant Wells may be a trained occultist of some sort, William. After a while, one learns to recognize the signs. When people start working in the esoteric disciplines, it's as if they've sent up a psychic flare. It's visible to anyone else with the psychic eyes to see, both around the physical person and on the Second Road. I don't read auras as well as Wesley, but those who do can almost always spot the signs, especially if the person is observed actually doing something."

"What was he doing?" William asked uneasily.

"It looked to me like he was trying to do a sending forth— a kind of telepathy," the brigadier said. "He seemed pretty desperate about it, too—which is good reason, right off, not to let him do it."

"Won't he just try again when he comes to?"

Ellis shook his head. "Not with the drug in him. A small amount might actually help, but Denny's given him too much for that. My question is, if he was trying to send forth, to whom, and why?"

William stared at the brigadier, mouth agape at this new aspect revealed, as Denton dragged his chair back to the side of Wells's now well-secured arm and sat down. The syringe, two-thirds filled with a pale, straw-colored fluid, was taped along the inner forearm, the needle hidden by a ball of cotton. Wells's eyelids were fluttering open again, and he gradually managed to raise his head under his own power, but it was obvious the drug was having its effect.

"He's about ready, colonel," Denton said, adjusting a last length of tape.

Graham brought another chair and set it backwards in front of Wells, straddling it in an easy, casual motion. William stood at his back and slightly to his right, and the brigadier settled in the wing-back chair to his left. Graham liked the direction this encounter was taking less and less.

"How do you feel, Mr. Wells?" he asked neutrally.

Wells gave his inquisitor a look of stony fury, but it was not nearly as effective as it might have been, had he not been drugged.

"You bloody bastard!" the man whispered through clenched teeth. "I might have known you'd be in on this. You're going to kill me, aren't you?"

"That depends a great deal on you, Mr. Wells," Graham said. "The problem is that this is wartime and you disobeyed a direct order. That certainly could be construed as a capital offense."

Wells snorted. "Not in any court in the realm, and you know it. That isn't why you're going to kill me, either. It's because of what I saw."

"And just what is it you think you saw?" William asked, folding his arms across his chest.

"I saw enough. I know who those people were. And you, Mister High and Mighty Prince—you were right in there with them!"

"Watch your—"

"Why don't you let me handle this, William?" Graham interjected smoothly. "Mr. Wells, if you know who they were, suppose you tell us? You had the guest list. Is that what you mean?"

Wells chuckled brokenly, a little hysterically, shaking his head. "Oh, no you don't. I know how you people operate. If I don't tell you, then you don't know for sure. Not going to get me that way...."

At Graham's glance and slight nod, Denton's thumb tightened on the plunger and injected another half cc. of the drug.

Wells bit his lip, eyes half closed, but he soon relaxed visibly. After another thirty seconds or so, his head began to nod. Quietly, the brigadier rose and went to stand behind him again, close enough to support the nodding head against his waist, hands resting lightly on the shoulders.

"Who were those people, Andrew?" Graham asked quietly, shifting to the man's Christian name. "Do you know anything besides their names?"

Wells nodded slowly. He was having trouble focusing.

"Yes."

"Tell me who they are, then."

"Freemasons," Wells breathed. "And Rosicrucians... magicians... witches.... One was even a Jew...."

Graham could feel William stiffen next to him, but he had no time to spare for righteous outrage just now. If Wells knew *what* the guests had been as well as who, he could not have learned that from any of them. The Freemasonry, yes—but not the others. Nor could he had inferred that much from what he might have seen and heard.

"Were they, now?" Graham murmured, glancing up at Ellis. "Who told you that was who they were?"

"I—knew. They told me."

"Who told you? Those people?"

"No."

"Who, then?"

"My chiefs."

He could feel William's eyes on him even more urgently, but he dared not interrupt the line of questioning now that Wells was talking.

"Are you a member of a secret organization, Andrew?" he asked.

Wells smiled dreamily but made no reply.

"He is," Graham muttered under his breath. "Andrew, is it one of those in the room?"

The tranquil face contorted in scorn.

"Not a chance."

Graham paused for a moment, frowning, watching Wells drift when he was not actively involved in responding to a question, then glanced over at Denton.

"I'm going to try something, Denny. Keep him at this level if you can. I don't want him to come up, but I don't want him much farther under than he is right now, either. Can you do that?"

As Denton nodded, Graham leaned forward and held his hand a few feet from Wells's face and slightly above eye level, snapping his fingers to catch the man's drifting attention. If Graham's growing suspicions were correct, Wells would have received extensive indoctrination and training in the use of trance, and likely of a far more submissive type than Graham would dream of using with his people. If such conditioning could be shifted to put Graham in control . . .

"Watch my hand, Andrew," he said softly, snapping his fingers again and noting the way the eyes tracked instantly to his fingertips. "No, just follow with your eyes. Don't lift your head. That's right."

Seeing what Graham was about, the brigadier slid his hands up to support the prisoner's head lightly. Wells's eyelids fluttered more and more erratically with fatigue and the drug as Graham brought his hand closer, a few inches above the bridge of the nose.

"That's right," Graham murmured. "Watch my hand. Your eyelids are getting heavier and heavier. It's an effort to keep them open. Relax, Andrew. Watch my hand. That's right. *Wache die Hand und schlafe nun. . . .*"

As he shifted into German, he touched Wells lightly between the eyes. The effect was almost electric. With a little whimper, Wells's eyes rolled upward and then closed, his body slumping almost bonelessly, head lolling against the brigadier's hands.

"*Ist gut, Andrew,*" Graham whispered. "*Erschlaffe. Es ist sehr gut. . . .*"

Cautiously, he withdrew his hand and glanced back at William, shaking his head and holding a finger to his lips when William would have spoken. Folding his hands along the back of the chair he straddled, he returned his attention to Wells. He hoped his German was up to a prolonged questioning.

"*Ich bin deiner Chef, Andrew. Kannst du mich hören?*" he asked.

"*Ja,*" came the scarcely breathed reply.

"*Gut. Höre gut zu. Du hast etwas wichtig gesehen. Sage es mir doch.*"

"*Nein. . . . Verboten. . . . Ich muß nicht. . . .*"

"*Du mußt. Berichte, bitte. Was hast du gesehen?*"

Haltingly, Wells began to answer in flawless German, re-counting a precise account of the night's meeting from part way through Graham's question-and-answer session. When he had finished, Graham asked him again about his membership in any secret organization. This time he was not refused.

Michael returned as Wells was beginning a detailed de-scription of his recruitment and initiation several years before as a member of the *Thule Gesellschaft*. He had already named several other highly placed British initiates and confessed that he and they had been relaying information back to Germany for over a year, often through psychic means. He had been trying to reach his chiefs when the brigadier caught the shift of his aura, though even *he* had not thought he had a prayer of succeeding under the circumstances. He did not know whether he had made contact.

After a few more questions, Graham turned the interrogation over to Michael, whose German was better than his own, and drew William aside. The prince was tight-jawed with outrage.

"I take it you followed most of that," Graham murmured, keeping his eyes on Michael and the prisoner. "I wasn't sure how rusty your German might have become."

"Not rusty enough, it seems," William replied. "I still can't believe some of the things I just heard. How did he get involved in something like that? More to the point right now, who vetted him before he came on my staff? I didn't even know he spoke German."

"I have some ideas I'll follow through on that," Graham said. "Considering who else he named, it shouldn't be too difficult to track down. Fascinating little exposé on the Thule Group, though. Charming folk, aren't they?"

William shivered and glanced at the floor. "It was sickening. How could anyone do that to another human being? I can't even imagine doing it to an animal! Could he possibly be making it up?"

Graham shook his head, remembering the Dieter photo-graphs. "Definitely not. Between the drug and our utilization of his own conditioning, he isn't capable of lying. At very least, he believes that's what happened, even if a lot of it were faked to look that way for the initiation, so they could blackmail him later on. That isn't likely, however. The Thulists are noted for their sadistic rituals. Ask Grubaugh about it someday if you want the really gory details."

"Jesus Christ!"

"I assure you, he has absolutely nothing to do with this. The question now is, what do you want to do with our friend?"

William snorted. "Have we really got a choice? Oh, I could cover his absence for a few days if you thought you could get anything more out of him, but it all comes 'round to the same decision in the end. He has to go—and the sooner it's done, the less chance of arousing outside suspicion."

"I'm forced to agree. Let's see if Michael and the brigadier concur."

Wells was still muttering in a broken mixture of German and English as they came back, but his words no longer made any sense. His head wove back and forth aimlessly between the brigadier's hands, his eyes focused with dread on something only he could see. Michael looked troubled as he glanced up at Graham.

"All I'm getting now is Nazi dogma and party slogans, sir— and something about eyes staring at him. Could someone be trying to link in with him?"

"If they are, they can't be getting anything coherent," Graham murmured. "Did you get anything else out of him?"

Michael drew a deep breath and seemed to pull himself together. "He did spill one other interesting bit. It seems he placed a trunk call to Scotland sometime in the past week— after you and Prince William set up tonight's guest list, since that's what he rang to report. Until this evening, he was convinced that the prince was the mastermind behind whatever is being planned—though he suspected all along that you were involved, Gray. Apparently, something about the Plymouth trip didn't set quite right, and he knew you'd made the arrangements. In any case, both your names were mentioned when he talked to Scotland. Sorry, sir," he concluded, glancing apologetically at William.

William's jaw tightened, but he only looked to Graham. Graham allowed himself a weary, resigned sigh.

"I don't suppose you got any names for 'them'?" he asked.

"No names, but I do have a number," Michael replied, looking a little more confident as he handed across a slip of paper. "He either doesn't know or won't say who it actually was. His contact used a code name which changed according to the date. Wells ordinarily receives his instructions by letter drop or post, but there wasn't time in this case. I got the location of the drop, and there's a code book in his room back at Buck House. Shall I try to trace the number when we get back?"

With a distracted nod, Graham memorized the number and gave back the paper. He was willing to bet a year's salary that it would connect with one of the high-born names Wells had already mentioned. That was not sufficient to save the unfortunate Wells, however.

"Good work, Michael. Please do. William, we'll need that code book as soon as possible. I'll ask you to collect it, if you will."

"Of course."

Graham folded his arms across his chest and sighed, then glanced down once more at the nearly oblivious Wells. He did not much like this part of his work.

"Is there anything else I should know, Captain Jordan?" he said formally, finally looking up at Michael. "Any reason to continue this questioning?"

Michael stiffened, immediately aware what Graham was asking.

"No, sir. Not in my opinion."

"Thank you. I know that was not an easy answer to give. Wesley, do you agree?"

"Regretfully, yes. If we let him come out of this, he'll spill his guts to his chiefs on the Second Road as soon as he's able." He sighed and dropped his hands to the condemned man's shoulders. "Poor lad, maybe he'll get things right in the next go-through," he murmured softly.

"Right. That's it, then," Graham said after a minute pause. With brisk efficiency and before anyone had time to think too much about it, he shouldered Denton aside and emptied the rest of the syringe into Wells's vein. Wells subsided almost instantly into unconsciousness.

"Denny, I'll need a lethal dose to finish this," Graham said quietly, beginning to remove the strips of tape that held the syringe in place. "Michael, I take it you found the Rolls?"

Only as Denton withdrew to prepare what was ordered did Michael rouse himself with a start, exchanging a slightly queasy look with the tight-lipped William.

"He hadn't hidden it very well, sir," Michael said, beginning to regain his composure. "He'd left it in a lay-by, less than a mile from here. I brought it around to the back entrance via the rear gate. None of the guests saw it."

"Fine. Where's your mother?"

"Seeing Dame Emma off. Everyone else has gone. She sent the servants off to bed, and the house is secure. Flynn stayed. He's patrolling the grounds with your other two men."

"Very good. Wesley, would you get his coat, please?"

As the brigadier complied, Graham left the last strip of tape in place and began untying Wells's slack arms.

"Now, Michael, here's what I want you to do when we're finished here," he continued. "There's a bad stretch of road with a diversion a few miles toward London. Do you know the place?"

"Yes, sir."

"Good. With the blackout, it would be very easy for someone in a hurry to miss a turn and go into the ditch. Make sure the car burns. Denny will go with you."

"Yes, sir."

As Graham pulled loose the last loops of cord and the remaining strip of tape, Denton returned with a full syringe; a stethoscope hung around his neck. Blood welled briefly from the needle still in Wells's arm as Graham switched syringes, and he wiped it off in a wad of cotton. Before his thumb could shift to the plunger, William laid a restraining hand on his arm.

"I'll take over from here, Gray," the prince whispered. "It's my job, not yours. He worked for me."

A little stiffly, Graham exchanged places with the prince and stood aside. William's face was unreadable as he bent over the syringe and its sure but merciful death. When it was done, William handed the empty syringe to Denton and pressed a cotton wad over the tiny puncture wound while his other hand sought the pulse point in the flaccid wrist. He closed his eyes when Denton moved in to slip the bell of the stethoscope inside Wells's shirt.

After a few minutes, Denton withdrew, and the brigadier bent to brush his lips lightly against Wells's hair, gently letting the head loll forward on the still chest.

"Go in peace, son," Ellis whispered.

William's eyes opened at the words. As he straightened and

let himself be eased aside, Graham's arm around his shoulders, his hands fell awkwardly to his sides. He watched numbly as Denton and Michael hoisted Wells's limp form between them and carried him out of the room. The brigadier followed with the dead man's coat, closing the door softly behind him.

William breathed out slowly, then pulled out a cigarette and sat in the wing-back chair the brigadier had lately occupied. His hands were shaking as he tried to light up, and Graham finally took the lighter away from him and gave him flame.

"You didn't have to do that, you know," Graham said, pulling his chair closer and dropping the warm lighter into William's hand before straddling the chair again. "I told you that before. I was prepared to do it."

Smoke wreathed around William as he shook his head and slouched in his chair. "No, it was my responsibility. I'd just forgotten how much I hated this part of the business. I thought I'd left the killing behind when they made me quit the service."

"I'm not sure we ever leave it behind," Graham replied, leaning his chin on his folded arms atop the chair back. "Hating it, I mean. I'm not sure we ever should. It's a weighty thing to take a life—and no one should enjoy being an executioner, even when the cause is just. You didn't do it out of vengeance."

"No."

The talk of killing reminded Graham of other lives taken, and he wondered again why it was only recently that more detailed memories of his own deeds should begin to surface. He shook the mood with a blink and a slight shake of his head—it had been a grim enough night already without bringing *that* in—and found William staring at him. He must have been away for longer than he thought.

"Where were you?" William asked, breathing out smoke. "You looked like you were seeing ghosts."

Graham smiled grimly, though he did not lift his head from his arms. "Perhaps I was. Does it matter?"

"Yes."

"Very well. I was thinking about other deaths for which I've been responsible. Does that make you feel any better?"

"Not really."

The ash on William's cigarette was getting long, and he rose with a cupped hand under it, looking for an ash tray. The only one was on the desk, next to the black bag and Denton's empty syringes. William stared at them for a moment, the cigarette dripping ash into his hand, then stubbed it out and came back to Graham, dusting off his hands, eyes downcast.

"So what happens next?" he asked.

"I have some loose ends to wrap up. You should get some sleep while you can." Graham glanced at his watch. "It's after one now. You may have four or five hours, at most, before someone finds your car and the authorities come inquiring. At least they'll know to ask here first, since it's known you were staying with Wesley for a few days. Until that happens, you ought to get some sleep."

"Sleep?" William snorted. "You don't really expect me to sleep after all of this, do you? Even if I hadn't just killed a man in cold blood, there was all that other."

He dropped heavily into the wing-back chair again, then cocked his head at Graham, eyes narrowing.

"You started to tell me something just before we found Denny and Wells. I asked if I'd said anything wrong, and you said that I might have unwittingly—what? You never got to finish."

Graham sighed, wondering now whether he should even mention it and give William one more thing to brood on. There had been no time to think about it while they resolved the Wells crisis, but now the imagery of those kneeling with their hands between William's snapped into clear focus. Even more chilling were the words they had spoken at the end: "God save the King!" If only he could be certain they were not referring to William.

"Gray, what is it?" William persisted.

Studying the carpet through the rungs on the back of his chair, Graham grimaced and resigned himself to the uncomfortable task of trying to articulate his worry without also putting ideas in William's head.

"Very well, it was the oath taking," he said softly. "I'm not sure you're aware how some people may have seen it. I think it might be construed as something more than a simple homage."

"Why? Was there some esoteric factor of which I wasn't aware?" William sat forward cautiously. "You know, of course, that I exchanged Masonic countersigns with Sir Robert when I took my oath. There was nothing unusual about that."

"No, of course not. What I was going to point out was that you might unwittingly have cast yourself in the role of another Edward III. It's probably remote—at least I hope so—but the parallel is an odd coincidence, in any case."

"Edward III? I don't know what you're talking about."

"Think back to that night in London when we discussed the founding of the Order of the Garter," Graham said. "Do you remember how you told me that a lady lost her garter and Edward picked it up and spoke his immortal words?"

"Yes, of course, but—"

"What did I tell you was the significance of that act, in esoteric terms?"

William leaned his head against the back of the chair, kneading at his eyes with the heels of his hands.

"Do you really want me to remember that far back?" he muttered. "Let's see. He—ah—had taken on the official protectorship of the old religion."

"That was the lesser possibility," Graham agreed. "What was the greater?"

"That he—ah—assumed the position of god incarnate for his people and actual head of the—" William sat bolt upright with a start. "Bloody hell, Gray, I didn't do *that*, did I?"

Graham smiled bleakly. "I certainly hope not. I can't say how they all construed it, but I'd be willing to bet you that at least some of them read it that way. You *certainly* assumed a kind of protectorship. That was inevitable, I suppose."

"But that's an entirely different—"

"Yes, it is. But don't you remember the look on Conwy's face? He said, 'In my religion we do not kneel to any man.' But he'll kneel to a god, Will. So would a lot of the others."

After a short, strained silence, William cleared his throat.

"That's—ridiculous. I'm not their god—and I don't know the first thing about magic so far as practice is concerned."

"I know that. Let's hope I'm wrong. Anyway, it isn't something we'll resolve by further discussion tonight." He glanced at his watch again. "You really should try to get some sleep. The others will be back soon, and then I'll have to get back to London. Mr. Wells has given us a lot of work tonight."

"You go ahead when you have to," William murmured. "I really don't feel like sleeping."

Graham gazed at him compassionately, then stood and moved

his chair around so he could sit on it straight on, knees nearly
touching William's. He did not really want to pull out the last
item in his reserve where William was concerned, but perhaps
it was time. The prince definitely should be asleep when the
authorities arrived. As William looked up at him quizzically,
Graham sat forward a little, fingers lightly intertwined, elbows
resting on his knees.

"If you want, I can help you to sleep," he said softly.

"With something from your black bag over there?" William
shook his head quickly. "No, thank you."

"Actually, that isn't what I had in mind at all. You don't
remember because I asked you not to, but that night at Oakwood, after we talked to Alix, you gave me a very special gift.
You gave me your trust," he added at William's look of question. "That trust is a very powerful tool. If you want to learn,
I can teach you how to use it now, to help you to sleep."

William stared at him incredulously. Graham could almost
hear the thoughts racing by as the prince reviewed that other
night and could find no hint of what Graham was talking about.
As William shook his head, still obviously unable to remember,
Graham knew that the trigger he had set would work. The
memory block would not be so complete if that were not so.

"I don't know what you're talking about," William said.
"Where were we?"

"In your bedroom. I won't go into details because you'll
remember them yourself soon enough, but you went into a
hypnotic trance for me. You can do it again if you want to and
remember everything that happened that night."

William squeezed his eyes shut for several seconds, then
opened them, still staring at Graham blankly. "I don't think
you're lying, but I honestly don't remember what you're talking
about. I went into a trance?"

Graham nodded slowly.

"What—" William swallowed audibly. "What did I say?"

"Nothing incriminating," Graham replied with a reassuring
smile. "I think you may have said 'yes' once or twice. Alix
had asked me to give you a sedative so she and I could work
undisturbed. I put it in your nightcap, but I wouldn't give it
to you without telling you first. Even after I persuaded you to
drink it, you were fighting it. Then you went into a trance,

just to show me that *you* trusted *me*, I suppose—even if you weren't sure we trusted you."

"Why don't I remember, then?"

"I felt it was better you *not* remember just then. I did leave you with a posthypnotic trigger like you saw me use with Michael, however. The very fact that you can't remember is proof positive that it took. Would you care to try it?"

A tiny smile was playing at the corners of William's mouth, as if he could not quite make up his mind whether Graham was serious, but the trust was there, too.

"All right," he said simply. "What do I have to do?"

"Just close your eyes for now," Graham said. "In a moment, I'll ask you to open them again, while you're in trance, because I want you to realize that you can. For now, just close them and take a deep breath."

As William obeyed, Graham leaned forward slightly and laid his hand across the prince's forehead.

"Let it out now and let go. Remember."

Immediately, Graham felt the initial rigidity dissolve. He let himself relax a little as he took his hand away, sitting back in his chair. A slow, lazy smile was spreading across William's face.

"It feels a little strange, doesn't it?" Graham said conversationally. "But I can see that you remember now. Stay in trance, but you can open your eyes if you want to. Tell me how you feel."

William opened his eyes and blinked several times, slowly. "I thought I'd feel groggy or something."

"No. You did the first time, but that was because of the drug. Right now, you probably feel—ummmm—perhaps a bit lethargic, like you haven't much inertia of your own. If I were to stop talking and leave you alone, with nothing to think about, you'd probably drift back into a sort of floating state. You might even go to sleep."

William seemed to digest that information, but he did not volunteer any comment. Graham knew that he was in deep.

"Do you remember that night now?" he asked.

"Yes."

"Good. In the morning, you'll find that you still remember it. For now, though, you expressed a doubt earlier that you'd be able to sleep. That's understandable, but I think sleep would be a good idea. It's been a very long day. Are you willing to let me arrange things so you'll be able to relax and get some rest when you go upstairs?"

William nodded slightly. "I don't want to forget, though."

"I understand, and I agree," Graham said. "Taking life should never be easy. We have to live with our responsibilities. Still, I think you can let your unconscious work on putting things in their proper perspective while you sleep, so that your nerves don't interfere with the other things you have to do. Would that be all right?"

"Yes."

"Fine. Why don't you close your eyes again, and in a little while I'll ask you to come out of trance. Before that, I want you to know that when you go upstairs and lie down on your bed, you're going to find it very easy to fall asleep. In fact, as soon as your head touches the pillow, you'll find yourself slipping into a deep, refreshing sleep. You'll sleep soundly until you're awakened. While you sleep, your mind will do whatever is necessary to sort out the many things that have happened tonight so that you can deal with them effectively. You'll probably find that you've achieved some distance and perspective when you wake up. That can help to sustain you through the difficult times which may lie ahead. Do you understand?"

"Yes, came the whispered reply.

"Is that all right?"

William nodded slightly.

"Very good. Take another nice deep breath, then, and let it out slowly. On the count of three, I want you to come out of trance, pleasantly drowsy and ready to go to bed but remembering everything. One . . . two . . . three."

William opened his eyes on "three" and looked at Graham, blinked, then grinned in spite of himself as he had to cover a wide, uncontrollable yawn.

"Remind me never to doubt you again," the prince said, stretching and shaking his head around another, lesser yawn. "That was very odd. Are you *sure* it wasn't magic?"

"Afraid not," Graham said with a smile. "It's useful in magic, but it's only a tool." He rose and gestured toward the door as William also stood. "On up to bed with you now. It really *has* been a long day. I'll look in on you in a few minutes, but I fully expect you to be oblivious. We'll talk more in the next day or two."

He saw the prince to the door and watched him disappear down the hallway, then went back to gather up the contents of his medical kit. He was nearly finished when the brigadier joined him.

"How's he doing?" the older man asked.

"Well enough," Graham replied, snapping shut the lock on the bag. "He didn't think he'd be able to sleep, so we worked in trance for a few minutes. What an incredible subject."

"That doesn't suprise me in the least," Ellis said with a gentle smile. "He's turning out to be an incredible man."

"Yes, you know, you're quite right," Graham murmured, resting both hands on the bag. "If I'd said a thing like that before this evening, I would have suspected my own bias in his behalf, but he really did do an incredible job. And the part with Wells—" He glanced distastefully at the empty swivel chair and fought down a shiver. "I didn't want him to have to do that, on top of everything else."

"He has a very strong sense of duty," the brigadier said, moving toward the door as Graham shook off the memory and joined him. "By the way, Michael and Denton got back a few minutes ago. They're waiting in your car."

"I assume everything went all right?"

"As planned. With the full moon, no one even noticed the fire. However, you may want to jog someone at the Admiralty about Wells being overdue, when you get back to London. That Rolls is altogether too distinctive. We shouldn't want some local to stumble on it in the morning who doesn't know William was staying with me and start a panic about *him* being the victim."

"Good Lord, no! That's the last thing we need." He paused just inside the door. "Incidentally, you'd better suggest that William try to arrange a sea burial or cremation as soon as is decently possible—and no inquest. I don't know what family Wells had, but I shouldn't imagine they'd object to a royal duke making the arrangements. Hard to refuse, in any case, and a gracious gesture on William's part."

"So long as they're not in on Wells's extracurricular activities, I should think you're right," the brigadier agreed. "If they are, perhaps I can bring additional pressure to bear. Don't worry about a thing. By the way, I dismissed your other two men before Michael and Denton left—sent them off by another road. No point chancing they'd see the Rolls leaving again and wonder later on. Flynn will stay the night just in case I need someone. You know, it's occurred to me that he might prove an ideal replacement for Wells eventually—provided he vets out suitably in other ways, of course, and that William agrees. What do you think?"

Graham nodded wearily. "I think it's a little premature, but it's possible—if Dame Emma doesn't hex us all for taking him away," he added with a grin. "At least he's one of us. I'll have Denny work up a dossier. Oh, and tell William that as soon as I receive official notification of Wells's death, I intend to send Michael over on loan. Hopefully, Mr. Wells's little Thulist cronies won't be able to prove a thing, but I won't have them taking potshots at William in retaliation, whether figurative or literal." He sighed. "Why do I have this sudden, awful feeling that Sturm is laughing right now?"

"Odd, I was thinking about him myself," Ellis replied, "but I hadn't pictured him laughing. Rather the reverse, in fact. I was thinking about Cousin Dieter, too."

"Dieter?"

As Graham stared at him in surprise, Ellis fished a pipe out of an inside pocket and sucked on it experimentally, one eyebrow raised.

"Oh, I know we'd agreed to break off relations with him," the old man continued, "but I wonder whether it might not be valuable to send a message, anyway, just to test how far back the ripples extend from tonight's piece of work. The Thulists aren't going to take Wells's death kindly."

"I don't take Wells's betrayal kindly, either," Graham said coolly. "I think I'll want to consider very carefully before I let on that I know anything about it." He glanced down at his feet, then back at the brigadier. "Am I being too rigid, Wes? Do you think it's possible to be as far into the dark as Dieter is and still retain a spark of light? I keep seeing those photos. . . ."

The brigadier fiddled with his pipe for a few seconds, then sighed and touched Graham's arm reassuringly.

"Let me put it this way, son. I'm not saying that what he's done is right—God knows. But if I were in your place, I believe I'd try very hard to imagine why he would have sent those photos in the first place, unless it was an expression of total honesty. Sometimes men have to do things they really don't want to do and which seem very wrong to those around them. Sometimes those things *do* turn out to be wrong—but not always, perhaps. I'm not saying that's necessarily the case with Dieter, but—Well, you're the only one who can decide how *you* feel about him, aren't you?"

Graham considered for a moment, then gave the brigadier a bleak smile.

"I'll think about it, Wesley." He paused just a beat, then went on. "I don't suppose you'd consider coming up to London for a few days until things settle down? I could use your advice."

"Why not?" Ellis grinned as he chewed on his pipe again. "I'll need to drive William and his valet back to the Palace in the morning, anyway, since you sacrificed his beautiful Rolls-Royce. I can see about that code book for starters, too."

CHAPTER 17

O N THE DRIVE BACK TO LONDON, DENTON AND MI- chael briefed Graham fully on their staging of Wells's car crash. Satisfied that none of them could be traced to the event, Graham dropped Michael at the Admiralty to ensure that a search began, with instructions to follow up afterward on Wells's Scottish trunk call. A quarter hour later, well before dawn, he and Denton entered the office building near St. James' Park.

He was reluctant to begin an official investigation of Wells's coconspirators until he had more solid evidence than Wells's accusations—the code book would be a start. For now, Denton could begin pulling what they had readily available on the four, and he could get his own report off to Selwyn. Grimacing at what passed for tea among the night shift, he sent Denton for a fresh pot for both of them and settled down for the rest of the predawn hours to compose a carefully coded account of the meeting and its aftermath. He decided to put off contacting Dieter, though he did mention the possibility in Selwyn's report. He wanted time to think a little more about the implications of Wells's betrayal before involving a man who, if he had not actually gone over to the enemy, was at least consorting with him.

One of the key points was that Wells had been aware of the occult connections of the attendees at the third reception. Not one man in ten thousand could have linked the eleven names on the third list in that context, especially with the other two

lists as blinds. But Wells had—or had help from someone like
Dieter. In any case, Wells had been well briefed, whether by
Dieter or some other master occultist, and had certainly con-
veyed his observations to his British controls in his call to
Scotland.

As a result, Wells's Thulist superiors in Germany almost
certainly knew that the Duke of Clarence had hosted a meeting
of many of his country's most powerful and influential occult
practitioners on the night of July eighteenth. Also, Wells had
undoubtedly presumed a far greater involvement on William's
part than had actually been the case—and Wells's death on
the very night of the meeting would certainly tend to confirm
the most extravagant of Thulist speculations about the King's
youngest brother.

Graham knew he had been implicated before tonight as well.
He wondered what had tipped Wells off about the Plymouth
trip. A needle mark perhaps? The headache the next morning?

If Graham were suspect because of Plymouth, then so were
almost all the rest of the Oakwood group by association. Richard and Geoffrey, son and nephew of Graham, flew the plane.
The brigadier, related to Graham and both young pilots, was
official host for the suspicious Laurelgrove meeting. If Wells
had also connected William's unexpected overnight visit to
Oakwood, only two days after returning from Plymouth, with
his sudden announcement the next day of plans to hold the
three receptions, then Alix and the rest of the Selwyn family
could also be linked to the occult conspiracy Wells undoubtedly
had seen brewing at the highest levels of British society.

That uncomfortable line of reasoning eventually brought
Graham full circle to the four associates Wells had named,
three of whom were capable of raising very embarrassing and
dangerous questions. The fourth was a smaller fish but was
protected by his association with the first three. Men of such
rank and social station could no more be rounded up and tossed
into solitary confinement to shut them up than Wells himself
could have been. Unless Graham was willing to risk a link
with Wells's death, his hands were essentially tied until he had
more tangible proof of their treason.

Partial respite came shortly before noon when Michael rang
to confirm that the number in Scotland belonged to the son of
a titled lord. Young Lord Hanfort also happened to be on

Wells's list of four. Graham had not yet received confirmation of the name from Wells's code book, but at least for this one, he decided not to wait. Within half an hour, he had concocted a plausible cover story about an anonymous informant and was briefing Ashcroft and one of his younger field agents. Ashcroft looked almost predatory as he and his partner left Graham's office.

By the time the brigadier rang, just on two o'clock, the Hanfort investigation was well under way, and Denton was making excellent headway on the three unofficial dossiers. As Graham picked up Ellis's call, Ashcroft was showing him records that suggested Hanfort's prior membership in several questionable organizations—and a background very similar to Wells, though Graham did not mention that to Ashcroft.

"Good afternoon, Wesley. How are you?" he said, signaling Ashcroft not to leave. "I can only spare you a few minutes."

"Ah." The single syllable conveyed immediate comprehension of the probable situation—that Graham was not alone and that appearances needed to be maintained. A witness would also help to establish Graham's innocence of prior knowledge of the news he was about to receive.

"Well, I'll try to make this brief, then, but I thought you'd want to know that the Duke of Clarence's aide was killed in a car crash last night. The duke wasn't with him, but he's rather upset about it, as one might imagine."

Graham let himself show surprised concern, shaking his head resignedly as he toyed with a pencil.

"I'm sorry to hear that. Wells, wasn't it? How did it happen?"

"Apparently, he missed a turn at some road works and went into a ditch," the brigadier said. "The car burned. H.R.H. had been staying out at Laurelgrove with me for a few days and sent Wells to pick up something or other from the Admiralty. When he didn't show, they rang me. We found the wreckage early this morning—a terrible thing, poor chap. Anyway, I drove H.R.H. and his valet back to the Palace a few hours ago."

"I see. How is he taking it?"

"Oh, well enough, now that the initial shock is past," the brigadier replied. "I'm in his sitting room now, helping with the funeral arrangements. Wells always fancied a burial at sea, you know."

Graham, relatively certain that Wells had fancied no such thing, had to bite at his lip to keep from smiling.

"No, I didn't know, but I'm not surprised. He was a naval officer, after all. When is the funeral?"

"Tomorrow morning at eleven at St. Paul's Cathedral, with sea burial out of Chatham in the afternoon. The boy's parents wanted to delay—the shock and all, you know—but His Royal Highness's schedule wouldn't permit if he's to attend. I don't suppose you could show up? You know how he hates these kinds of things."

"Of course. Please tell him to expect me," Graham replied, jotting the time and location on his desk calendar and making a mental note to inquire further about the parents later.

"Right. I'm certain he'll appreciate it. Incidentally, was there anyone you can think of who should be notified? Any of the boy's friends?"

Graham considered for a moment, pencil poised above the calendar. This could be a lead-in about the code book.

"Not off hand, Wesley. I didn't really know him that well. When I've occasionally had to arrange such things, I've always looked for an address book or diary and used that as the basis for notifications."

"Oh, well, we've got that, then," Ellis said easily. "It appears to be quite complete. We'll just work from that."

Graham nodded, containing a grim smile. With the code book in hand and the names confirmed, he could now start on the other three men in earnest.

"That's what I would do," he said. "Let me know if there's any way I can help, but you seem to have things under control, as always."

"Yes, well, it's always so tragic when such a young man dies," Ellis returned with a note of genuine sorrow in his voice. "I'll certainly tell His Royal Highness you offered. Listen, I do have several other calls to make this afternoon—sad, sad business, this—so I'd best ring off. If you're free this evening, why don't you join me for a bite of supper at my club, say, around eight? In fact, I thought I might invite H.R.H. to join us—take his mind off things."

Graham nodded, seizing the opportunity to offer Michael's services.

"That sounds like a fine idea, Wesley. I believe I will. Incidentally, until he can select another aide, do you think he'd like the use of one of my men? I could send Michael over later this afternoon. He's still on light duty, anyway."

"I'm sure he'd appreciate it," Ellis replied. "We can make it four for dinner, then."

After Ellis rang off, Graham sighed and scribbled Wells's name beside the time he had written on his calendar, circled it, and tossed down his pencil.

"Well, that's a nasty blow for His Royal Highness," he said to Ashcroft. "His aide was killed in a car crash last night."

"Clarence's?"

Graham nodded.

"Sorry to hear it," Ashcroft said. "I'd gathered something of the sort. I take it the duke is all right?"

"Oh, yes. Just a little shaken. Fortunately, he wasn't in the car. When Michael checks in or calls, tell him I need to see him, please."

"Of course."

"Also, I'll be gone all day tomorrow. The funeral is at St. Paul's, with sea burial out of Chatham. Are you on for the weekend, or is Basilby?"

"I am. I'll cover for you."

"Thank you. Now, where were we on young Lord Hanfort? Some club when he was up at university, wasn't it?"

Ashcroft returned to the file he had been reviewing with Graham, scooting his chair a little nearer.

"That's right. Ostensibly, it was a Teutonic study group, but we think they may have done some recruiting for the Nazi party as well. Interestingly enough, one of those other chaps you asked about was also once a member."

"Was he, now?" Graham said. As Ashcroft showed him another sheet, he scanned its contents with interest and nodded.

"I think that gives us sufficient cause to make this official, then. Let's go ahead and open files on all three of them, shall we? If my informant's suspicions about Hanfort are correct, he may well be right about other things as well."

That evening, Graham dined with the brigadier, William, and Michael and told them of the progress so far. They made

an early night of it, for all of them were still exhausted from
the night before. After the brigadier passed on the code book,
they went briefly over the logistical arrangements for the next
day. Graham was uneasy to learn that one of the pallbearers
enlisted by Wells's father was adjutant to one of their Thulist
suspects, a fairly prominent member of Parliament.

"I didn't know that when he gave me the list," William
muttered, shifting restlessly in his chair. "Can't we find some
reason to replace him?"

But they could do nothing too overt, lest they create suspicion where none yet existed. Graham did find an excuse to
pull Michael aside before they parted and warn him to be
especially wary. After that, he spent several more hours re-
checking security for the next morning, even assigning one of
his own agents to shoot high-speed photographs of all the mourners from a side gallery. He hoped there would be no need for
anything more, but he had the man armed just in case.

The funeral went off without a hitch. Dozens of friends and
acquaintances of both Wells and the prince showed up to pay
their final respects, including one of the four suspects—an
aging baronet who worked in the Ministry of Finance. But the
man did not accompany the smaller cortege that made its way
to Chatham for the burial at sea. Nor did Wells's parents accompany their son's body for the final services.

Heavy weather was brewing as the pallbearers brought
Wells's coffin aboard the minesweeper. The naval ensign draped
over it was the only splash of color against the grey-painted
decks and the even greyer sea and clouds. Thunder rumbled
along the horizon all the way into the Channel, a stiff breeze
prickling everything with spray as the ship ploughed through
the swells, the temperature falling.

By the time the last words had been read by the ship's captain
and the body was committed to the deep, the weather had
worsened considerably. As the crew battened down for the run
back to port, the pallbearers and the few other mourners went
below to get warm, but William turned up the collar of his
naval greatcoat and wandered far up on the bow with Graham.
Michael lagged a little behind to see that they were not disturbed.

"Thank God that's over," William murmured, gloved hands
locked around the cable rail as he squinted into the wind. "I

hope you don't think I'm being too paranoid, but I really didn't feel like being cooped up below with that pallbearer. Do you think he's involved?"

Graham hunched down farther in his overcoat and shrugged. "It's too soon to say. I'm having everyone checked out on all four men's staffs as well as vetting all their regular acquaintances. But we mustn't start seeing Thulists under every bush. The master's affiliations don't necessarily carry over to his servants, after all. Look at Wells."

"I suppose you're right," William said with a sour grin. "I've been doing a lot of worrying about where all of this leaves me, though, since we had that talk last Thursday night."

He glanced over his shoulder, where Michael was lounging against the rail a few yards out of earshot, but there was no one closer. Most of the crew were not even in sight.

"Gray, you've said that part of your role seems to have been determined by your past lives—Drake and such. I was wondering whether I might persuade you to do some past-life regressions with *me*. I'd certainly like to find out a little more about where I'm headed."

Graham braced himself against a particularly heavy swell and held onto his hat with a gloved hand, avoiding the blue eyes. He hoped William would not pursue this. It touched too closely on that chilling conversation with Alix about past lives and sacrifices and the possible role Conwy and some of the others had ascribed to the prince at the end of the Laurelgrove meeting. Though Graham was as determined as ever that *he* should be the Victim, if it came to a choice between the two of them, he was no longer entirely certain the choice lay within his power. That uncertainty produced a very great temptation not to tell William *anything* further—to cut him off entirely from future involvement by keeping him in ignorance.

Yet ignorance was not an answer. Only knowledge was an honorable weapon with which to fight the Enemy. William was already involved, whether Graham liked it or not—though at least they could hope the assigned role would be minimal. Whatever the fates had in store, the prince deserved to face it armed with the best information available. It was his right, by blood and by birth as well as by trust, even if Graham might mistakenly have been tempted to deny it to him out of love.

"Are you sure you want to find out?" Graham asked, making

one final try to turn William aside. "I'm not sure I do. I've been worrying, too. I think you're in deep enough already."

"Deep enough for what?" William replied. "I still don't know a great deal more than when all this started. Oh, I've certainly seen and heard some strange things, but I feel like— like I'm on the outside of a sweet shop with my nose pressed against the glass. Now I'll grant you I'm not fond of all kinds of sweets, and I'm not sure I could afford the price of some of them, but several of those pieces seem to have my name on them. I think I ought to at least have a closer look—maybe even a taste."

Graham shook his head slowly, but he could not help a resigned smile. Despite all his efforts, William was being drawn closer for *something*. Graham had no choice but to give him all the help he could.

"If I said no, you'd just keep badgering me until I changed my mind, wouldn't you?"

"Yes."

"Very well, then, I'll save us both the argument. I need the energy for other things. What's your schedule like in the next week or so?"

"Full—but I won't be put off, Gray. I'll adjust to suit yours even if I have to cancel something else."

"You'd do it, too, just to spite me, wouldn't you?" Graham replied, echoing the prince's bemused nod. "Early or late in the week, then?"

"Early if possible. Tuesday would be best. Bertie has asked me to tour with him later in the week. You'll want an evening, anyway, though, won't you?"

Graham shrugged. "Tuesday it is, then."

"Fine. When and where?"

Graham smiled at the prince's enthusiasm despite his own lack of it. He wished he felt more confident that he was doing the right thing, that he was not leading one or both of them to their deaths.

"Come 'round to my flat around seven," he said. "I'll have Denny whip us up a light supper before we get started. I'll bet you didn't know he's a gourmet chef, did you?" he added, almost as an afterthought.

"Denton?"

Graham nodded distractedly and gazed out through the spray at the nearing point of Sheerness.

"Oh, I think you'll find we have all kinds of unexpected talents," he said softly.

For Graham, the intervening days continued much the same as the end of the previous week. Surveillance was discreetly extended to all four Thulists. He assigned both Grumbaugh and Basilby to back up Ashcroft's surveillance task force while he and Denton ferreted away at the even more delicate question of how Wells had managed to get security clearance for royal service without his German connections coming to light. By Monday, Graham had amassed enough evidence to transfer several lesser clerks and background investigators to nonsensitive departments for their parts in Wells's clearance, since wartime dismissals might tip his hand to their Thulist superiors prematurely. By Tuesday evening, when Graham left to meet the prince, no one had yet been able to pin down anything serious enough on the four to warrant action beyond continued surveillance and investigation.

William arrived at Graham's alone on Tuesday evening, smoking a slim cigar and carrying a bottle of vintage port under one arm, which he presented with a flourish. After a simple but elegantly prepared supper, Denton brought them coffee and the port in Graham's sitting room, accepting the royal compliments with a deferential nod before retiring to his room. William had a cigarette with his port and did not seem to notice that Graham had largely abstained. He started a little as Graham turned out a lamp on the table behind them.

"Well, I suppose we ought to settle down to work," Graham said, setting his wine glass aside as William turned to peer at him owlishly. "Why don't you take off your coat and tie and lie down? Take off your shoes, too. It helps to be as comfortable as possible, especially in the beginning."

Caught a little off balance by the abruptness of it all, William tossed off the rest of his wine in a single swallow, then wormed awkwardly out of his coat. He hesitated over the tie as Graham hung the coat neatly over the back of a chair, but then he stubbed out the last of his cigarette and yanked loose the knot, draping the tie over the coat.

"There's just no point dressing properly when I do things

with you, is there, Gray?" he muttered, making nervous conversation as he sat to remove his shoes. "In Plymouth, it was
a polo sweater and baggy trousers—and now you've got me
in shirt-sleeves and stockinged feet. You aren't conventional
about anything, are you?"

Graham smiled, defusing a little of the tension.

"I didn't think you'd come here tonight to be conventional,"
he replied, waiting until William had swung his legs up on the
couch to cover his feet with a tartan lap rug. "Just lie back and
make yourself comfortable. Put a pillow under your head if
you like. There's nothing particularly complicated about getting
started. As soon as you're settled, close your eyes and take a
few nice deep breaths to relax."

As William adjusted his pillow and settled down, Graham
pulled a straight-backed chair closer to William's head and sat,
reaching across to touch his forehead gently as soon as the
prince's eyes closed.

"Let go like you did before. That's right. Another deep
breath, in . . . and out. Good."

All of William's previous nervousness and tension seemed
to melt away as he let himself sink into trance. Graham watched
him for several seconds, considering various strategies, and
decided that a little reinforcement and practice would be good
for both of them. Excursions into past lives could be unsettling
enough, the first few times, without asking for something odd
to happen. Already he dreaded what William might recall.

"Before we try anything more advanced, I thought we might
work our way up by talking a little about hypnosis in general,"
he said conversationally. "Doing it with you already in trance
helps take the edge off any nervousness. You can open your
eyes now if you want to, though you'll remain in trance."

As William's eyes slowly opened, Graham leaned back in
his chair and smiled. There was surprise in the prince's slightly
unfocused gaze. He clearly had not expected that they would
jump right into the night's work this way, and Graham deliberately had not warned him.

"Are you comfortable?" Graham asked.

"Yes."

"Are you aware that you're in a fairly deep trance?"

William blinked sheepishly. "Am I? I still keep thinking I
should feel sleepy or groggy or something."

"I thought you'd agreed never to doubt me again," Graham said with an easy grin. "Relax for just a minute. I'll be right back."

The pungent smell of medicinal alcohol accompanied Graham when he returned, but its source was hidden casually in his left hand. William wrinkled his nose in question, but he could not quite seem to muster enough energy to ask about it.

"This is just for a little demonstration of the power of your mind," Graham said, answering the unasked question as he sat and moved William's right arm along his side, where he could not see it. "As I stroke your hand with my fingertips, I want you to feel all sensation going out of it. It's becoming completely insensitive to pain—numb and cold, as if you'd plunged it to the wrist in a bucket of ice and held it there for a minute or two. Can you feel that?" he asked, pinching up a fold of skin on the back of the hand, out of William's line of vision. "I'm pinching rather hard."

William shook his head, looking vaguely puzzled.

"No."

"Good. You'll continue to feel nothing. Close your eyes now, and I'll show you something else."

As William obeyed, Graham swabbed the web of skin at the base of the prince's thumb and forefinger with the wad of alcohol-soaked cotton he had hidden in his hand, then gave another wipe to the fine hypodermic needle he had also brought.

"You won't feel this, either," Graham said, thrusting the needle deftly through the web of skin.

William did not even flinch.

"Very good. It's done. You can open your eyes and look at your hand now. You feel no sensation in your hand, and what you see doesn't bother you at all. That's right. Open your eyes."

As William turned his head, his eyes opened and then widened momentarily as he raised his hand and saw the needle sticking through his skin. But as he moved the hand closer to examine it, he obviously felt no discomfort.

"Do you feel anything at all?" Graham asked.

William shook his head slowly, his expression vaguely incredulous.

"You can't feel it when I do this, either," Graham said, gently wiggling the nub of the needle and watching as William did not flinch or even blink. "Nor will it bleed when I pull the needle out," he continued, suiting action to words and wiping off the puncture site again. "It's the same kind of thing I did with Michael that time in Dover: blocking pain. To a certain extent, you can also control bleeding. If you need to, you should be able to duplicate this in the future. As you saw with Michael, it can be a very useful talent."

Only two faint puncture marks were visible as William held the hand closer to his eyes again and peered at it—and no blood at all. Graham laid aside his needle and cotton, then touched the hand lightly again with his fingertips.

"You'll feel no discomfort as your hand goes back to normal now, and none in the future as it heals. Tell me, though, do you think you could have done what you just did if you hadn't been in a trance?"

"No."

"Then you'll agree that you *are* in a fairly deep trance?"

William managed a wan smile, laying his hand back on his chest. "I suppose I must be."

"Good. Close your eyes, then. When I touch your wrist lightly, I want you to go at least twice as deep as you are right now." He touched the wrist. "Are you there?"

The answer came more thickly. "Yes."

"Good. Now let's try an easy regression into your memories of childhood just so you can get the feel of what it's like to go back. You can imagine the pages of a calendar flipping backwards or a film running in reverse—whatever seems to carry you in the right direction. Why don't we start when you were a cadet at the Royal Naval College? You pick the specific time. Imagine yourself there now and tell me what you see."

After a few seconds, William's eyelids began to tremble. Briefly, Graham laid his hand across William's eyes and forehead.

"Just relax and let it flow," he whispered. "You're perfectly safe. Tell me what you see."

William's trembling subsided almost immediately, and Graham withdrew.

"I swamped the boat," William soon murmured in a voice that did not sound quite like his own.

"What boat was that?"

"A sailing dinghy."

"How did it happen?"

"Some of us were racing. A swell caught me just as I jibed around the downwind marker buoy." He frowned. "I saw some of the upperclassmen laughing."

Graham nodded sympathetically. He could remember similarly embarrassing moments in his own youth and knew how much more painful they must have been for the far more sensitive and sheltered William.

"Were you the only one to swamp?" he asked.

"No, but I'm a prince. I should have known better."

"Hmmm, perhaps. How old were you?"

"Sixteen."

"Well, these things do happen sometimes. Even princes make mistakes. Why don't you go back a little farther and tell me what else you see? Don't just remember it this time. Try to actually *be* there."

They worked in trance for nearly half an hour, William eventually recalling incidents from far back in his childhood. He relived the grief-choked winter afternoon his twin had died at Sandringham; the color and pomp of a more joyful day eight years before that when his brother David had been invested as Prince of Wales; his grandfather's funeral, the coronation of his parents; and even earlier memories from nursery days and his illness-plagued early years, though Graham did not attempt to take him back any farther this first time. After setting up a series of signals to go even deeper when they resumed, he brought William out of trance and let him talk about the experience.

"I'd forgotten how beautiful my mother looked when she left for the coronation," William mused, hands clasped behind his head as he gazed up at the ceiling. "And those silly sailor suits they made John and me wear when we heard Papa proclaimed as King at St. James' Palace. Of course, I suppose they were quite the thing for five-year-olds. Odd, what one remembers. . . ."

After a short break to stretch, William settled back on the couch again, this time much more at ease and confident. Quickly, Graham took him in and out of trance several times in rapid succession, each time pushing him deeper than the one before. By the time Graham judged him ready to try for a past life regression, William was so relaxed that he seemed to be de-

tached from his body, floating, with only Graham's hand on
his wrist to anchor him to the room. Graham started him back
slowly, but then he went by fits and starts, gradually picking
up speed.

"Look for something in your past which has meaning for
what is happening to you now, in this life," he heard Graham
say.

William felt himself tense, his hand twist around to grasp
Gray's wrist and cling with an iron grip. With that security,
he sensed himself plunging even faster, deep into a before-time
that flashed past so quickly it almost took his breath away.

Suddenly, he was in another body, looking through another
man's eyes. He opened his physical eyes, but he was not seeing
the familiar room. He was not even in a room at all.

He stood on a darkened hilltop, his Garter mantle whipping
against his ankles in a wind tangy with salt, the heavy velvet
almost black in the firelight. His hand was clasped wrist to
wrist with Gray's, but both of them wore different faces and
different names. At his elbow stood another Garter Knight,
also known in both lives, though he could not place the modern
one just now.

"Where are you, William?" a low voice asked out of limbo.

He ignored the voice, for that was not his name, and tried
to see more clearly what was going on around him. He was
masked, as was the other Garter Knight beside him, but the
people foregathered on the hillside all around knew them by
function and office, even if not by name. The garters bound
around both men's knees spoke far more eloquently than words.
More important, the assembled folk now knew Francis, flanked
by England's chancellor and her lord admiral, for what he was.
The royal sanction could not have been more firmly put unless
the Queen herself had come to the point above Plymouth Sound.

"William, try to tell me what you're seeing," came the
outside voice again.

But he jerked his head in denial, wishing the voice would
leave him alone. He had work to do, things and places to see.
Even in his slight irritation at the intrusion, he felt time ripple
again.

He closed his physical eyes, but the images still came:
kneeling before the Queen to present the gilded sword . . . the

sword set flat-bladed to the shoulders of the man whose link even now kept some part of him anchored in another time....

William knew the meaning of the garter the Queen dropped that day on the deck of the *Golden Hind*, just as he understood the role laid upon Francis when he picked it up. Like many other men at court, he and Francis had long been students of the occult. Over many a pint of good ale, the two of them had sat and talked of such things well into the night, even as he and Gray had begun to do of late, though in modern terms of cognac, coffee, and cigarettes. His lips curved upward at the memory, savoring the dual flavor of strangeness and familiarity, but he tensed as the scene began to shift again.

The images came more swiftly now, moving steadily backward in time: greeting Francis at the New Year's court earlier that year when the Queen wore the crown of emeralds that her bold captain had brought back from the New World; the day he received his own commission as captain of *her* guard; and his first appearance at court, that Twelfth Night masque nearly twenty years before when he first had caught the Queen's eye....

But there was no time to dwell on that. With a suddenness that made him gasp, he was plummeting backward again, going even deeper than he had ever been before.

William knew in some shadowed part of himself that he was not really climbing stone steps inside some vast, dim-lit cathedral, but the sensation was so real that his feet twitched under the tartan lap rug, and he shivered with the cold. The winter chill penetrated even the heavy vestments he wore. Ahead of him, carrying a processional cross, walked the young monk who had helped him vest only a few minutes before. It was dusk. Somewhere in the crypts below, voices were chanting the Office of Vespers.

The whole scene was wavering, threatening to slip away before he could read it, but he tried to hold on, sensing that it was important. The effort distracted him, though, and the next clear image he could focus on was of three armed knights approaching him by the steps, naked steel in their hands—and cold stone at his back as he faced men he knew had come to kill him.

Words were exchanged in a strangely accented language he could not quite follow, but the sense was clear enough. All of them, including himself, were following a familiar script. When the men laid hands on him, he made only token resistance, his eyes meeting those of one of the men and seeing Gray's eyes. The rest was lost in the stunning pain of that first sword blow— Gray's blow!—and utterly shattered in the ones that followed.

He clawed his way back to the present and found himself gasping for breath in Gray's arms, rolling his head wildly from side to side but not really seeing. Only gradually did Gray's voice begin to seep through to his terror.

"It's all right, Will! It's all right. Look at me! Focus on my eyes!"

"No! No eyes!" he managed to whisper.

"Then *close* your eyes," Gray commanded. "Relax. Take a deep breath and let go. It's all right. You're safe. We'll take you down and bring you up slowly. You're all right."

Still shaking, William managed to draw the ordered breath and obey. He felt relief wash over him like a wave as he sank back on the couch. Gray's hands on his shoulders helped pin him to the present. For what seemed like another lifetime, he listened to Gray's voice soothe and reassure, grounding him back to the here and now, blurring the past memories for gradual remembering, taking away the blind fear.

He was quite calm when Gray finally brought him out, feeling a little silly to have put up such a fuss. As he opened his eyes, Gray was sitting back in his chair and looking as if nothing particularly out of the ordinary had happened. Somehow William knew better.

"Feeling better now?" Gray asked.

Slowly, William drew a long, careful breath and let it out with an audible sigh.

"Yes."

"Good. Just stay where you are and don't try to get up. I'll be right back."

Very shortly, Graham returned with a tea tray laden with sandwiches and biscuits. He let William sit up then, but he would not let him stand. He poured strong, sweet tea for both of them and made William drink a cup and eat most of half a sandwich before he would allow him to talk. Graham himself managed to get down a cup of tea and tried nibbling on a biscuit, but food was out of the question. His stomach was only barely tolerating the tea, churning with a sick apprehension over what the prince had seen.

"So, do you think you have both feet firmly back on earth?" Graham asked, trying to keep his voice casual and confident.

"I was that bad, was I?"

"On the contrary. So far as I can tell, you had a devil of a regression—if you'll pardon the expression. Want to tell me about it? You weren't too talkative at the time."

William gave a derisive snort. "I do seem to remember someone nagging at me to talk. It just seemed like too much of a distraction."

"Now you know how I felt at Buckland," Graham replied, managing a wan smile. "You may recall Alix badgering me, trying to get me to stay in touch. I know from experience that it's sometimes unavoidable, but it's a little tough on the operator, who has no way to know what's going on in the subject's head. You must have been working on something very important."

"I think I was," William said slowly. "I can't seem to remember the last bit—you know, the part that was so frightening. Did you do that—make me forget?"

"Yes. If you'll start at the beginning, the rest will come back as you're ready. For that matter, you don't have to tell me about *any* of it if you don't want to," he added, though he had no idea what he was going to say if William *didn't*.

"No, I want to," William said, to Graham's intense relief. "As a matter of fact, it may help to explain a lot of what's been happening. I think I understand now why I offered you my services as a Garter Knight. I'd done it all before."

"Oh?"

"I was Hatton, Gray. I knew you when you were Drake." The prince grinned self-consciously. "Does that sound silly? I don't think I'm just making it up."

Graham pursed his lips thoughtfully, wondering whether he dared relax a little. Alix had said William might have been one of Drake's Garter Knights. If the prince had been Hatton, it would certainly explain a great deal. Nor was it difficult to check. When he had told William of Hatton's role in his own flashback of Drake and the Garter Knights, he had not given much in the way of detail. He wondered whether William could. At least it would delay the other recall.

"No, I don't think you're making it up, either, William,"

he replied. "Why don't you tell me what you saw? Where were you?"

"I was standing with you on a hilltop at night. I could smell the sea." William's eyes shifted from his and took on a faraway look. "Howard of Effingham was with us, too. He and I wore our Garter mantles—only they were a darker blue than the ones we wear today, almost black. I remember being aware of the garters buckled around our left knees and the fact that we were masked—Howard and I, not you, though everyone knew who we were. I clasped hands with you, wrist to wrist—though maybe that part was from here, because I think I remember twisting my hand around to grab your wrist."

Graham felt a chill run up his spine, for William was describing precisely what he had seen in that other flashback at Deptford, giving details Graham had not mentioned. He was sure he had never spoken of the masks.

"Go on."

"Then I was on the *Golden Hind*, watching the Queen knight you," William continued. "She asked for my sword. I understood what the garter meant, too, even though I was only captain of her guard at the time—but there was more before that. You and I used to talk together after a good meal, just as we do now—and about some of the same kinds of things, too—magic, and such."

He shook his head, passing one hand over his eyes.

"There was more about my earlier life, too: receiving my commission from the Queen—and the first time she noticed me, when I performed in a court masque at Twelfth Night. . . ."

He blinked and looked at Graham again, his eyes once more normal.

"Do you think I *was* Hatton, Gray? Did we know one another before, and that's why we've come together this way now? Is that what you started to tell me when you read my horoscope?"

Graham controlled a shiver and poured another cup of tea for each of them, busying his hands with sugar and milk while he tried to think. He was reasonably convinced of the Hatton incarnation now, and that could certainly account for everything William had done so far, but what of the future? What of the other recall, now temporarily blocked?

What of Graham's other lives besides Drake?—Tyrrel and FitzUrse, in particular. Was it possible that William also fit into those, since he fit into Drake's? Who else had William been?

"Well, I don't think there's any question that you were Hatton," he said, toying with his spoon. "The parallel has been close almost from the beginning. The relationship would even account for what happened at Buckland when I thought you were Selwyn. Incidentally, did you know that even though he and I are absolutely certain we've been linked in past lives, we've never managed to track down who we were?"

"Really?" William looked pleased. "I must be doing better than I thought, then. Maybe there *is* something to this old-line inheritance you keep mentioning."

Graham wished William had not said that, for the links Graham was worried about had precisely to do with old line inheritances, more literal than even William dreamed. He wished there were some way around it, but he knew he had to ask about the rest of William's recall. Denying it would not make it go away.

"You're doing fine," he said neutrally. "If you're up to it, how about looking at the rest of your recall, though? I'd like to know what frightened you so. Neither of us has seen anything in the Drake-Hatton relationship to account for that kind of panic."

"All right."

William sounded confident, and he did not draw away as Graham reached across to touch his wrist lightly in posthypnotic trigger, but he shivered a little as the memories came flooding back and closed his eyes. After a moment, he looked up at Graham warily.

"Do you remember?" Graham asked.

"Yes. I'm not sure what to make of it, though. I—think you were in it again, only—" He lowered his eyes in confusion. "We weren't enemies, I know that. I think we were friends, or maybe vassal and lord, but you—"

As he broke off, shaking his head, troubled, Graham had a flash of prescience and suddenly *knew* what William was going to describe.

"Why don't you take it from the beginning?" he said softly, hoping desperately that he was wrong. "Tell me the first thing you remember."

William closed his eyes. "I was a—a cleric of some sort.

I could hear voices chanting Vespers as I climbed some steps in a church or cathedral. . . ."

Instantly, Graham's own memory of the scene came flooding back, seen through the eyes of Reginald FitzUrse as William sketchily described the scene from Thomas Becket's point of view. William, not as experienced at recall, could not bring back as much detail as Graham had—and, indeed, did not even realize whom he was describing, much less the true reason for the killing—but he had been Becket. Graham was as sure of that as he was sure that *he* had been Drake and FitzUrse. Graham had never even mentioned his own FitzUrse and Becket memories to William.

He forced his own stunned suspicions aside and willed himself to listen impassively to the end of William's account. The prince was trembling by the time he finished, shaking his head in denial as he looked for reassurance that it had *not* been Graham who had slain him in that other life, already making up rationalizations to account for what he could not accept.

"Maybe I was dreaming there at the end," William ventured. "Didn't I read somewhere that one will sometimes shift from a trance into sleep? It's very late, after all, and I'm very tired. You don't think you *really* killed me in a former life, do you?"

Graham drew a cautious breath and did his best to cover his own uneasiness. He was beginning to be afraid he might have done just that, though now was hardly the time to go into details on why. For if he and William had been FitzUrse and Becket, slayer and slain in the sacred ritual, where did that put them now? He no longer doubted that they had been linked in their Drake and Hatton incarnations, but he would like to believe that only that parallel was intended in this life—one recognizing the other, to continue the sacred dance.

But if that was *all* that was intended in their current lives, then why had both of them fastened on the Becket-FitzUrse episode as well? It smacked too strongly of the Hanged Man and old Conwy's acclamation.

What of Graham's other memories of slayer and slain? Might William eventually recall those, too? Where did it end? Why did it have to start coming to a head right now, when Lammas was little more than a week away and Graham had no time to deal with it?

"Perhaps that last part *was* a dream," he finally agreed,

trying as much for himself as for William to put out of mind the potential endings he had been imagining. "Perhaps the idea of seeing your own death was too frightening to deal with, undisguised, so your mind substituted a familiar face for the unfamiliar one of death."

"But why yours?" William persisted. "God knows, if I don't trust you, Gray, whom do I trust? That just doesn't make sense."

"Well, there *are* unknown, frightening aspects of me that you don't know about," Graham replied. "All this magic—it would be unusual if you *weren't* afraid of me just a little, if only because I represent part of the unknown. That's probably all it was."

William seemed to accept that explanation. At least that was what he said. He soon hit on the similarity of his "dream" to the murder of Thomas Becket and wondered whether Graham had noticed it, but Graham was noncommittal. After another half hour or so and a glass of port apiece, Denton drove the prince home to get some sleep.

Graham did not sleep for some time after William left, however; and when he did, he dreamed that he was FitzUrse again, killing Becket—only this time the archbishop had William's face.

When he woke, in a cold sweat, he had to turn on the light and look before he could convince himself that he did not have William's blood on his hands.

CHAPTER 18

GRAHAM WAS STILL HAUNTED BY THE DREAM WHEN HE went in to his office the next morning, slightly later than usual and with a dull headache from having slept so badly. He rang William to see how he was doing but was informed that the prince was out for the day, inspecting troops with His Majesty. Graham's mental state was not improved when, just past noon, Denton handed him an envelope marked *personal and urgent*. The Yorkshire postmark was two days old, but the handwriting was almost certainly Dieter's.

"Did this just come in?" Graham asked, glancing up at Denton in surprise as he slit the envelope with a paper knife.

Denton paused in the doorway. "Yes, sir."

Graham scanned the lines penned on the stiff, single sheet, then turned it face down on his blotter and began rummaging in a desk drawer for paper and a pencil.

"Thank you, Denny. Please hold all my calls for the next hour or so."

As soon as Denton closed the door, Graham settled down to the tedious task of decoding, a part of his mind asking disturbing questions while eyes and hands made the required substitutions.

The hand was unmistakably Deiter's, signed with his sigil at the bottom, but the letter had been posted in England on the twenty-second. Dieter could not possibly be in England. Someone else must have mailed it for him, perhaps even one of

Wells's Thulists—which meant that whatever prompted the letter had occurred at least a day or two earlier than the postmark, right around the time of Wells's death.

But Graham had never contacted Dieter since the Wells affair. When he sent Selwyn's report, he had asked advice, but communications with Selwyn were often sporadic now that his flotilla was on convoy duty. Though nearly a week had passed, Graham still had received no reply. That Dieter initiated contact with Graham, apparently on his own, seemed distinctly ominous—and appeared even more so, when Graham had the clear text of the letter before him.

> IMPERATIVE WE SPEAK FACE TO FACE BEFORE ONE AUGUST STOP YOUR FRIEND IN GRAVE DANGER STOP ISAIAH FORTY THREE FOUR STOP CONFIRM YOUR AGREEMENT TO RENDEZVOUS SECOND MIDNIGHT AT BELOW COORDINATES BY SENDING SIGNAL AFTER BBC NINE NEWS ANY NIGHT AS FOLLOWS STOP WOOZLES WAIT IN THE HEFFALUMP PIT TO GOBBLE CHARMING BILLY STOP

The coordinates that followed pinpointed a very precise location off the coast of Brittany.

As Graham pulled down a copy of the Bible to look up the Isaiah reference, so many points clamored for attention that he hardly knew where to begin. Most disturbing on the face of it, besides the mere fact of a message from Dieter, were the urgency of meeting before Lammas and the phrase *Your friend in grave danger*. No matter how Graham read that, the friend had to be William. If anyone else were intended, the warning would have gone to Selwyn or Alix—not to him.

The reference to "charming Billy" seemed to be the clincher. What was the line from the old ballad? *"O where have you been, Billy-boy, Billy-boy, O where have you been, charming Billy?"* If Dieter had heard about the Wells affair, he might well ask that question. The Milne allusions to Woozles and Heffalump pits, juxtaposed with the ballad, only heightened the sense of danger.

He found the Isaiah quotation and had to read it twice to make certain he had it right. It *might* refer to Dieter himself and an offer to form an alliance, but the sense tallied all too closely with things he had already been worrying about. With

a sick churning in his gut, he wondered whether it was possible
Dieter knew:

*"Since thou wast precious in my sight, thou hast been hon-
ourable, and I have loved thee: therefore will I give men for
thee, and people for thy life."*

Graham did not waste time on intermediaries. He needed
to find out what Dieter was talking about. Within an hour, he
wheedled the location of Selwyn's convoy out of a contact at
the Admiralty and arranged to meet a flying boat at Calshot to
fly him there. He gave Denton instructions to ring William that
evening and tell him Graham had been called away unexpectedly for a few days. He was on the train to Southampton before
two and in the air by half past four.

By dusk, Graham was boarding Selwyn's destroyer from a
bobbing whaler. Selwyn was not expecting him, but he led
Graham below without a word, as if it were the most usual
thing in the world to have visitors arrive by aircraft. All around,
the ships of Selwyn's flotilla were going dark as they rigged
for night running.

"I'm going to agree to the meeting, and I want you there,"
Graham said when Selwyn had read Dieter's message. "I don't
know what he's trying to pull, but I want to have it out face
to face as soon as possible. The August first deadline suggests
that something is going to happen on Lammas besides what
we're planning, and it looks to me like William's safety is
involved. They *must* know about the Wells affair, David."

Selwyn skimmed through the decoded message again, nodding several times as he read, then sat back in his chair with
a sigh as he removed his glasses.

"I agree that it has to be investigated, but I'm afraid you're
asking a lot. Even if I could leave my ship at a time like this—"

"I don't think you understand, David. I'm going to ask
for your ship, too," Graham responded before Selwyn could
finish. "I want the clout of a British warship behind me when
I talk to Dieter, as well as your support and advice. You can
reach the coordinates by Friday—we'll say Saturday, to be
on the safe side. I'll make the arrangements with your flotilla
leader before I leave in the morning. Besides, there's no other
way to get that close to the French coast and be sure of
coming out."

"If it's a trap, you won't come out, anyway," Selwyn said

gloomily. "Dieter could have that whole sector crawling with U-boats and other unpleasant surprises by the time we get there."

"Yes, but if he's on the level, he could have it deserted, too. He doesn't know what kind of transportation I'd arrange, David. He's probably expecting a fast torpedo boat or something of that ilk."

"Yes, but wouldn't a destroyer be a prize?"

"At least it could put up a fight if there *were* a double-cross."

Selwyn dropped his head into his hands and sighed. "All right, Gray. If you can get my boss to agree, I won't argue with you. You're calling the shots now. I'd hoped I'd never have to look at Dieter again, though. If Merilee were still alive, she'd die of shame to know what he's done."

"I'm certainly not condoning his actions," Graham replied. "I don't trust him any more than you do. But there's something else you should be aware of."

"What's that?"

"There's more than one way to read that verse from Isaiah. The key idea is sacrifice. Now it's possible Dieter meant it to refer to himself—a willingness to help us, and William, even at the risk of his own life and those he's pretended to work with—but what if the verse actually refers to William himself? The subject of William as sacrifice has come up independently before."

Selwyn's face went as white and still as a waxen mask.

"What are you talking about?"

Graham told him about the FitzUrse recall and William's more recent parallel recollection of Becket.

"I haven't even mentioned that one to Alix yet," Graham concluded. "It only happened last night. After the discussion she and I had about the Hanged Man and everything, the whole thing begins to connect all too readily. I won't allow it. If anyone is going to die, it's going to be me, not William."

"If it's up to me, it isn't going to be either of you!" Selwyn retorted, but fully agreeing that they must confront Dieter.

Graham slept on a cot in Selwyn's cabin that night, for he did not wish to advertise his presence aboard ship any more than his unusual arrival already had. The next morning, Selwyn brought his ship alongside the one serving as flotilla leader,

and Graham transferred across by breeches buoy. The day was
fine but hazy enough to make it difficult to spot approaching
aircraft; the convoy spread across several square miles to the
north and west. Graham could see Selwyn's ship dropping back
to run half a mile behind and to the west as he followed a
young midshipman up to the bridge.

This destroyer's skipper was the same Royal Navy captain
who had called Graham to the Admiralty little more than a
month ago. The man lowered a pair of field glasses and turned
to raise one dark eyebrow in surprise as Graham gave formal
salute. He took his time about returning it, blue eyes noting
every detail of Graham's salt-stained battle-dress, beret, and
the black polo sweater visible at the neck, in stark contrast to
his own immaculate service dress uniform.

"So you're the mystery guest that Sunderland brought in last
evening, colonel," he said with a slight smile. "I'd wondered.
Back to your usual state of undress, I see."

"Yes, sir. I need another favor," Graham said without further prelude. "May we talk?"

Frowning a little, the man led him out of the enclosed portion
of the bridge to an open platform in front that was still in plain
sight of the bridge watch but out of casual earshot.

"I'm sorry, but I can't leave the bridge right now," the man
murmured, raising his field glasses again and scanning the
eastern horizon. "We're expecting a German raid. Can you
keep it short and sufficiently vague that we don't try the patience of my junior officers inside?"

"I'll try, sir," Graham replied. "Put briefly, if not vaguely,
I need to borrow one of your captains and his ship for the rest
of the week."

"You need to borrow a destroyer and its captain for the rest
of the week," the man repeated slowly, not lowering his glasses.
"I assume you have someone particular in mind."

"I think you know who, sir."

The man let his glasses dangle from their neck strap and
glanced at Graham sidelong, then laid both hands precisely
along the metal rail in front of them.

"One would need a very good reason for granting such a
favor," he said, looking out to sea again. "Ought one to assume
that this has to do with—ah—the matter we discussed before?"

"The same, sir. And with the man who was responsible for

having me 'out of battle-dress' that night, as I believe you put it."

The other's features stiffened, but he only continued looking out to sea. This time, Graham had the distinct impression he was no longer worrying quite so much about a German raid.

"I see," the man said after a slight pause. "Is—ah—*he* involved in this?"

"Yes, sir."

"May one ask how?" This with a slight edge of ice.

"The—ah—other thing you arranged for me, sir," Graham said cautiously, hating the necessity of having to speak in shorthand. "He was there, at his own insistence, and things have progressed since then. I didn't start out to involve him, sir."

"I should hope you didn't," the other man muttered, the blue eyes glancing at him furtively as the fingers of one hand drummed on the metal rail in consternation. "What about this—future thing, then?" he continued. "He isn't going to be involved in that, is he?"

"I'll certainly try to prevent it, sir," Graham replied carefully. "With my own life, if necessary. I mean that. I have reason to believe he's in very grave danger unless something drastic is done. I need your destroyer—and its captain—to find out whether that's possible."

"Where do you want them sent?"

Graham handed him a folded piece of paper without a word. The man studied the coordinates and timetable for several seconds before slipping them into an inner pocket.

"You know, of course, that if anything happens, he'll have acted without orders and my name will never be mentioned. Officially, I can only send him close enough to continue there under cover of darkness—and he'd jolly well better be out of there by dawn."

"We're aware of that, sir."

"Very well. I'll have the new orders cut before you leave, provided the Jerries don't keep us too busy this morning. I assume another flying boat is coming to collect you?"

"Yes, sir, sometime after two."

"Humph. We'll see."

Graham just about determined that the long silence that followed was a dismissal, but then the man laid both hands on

the rail and threw his head back to squint up at the sun, casting
a faint smile in Graham's direction before putting glasses to
the horizon again.

"Incidentally, Gray, how would you fancy having your captain and his ship sent back to flotilla HQ for a few days when
you're finished?" came the low-voiced question. "He could get
a train south from there and be home in a few hours. I believe
I might spare him until after the first if you think that might
help."

Graham closed his eyes briefly and allowed himself a faint
sigh of relief at the sheer offhandedness of it all. He had wondered how he was going to get Selwyn back to Oakwood for
the Lammas working and had more or less resigned himself to
his chief's absence until receipt of Dieter's message. Now this
remarkable man had turned all of that around with a few well-
chosen words.

"I think it might help a great deal, sir," he whispered. "And
thank you very much."

By the time Graham returned to London that night, he had
dodged several German air raids, both on the convoy and in
the Sunderland, en route home. He found Ashcroft and Basilby
working late when he checked in at his office, with no progress
to report on their elusive Thulists, so he went on to his flat
and poured himself a stiff drink before ringing William. He
was astonished to learn that the prince's day had been hardly
less eventful than his own.

"Bertie and I went to Portsmouth to inspect the ships and
barracks, and we had a gigantic air-raid warning," William told
him gleefully. "We had to wait in an underground shelter until
the 'all-clear.' The raid never did happen, but I think we must
have been a great trial to Bertie's security people. While they
were all worrying about what would happen if a bomb fell near
the King, Bertie and I were enjoying our cigarettes and making
jokes!"

William was in such good spirits as he recounted his ad-
venture, close to the action at last, that Graham could not bear
to spoil it by intimations of danger that might never materialize.
Graham shrugged off his own activities of the past thirty-six
hours with vague hints of intelligence matters that were best
not discussed over the telephone and left it at that. His impending absence over the weekend elicited no particular re-

action from William other than the remark that perhaps they might dine together sometime early the next week, since William's Friday schedule was utterly impossible.

Graham could only conclude that the prince had taken his experience of last Tuesday totally in stride and felt no urgent need to talk more about it, for which Graham was exceedingly grateful. Much relieved, he rang off to get some much-needed sleep and spent Friday catching up on the week's more general war developments.

From his own experience in Selwyn's convoy, it was clear that Channel shipping raids had increased dramatically in the past few weeks. Enemy action had escalated all along the Channel coast, with Dover being especially hard hit. In an effort to seal off the major British ports of Plymouth and Portland as well as Dover and Portsmouth, the Luftwaffe stepped up their bombing strategy all along the southeastern seaboard, with mine-laying runs night after night along the Thames and Severn estuaries in particular. RAF reconnaissance continued to note the steady buildup of ships and other materiel in French ports for a possible invasion force. Reports leaked from agents close to the German high command confirmed that plans for *Seelöwe*—Operation Sealion—were still going forward.

Graham's plans to stop *Seelöwe* were still going forward, too, though he had not counted on having to take time out to deal with Dieter. Denton drove him to Oakwood early Saturday morning to advise Alix of developments. She, in turn, assured him that everything else about Lammas was going smoothly. By three, he and Denton were airborne and headed out over the Channel to hunt for Selwyn, with a different air crew from either of Graham's two previous flights.

Finding Selwyn's ship proved more difficult than Graham had envisioned, for the weather worsened the farther out they went. Low-roiling thunder clouds churned the air and made the flying very rough. Even when they sighted the destroyer, Graham feared he and Denton might never be able to board it. He asked about the possibility of parachuting down if all else failed, but the horrified looks on the faces of the Sunderland crew answered his query.

"You'd never make it, sir, even if you managed to get clear of the aircraft," one of the flight crew told him. "You'd drown before they could pick you up."

But their intrepid Sunderland skipper finally found a hole in the weather and set them down less than a quarter mile from the ship. He was in the air again before the whaler sent to fetch his passengers was even halfway back. He circled for several minutes to see them safely aboard, then signaled, "*Ta-Ta*," with his Aldis lamp before heading west for clearer skies. Graham spared a few seconds to watch the aircraft disappear into the twilight before following Selwyn and Denton below to the captain's cabin, thinking of Richard and Geoffrey.

The next hours seemed to crawl as the ship changed course and steamed east toward her midnight rendezvous, but they entered calmer waters. While Graham and Denton ate a meal washed down with mugs of steaming cocoa, Selwyn briefed them on the procedures that would be followed for making their German contact and then left them alone to catch a little sleep. He woke them at half-past eleven, taking Denton topside with him to escort their expected guest.

Graham left the lights off and watched through a spy slot in one shielded porthole until the small, pale blur of an inflatable dinghy had come alongside and disappeared from his line of vision. After securing the porthole, he turned on the lights and paced for several minutes, thinking about the German U-boat out there and the consequences if Dieter had set them up. As the tiny clock by Selwyn's bunk chimed the quarter hour, he sat warily in Selwyn's chair, at the head of the table. Soon he heard footsteps approaching.

Graham stiffened slightly, but he did not rise as Selwyn ushered in a man of similar height and build wearing a ski mask and dark oilskins that dripped on the pale-green carpeting. The newcomer paused just inside the door to stare at Graham, to give the room a cursory inspection, then pulled off the mask and continued on into the room, shedding his outer garments as he came. Graham caught just a glimpse of Denton taking up position outside as Selwyn closed the door behind them and leaned pointedly against it, arms crossed over his chest, pale eyes unreadable beneath his peaked naval cap. Dieter ran a hand nervously over close-cropped fair hair and tried a shallow smile.

"Well, David, you didn't tell me your second-in-command had become so dour of late," he said with a slight Austrian accent, tossing his oilskins negligently on a chair and glancing back at Selwyn. "Why don't you offer me a drink and we'll sit down and discuss it like gentlemen?"

"You'll have to take that up with Gray," Selwyn replied. "In this particular operation, he's in charge. I'm only providing the meeting place."

Dieter, poised, aristocratic, and far younger looking than his fifty-plus years, raised one almost invisible eyebrow and pursed his lips.

"I see," he said after a moment. "So that's the way it's to be, is it?"

"Did you expect some other reception?" Selwyn retorted coldly.

As Dieter turned back to Graham, raising both palms in query, Graham tossed a pile of oversized photographs on the table between him and the German. Dieter's face went very still as he recognized his own image on the top print. After a few seconds, he signed and nodded, moving slowly toward the table and the chair at Graham's right.

"May I sit?" he asked, elegant hands resting lifelessly along the back of the chair.

Graham inclined his head. "If you wish."

"Thank you."

When Dieter had taken his seat, Selwyn came around and sat on Graham's other side, tossing his cap on an empty chair and unbuttoning his mac. Dieter offered a silver cigarette case around, and when refused, shrugged and lit up for himself, inhaling several long, steadying lungfuls of smoke. After a moment, he reached across and turned the top photo face down on the rest of the stack, his pale eyes touching both of them.

"I'm not proud of that," he murmured, breathing out smoke. "God knows, I'd hoped you'd realize that. It was the only way I could infiltrate Sturm."

"By killing an innocent man in cold blood?" Graham asked.

Dieter took another slow, careful pull at his cigarette and studied Graham over its top through narrowed eyes, nodding slowly as he exhaled. "That's right. The same way you undoubtedly killed the unfortunate Mr. Wells—in cold blood."

"What makes you think I had anything to do with Wells?" Graham said softly, refusing to rise to the bait. "As I heard it, Wells died in a car crash. Where did you hear otherwise?"

A grim smile flickered across Dieter's lips, but it did not

light his eyes. "Let's not play games, shall we, Graham? I
don't have all the facts because Wells never got to report what
he found out at that meeting, but I know who was supposed
to be there, and I know that your Duke of Clarence hosted it.
I also know that you have been involved up to your eye teeth
in whatever is going on. Sturm knows all of this as well. If
you're interested, I can tell you what Sturm is planning for
August first as a foil to what David's—pardon me—*your* group
is planning. I can also tell you what plans Sturm has for your
precious duke. Now, did you come here to listen to me, or did
you come to moralize and make accusations?"

If Dieter had expected a reaction out of either of them, he
was disappointed. Graham stared back unblinking for several
seconds—though it was not for want of shock—then shifted
his gaze slowly and deliberately to Selwyn, just as deliberately
back to Dieter. As he had hoped, Selwyn was not giving any
clues, either.

"Very well, we're listening."

Dieter inclined his head in mocking parody of Graham's
earlier gesture, shifting indolently in his chair.

"Thank you. I shan't belabor you with justifications that
you won't believe, anyway. Suffice it to say that I've done
what I've done for a greater good which meets my own criteria
of morality. I did not expect it to be complicated the way it
has been."

He drew at his cigarette again, searching for words.

"Your concern, however, lies with the success of what you
plan for Lammas and the fate of your Duke of Clarence," he
went on. "Because of Wells's information—whether true or
not—plus other intelligence which has been made known to
Sturm from other sources since then, Sturm believes that Clarence is behind a powerful and concerted British effort to strike
at the Führer magically on Lammas night."

"Quite apart from the fact that Clarence is not involved, one
must wonder how Sturm found out something was happening
Lammas night," Graham muttered darkly. "Wells never knew
that—but you did."

"You think I told Sturm?" Dieter blew smoke derisively.
"My dear fellow, it's the next major Sabbat. Everyone knows
that. You must admit there was a certain urgency about your
duke's little meetings—only a week's advance notice for royal

invitations? Given the third guest list, what other conclusion was possible?"

He smiled. "On the other hand, who would have thought it possible that your Clarence would be behind such a thing? I, knowing what I do of your Royal Family and of your own scruples, think the entire scenario highly unlikely, but nonetheless, Sturm believes that it is so. I have not misapprised him of this notion."

"No, you're perfectly willing to let 'my Clarence' take the heat to save your own neck," Graham retorted.

"To protect my own cover for a while longer, yes. Because with my help, there is another way to handle this which could save him and incidentally accomplish both our goals.

"Which way is that?" Selwyn asked suspiciously. "And what possible goals could we have in common anymore?"

"Just this. The Führer is presently under the not inconsiderable protection of Sturm. Thanks to your very inconvenient Mr. Wells, *Magister* Sturm now expects a direct attack against the Führer on Lammas night, spearheaded by your duke—which means that Sturm will almost certainly detect and counter *any* magical working aimed at Hitler on that night, whether direct or indirect. Thus, your very well planned effort, while it might well have accomplished a great deal had it remained unanticipated, now stands little hope of going undetected—unless Sturm is given something else to think about."

"Just what kind of a 'something' did you have in mind?" Graham asked. "Yet another betrayal?"

Dieter gave a crooked little smile. "You anticipate me, colonel, though not in the way you suspect. I propose that since Sturm *expects* a direct attack, he should *receive* a direct attack—not against the Führer but an attack against *himself.* From *me.*"

"What the—"

"Please hear me out!" Dieter snapped, leaning forward to point with the butt end of his cigarette. "Only Sturm's death can ensure that the Führer is vulnerable to what the rest of Britain's enlightened ones will be working toward on Lammas night. I am not joking, David. I say 'the rest' because I must ask you of the Oakwood family to assist me if we are to be certain of killing Sturm. It is also the only way to keep your royal duke from danger," he added, looking from Selwyn to Graham hopefully.

Dieter's sheer audacity so stunned Graham for the first few seconds that he could only stare aghast. That the man could actually expect them to work with him and trust him, after consorting so deeply with the very man he now claimed ready to betray, left him speechless. Not so, Selwyn.

"Goddamn you for a bloody, rotten liar!" Selwyn muttered, so low that Graham almost could not hear him. "How in the name of all you've profaned—"

"David, David, if we start calling one another names, we are lost!" Dieter whispered, shaking his head and raising one hand in negation. "David, listen to me. You're perfectly within your rights to be outraged. I don't blame you. In defense, I can only say that the Isaiah verse I sent in my signal was sent for a reason. It was meant for your duke as well as the rest of you. I am willing to die to do this, David. It has been my intention from the beginning to give my life, if necessary, to stop Sturm."

"By torturing and murdering innocent victims?" Graham asked, angrily shoving the pile of photographs in front of Dieter again. "Ask the man you slaughtered whether he was willing to die, Dieter!"

"Sometimes sacrifices are necessary."

"Yes, *willing* sacrifices!"

"Is your duke a willing sacrifice, then?" Dieter countered. "He had better be. Because if I fail and Sturm does not die on Lammas night, your royal William will be offered up on the altar of Sturm's black intentions like a helpless lamb, both figuratively and literally, and the Führer will grow stronger on his blood!"

Before Graham realized what he was doing, he was on his feet and going for Dieter's throat, only to be pulled up short by Selwyn grabbing at one shoulder, yanking him back with a wordless cry, forcing him to sit. Dieter, shaken, settled back in his chair and stubbed out his cigarette, all taste for it gone.

Still almost rigid with rage, Graham closed his eyes and forced half a dozen deep, shuddering breaths, shaking his head as scenes of slayer and slain flashed behind his eyelids. He was still trembling when he looked up, but in control. He nodded curtly at Selwyn, for he still did not trust himself to speak to Dieter. He could almost feel the chill as Selwyn gazed across the table at his former brother-in-law.

"All right, let's hear your plan, Dieter," Selwyn said. "And it had better be good. Next time I won't be responsible for anyone's actions but my own."

Dieter nodded, toying uneasily with his cigarette case.

"Understood. I shall try to go directly to the point." He drew a deep breath and let it out. "In order to be sure of killing Sturm, I need more power than I can raise by myself. I propose a psychic bonding between myself and Graham on the Second Road to permit focusing the power of the Oakwood group on Sturm."

"Why Graham?" Selwyn asked.

"Your antipathy for me—his personal stake in what happens to Clarence. He is also your man in black, for purposes of the grand coven, is he not? It is therefore fitting that he focus the power of the group for my attack on Sturm."

"*Your* attack?" Graham began hotly. The notion of Dieter controlling the psychic link he proposed was unthinkable.

"Of course. I will be there; you will not. I know Sturm; you do not. With Oakwood's power at my command, I can turn it against Sturm when he least suspects: stop his heart, perhaps cause a stroke—any of a number of fatal possibilities."

"You could also turn it against me," Graham said.

Dieter shrugged. "If Sturm should prove too strong, *he* could turn it against you—against all of us. With the kind of link I'm asking, a backlash is always a dreaded but very real possibility."

"And the backlash might not necessarily be at Sturm's instigation," Graham persisted. "Suppose you're lying? You've lied to him, after all—or have you?"

"My dear Graham—"

"I'm not your dear anything, Dieter! I want to know what's to stop you and Sturm from turning our own power against us—augmented by whatever *he's* capable of—to destroy everyone at Oakwood. And if Oakwood goes, what about the grand coven? What about the duke?"

"What *about* them?" Dieter snapped. "Hasn't it occurred to you that Sturm, by himself, might be powerful enough to do whatever he wants *despite* anything we could do to stop him?

What must I do or say to convince you of my honest intentions? I can't undo what's already happened."

"No, you can't," Selwyn said quietly.

Shoulders slumping in defeat, Dieter sighed and lowered his eyes, turning his cigarette case several times in his hands.

"I have only one hope," he said after a moment when neither Selwyn nor Graham spoke. "I've brought a surety for my good behavior. If you were to agree, this would be Graham's link to me. It is also a good deal more, as you know."

Opening the cigarette case, Dieter pried at the back of what Graham had presumed to be an empty compartment and extracted a skein of thin scarlet cord wound loosely back and forth on itself many times, stained across one end with rusty brown. His measure: the length of cotton or silken thread laid 'round the measurements of an initiate's body at the time of reception into the old faith and sealed with his own blood as a mark of dedication to the elder gods. The measure was a profoundly powerful talisman, with arcane bindings to its owner that could be harnessed by the possessor for good or ill. This Dieter laid on the table before Graham as a pledge of his faith.

Graham stared at it for an instant in shock. His first thought had been that it could not possibly be authentic, for he could not believe Dieter would give anyone that much power over him. Before he could pick it up, however, Selwyn's hand clamped around his wrist.

"Let *me*," Selwyn whispered, his eyes fastening on Deiter's. "Alix and I took this when he and Merilee were handfasted. If it's really his, I'll know."

As Graham nodded minutely and withdrew, Selwyn extended his hand flat above the measure for several seconds and stared at Dieter, neither man wavering. Then Selwyn cupped his hand over it and closed his eyes.

For nearly a full minute, no sound intruded save the tiny clock and the muted, muffled noises of the ship outside—and then footsteps approaching hesitantly and the low buzz of voices, Denton's and someone else's. For the first time since Dieter entered, Graham thought of the U-boat lurking in the dark waters outside.

The sound roused Selwyn, too, and he stirred to brush at

his eyes with one unsteady hand, half turning his face away from the skein of scarlet cord.

"It's his," he whispered, rising to turn away completely and lean heavily on the nearby desk.

Graham stared after him for a moment, sensing the pain felt for the sister who was no more, whose essence yet remained in the measure with Dieter's, then looked back at the German. Dieter, too, looked white-faced and drained. Though Graham did not want to believe it, he was suddenly hit with the awful possibility that everything Dieter had said might be the truth.

"I hope you realize I can't give you an answer tonight," Graham said. "What you're suggesting would require a great many changes in our plans—*if* I decide you haven't been lying through your teeth. What will you do if I refuse?"

Dieter seemed to pull himself together with an effort. "Go ahead, regardless. And so will Sturm, if he isn't stopped. I only pray I can do it alone."

"Humility doesn't sit well on you, Dieter," Graham said coldly. "Perhaps it's because you've used it so often in the past as cover for something else."

"I deserve that," Dieter agreed, starting a little as Denton tapped on the door outside.

"My lord, the bridge requests me to tell you the sub is standing by."

"Thank you, sergeant," Selwyn called. "Tell them we'll be there directly."

With a laconic little smile, Dieter rose and retrieved his oilskins and began pulling them on, looking many years older than when he came in.

"Unfortunately, I can't tarry to plead with you anymore. If you decide to join me, you'll be most welcome, just as in the old days. If not—well, in either case, there's my measure to do with as you see fit. I can do nothing more."

Graham rose slowly as Dieter finished donning all but his ski mask, but when the German started to extend a hand across the table, Graham merely folded his hands behind his back and inclined his head slightly. Dieter smiled and turned his own motion into a raise of one hand in farewell.

"I'll say *auf wiedersehn* rather than good-bye, then, Graham," he said softly, following Selwyn to the door. "Perhaps, if I am very, very fortunate, I shall see you on the Second Road as an ally, come Lammas night, eh?"

When he and Selwyn had left, Graham sat back heavily with Dieter's measure on the table before him as the little clock across the room chimed one.

CHAPTER 19

GRAHAM DID NOT RETURN TO LONDON IMMEDIATELY as planned, though he sent Denton back to cover for him. He needed time to think. He did not want his decision making clouded by William's close proximity even though the prince was a prime factor in his consideration. He stayed aboard Selwyn's ship in a kind of retreat, telling Denton to expect him no later than the thirty-first. In the meantime, William was to know only that Graham was still in the field.

Graham's evaluation of William's mental state was perhaps less accurate than he believed. The prince had, indeed, managed to put things out of mind for the first few days after his session with Graham despite his own nightmares of the night itself. But by the weekend, the notion of a connection with the martyred Thomas Becket began to haunt him. Nor would the spectre of Gray's eyes in his murderer's face be exorcised.

Torn between caution and foreboding, William thought about seeking advice from the brigadier or even the Countess of Selwyn in Gray's absence, but he did not know how much Gray had told them. With Lammas but days away, he assumed they would be increasingly preoccupied. Michael, though at hand and apparently uninvolved in the actual Lammas preparations, seemed reticent about discussing anything to do with the occult, probably on Gray's orders.

William understood that. Obviously, the trained energies of the Oakwood folk must be directed toward the more important

considerations of the work to come in preference to a prince's
self-induced nightmares. Besides, William had his own rounds
of royal duties to attend to—activities that occupied his days
but rarely his nights. Increasingly, he found himself reading
late to bring on sleep, assimilating everything he could find on
Thomas Becket, unsure whether he wanted something to strike
a more familiar chord or not. He learned a great deal about the
historical circumstances of Becket the archbishop and his classic confrontation with a king, but Becket the man continued
to elude him.

The fascination would not be put aside. By Thursday morning, the day of Lammas, when William still had not heard from
Gray, he was so convinced of an affinity that he had Michael
drive him to Canterbury. He did not tell the younger man what
he planned, for he was not sure himself. All he knew was that
he wanted to visit the cathedral again, to look through new
eyes at the place where Becket had died. If Buckland and
Deptford had worked to trigger deeper memories for Gray,
perhaps Canterbury would do the same for him.

The day was cloudy and brisk but clearing as they headed
east, arriving midmorning. Though the town of Canterbury
received its share of air raids like the rest of the southeast coast,
the cathedral thus far had escaped any direct hits. It was rumored that Hitler was sparing many such historic sites so that
he might enjoy them intact when he occupied England. Besides,
German pilots were said to use the cathedral's distinctive towers
as a navigation landmark for bombing runs farther inland. Sand-
bags were stacked neatly around the lower levels of the cathedral to protect the stonework. All the stained glass not blown
out early on by nearby concussions had been taken out and
stored for safety, the now-blind windows boarded up.

The interior was quite dim as a result, but that suited William
very well. This was a private pilgrimage, and he hoped to avoid
recognition. Both he and Michael wore duffle coats to hide the
rank insignia on their uniforms, but he still felt exposed with
his cap tucked under his left arm. At least that hid the oak
leaves on the peak. Had it been proper in a church, he would
have raised his hood for further anonymity.

Fortunately, the small but steady stream of visitors seemed
more intent on the beauty of the cathedral or on prayer than
on the faces of fellow pilgrims. Even so, William kept his head

down as he and Michael walked briskly down the south aisle of the nave and up the first set of worn steps. Skirting the quire and chancel, they climbed the Pilgrims' Stairs and paused to gaze up at the tomb of the Black Prince, behind its black iron railings. This Edward had been one of the founding Knights of the Order of the Garter. Beyond his tomb, in the Trinity Chapel behind the high altar, lay the former site of Becket's shrine.

Nothing remained of the shrine, of course. The eighth King Henry had seen to that four centuries before. A placard on a stand at the rounded east end of the chapel displayed an artist's rendering of what the shrine probably had looked like at the height of its glory, but today only a difference in the tesselated pavement at their feet marked its former location. William circled around and stood for several minutes with his back against the tomb of Henry IV, nephew of the Black Prince who lay across the way, but he could divine no new insight from merely staring at the floor. He would find no answers here.

With a sigh, he slipped out of the chapel and down the other set of Pilgrims' Stairs, head ducked in thought as he led Michael along the north quire aisle. There was still the place of martyrdom. He glanced over the railing and into the transept as he went down the last set of stairs, but the area was deserted. He paused by the door that led out to the cloister—the door through which the knights had come in his misty recall—then crossed slowly to the door of a chapel that extended to the east. There was no one there, either. Words chiseled in the wall to his right declared this to be the spot where Thomas Becket, archbishop, saint, and martyr, had died on Tuesday, the twenty-ninth of December, 1170.

This was the place. Casting a surreptitious glance up the way they had come, he stooped and laid both hands flat on the floor beneath the inscription for a few seconds, Michael watching him oddly. He was not sure why he was doing it or what he was supposed to feel as a result, but he detected nothing. Dusting his palms together distractedly, he stood and beckoned Michael closer.

"Did Gray tell you anything about what we did last week?" he murmured, craning his neck to glance down a passage farther to the right that led into the undercroft.

Michael shook his head, mystified.

"No, sir."

"Well, we did a past-life regression that seemed to touch on Becket. I think I need to find out a few more things. I'm going into the chapel to see what I can do, and I'd like you to see that I'm not disturbed."

Michael looked very doubtful. "Does Colonel Graham know what you're planning, sir?"

"No. But he didn't say I shouldn't."

"With respect, sir, I doubt he said you shouldn't conjure demons, either, but one would hope you'd know better than to try. You can't possibly have a great deal of exper—"

As a young couple emerged from the crypt, lost in one another, Michael smoothly shifted into a low-voiced explanation of some feature of the carved screen separating the chapel from the transept where they stood. William glanced at them in surprise and caught back a pang of bitter grief and loneliness, for the young man's lady reminded him very much of Caroline Marie. But the two did not even seem to notice him and Michael as they passed through and out the cloister door.

Before he could pick up the thread of his earlier conversation with Michael—which was fast assuming the scope of a major disagreement, he suspected—three men in uniform wandered down from the nave and spent several minutes exclaiming quietly on Becket's place of martyrdom. As Michael continued to dissemble about architecture, keeping himself between William and the men to shield him from full view, an organist somewhere deep in the undercroft began running arpeggios up and down the scales, soon soaring into the Bach Toccata and Fugue in D Minor. The opening chords sent chills up William's spine, making him flash again on the face of the girl who looked like Caroline Marie and underlining Michael's warning. He was more subdued when he turned back to Michael again, after the men finally moved on, but more firmly resolved.

"Michael, it's true that I don't have a great deal of experience, but this is something I feel I must do. If I get into trouble, I'll simply have to trust that you can get me out. Gray has a great deal of confidence in you, so I do, too."

"I still wouldn't advise it, sir."

"Very well, I take your meaning. Now kindly do as I say. That is only just short of a command, Michael."

Before Michael could reply, William turned on his heel and entered the chapel. He regretted having to put it on those terms, but Michael had left him no choice—even though he knew the young man meant well and was very likely right. Still, as he slipped into the back row of chairs on the right, as close as he could get to the actual spot where Becket was supposed to have fallen, he was relieved to see Michael taking up a post in the doorway, leaning casually against the door frame as if he were simply contemplating the beauty of the chapel beyond.

Smiling a little, William drew up the hood of his coat and laid his head back in the corner, hands clasped loosely in his lap. With luck, if anyone did see him, they would think he was simply meditating. He only hoped that nothing would come up from yet another life. If he had multiple incarnations, like Gray, he would just as soon tackle them one at a time. Now that he knew more about Becket and his circumstances, he thought he could handle that one by itself.

He closed his eyes and let himself settle for a few seconds, trying to make his breathing slow and even, the way Gray had taught him. He took a deeper breath and let it out slowly, imagining the touch of Gray's hand on his forehead. The now-familiar sensation of detachment he had learned to associate with trance came easily, as if Gray himself had been there to direct it. That reassured him.

He let himself go deeper then, concentrating on whatever essence of Becket might still permeate the walls of the cathedral all around him—some essence of *him* with which he could make connection, if he had, indeed, been Becket. He nudged himself backward and felt a stirring, halfway between a flutter of anticipation and the sinking sensation Gray had once described to explain how *he* felt when he was slipping into deeper trance.

Then, with a twinge of vertigo, William was in that other set of memories—deeper, yet enough removed to realize that part of him remained with his body in a cathedral quite different from the one Thomas Becket had known.

In memory, he stood with his back against a column not far from where his present body sat. A young monk stood at his side bearing the great primatial cross, but Becket's eyes were only for the three knights slowly mounting the steps from the cloister door, where a shadowed fourth moved to cut him off from his men in the back of the nave.

Fools! Did they not realize he would not run? He had received the kiss of peace from Henry and assumed the sacred mantle. King and archbishop had long been one in sacrificial worth. FitzUrse knew that even if the others did not. FitzUrse was his own vassal and follower of the same path. FitzUrse would see that his suffering was no more than it must be.

His would be a good death, fulfilling the several needs. He would be a martyr for the Christians and a god incarnate for the old faith. The taking of his life would light a spiritual beacon in Christendom, but the spilling of his blood would fecundate the land. It was a role he had played before, though never in this fullness, doubly blessed for serving double needs. To shrink from his destiny was not even thinkable. . . .

"Do not try to escape, archbishop," FitzUrse called. This time, William knew he spoke in Norman French—his own tongue, the language of his birth. "Will you raise the anathema you pronounced on the King's men or no?"

As Becket shook his head, William shook his. Though the William part of him did not fully understand what was about to occur, Becket did. It was all a part of the sacred dance.

"I may not, for the sake of my office," Becket replied, speaking of more than one office.

One of the other knights took another step forward, brandishing his sword. "Do not provoke us, Thomas of London. You force us to drastic measures by your stubbornness."

"Here am I, the priest of God," Becket/William breathed, opening his empty hands. "Do what you must. I will not be moved."

As he turned his back on them, he knew what they would do. Mailed gauntlets clutched at his pallium, his vestments, twisting him around, and he knew brief anger at the presumption of the other two knights. He had chosen FitzUrse.

"No!" he protested. "Reginald, you are my man!"

He saw what he took to be an instant of reluctance in FitzUrse's eyes—in *Gray's* eyes!—as the others took other meaning from his words and hesitated, and he contrived to stumble closer into FitzUrse's grasp. Could the man not see that death's embrace was welcome in such a cause?

"FitzUrse, you pander! I am your liege! Remember your

duty!" he shouted, at the same time imploring FitzUrse with his eyes to strike and be done with it. Mortal courage and resolution could last only so long!

The knight's hoarse cry reverberated in the cathedral as he jerked Becket around, the clerical skullcap flying off with the force of the turn.

"Take him! In the King's name, strike!"

He saw the eyes no more—only Gray's sword descending. In that last instant, he managed to raise one hand to shield his sight, that battle-trained reflexes might not betray him into flinching from his fate. The first stroke stunned him past all further pain, the second following so closely that he was already dying as he sank to his knees. Neither as Becket nor as William did he feel the other blows.

An odd sense of fulfillment surfaced briefly and then was gone as awareness of Becket faded. Still, William felt a surge of vertigo as he catapulted back to waking consciousness, and his breathing was ragged. He found Michael sitting anxiously in the chair next to him when he opened his eyes. His light-headedness must have shown because Michael immediately forced his head between his knees and pulled back his hood, beginning to knead the back of his neck with both hands.

"Keep your head down for a few seconds, sir, or you're going to have God's own grandfather of a headache," Michael murmured. "You just came back a little too quickly. It happens to the best of us. Take a few deep breaths and let yourself reconnect."

William obeyed, gratefully surrendering to Michael's ministrations, and after a minute or two, the dizziness eased. At least this had been better than the time at Gray's flat. As he finally straightened cautiously, feeling no hint of the threatened headache, he staved off Michael's queries with a gesture and a reassuring shake of his head. He was all right, but he needed to sort out what he just experienced.

It had been about sacrifice, not murder, he realized now. Murder had been the outward form, but that had not been the real reason. All the political motivations for Becket's killing had been contrived as a cover-up for something else far more convoluted.

Clearest was Becket's almost joyful resignation to his fate as a Christian martyr, slain in affirmation of certain prerogatives

of his office as archbishop that could not be surrendered to any
earthly king, however close the two had been. The controversy
with Henry over that point had been long-standing and quite
expected, given the two men involved.

Less clear was the dual nature of the killing, aspects of
which overlapped quite strangely with what William thought
he understood. One part whose importance he sensed was the
ritual kiss of peace the two had exchanged in private. Both
men had attached some mystical meaning to it, but William
did not know what it was. The significance of the kiss was
doubly puzzling because William had thought, from his perusal
of historical sources, that the King's refusal to give the kiss
had been a major bone of contention leading to Becket's murder. Now it appeared that as a result of privately accepting that
kiss, Becket had also accepted some kind of sacrificial role in
Henry's place, in addition to the almost incidental role of martyr. It was all very vague, but throughout ran the thread that
the archbishop and the King were somehow interchangeable in
this context.

"Michael, is there or was there something in your religion
having to do with human sacrifice?" he whispered almost inaudibly, not sure he really wanted an answer to the question.
"Was Thomas Becket somehow involved in the old religion?"

Michael stiffened, then stood and gestured toward the doorway with his chin. "I think such matters might be better discussed in the car, sir."

Their conversation on the way back to London was guarded
at first, for Michael did not know how much the prince had
been told about the elder faiths. But William's obvious familiarity with much of the terminology soon had the young agent
talking freely about the idea of the sacred king, who was wed
to the land and whose blood must be spilled at intervals to
ensure prosperity.

"I'm not the expert Gray is, but I do know that it was on
a seven-year cycle," Michael said, picking up speed as they
left the outskirts of Faversham. "As long as the king was strong
and in good health, substitutes were sometimes ritually slain
in the king's place, though it was usually made to look like
something else. Generally, they were raised to royal rank or
the equivalent—archbishop in the case of Becket—and actually wielded the power of a king for a while."

"Like Becket being chancellor before he became arch-bishop?" William asked.

"That's right, sir. After a period of weeks, months, or even years of power, the surrogates eventually appeared to fall from grace and were charged with some capital offense, of which they were almost always innocent. Treason was a particularly convenient charge since the penalty almost always involved the shedding of blood—beheading, or else hanging, drawing, and quartering."

William grimaced, rubbing the back of his neck. He was getting a headache despite Michael's earlier attentions.

"Let's go back to Becket," he said. "Was there some kind of tie like that between him and Henry so that Becket could have been killed in place of the King?"

Covering a yawn, Michael nodded. "For sacrificial purposes, I think the King and the Archbishop of Canterbury were often interchangeable. The association goes back to the days when the king was also a priest."

"Ah, yes. Gray mentioned the remnants of that in the coronation ceremony."

"That's right, sir. Some of the elements are close to an actual ordination, I'm told. Anyway, it's pretty much accepted among our people that Becket was a substitute victim." He smiled. "It's said that William Rufus had tried to get Saint Anselm to do the same thing for *him* when he tricked him into becoming Archbishop of Canterbury, only Anselm wasn't having any of it. Maybe that's why Rufus ended up in the New Forest with an arrow in his chest instead of the archbishop—though they say he knew he'd been chosen from a very early time and was well aware of his duty when the time came to die. A willing victim was always best."

"Like Becket," William murmured. "One would almost think he sought death."

Michael shrugged. "I don't know that I'd put it that strongly, sir, but I think he probably saw it as his duty and accepted that, the same as Rufus. For that matter, Jesus fulfills all the requirements. As you may recall, he wasn't too fond of the idea of dying, either, though he did what he had to in the end."

"Let this cup pass from me . . . ," William murmured. "That's right. It's difficult for me to think of Him in this context. Who else?"

"Ummm, Cardinal Wolsey, I think—and I'm pretty sure there may have been some Anglo-Saxon examples, but I can't recall any specific—"

He broke off to yawn again, shaking his head in apology, and William caught himself yawning, too. Feeling more groggy by the second, William started to remark about how stuffy it had got. He started to crank down his window for some air when he noticed that Michael was slouching over the wheel and yawning yet again. His window control was not moving. Even as William opened his mouth to tell Michael, he saw that his companion was frowning and trying unsuccessfully to open his own window.

"What the—?"

"Can't—open—mine, either!" William managed to mumble, catching himself clumsily against the dash and trying to help steady the wheel for Michael as he gave up on the window.

But Michael was already applying the brakes and skidding the car erratically across the center line and onto the opposing shoulder, one hand fumbling at the ignition to shut off the motor.

"Got to get out!" Michael gasped, trying futilely to open first the door handle on his own side and then the window again.

William tried his door, too, but had no better luck. His vision was tunneling and blurring as he flung his shoulder repeatedly against the door panel and wrestled with the latch, and his head seemed stuffed with cotton wool, which made it impossible to think, muffling the pounding in his temples. He turned in what seemed like fighting through thick red honey to see Michael beating on the window with the butt of an automatic pistol, finally shattering the glass only after the fourth or fifth desperate blow.

Panting, Michael forced his arm and shoulder through the shards of the safety glass still clinging to the lamination and managed to open the door from the outside, nearly tumbling out on his head as it finally gave. Immediately, he lurched back to grab William by the lapels and drag him out onto the grass. Both of them lay gasping for breath for several minutes until William finally turned his head to glance at his rescuer.

"Mr. Jordan, I ordinarily find your company highly stimulating," he said with a weak grin. "I *know* it wasn't the conversation that was putting us to sleep."

Michael's answering chuckle had an edge of near hysteria to it, but then he shook his head and sobered as he sat up. "No, sir, I don't think it was. Are you all right?"

Wincing, William rolled over on his side and struggled to a sitting position with Michael's help, cradling his head in both hands as the pulse began pounding again behind his eyes.

"Damn! That headache you threatened earlier just materialized. What happened?"

"A carbon monoxide leak, I think," Michael muttered. He heaved himself to hands and knees and dragged himself over to peer under the rear of the car. "Exhaust manifold seems to be intact, but—hello, what's this?"

William twisted around painfully to look, still trying to slow his breathing and cope with his throbbing head. Michael unlocked the back door and opened it, then bent to peer underneath and on the floor of the back seat several times. After a moment, he sat down cross-legged, hard, stretching to collect his weapon from the grass as he shook his head disbelievingly.

"The bloody sods must have done it while we were—begging your pardon, sir, but this was no accident! Take a look for yourself. . . ."

As his voice trailed off, William mustered enough energy to crawl closer and look where Michael pointed. Extending from the exhaust and back up into the passenger compartment in the back seat was a length of one-inch black rubber hose.

CHAPTER 20

THE ODDLY PARKED DAIMLER ATTRACTED A FAIR AMOUNT of attention in the next quarter hour. Several drivers slowed to eye them curiously, a few even stopping to offer assistance, but Michael politely but firmly declined all aid as he and the prince worked to make the car safe to drive again. If the tampering had been done in Canterbury, as was almost a certainty, then someone must have followed them there from London, for no one had known of their destination beforehand besides themselves. They might have been under surveillance for some time—and could still be. The perpetrators might well try again.

"Thank you, no," Michael said as yet another would-be Good Samaritan pulled alongside. "If you'd be so good as to send the first police constable you see—Yes, thank you."

As the car drove away, William peered over Michael's shoulder to watch him blocking up the hole in the floorboards.

"I'll bet this was a retaliation for Wells," he muttered dismally. "Gray was worried something like this might happen."

Michael finished with the hole and tossed the length of hose under the driver's seat.

"I suspect you're right, sir. On the other hand, this is wartime. Maybe some Nazi thought he'd strike a blow for the fatherland by doing in a member of the Royal Family. For that matter, there's always the odd maniac who feels compelled to kill someone with a royal title."

Further speculation was cut short as a black police Wolseley pulled up and two elderly constables climbed out. A second car was not far behind. Once the officers recognized William, there was no question of keeping the sabotage attempt from official notice. The smashed glass in the driver's window spoke for itself, as did the still-jammed door locks and the obvious shakiness of the prince and his bodyguard. The hose and the plugged hole clinched it. The constables knew their duty to their royalty even though both victims insisted they were fine. More reinforcements arrived before William could insist otherwise.

By the time the official uproars subsided, several hours had passed. The prince and Michael were whisked to the nearest hospital for medical evaluation, and Scotland Yard took a report and towed away the Daimler for further investigation. A Palace liaison officer was also notified of the incident, all over William's objections. Had the King and Queen not been away from London, more stringent measures might have been imposed.

As it was, William had to threaten a royal scene to prevent the doctors from keeping him and Michael overnight for observation. An offer of 'round-the-clock detective protection from the Yard was less emotionally but no less firmly declined. As a compromise, William and Michael spent half an hour flushing out their lungs with oxygen, assuring the hospital staff that they would see a Palace physician when they got back to London, and then let the Yard's chief inspector drive them back to the Palace, since they had no other transportation, anyway. A royal surgeon was waiting for them in William's quarters. After admonishing them to get a good night's sleep and maintain a relaxed schedule for the next few days—advice that made both men laugh—the doctor at last gave them a clean bill of health and departed. It was nearly four by the time they could start trying to track down Graham.

But Graham was not immediately reachable. He had tried several times that day himself to contact William without success. The train he and Selwyn had taken south from Humberside the morning before had been crowded and slow; both of them had spent most of the trip sitting in the aisle. By the time Denton collected them at Victoria Station, it was after midnight and far too late to ring the Palace, and Graham was far too exhausted to deal with William's inevitable questions, anyway.

While Denton drove Selwyn on to Oakwood, Graham spent a fruitless few hours in the office trying to catch up on a little of what had gone on in his absence, then gave it up as a lost cause until he had gotten some rest and went home to bed.

He did not sleep immediately. When he finally did drop off, he dreamed variations on the same nightmarish images of the past week. In the one he remembered most vividly, he and William were galloping lightheartedly in Windsor Great Park— only suddenly their clothes were wrong, and Graham carried a longbow. All at once, Graham drew the bow and loosed an arrow into William's breast.

He woke gasping, looking for blood on his hands as he had so many nights in the past, but of course there was none. At least when he finally fell asleep again, the dreams did not return.

Despite instructions to the contrary, Denton let him sleep in on Lammas morning—he had his own instructions from the Earl of Selwyn. As a consequence, by the time Graham got back to the office at eleven o'clock—in sour temper despite the fact that he knew he had needed the rest—William had already left for the day. No, he had not gone on any official engagement, the prince's secretary informed Graham, but Capt. Jordan had been in attendance.

Their intentions were unguessable after so long a time without contact, so Graham gave up on William for the moment, trying to put both him and Lammas out of mind while he settled down once more to the business of catching up. In the days of solitude and soul searching with Selwyn, he still had not reached a decision about tonight, though he carried Dieter's measure in a breast pocket.

Some of the war developments he could have deduced from news that filtered through to Selwyn's ship en route to port. The Dover destroyer flotilla had lost three of its number in the past five days, along with eight war-laden merchantmen, and had finally been ordered to Portsmouth for greater safety. Desultory bombing raids over much of the southern half of the country had probed far inland, as seemed to fit an increasing pattern—though so far, the Germans had assiduously avoided London.

In addition, clear weather the night before permitted German mine-laying runs along much of the east coast from Dover to

Tyneside, once more endangering shipping. Long-range weather forecasts were predicting more of the same—which was good news for Richard and Geoffrey, flying in from Pembroke Docks for tonight's working, but also good for the Germans. Against the Luftwaffe's losses of five planes the day before, Fighter Command had lost three—a far worse than average score. Even as Graham read, a report came in of another convoy attacked off Dover and more planes shot down.

The day continued on the note set early on, the capper a cipher translation that Grumbaugh handed him just as he was heading out the door for Oakwood at midafternoon. Hitler's latest directive on the proposed invasion had come through only minutes before. Indirectly, it underlined the reason for everything now in progress.

> *The German Air Force will use all available means to destroy the British Air Force as soon as possible. Attacks will be directed primarily against the flying units, ground organization, and supply installations of the Royal Air Force, and, further, against the air armaments industry, including factories producing anti-aircraft equipment.*

There was more, but Graham had no stomach to read it just then. Torn by the double dilemma of trying to stop the invasion and protect William and not knowing whether refusing Dieter would help or hinder either effort, he stuffed the copy in his pocket and stalked out of the office for the night. He could feel the tension tightening in his gut all the way to Oakwood.

"This only makes it clearer in my mind that tonight's working *has* to succeed," he told Alix and the brigadier bleakly as Selwyn read through the new directive for himself. "But it isn't *going* to succeed if I make the wrong decision. I've been agonizing over it for days—just ask David. It still boils down to one ultimate question: is Dieter telling the truth?"

"What are the options as you see them?" the brigadier asked. "David has told us about Dieter's proposition. How many choices do we have?"

Graham sighed and laid both hands flat on the table in front of him, studying their backs. He had rehearsed the different combinations in his mind so often in the past few days that he hardly had to think about the words.

"One: if Dieter's lying about wanting to work with us and we join him, there's an awfully good chance that by the time I know that for sure, it will be too late to pull out in time. If I absorb the backlash, I can *probably* keep him from getting through to you right then—which would at least give you time to prepare—and I might even be able to deflect some of the attack back on him, but I may not survive it myself. I could accept that if it meant you and William would be safe, but with me dead, Dieter and Sturm could regroup and still make a try for you. I have no way of even guessing what their combined strength might be."

"Well, I can't say I fancy that option," Alix murmured. "Suppose we *don't* join him?"

Graham shrugged. "Two: if he's lying and we *don't* join him, there obviously can't be a backlash problem—but he and Sturm will probably launch a direct attack on us, anyway—or on William, which frankly terrifies me even more. Dieter hinted that Sturm has definite plans for William, but he either didn't know or simply wouldn't say what those plans are. In any case, I'm afraid we have to face the fact that an attack of some sort may occur whether Dieter is lying or not."

"And if he's telling the truth?" the brigadier asked.

"Three: if he's telling the *truth* and we try to help him, we're deliberately pitting ourselves against a master black magician who is even farther out of our league than Dieter himself— maybe even more powerful than Hitler, for all we know. Sturm is supposed to be Hitler's protector, after all. But at least we'd know what we were getting into; we wouldn't be taken by surprise. If we lose, it's an honest defeat; and if we win, then William is safe, and what is even more important, what the grand coven is going to do tonight has a reasonable chance of succeeding."

He rocked his chair onto its back legs and glanced at the ceiling. "Option four has almost the same result as if he were lying. If he's telling the truth and we *don't* help him, he may not be able to stop Sturm by himself, and we may *still* have to counter a direct attack from Sturm. Again, William is in danger. I don't like any of those choices—and there are no others."

"What about William?" Alix asked after a moment. "David says you haven't even told him what's going on."

Graham shook his head. "It was pointless to tell him anything before I left. Even we had no idea it would get this bad. Now that we know—well, I don't know if he could handle it or not, Alix. I certainly don't know if *I* can be unbiased where he's concerned. That's one of the reasons I stayed at sea with David. I needed time to work out all the angles without worrying about him getting any odd notions. David, you told them about his Becket recall, didn't you?"

"Yes."

"Well, it goes a litttte farther than I told even you," he said, letting his chair down on all four legs with a thump. "Alix, I'm terrified that no matter *what* I do, I'm going to kill him! I even dream about it! I'm FitzUrse to his Becket—or I'm *myself*, which is far worse. When I wake up, I have to look to be sure I don't really have his blood on my hands!"

"Don't let your fears get out of hand," Alix answered sharply. "You're dwelling too much on the past. Just because you fear, it doesn't make you his slayer in *this* life."

"You haven't had to live with my nightmares the past week, Alix. How else can you read it? The Drake and Hatton lives were certainly a direct parallel, and the cards—you yourself said that the Hanged Man was a literal card of sacrifice. Why else are both of us remembering FitzUrse and Becket now if they don't have also some bearing on the present? FitzUrse isn't the only slayer I've been, you know. I've been Walter Tyrrel and a monk named John. Who else has *he* been?"

"I'm not sure we've yet proven that he's been *anyone* besides himself," Ellis replied, aromatic smoke wreathing his head as he puffed calmly on his pipe. "It's entirely possible—probable, in fact—that both you and William have simply been projecting your own fears for one another on your various regressions. You know it happens, Gray. You even told him so, when you gave him a reason he saw your face on his killer. It was a perfectly logical explanation, too. But he's not the only one who's been afraid of the unknown. You've been anxious about involving him in the old ways—as well you should have been—and your anxiety has started to color your own fears. That's only natural, but you mustn't let it interfere with your functioning."

"Don't you think I've tried to tell myself that?" Graham whispered.

"I'm sure you have," said Ellis. "But let's look more closely at an example which you yourself mentioned. The Drake-Hatton relationship certainly was not one of slayer and slain—if it ever even existed outside of William's wishful thinking, which is not at all certain. You did tell him quite a lot about the background of that situation before you did the regression and he 'remembered' being Hatton—perhaps more than you recall. He also could have read a lot and simply neglected to mention it. He wanted very badly to be of help, after all. Remember how moved he was after being acclaimed at the meeting?"

"Yes, and at least a few of them acclaimed him as a royal substitute," Graham pointed out. "That's only one step away from a substitute victim."

"It is if that's what was *meant*," Ellis said softly, "but we don't know that."

Graham sighed heavily and tried to tell himself he believed it, much preferring Ellis's explanation to his own, but the dull dread was still there.

"I suppose you could be right," he said after a moment. "Maybe I *have* been blowing things all out of proportion. I *want* to believe you. However, that still doesn't remove the threat from Sturm. You must admit, *that* isn't a figment of my imagination."

"No, it isn't," Alix said, shifting uncomfortably in her chair. "Where is William now, by the way?"

Despite an earlier resolution not to take out his own frustration on the others, Graham found himself glancing at Selwyn resentfully.

"That's a good question. Since someone allowed me to sleep too late this morning, he'd already gone off with your son by the time I could ring him to check in. I'm sorry, David. It just really started the day out badly."

"I don't think we have time to start blaming one another for anything, Gray," Alix replied sharply, glancing at her husband to cut off any argument on his part. "They knew how important tonight was even without Dieter's complication. Where do you suppose they might have gone?"

"I haven't the foggiest notion."

"No official function?" the brigadier asked.

"Not that his secretary knew about."

"Well, he was supposed to end up at the Garter Chapel for this evening," Selwyn said. "Maybe Michael's driven him— though Michael should have been here by now," he added, glancing at his watch.

"Maybe Michael ought to stay there with him, then," Graham said wistfully, folding his hands and leaning his chin on them. "The more I think about it, now that we *do* have the Dieter complication, the less I like the idea of him being alone tonight. And I *certainly* don't want him here."

"Well, I don't see how Michael can be both places at once," Alix said, "and we're already short a full complement at this end. Don't you think William would be safe enough by himself at Windsor?"

As Graham waggled one palm in a yea-nay gesture, the brigadier disengaged from his pipe and blew a smoke ring ceilingward.

"Oh, it's probably as safe a place as any, as far as places go, Alix. Anywhere that's been used for six centuries by an order as powerful as the Garter has to have built up a certain amount of protective energy for its members. However, I think I have to agree with Gray that I'd feel better if I knew there were someone there with him who knew what they were doing."

Selwyn was called to the phone while they continued the debate, but he reappeared almost immediately with a shocked, incredulous expression on his face.

"You'd better take it, Gray," he said in an oddly strained voice. "Everyone is all right, but that's Michael on the line. Someone tried to kill the prince earlier this afternoon."

Graham never remembered how he got to the phone. One decision, at least, had been made for him. When he heard William's guarded account of his and Michael's close call, he got Michael back on the line and told him to go with the prince to Windsor and stay there. It had not been necessary for either of the younger men to mention who they thought responsible. As soon as the two rang off, Graham rang Denton to order the roundup of all four of their Thulist suspects for overnight detention and questioning.

It did not occur to him until he was back in the library telling the others what he knew that while it was almost certainly a

Thulist attempt to kill William, it was not necessarily a mere retaliation for Wells's death. Even then, it took the brigadier's comment to trigger another possible motive.

"You know, it's a trifle odd that William should have picked today to go to Canterbury," Ellis said, sucking thoughtfully at his pipe. "Whatever else it may be, Canterbury is and has long been a place of sacrifice. Christian sacrifice continues there daily, as symbolized by the Eucharist—and regardless of our previous discussion about parallels, we all do know what happened to Thomas Becket there, don't we, Gray?"

Graham, who still had not unwound from the initial shock of Selwyn's summons to the phone, felt a hard lump of dread congeal in his chest.

"Are you saying William went there because of the Becket-FritzUrse connection?" he asked. "Do you think he *knows*?"

"Hmmm, I'm not sure I'm ready to speculate about *why* he went there," Ellis replied. "It was very convenient for *someone*, however. In case anyone has forgotten, Lammas is one of the four traditional days of sacrifice in many traditions. Some would say it was one of the two."

"What are you driving at?" Selwyn muttered.

"Well, we have a very important working scheduled for tonight. We know that others across the Channel have similar plans—and they think William is behind ours. What if today's little episode with the car wasn't a Thulist revenge on Wells at all but an attempted sacrifice to seal the success of *their* night's venture? We know that human sacrifice is part of their stock in trade—and they don't care whether the victim is willing or not."

With a groan, Graham buried his face in his hands, only dimly aware of Alix slipping an arm around his shoulder in comfort. If Ellis were right, there remained only one thing for Graham to do, but the actual recognition of that fact left him cold and desolate.

"You've presented a very frightening theory," he heard Selwyn say. "Would you care to elaborate?"

"No, but I will. If the Thulists *did* believe a sacrifice necessary to ensure the success of their working against us, who better than the leader of the opposition? It would also eliminate his supposed strength from our complement."

"I'll agree with that last," Alix spoke up beside him, "but why do you think it was an attempt at a sacrifice?"

"Aside from the day, the method was right."

"Carbon monoxide poisoning?" Selwyn asked with a note of disbelief.

"No, asphyxiation. It was the next most acceptable manner of slaying after bloodshed and burning. Hanging was the usual form, but we know that sacrificial victims were also smothered with pillows, strangled, and drowned. It's the effect that's important, ritually speaking. The end result is all the same."

"Well, the end result they're going to get isn't going to be the one they were after," Graham said, raising his head to look at them, "because William isn't going to be the sacrifice—I am. And it will be on *my* terms, for *our* purposes—not theirs."

As they stared back at him, no one apparently willing to be the first to try to dissuade him, Graham drew himself up and let out a heavy sigh.

"Look. We've been avoiding this question for weeks even though we've talked from the beginning about the possibliity of a sacrifice. The past-life parallels have nothing to do with that. I accepted the possibility when I took over from you, David. I did *not* accept the possibility that William might somehow get substituted in my place."

"No one's saying that he should be," Selwyn objected.

"The Thulists are. It also seems to me that the potential has been building all along, whether we were thinking about it or not—perhaps because we *weren't* thinking seriously about the possibility that *I* might have to rise to the occasion.

"Well, we can't avoid addressing the question any longer. It's clear that *someone* is being set up to be a sacrifice— William, if the Thulists have anything to say about it. I don't accept that. Nor will I be FitzUrse to his Becket this time around. I've been the slayer before, but I've also been the slain—and that's the way it's going to be tonight if anyone's going to take that role."

Alix drew back to stare at him. "Do you honestly see that as the only option?"

"I do. I'm going to work with Dieter, Alix. I've already told you how I see my chances in that regard, so the rest of you are free to join me or not, as you choose. If he's lying, I intend to rebound every ounce of power I can muster back onto him. I don't expect I'll survive—but he won't, either. If he's telling the truth, then one or both of us *may* live through it. If we're lucky, we may even take out Sturm. In either case, it's the best chance I can give William—and the best chance for the grand coven to get through to Hitler, which is what tonight was all about in the first place, in case anyone had forgotten."

Stunned and sobered by Graham's cold recounting, they had no argument to offer. Nor would they even consider leaving him to fight his battle alone. After discussing specifics of the link Graham would make with Dieter, they called in the three younger members of the group, and Alix told them of the change in focus for the night's work. She did not dwell on the particular danger to Graham or even mention that William was a consideration.

Richard seemed to sense something left unsaid even though Geoffrey and Audrey took the news in stride. When Alix suggested that everyone retire for an hour before supper, he lingered until only his father and grandfather were left in the room. Ellis, seeing the look on Richard's face, wisely bowed out, closing the heavy door behind him.

"We haven't been told the whole story, have we?" Richard said softly, searching his father's eyes.

Graham sighed. He had not realized that this would be one of the hardest tasks of all.

"It isn't really anything I should talk about, Richard," he finally said. "If it works—"

"But you're not sure it will, are you?" Richard breathed. "And it isn't just you." He paused. "Is the prince in danger?"

Graham bowed his head, unable to lie to his son any more than he would have been able to lie to William.

"Terrible danger, Richard," he whispered, "and it's partially my fault."

As he looked up again, Richard was staring at him in disbelief, the hazel eyes stunned. His son's lips parted several times as if starting to speak but deciding against it. Then Richard came close enough to gently lay his hand on his father's forearm.

"Let me help."

Graham's tight-leashed control broke at that. With a stifled groan, he caught the boy to him in a fierce embrace, burying his face against the blue-uniformed shoulder as his body shook with dry, soundless sobs. Richard held him tightly in return, not saying anything, his hands making awkward little patting motions, touching his father's hair and stroking it uncertainly as Graham had done for him so often in years long past, waiting until the emotion spent itself.

"I—meant what I said," Richard murmured, his voice catching in his throat as Graham regained enough presence of mind to pull back a little and look across at him dazedly. "I want to help. I know there are things you can't tell me, but I want you to know I'll be with you, whatever you have to do. I love him, too."

Still shaking a little despite the other's support, Graham drew a long, shuddering breath and nodded, forcing himself to swallow and get himself together as he looked into his son's eyes.

"Thank you," he murmured, breathing again and feeling himself untense a little more. "And thank you for staying. If I—shouldn't make it back tonight, promise you'll serve him the way I've tried to."

"Even if you *do* come back, sir," Richard whispered, tears glistening in his eyes. "I promise."

"Bless you, Richard," Graham murmured, averting his gaze, feeling awkward now that the moment was past. "You'd better go get some sleep now. It's going to be a long night."

Reluctantly, Richard left him, turning to gaze back with a wistful but proud hesitation before pulling the door closed behind him. After a few minutes, Graham went up to the room he used when he stayed at Oakwood. The brigadier was sitting in a chair on the other side of the bed, waiting for him.

"Did you tell him?" Ellis asked.

"No, but he knew. Not the details, but he knew." Graham sat wearily on the bed and pulled off his boots. "He's one hell of a kid, Wesley. I guess he must take after his grandfather."

Ellis came around to Graham's side of the bed and gently pushed him back against the pillows.

"I think he takes after his father," he said softly, "and I think you should get some sleep."

"I can't. There's too much to think about."

"You can—and I'll insist if I have to. Let me help you, Gray. Just relax and let me handle this part."

Graham did not really want to sleep, afraid of what he might dream again, but Ellis's touch was insistent and the offer of escape too tantalizing to resist. Sinking back into the pillows, he let himself plummet into deep, dreamless slumber, awakening refreshed shortly after dusk. He thought he remembered Ellis talking to him for a while, but the sense of whatever he had said was blurred—probably at Ellis's suggestion and certainly with good effect, for he was no longer haunted by active fears for William or himself even though his mind knew the dangers were no less real.

When he joined the others for a light meal, the talk was all of the details of the war and speculation about the other groups joining the work tonight. Expectation grew as darkness settled and the appointed hour approached.

CHAPTER 21

Lammas Night, 1940

THE APPOINTED HOUR APPROACHED. NOT ONLY OAKwood prepared. Outward appearances as well as the stated beliefs of the participants might differ from place to place, but the intent was always the same: the invasion must be prevented; Hitler must be stopped.

In Plymouth, men and women whose forebears danced the sacred round with Drake to stop an Armada foregathered on a wooded promontory across the sound from Devil's Point, for the old meeting place was habited now by gun emplacements and sentries. Some carried picnic baskets and blankets like any other folk on summer holiday, but one man lugged a wide, flat Irish *bodhran*, reminiscent of a larger, older drum at Buckland Abbey. Some of them sang or hummed under their breaths as they approached the ancient wood, calling soft greetings to one another as they came. Perched on a tree stump at the meeting place, a young boy piped a haunting melody on a penny whistle....

A ceremonial magician in a Yorkshire attic, aloof and solitary, stepped into a chalked circle and bowed his head in reverence, then spread his arms in the opening salute of the Qabalistic cross, summoning the forces of light to guard and guide him in his work:

"Ateh...Malkuth...Ve Geburah...Ve Gedulah...Le Olahm...Amen," he intoned as his hand traced out the ancient sign.

In a grove atop Chanctonbury Ring in Sussex, witches of

a coven old before the coming of the first Conqueror huddled around a fallen tree-trunk altar to shelter from the wind as their priestess scribed a circle around them with her athame and earthed the ritual blade with a cry. In that instant, the wind died down in that area alone, not to resume until the work was finished, the power contained and sent.

In a Gnostic Christian temple in Scotland, twelve Anglo-Catholic canons and their master prayed in preparation, fingering the seven-colored cords called quipus, whose mystery held awesome powers.

Far to the south, on the island of Anglesey, where Druid priests and priestesses had cursed the Roman invaders across the Menai Straits nearly two millenia before, white-robed contemporary Druids gathered by a ring of standing stones. At their head, their flamen held a ceremonial sword aloft by its point, proclaiming the readiness of all of them to suffer, if need be, in the cause of truth. As they processed from the ring and into the sacred grove, circling a center stone, they raised sprigs of oak and mistletoe aloft while the chief bard sang an invocation:

"Grant, O God, Thy protection; and in protection, strength; and in strength, understanding; and in understanding, knowledge; and in knowledge, the knowledge of justice. . . ."

A depression in the rock held rainwater, sacred from its source. A priestess in white linen robe and headdress dipped a pine cone by its stem and sprinkled each participant as he or she passed. Consecrated fire burned on a flat hearth near the water, sheltered from profane eyes outside their sacred site. . . .

At selected Masonic temples, aproned worshipful masters enjoined hand-picked brethren to join in prayer and meditation upon a worthy work:

"Now may the Wisdom of the Great Architect of the Universe be upon us and prosper the Work of our hands and minds upon us. . . ."

In Glastonbury—for untold centuries a seat of Britain's Mysteries—an adept known as Dion Fortune closeted herself as she had each day since the outbreak of war and went out on the Second Road to summon ancient guardians: the four great archangels towering from the sea surrounding Britain, patrolling her shores, overshadowing the land with the protection of their wings and barring the way across the water with fiery swords.

In Hampshire, near Christchurch, Dame Emma and a dozen other men and women picked their way down a stony path toward a cove on the Solent, where others already laid the kindling for a bonfire, sheltered from view by sea or air. On the cliffs above, others kept watch for the Home Guard and other regular patrols, though one of their number was a warden and had ensured that they would not be interrupted. . . .

It was nine o'clock, and the guardians of England were settling down to work in scores of places and in scores of different ways. For the next four hours, their combined abilities would build and augment one another's strengths, uniting in a commonality of will to make a madman doubt himself. It had been done before; it could be done again. As the minutes ticked by, more of them joined the growing group mind, the promise of power discernible to those who knew how to look, as it spilled onto the Second Road. . . .

At Oakwood—the source of the night's effort—Sir John Graham roused groggily from his astral scouting, confident that the work was progressing satisfactorily, and slipped a skein of scarlet silk into the pocket of his robe before going outside with the brigadier. The rest, save Selwyn, were grouped around the heavily shielded lantern that Alix had set just outside the entrance to the maze, and they made room for Graham and Ellis without speaking. The silk in Graham's pocket might have been cold iron, so heavily did it weigh on mind and soul. He was very much aware of Richard's presence in the shadows to his left.

No light showed at any window of the house. The moonless night grew steadily darker as they waited in silence, each alone with his or her own thoughts, steeling nerves and souls for what might come. Black-robed bodies were but shapes of denser dark against the variegated greys of the shrubbery, averted faces paler blurs inside cowled hoods as each meditated on the work to come.

A door opened and closed softly in the direction of the library. The muted crunch of gravel underfoot announced an approach, and then Selwyn was moving easily among them, smelling faintly of soap as he touched hands and shoulders in reassurance and made his way to Alix's side, slipping an arm around her waist.

"Sorry to keep you waiting," he said to all of them as he glanced around the circle. "In view of everything that's happened and the importance of tonight's work, I wanted to leave Jennings with instructions that were more than usually complete. Gray, I've told him not to interrupt for anything unless he checks with Denton in London first, and Denton says he should. Will that cover your department?"

Graham nodded. "It should. I've given Denny strict instructions myself."

"Very well, then. Geoffrey, have you and Richard checked all the gates?"

"All in order," came a reply from beyond the faint circle of light.

"I think," said Alix after a slight hesitation, "that we're ready to walk the maze, then. Even more than usual, let's use this time to good advantage."

Picking up the lantern, she took her husband's hand and led them slowly into the darkness between the yew hedges, the others falling in behind in customary order: first Richard and Geoffrey, then Audrey, and finally the brigadier and Graham. The dim light did not penetrate far beyond Alix herself, especially once she entered the maze, so each person laid his or her right hand on the shoulder of the person ahead for guidance, though the path was well known to all of them. Graham pulled the outer gate shut and locked it before linking with Ellis, then closed his eyes and let himself be drawn physically and psychically into the labyrinth. He tried not to think about William or what else might lie ahead.

He felt the gravel smooth and cool beneath his feet as he walked, the brush of leaves against one sleeve, sniffed the faint summer scents of jasmine, roses, and sun-warmed earth. He knew when they had passed the first internal gate by the distinctive tingle that began to build at the base of his skull as they doubled back along a series of switchbacks—a faint itch of psychic hackles stirring along his spine, familiar yet ever new.

He had first walked the maze as a very young man more than twenty years ago, but repetition had never dulled the experience. The effect defied all rational explanation, for to

most Oakwood visitors the maze was childishly simple, remarkable only in the precise beauty of its close-clipped yew
hedges. Unless the proper gates were pivoted to new positions
inside, the path among the seven-foot hedges meandered in
pleasant but unspectacular fashion until it came out before a
quite conventional Victorian gazebo.

The path they walked tonight, however, was not the one on
which visitors strolled by day. The pattern was ancient; no one
knew how old. Norman ancestors of the Jordan family had
brought the design with them from France at the time of the
Crusades, long before there had been earls of Selwyn, and cut
the original maze in turf. Hedges and the camouflage of false
paths had come with the repressive atmosphere of the Tudors
and Stuarts, the current hedges dating only from the 1800's.

But once the gates were changed, the usually simple maze
was transformed into a complex labyrinth that, when walked
with magical intent, became an analog of the sacred dance,
weaving unseen barriers to prevent the entry of outside psychic
forces and to contain those raised within them. So powerful
was the completed network of energies that often they did not
even bother to cast an additional circle at the temple, though
they would do so tonight.

The patterning intensified as they wound back and forth and
around, finally peaking and leveling out as they emerged into
the flagstoned center of the maze. The gazebo glowed very
faintly from inside, lit by three more shielded lanterns like the
one Alix carried, trellises nearly obscured by climbing roses
and ivy trailers. As Alix and Selwyn mounted the weathered
steps hand in hand, disappearing inside, Alix set her light just
inside the entrance. In silence, the rest of them waited at the
foot of the steps for the circle to be purified and cast.

Though lattice and roses permitted no clear view inside,
Graham did not need to see with his eyes to know what was
being done. He had stood in as Alix's high priest when Selwyn
was away, as had most of the other men. He could follow their
progress by memory and the faint sounds of movement within,
quite aware when they raised the circle's boundaries and invoked the guardians at the four quarters. The rites were even
more ancient than the pattern they had walked.

Shortly, Selwyn appeared at the threshold transformed, sword
in hand and a staghorned crown on his head. His lean, hard

body gleamed against the faint back light like the polished stone of classic statues, for he and Alix both had shed their robes for the opening of the temple. In that moment, Selwyn *was* the Horned God of forest and hunt, consort to the Goddess who moved into place at his side. Alix's hair tumbled to her hips from a garland of wheat and wildflowers, veiling her breasts like misty sunlight. A silver crescent moon was bound upon her brow, and in her hands she held an earthen goblet and a tuft of pine needles.

The response that rippled among those who waited was almost a physical ache of awe and joy. Dry-mouthed, Graham watched as the others began to move in turn to the top of the steps and seek admittance, drinking in the beauty and majesty of the pair and trying to put from his mind the possibility that this might be the last time he would enter such a circle. The skein of red silk weighed more heavily than ever as the others left him, one by one.

Incense drifted lightly on the chill air and mixed with the scent of roses as challenge was given and answered and the company admitted. At last, only Graham remained, to climb the four steps and pause before the threshold. The psychic silence was almost deafening, for he was truly alone between the worlds now: within the maze, yet outside the circle's womb. As the point of the god's sword pressed against his throat, steel against flesh, he could feel the power resonating through the blade from the one who challenged.

"Who comes?"

"*Din*, a friend of the Old Ones, duly sworn."

The sword dropped away, and Graham blinked as water spattered his face and hands, a shock in the growing chill of the night even though it was expected. Then he was bending to Alix's kiss and being drawn into the circle, the taste of her mouth lingering sweet and almost painful as he took his customary place. The scrape of Selwyn's sword across the threshold, closing the final breach in the circle, set up a resonance in his mind that echoed for several heartbeats like an immense, voiceless gong, leaving only a sense of peace and security as the impression faded. Even the weight of the silk in his pocket seemed lighter as he closed his eyes and waited for the human circle to be made complete.

He was barely aware of Alix and Selwyn stripping off their

ceremonial accoutrements and donning robes again behind him: Alix, quintessential priestess, woman and goddess in one; and Selwyn, strong, practical, sometimes stern, reminding him a little of what he remembered of his father—a fitting one to represent the god. Not for the first time, Graham felt awed that he should have been asked to take Selwyn's place, regardless of the peril now attendant upon that role. For it was he who would be the arbiter of tonight's working—not Selwyn or even Alix—and on his judgment could depend all of their lives, not just his own.

For a moment, all of them joined hands, eyes closed and heads thrown back, casting off the last of their outside concerns and affirming their unity. Then Alix and Selwyn together laid the sword across Graham's hands as a symbol of the shifting of authority, and Graham touched the hilt to his lips before laying it beside a cushion in the center of the floor.

He sank cross-legged onto that cushion as the others settled all around him. As he tucked his robe around his knees for warmth, he fixed the others' positions in his mind: Alix and Selwyn; Wesley, a cool reserve of calm and courage and vast experience; and lighthearted Geoffrey, whose true depth never showed except under pressure. Audrey, sometimes shy and hesitant about her abilities with Peter away at sea, for they had worked together as magical partners since childhood, but able enough alone to track Michael a few months ago. And his own Richard, who had somehow sensed without being told what the true cost of this night's work might be.

He had them join hands around him and run through a brief breathing exercise first, for it was best always to begin with the familiar when about to embark upon the unknown. Palms upturned and relaxed upon his knees, he closed his eyes and let himself center, gradually settling to a solid working depth and reaching out with his mind. He could feel the psychic links beginning to mesh around him as the group stilled and attuned to one another in the ancient, time-worn patterns. Slowly, he began reeling them in, shaping their offerings to his will, teasing their potentials into the necessary channels.

He sensed that his guidance was a little sluggish at first, but he found his stride quickly, soon nudging the proper balance and compensations into play without the need for conscious thought of how to do it. With increasing confidence, he re-

combined their individual resonances, plaiting the energies into
different configurations and getting their feel, testing, gradually
binding the bright strands into a smooth, cohesive beam, ready
for focus. He could feel the power rising in a steadily growing
cone of brightness above their heads as he stretched and con-
tracted the cords of power, trying their limits and his own
controls and searching for weaknesses. There were a few, as
he had known there must be, but with luck and a little skill he
thought he could work around them.

When all his resources had been tallied and set in the se-
quences he wanted, he withdrew enough to slip Dieter's measure from his robe and close it in his right hand. The silk felt
warm against his palm now, throbbing with power, to his
heightened senses. Slowly, so as not to jar himself physically
from the psychic detachment he had already achieved, he lay
back and stretched his legs and body out across the circle, bare
feet slipped close between Audrey and Geoffrey and his head
in Alix's lap. Her hands were cool on his temples, Ellis and
Selwyn like pure white flames guarding him to either side, the
cold of the sword blade along his left arm balancing the growing
warmth of the measure in his other hand as he closed his eyes
and eased back into full rapport.

A moment he spared for one final, fleeting thought of William and Michael, alone and unaware at Windsor, then returned
his intent to the skein of scarlet silk now resting feather light
in his flaccid hand. As he began reaching into the measure for
the psychic strands that would lead him back to Dieter, he was
aware of the potential of the group's power surrounding and
protecting him like shielding wings of sun and starlight.

William and Michael, unaware of the change of plans at
Oakwood, were only then making their way toward the Garter
Chapel. By the time they finally arrived at Windsor, answered
yet more questions about the afternoon's misadventure, and
could escape for a casual walk and a smoke inside the castle
grounds, it was already ten o'clock—far later than they had
planned.

Even then they must go warily. They chatted with several
guards as they worked their way into the lower ward, William
confiding to the last one that the day's events had made him
far too edgy to sleep and that he thought he and his aide might

stroll about the grounds for several hours. He tossed his cigarette as they moved on, both of them listening for the guard to change direction and head away before they slipped into the porch between the Albert Memorial and the east end of the chapel. The chapel door was locked, but William had a key.

They paused to listen just inside the door before locking it again, eyes and ears straining into the darkness, but nothing stirred. Pale illumination from a presence lamp inside the sanctuary spilled across a threshold ahead and to their left, but the single light source did little to dispell the dark even when their eyes adjusted. Furtively, they lit the extra candles they carried, shielding the flames with their hands as they began creeping down the north aisle on quiet rubber soles.

They parted at the transept, where William headed toward the entrance to the choir, for they had agreed that the choir, with its profound Garter associations, should be the exclusive province of the prince. As Michael receded down the nave in a faint glow of candlelight to find some other place, William moved through the choir doorway and set his candle on one of the tiles at his feet, quietly closing the doors behind him.

It was not that he did not trust Michael; nor would closing the doors prevent Michael from entering by the east end if he really wanted or needed. But William sensed that his own part in tonight's work was somehow Garter business as much as any incidental support he might conceivably give to Gray's endeavor. He had even brought his Garter, though he had only dim notions why. He could feel its metal fittings cold against one palm as he shoved his hands in his pockets and cupped the coil of it for reassurance.

With his back against the ancient doors, he let his mind rove back across the centuries of Garter history encompassed by these walls while his eyes sought newer clues in the shadows. The carved stalls to either side loomed dark and indistinct beneath their canopies and banners; the expanse of black and white floor tile extended from the pool of candlelight at his feet into the dimmer reaches of sanctuary and presence lamp guarding the high altar. He pulled the Garter from his pocket, fingering the velvet and silk and gold thoughtfully, and was reminded of what Gray had said about the Garter Knights of long ago bowing first to the King, who embodied the Living

God, and then to the Resurrected God symbolized by the light
above the altar.

He glanced at the Sovereign's stall, so close on his right
that he easily could have reached out to touch it, and he thought
about the two god-kings, living and resurrected, as he continued
to play with the Garter in his hand—the Garter Gray said was
also an emblem of magical rank.

He knelt to retrieve his candle then; but before he rose, he
paused to glance up at the Sovereign's stall again, dipping his
head in deliberate salute before moving on toward his own
place on the other side. He made a proper reverence toward
the altar before mounting the three shallow steps, but he thought
it rather interesting that he had, indeed, felt—not *compelled*
but—*inclined* to offer acknowledgment to the living king first.

He gave the idea more sober reflection as he knelt to pray,
setting his candle on the edge of the prayer desk in front of
him and laying out the Garter flat. His watch read half-past
ten. He wondered what Gray was doing.

Graham still had not made his link with Dieter, though
through a fleeting touch he sensed that the reason was benign,
having to do with the danger of Dieter's location at present,
and not with any duplicity. It was still a little while before the
German working was scheduled to begin; Dieter would not
wish to risk tipping his hand too soon. As Sturm's black lodge
gathered, it would be all too easy for one of them to catch
anything more than a very brief contact, just as Ellis had detected Wells's less adept attempt that night at Laurelgrove.

Graham pulled back and cast about more randomly for a
while, first in the direction of Germany, to see whether Dieter
was ready for him yet, and then over Britain itself, to monitor
the progress of the grand coven. The latter's cone of power
rose gradually and carefully over the island like a slowly unfolding umbrella of faint blue light, discernible only from the
Second Road and then only to those who knew exactly what
to look for—stronger each time Graham returned. As he shifted
his focus out over the land, it seemed to him that the very hills
and fields and ancient stones took up the pulse and rhythm,
shaping the power, forging the will of Britain:

You cannot come....The Channel cannot be

crossed. . . . Useless to try. . . . You will fail, you will fail. . . . You cannot come. . . . You cannot come. . . .

Heartened despite his own coming trial, Graham basked in that rhythm for a short while, even eking out a little of the Oakwood energy to assist it, though he dared not spare too much, with his own work still ahead. All too soon, it was time to narrow and extend his focus, to head once more for that other land across the water. As he began to move—and then so quickly that he almost missed it—he caught the clear, familiar beacon of the much-missed Michael, raising his own modest nexus of solitary power and offering it triumphantly to Graham's use despite the separation of miles: a shining spindle of new energy to add to the strands already issuing out of Oakwood, while his body lay curled in a tight fetal ball in a corner of a side chapel at Windsor.

Graham was able to impart only a hazy notion of their altered plans, but Michael never faltered. Gratefully, Graham bound the new energy into the existing strands to fashion an even deeper reserve of power, feeling the joy of the rest at Oakwood in an almost physical ache as they sensed Michael's presence among them.

A moment more Graham tarried before leaving Windsor, hovering protectively over the bowed figure of William at his prayers, brushing the shy, shaky tendril of the prince's concentration with a fierce affection—for this man, as much as any other reason, was why Graham went forth to do battle with the enemy tonight, whether that enemy be Dieter or those even Dieter feared.

Then, with Dieter's measure in his hand and his heart resigned to death if it would save the man kneeling at Windsor, Graham stretched his mind along the strands that led to the measure's owner, speeding back toward Germany and his destiny, where the enemy waited.

His quarry played no game of coy avoidance this time. When the contact came, Graham found himself sucked into the link so swiftly that there was no time for caution, drawn as much by his own volition as by Dieter's sheer force of will. He did not try to resist Dieter, for in case the German played them false, Graham had damped the full potential of his strength and held some in reserve. With that edge, there was a chance of getting out alive despite Dieter's incredible control.

But Dieter seemed open enough, even if the bonding wavered a little in the first few seconds as the two weighed one another and Dieter tested his control. At first, Graham could sort out only tactile impressions: the rough texture of Dieter's robe, the grit of sand beneath boots as he descended a spiraling stone stairway, the sleek chill of a newel post trailing past his fingertips as he kept circling down, down. . . .

But then, as Dieter paused before a massive entryway, catching the weight of an ill-balanced door against his palms as it started to swing shut, Graham could suddenly see through Dieter's eyes.

His vision was somewhat restricted by the mask that Dieter, like the men around him, wore over the upper part of his face. In the dim-lit hall into which Dieter now entered, Graham could sense perhaps twenty or thirty more men waiting in an unnatural silence. Sturm had told his inner circle that they would be joined by a few others tonight, the better to protect the Führer, but he had also brought them from Vogelsang to the Berghof, Hitler's own mountain eyrie in Berchtesgaden. The new location made Dieter uneasy.

The newcomers raised his hackles, too, as he eased into the room with them. Most of them wore uniforms beneath their robes, collar tabs showing the lightning runes of the SS or the silver death's heads of the *Totenkopf* Division—hard-eyed men with the short-clipped hair, lean bodies, and arrogant bearing of Hitler's crack elite. Dieter despised them. Abruptly, Graham was sure that Dieter had not been lying, at least about his affiliation with the black lodge. The German master magician, whatever his personal justification for what he had done in the past, hated these men with a vehemence that exceeded even Graham's own.

Dieter sensed Graham's new perspective at once, and in that instant, his hold on their link shifted almost imperceptibly from one of iron control to one approaching partnership, though it still was Dieter who would direct. The German now turned his attention to a brisk but thorough survey of the chamber and its inhabitants to enable Graham to get his bearings. At the same time, he probed subtly for a closer reading of the potential Graham might tap. Graham ignored the probe, concentrating instead on his own orientation, and after a moment, Dieter subsided. Graham caught a distinct impression of resigned mirth.

The chamber was much larger than Graham first had thought—long and narrow, with a barrel-vaulted ceiling nearly lost in shadow, but it had the same heavy feel of that other room in Vogelsang. The air smelled just a little stale; the red-tile floor was not quite damp beneath Dieter's boots. The walls bore the same kind of red, black, and white hangings, but they fell limply in this stillness, the lower edges weighted with a hint of condensation.

No torches guttered on these walls. Instead, squat black candles in holders as high as a man's waist formed a large circle at one end of the vaulted hall. At the center of the circle stood a chair draped with the same red, black, and white of the walls. A few of the men were already gathering around it in expectation.

At some prearranged signal that Graham did not catch, the rest of the men began to congregate inside the circle as well. He flinched with Dieter at the dark chill as they passed between the black candles and took a place in the first row of a triple ring. After a long silence, increasingly oppressive, a door opened at the other end of the hall, and all eyes turned in that direction.

The men who entered were black-robed like the rest, the first two bearing torches whose light somehow did not illuminate the masked faces inside the raised hoods. Behind them, two more half led and half carried a bound and naked figure whose superficial resemblance to William was so startling that Graham's psychic gasp almost provoked a physical reaction from Dieter. The man's arms were lashed cruelly behind his back, but he seemed not to feel the pain his bonds must surely have caused him or to notice his surroundings.

Drugged, came the reason, as Dieter caught a glimpse of the eyes.

Another man walking behind the sacrifice—for such he surely was—bore a large golden chalice with handles on either side.

Sickened, Graham flashed for an instant on the old photographs, for he knew the man's intended fate, but no reaction came from Dieter. The German's attention was locked firmly on the last two figures in the procession, shocked astonishment growing as the first two entered the circle.

One of the final men was Sturm—the same heavy-set figure, the same casual assurance of motion, the same scar extending below the mask, the same rune-carved dagger held before him as if in salute. It was the other man who caused Dieter to stiffen minutely as he watched, fear mingling with surprise even as a murmur of anticipation and awe rippled among the men surrounding them.

Black-robed and masked like Sturm but not so tall and perhaps a little more lightly built, there was no mistaking the walk, the arrogance of bearing, the mad, hypnotic glitter of the eyes, the telltale mustache that bristled below the mask.

It was the Führer himself!

CHAPTER 22

IN REFLEX HORROR, GRAHAM REBOUNDED FROM THE LINK with Dieter and slammed back into his own body, curling onto his side with a groan and gasping for breath as he struggled to sit up. His eyelids felt like lead as he fought to open them, and even when he succeeded, he kept seeing the hated image in his mind and felt the panic rising.

"What is it?" Alix whispered, seizing his shoulders with a little shake as she turned him around to face her. "Gray, what's happened? Are you all right?"

"*He's got Hitler himself in there tonight!*" Graham gasped, his voice harsh and rasping as he tried to bring her into focus. "Goddamn bloody sonofabitch!"

"Who, Dieter?" Selwyn demanded.

"No, *Sturm*! He didn't warn *anybody* in advance. God, I'm no match for Hitler! I can't take *him* on!"

Muttering under his breath, Ellis shouldered the stunned Alix aside and grabbed Graham's wrists, signaling Selwyn to support his back as he forced Graham to recline. Selwyn pulled Graham against his chest, holding him when Graham would have resisted, and Ellis released one wrist to snap his fingers repeatedly in front of Graham's face.

"Gray? Gray, look at me, damn you! Take a breath and pull yourself together!" Ellis ordered, touching him between the eyes when Graham at last tried to comply. "Again!—and once

349

more. Now, tell us exactly what you saw. We haven't much time."

With another profound heave of his chest, Graham managed to trigger the response he knew Ellis was looking for, abandoining himself to the flood of blessed calm as Ellis's direction interceded. The tension drained out of him so quickly that he was lightheaded for an instant, but at least he got a grip on his panic.

Then he was blinking dazedly and staring at the end of the measure protruding from his fist, sanity and reason restored. The dual reinforcement of Ellis and Selwyn kept him calm even as he conjured up the known but feared face. Richard was kneeling beside him, holding his left hand, and Geoffrey and Audrey also moved in closer around his feet. Graham took another deep breath as his eyes flicked across their faces.

"They're at the Berghof. Hitler's there," he said haltingly. "There must be—thirty or forty of them, all Hitler's elite—SS and such, besides Sturm's core group. They've got a—a human sacrifice who—looks like William."

As he shivered despite their support, he felt Selwyn's arms tighten around his shoulders in comfort, his chief's head resting briefly against his own.

"God, I'm sorry, Gray," Selwyn whispered. "*I* should have been the one. And even Dieter shouldn't have to face *that* alone. Give me the measure. I'll go."

The offer jolted Graham back to stark reality with a speed that left his head incredibly clear. He was almost calm as he shook his head and clutched the measure more closely to his chest, now thoroughly resigned to what he knew he had to do.

"No, you won't," he said steadily. "It's my job. We've known all along that it might come to this. And after this afternoon..." He sighed. "I'm willing. It won't be the first time. Tell him for me if I can't, Wesley."

At Ellis's nod, he glanced beyond to Richard, but before he could even speak, Richard squeezed his hand and nodded solemnly.

"I promise," Richard said.

With a grateful smile, Graham reached across to touch their joined hands, then, with Richard's help, pulled the sword up to rest in the crook of his left arm.

"We'll be with you, Gray," he heard Alix whisper. And as he turned to look at her, he saw the tears starting to well.

Slowly, he reached up his right arm and drew her down to him, heedless of Selwyn's presence behind him as their lips met. Abruptly, he knew that Selwyn had always recognized the love he felt for Alix and that it was accepted as part of that perfect bond of love and trust that bound all of them.

Thoroughly at peace now and prepared for whatever might come, Graham let himself sink into the sweet bliss of this one last kiss. He felt the power potentials surge back to their previous levels and beyond as the others settled into rapport once more and the old links fell into place, and he used the energy as a launching point to hurl him back to Dieter. He was hardly aware of hs body, slumping bonelessly back against Selwyn's, as he soared out onto the Second Road again, but he felt the sure support of all of them as he began to focus in on that other place.

William sensed nothing of what was occurring at Oakwood or in Germany. Kneeling still in his Garter stall at Windsor, the prince had spent the past half hour in fervent if fitful prayer: calling on votive patterns learned as a child, using his candle as a focus as he had seen Gray do, trying to keep his mind on visualizing a weak and vacillating Hitler. His attention kept wandering. He quickly realized that there was more than he thought to the mental discipline Gray and those like him seemed to take for granted.

He was disappointed in himself for not being able to concentrate any better than he had but realized the limits imposed by lack of experience over which he had no control. Needing a break from the unaccustomed tension, he sat back in his stall and allowed his mind to wander to more immediate and unsettling thoughts.

Events of the afternoon were the most vivid. Even dismissing the assassination attempt, disturbing enough in its own context, there was still that mind-riveting recall of Becket, at Canterbury, and William's growing perception of what the great archbishop really had been about, in addition to all the pious motives generally ascribed to him by history. Somehow it was not enough only to say that Becket, in addition to his role as martyr for the authority of the Christian church, had also been a sacred victim for the land. Something else was involved that thus far eluded him.

He understood what Michael had been trying to tell him about the essence of the king and the archbishop being linked. Nor was the periodic sacrifice of the sacred king or his substitute any longer a wholly alien concept, the way both Gray and Michael had explained it. Jesus Himself could be seen in that light, after all.

But there had been more to it than that. He knew now that *he*, as Becket, had been the victim in that other life—slain in the place of the king for the good of the land. He had welcomed it, in the end, and had gone to his death with dignity and full awareness of the many-faceted role it had been his privilege to play. But somehow it also mattered that his slayer had been Gray.

Gray. William was quite sure of that now, just as he was sure that Gray knew the Becket dream had been no dream at all but memory of past lives shared between them. Gray had been the leader of those knights in the cathedral—Reginald FitzUrse; the name came, unbidden—personally chosen by Becket to strike the first blow. That had been nearly as much a privilege and honor to FitzUrse as it had been to Becket to die in that manner. William wondered why Gray had tried to deny it. The bond between slain and slayer was an indispensable one, without which there could be no sacrifice. Even Christ could not have been delivered to His glory without His Judas. William understood now why he had always held a soft spot in his heart for the miserable disciple who had betrayed his Lord. There had *been* no betrayal. Judas, too, had been playing his part—an honored and essential, if unappreciated role. And Gray?

William sighed. If he hoped to gain any further insight without Gray to turn to, the only thing he could think to do was to try another regression. The key, he was certain, lay back in that life as Becket. He was not certain he ought to attempt two such operations in the same day or whether he could even get back to Becket again, away from Canterbury and its associations, but the only way to find out was to try. Any qualms he might have had after his difficulty grounding earlier in the day had utterly vanished in light of the even more disturbing notion of himself as sacred victim and Gray as his slayer.

Gingerly, he shifted position and got as comfortable as he could, though the straight-backed choir stalls were hardly designed for ease of body. Closing his eyes, he concentrated on his breathing for several minutes, searching for and finally finding that inner stillness he had learned to associate with trance. It was easier this time.

Going backward was more difficult, especially after his earlier experience, but by remembering Gray's words of guidance and imagining his touch drawing him deeper and more closely centered, he felt his aimless drifting shift to purpose. Abruptly, he hit on the right procedure and found himself hurtling back through time again—though his control was less than sure.

He flashed on Becket and the knight with Gray's eyes, but he could not hold either one. Even further back he went. In a surge of lightheadedness, he came to a halt in a chamber he knew he had never seen before in his current life—but again, the man seated across from him had Gray's eyes. . . .

The white-washed walls were hung with tapestries. Sunlight streamed through the open window and onto the benches where he and the man sat facing one another, the other wearing a scarlet tunic. He saw a hand he knew was his lift a jeweled goblet and hold it to the sun in salute, the gems catching the light. Then he drank deeply and held it out to his companion. The man flinched as William put the half-drained goblet in his hand.

"Drink thou of the cup. I would not have it pass," William murmured, in memory studying the man who lowered his eyes over the goblet's rim. "Canst thou not recall the good times between us? Who better should I ask to do me this last service?"

The man with Gray's eyes sighed, staring at their booted feet set toe to toe, then shook his head in resignation and drained the cup in four great gulps. When he had set it upsidedown on the bench beside him, he buried his face in his hands, his breathing harsh in the silence. William gave a sympathetic shrug and sighed, lacing his fingers between his knees.

"Let be, Wat. I know 'tis not an easy burden to accept, but thou knowest the law. For this was I chosen long ago. The cycle must be observed. The succession shall pass in orderly fashion. I have made all the arrangements. Wouldst have some other hand less loving strike the sacred blow?"

"No." The other man leaned his head against the wall and finally met William's gaze. "I recognize the honor you do me, Lord, and my hand shall not falter when the time comes. It is my mortal heart which aches, heavy in my breast, for I shall miss you. The slayer goes not with the slain."

"Alas, no."

Wistfully, William took a long, skin-wrapped bundle from the floor at their feet and laid it beside him on the seat cushion, untying the thongs with steady fingers. Inside were six new crossbow quarrels, the points keen-honed and deadly. Two of these he took out and fondled, testing the sharpness of the barbs against his thumb before holding them out to the man before him.

"To the best shot must go the finest arrows," he said softly. "I hope that two will be more than sufficient, for I have no more love of suffering than the next man. I rely on thee to do the task with dispatch. This role of God does not come easily, in its ending."

The man with Gray's eyes took the quarrels and touched callused fingertips to each point, then sighed and saluted with the shafts as if they were a sword.

"I shall not fail you, my liege. Only, let us speak no more of this until we must again."

William smiled and nodded gently, then stood and laid an arm around the other man's shoulders as he, too, stood, and the two of them headed for the door.

Everything was done. The horses were waiting. The last preparations had been made, and the stage was set. So long as neither's courage faltered at the end, all would be well. This life was cycling to its end, but the ending would serve its purpose. The Norman line established by his father must be wedded to the land with Norman blood. Though not his father's eldest son, he had been born in this land to be its king. The people had known it from the beginning, and so had he. Even through the foolish, futile tries to perhaps avoid it, to set another in his place, he had known that it must come to this. He was ready. . . .

* * *

In Graham's short absence, the very air around Dieter had changed. It was not easy even to find him again, for the closer he got on the Second Road, the more thickly was the atmosphere charged with malevolence, made foul with the psychic stench of power raised for unspeakable intentions.

Approaching that ill-hallowed circle with dread resolve, Graham gathered the strands of the Oakwood potential into a shining knot and set it unreservedly into Dieter's use as he locked back into the link forged before, his own commitment adding yet another glowing skein to plait into the rest. With an answering surge of relief, Dieter bound his own enormous ability around the shining power Graham had brought. Confident now, Dieter returned his attention to his coming need as he wound and coiled the power, ready to be unleashed. Something else about Dieter had changed, but Graham could not quite pin it down. The instant of reckoning was approaching very, very fast.

Again, Graham caught snatches of visual impression: the triple ring of Sturm's black adepts, grim mouths set in obscene anticipation, hungry-eyed behind their masks . . . the Führer seated in their midst, stiff and almost rigid with the power being raised—a satanic overlord holding court, masked face lit eerily by torches and candlelight . . . Sturm himself bowing low before the satanic throne, SS blade held horizontal above his head in both hands in terrible salute. . . .

The cupbearer kneeling between Sturm and the Führer, raising the golden cup in offering . . . and the doomed victim forced to his knees before it, chest thrust rigidly forward from the pressure of a warder's knee in the small of his back, neck bent back taut and straining, mouth agape, the eyes dulled past caring, as Sturm laid one hand on the pulsing throat and raised the knife in his other—

God, how long would Dieter delay?

Only as the blade started to flash downward did Graham sense Dieter's full intent—not *only* the psychic assault for which he had begged their aid but destruction less subtle than magic emerging from beneath his robe in a desperate attempt to make the most of what the fates had dealt.

Fire spat from the cold iron in Dieter's hand: once through the victim's heart in mercy, once at the man in the chair. The second shot incredibly pinged off the golden cup, hitting one of the torchbearers as he bowled over chair and occupant, flinging himself across his Führer's body in death.

Another shot went wild as men tackled Dieter from either side and manhandled him to the floor, but he twisted the gun into the belly of one of his assailants and fired a fourth time at point-blank range. As he squirmed out from under the body that collapsed across him, he backhanded another man brutally with the barrel and managed to wrench free as the others faltered before his defense. Rolling to his knees, Dieter fired again in the direction he had last seen Hitler.

Black-robed bodies amassed over the spot where the Führer had disappeared, becoming human shields to save their leader's life. Though Dieter continued to pump round after round into their midst, heedless of their screams and the hands dragging him down again, he knew that it was futile. Another weapon spoke—this time from Sturm's hand—but Dieter's clip was empty, the Luger being twisted from broken fingers, useless against Sturm's gun. Now he shifted focus for the other assault, the last one, the one for which he had summoned Graham in the first place.

Dieter hardly even felt the crippling bullets that slammed into both his legs, for he was out of his body with a snap, yanking Graham with him, his will a burning lens focusing all their power on Sturm.

Now! came Dieter's sharp command, cutting through Graham's shock and hesitation. *This chance we still have!*

The order helped Graham concentrate. Detached with Dieter now, he gathered the plaited strands of the power he bore and fed them all to Dieter—pulling the energy from willing sources, deep, deeper, ramming it through the nexus of Dieter's intent with a force that would not be turned aside. The bolt went straight toward Sturm on the Second Road: a clear, sun-bright beam of cleansing psychic fire, burning through all resistance and subterfuge.

Sturm seemed not to feel it at first. Scarred face contorted with rage, he waved his men aside with a curt gesture of his weapon and took three swift steps toward the motionless Dieter, sighting along the barrel to take deliberate aim. His first shot shattered Dieter's right arm at the elbow, but Dieter was beyond pain now, eyes only glaring back defiance as the power continued to pour through him from Graham.

Sturm faltered as his finger jerked a second time, the shot going wild. Then he clutched at his chest and staggered, collapsed, his eyes glazing over. The gun, which slipped from lifeless fingers, skittered to a stop at the feet of Adolf Hitler.

Dieter might expect no second victory over such as this. The sudden flare of Sturm's dying was enough to catapult him back into his bleeding body, and Graham with him. Contorted and paralyzed, he groaned aloud at last, giving release to the pain so long denied.

He was dimly aware of hands roughly turning him on his back, stripping off his mask—the ripple of reaction at his identity, the loathing—but all that was as nothing. Through a haze of distant pain, Dieter watched Hitler yank off his own mask and swoop to pick up Sturm's gun, eyes wild with impotent fury. Dieter felt no fear as death stalked him—only a profound sense of fulfillment: Sturm, at least, was dead.

As the Führer bent over him and raised the gun two-handed, shaking with rage, Dieter smiled a little and closed his eyes. No longer aware of Graham, he commended his life into the judgment of the lords of karma. Graham, too stunned to pull out from the link, felt the cold barrel of the pistol against Dieter's temple and even heard the faint click just an instant before the bullet exploded into Dieter's brain.

The force of the shot reverberated all the way back to England, catching Graham even as he tried too late to disengage. No cry escaped his lips, but his body convulsed in echo of all the agony felt by Dieter in that final instant. Then merciful blackness claimed him.

A single low moan was the first thing William heard as he dropped back to his own body and time with a jolt, but it did not occur to him that the faraway sound came not from himself but from Michael, lapsing into deep unconsciousness with the shock of Dieter's passing. William found himself gasping with his own terror, fingers locked around the carved animal heads of the stall's arm rest in mute appeal for some reprieve. Surely what he had seen had been part of some terrible dream!

But as he stopped gasping at the air and ceased his shaking, he knew that in lives past he had played the sacrificed king himself as well as sacred substitute! Not only had he been Becket but also that other William, the very Rufus whom Gray had often cited as a slain sacred king and with whose tomb William himself had held idle converse not many weeks before. Had some deep part of him suspected even then?

And Gray had been with Rufus as well as Becket! Did he know? Had he read his own role as king slayer and simply not told William, fearing at some deep level, perhaps not even conscious, that the two of them were scheduled for a repeat performance of old, familiar roles? Was that what the Rufus and Becket memories meant? Was Gray fated somehow to slay him in this life as well?

The connection came to him so abruptly that he gasped aloud. The notion terrified him, suddenly taken out of the realm of the abstract, but all at once a great deal seemed to make sense.

He had been Rufus in some other lifetime, and he had also been Becket. Becket had been the substitute victim for his king, who was acknowledged as the incarnate god by the very fact of his anointing and recognition at his coronation.

But William had *also* put himself in the role of the incarnate god in *this* lifetime, when he offered himself as the focus for the oaths taken by the grand coven leaders. Gray had seen it and had warned him at the time that the others might have seen it thus, but the impact of that warning had been lost on both of them in the urgency of Wells's betrayal and because they did not want to see it.

The signs had been present even earlier than that, when William handed Gray his Garter star at Deptford and offered to bring the grand coven together in the first place. That had been but a parallel of his Hatton role—but now he knew he had been the sacrificed Rufus as well as catalyst to Gray's defender. If he had also been Becket, who had combined functions in his martyrdom as Christian saint and sacred substitute, was it possible that he was being called upon to combine roles again, as Becket had already done? Having already catalyzed the work necessary to protect England, as Hatton had done, was he now destined once again to substitute for his King to seal that work, after having taken on the role of god in the eyes of those who still observed at least a part of the old faith that protected England? Was that where it was all leading?

He shivered and hugged his arms across his chest, refusing to believe it. The very idea was absurd. The old gods did not demand the sacrifice of their kings in these modern times. He was not even certain he believed in the old gods. One God was enough for him.

But as he re-examined all that had happened in the past few months, he had to admit that everything *could* be interpreted that way. And if it was needful for the king or his substitute to die periodically, perhaps to ensure the success of the very venture now in progress all around him, then who was better suited?

Not the King himself, whose leadership and example were so badly needed and whose death would put a defenseless young girl on the throne prematurely to bear burdens that might well crush her. Not his brothers, Gloucester and Kent, both of them vitally involved in the war effort and, furthermore, married and one of them with children. Not his sister Mary, also married and with little ones. And David had already been offered the chance and refused. The sacrifice must be willing.

Of the immediate Royal Family, that left only William, who met all the requirements of a royal substitute: son and brother of kings; an extra prince, as he himself so often lamented; deprived of the likelihood of wife and children, at least in the immediate future, by the death of a much-loved and much-missed fiancée. Had it been for this, he wondered, that she had met *her* fate? Most importantly, he knew he had done the job before—and so had Gray.

William shivered again at that, for the thought of being slain by Gray in this life was inconceivable. Yet try as he might, he could not dismiss the other factors. There was too much coincidence—and Gray often said that there was no such thing. A pattern had formed, and he and Gray seemed to be at the heart of it.

Vainly, he tried to put it out of mind, to concentrate instead on what was being done elsewhere for England's sake, but the images persisted—haunting, horrifying, and yet oddly familiar—the king or his proxy slain for the good of the land. As his eyes strayed to the image of the Christ carved above the altar, his thoughts returned time and again to sacrificed gods and sacrificed kings and memories of other lives and Gray—and his brother the King, who even now was probably on his way back to Windsor, heavy-hearted with the burden of the

war, not dreaming of the other burden awaiting—*someone*—
if the land was to be preserved....

After a while, William rose and made his way down to the
checkered floor, now reconciled with his destiny. He stood in
the aisle before the closed choir doors for a long time again,
fingering the Garter in his hand and taking in every detail of
the Sovereign's stall, remembering his brother kneeling there
the last time the order met in chapter—gentle, shy, loving
Bertie, who had never wanted or expected to be King.

When, at last, he laid his hand on the gate and swung it
wide, mounting the few steps into the Sovereign's stall, no
doubts remained. He sat long enough to raise his trouser leg
and buckle the Garter above his left knee, then slid to both
knees on the velvet cushion and bowed his head in prayer,
palms upturned in selfless offering.

CHAPTER 23

THE PRINCE WAS STILL BOWED IN THE SOVEREIGN'S STALL when, nearly half an hour later, he was startled from his meditation by the sight of Michael staggering into the choir by the sanctuary entrance, obviously in distress. By the time William could reach him, Michael had crumpled to a sitting position beside the communion rail, one hand and his forehead braced against the cool wrought iron.

"Michael, what's wrong?" William whispered, crouching to steady him.

Gasping, Michael shook his head. "I think—some kind of—psychic backlash."

"You mean something went wrong?"

Michael winced at the sound of William's voice, lowering his head between his knees until a wave of vertigo passed.

"I think something's happened to Gray," he murmured when he could see again. His voice was so low that William could hardly hear him. "They—didn't do what they were supposed to do. There was—some kind of—change of plan at the last minute."

"A change of plan? What kind of change of plan? Is he all right?"

Michael's face was pinched and very pale as he shook his head.

"I don't know, sir. Whatever it was, it knocked me out for

361

a while." He glanced at his watch and grimaced. "Christ, I didn't know it'd been that long! We'd better ring Oakwood."

As soon as Michael could walk without obvious assistance, the two of them made their way stealthily back to the royal apartments, where William immediately rang the Oakwood number. He tried to keep in mind that it was almost two in the morning, but even so, it seemed to take an unconscionably long time to get anyone to the phone besides a servant. He got more and more worried as he watched Michael sitting in a nearby chair, head cradled on knees. Even when Brigadier Ellis finally came on the line, he could get maddeningly little information.

"Wesley, is that you?"

"Sorry to have kept you waiting so long, sir," Ellis said coolly. "I'm afraid everyone had already retired for the night. How may I help you?"

The formal, guarded wording only confirmed to William that something was wrong. Pulling out a cigarette and trying to light up, he realized that his hands were trembling. He had to concentrate to keep his voice calm as he pursued the conversation with Ellis.

"Actually, I wanted to speak to Gray," he said, slipping the lighter back into a pocket and exhaling smoke. "We've—had an interesting evening at this end."

"Have you, indeed?" Ellis murmured. "I trust everyone is all right."

William glanced at Michael, who was groggily raising his head in question, and wondered whether they were.

"Well, Michael isn't in too good a shape, but I suppose it could be a holdover from this afternoon," he replied, knowing it was no such thing and suspecting Ellis knew it, too. "Nasty business, that. He has a devil of a headache. I'm all right, though. Would it be possible to speak with Gray?"

The silence at the other end was finally broken by a nervous cough.

"I'm afraid not, sir. As a matter of fact, he's down with a beastly migraine himself," Ellis answered, his voice curiously flat and emotionless. "The doctor's just given him a stiff sedative to knock him out for a while, and I shouldn't be surprised if he sleeps until noon. Could you ring back late in the morning, do you think? Or if you wanted to run down and see him tomorrow afternoon, I suspect he'll be feeling better by then."

William's mind churned with imagined reasons for the cause of Gray's condition, but there was nothing further he could do except agree to come. Michael was staring at him intently, starting to get out of his chair as he read the concern on William's face, but William shook his head and jabbed his cigarette emphatically in Michael's direction for him to stay put. He did not like the way things were developing, but he had no choice but to play it Ellis's way.

"I suppose that sounds fair enough," he said, feigning nonchalance. "Tell him I hope he feels better and that I'll drop by after lunch tomorrow—or today, actually. Sorry to bother you so late."

There was little to relate to the anxious Michael beyond what he had already heard, but William reiterated all he knew. After that, he took a clue from the mention of Graham's treatment and persuaded the younger man to take a sedative. Only when Michael was resting comfortably did William return to his own room and collapse on the bed shaking. After a while, he, too, slept and for the first time in weeks did not dream.

William's concerns the next morning were as much for Graham as for himself, though he did not intend to relent in telling Graham of the decision he had reached. Other than the facing of the deed itself, William suspected that this afternoon would be the most difficult time of all: convincing Gray of the inescapable logic of it and that Gray's part was as vital as his own. He was greatly relieved and encouraged to find Michael almost fully recovered as the two of them drove to Oakwood.

To William's surprise, the brigadier was still there when he and Michael arrived. It was Ellis, not Lady Selwyn, who greeted him and ushered him into the garden. He soon learned that Alix was taking a nap, having nursed Graham through much of the night, and that Lord Selwyn had already left to return to his duty assignment, as had Ellis's three grandchildren. Michael immediately disappeared upstairs to inquire after Graham and his mother.

Ellis did not go into great detail on what had occurred, but William gathered, by reading between the lines, that the focus of the group's working the night before had been shifted. Graham had mentioned Sturm before and his fear that Sturm's

black adepts were working against British interests. After Wells's
betrayal, all of them worried that Sturm might have discovered
the plans for the Lammas working and would take action to
try to counteract it.

Now he understood that Sturm had, indeed, been intending
to interfere and that his defeat had been the object of Graham's
work the night before. The venture had been complicated by
the unexpected presence of Hitler himself at the place of Sturm's
working. Ellis never made it clear just how Graham had learned
of this or how he had gone about neutralizing Sturm's influence,
but however it had happened, Ellis now believed Sturm to be
dead. Unfortunately, the same could not be said for Hitler. The
episode did not seem to have a great deal of bearing on what
William had come to talk about, so he did not give it too much
thought other than to realize that Graham's resultant condition
might make him less likely to succeed in talking William out
of his decision.

After a while, Graham came downstairs, haggard and un-
shaven and a little unsteady on his feet, wearing a dark-blue
bathrobe over a pair of Selwyn's pajamas. He had little real
desire to talk to William yet, especially with his head still
aching the way it was, but Michael's quick briefing convinced
him that it should not be put off. There was no time to think
through the full implications of his own survival and its impact
on the prince. His only goal, as he joined William and Ellis
in the garden, was to get through the visit without having
William realize the true reason Graham had put himself in such
jeopardy the night before. After Jennings brought them tea and
biscuits beside the fish pond, Ellis left them alone.

"Now *you* tell me how you are," William demanded. "I've
had enough of Wesley's vague reassurances."

Graham managed a shaky smile and launched into reassurances of his own. He gave William a brief account of what he
could remember of the assault on Sturm between careful sips
of tea and bites of dry toast, but he scrupulously avoided any
intimation that William had been at all the cause of his action.

But everything Graham ate and drank suddenly turned to
lead in his already queasy stomach as William began relating
his own night's experience. The prince unfolded the evolution
of his logic with cool detachment, not meeting Graham's eyes
as he described his regression and subsequent decision. In the

ten short minutes of the royal recitation, all of Graham's most dreaded speculations gradually took tangible form. William was aware of the need for sacrifice.

"So you see, I'm the only logical choice," William concluded as he ground out a cigarette in a Wedgewood ash tray and dusted off his fingers. "You yourself said that Bertie is too valuable to the country as a rallying point just now, though the lot would normally fall to him. Besides, if it were he, think who comes next. She's hardly more than a child, Gray. She's fourteen years old. And my other brothers and my sister all have families; I don't. Remember? I'm the extra prince, that fifth wheel. For the first time in my life, that's a useful thing. You have to admit, I'd be least missed."

"Not by me," Graham whispered, absolutely stunned.

William shoved his hands in his pockets and glanced away uncomfortably.

"Well, I'm not that keen on the whole thing, either," he murmured, his voice a trifle unsteady. "The whole notion scares the hell out of me, when you get right down to it. I simply don't see any other way to read the evidence. If your sacred-king theory holds any water at all, then all the signs point to a sacrifice being necessary at this time. And are you going to tell me now that you *weren't* Reginald FitzUrse or Walter Tyrrel and probably some others that you haven't bothered to mention? You can't have been unaware of all this, Gray. And I know that *I* was Becket and Rufus. How much clearer does it have to be?"

Graham dropped his head into his hands, unable to refute it, pain throbbing in his temples. He had come close to dying along with Dieter last night, and now he almost wished he had. He *had* been FitzUrse and Tyrrel and other slayers, not to mention Drake and doubtless others yet unremembered. Just as surely, it seemed, William had been Becket and Rufus and the gods alone knew who else. And despite everything Graham could do, the two of them were being drawn inexorably toward the same relationship played out so many times before. Was there no way to break the cycle? Surely this cup might yet pass.

"It's clear that you believe what you're saying, Will," he said, rubbing at the space between his eyes and wishing he could make his head stop pounding. "I *don't* necessarily accept that it's the only way of looking at the evidence. You're talking about a—a propitiary sacrifice to seal the success of what was done last night by the grand coven. This is the twentieth century. Propitiary sacrifices haven't been a part of our British tradition for—at least a thousand years."

"Perhaps not, but you yourself said that the seven-years were still observed."

"In *theory*, William—in *theory*!" Graham murmured. "But in *fact*, maybe not for several centuries. Even if they were, we aren't in anyone's seven-year cycle right now. The King is— what?—forty-four? And this is his *fourth* regnal year, not his seventh."

William's chair squeaked as he leaned it on its back legs. "That's true. But if you're going to use that argument, you have to take it the rest of the way. I've done a little calculating myself on the way here. My brother David was forty-two the year he became King and abdicated. Now I'm beginning to wonder if I understand part of the reason he did it. Don't you think the abdication was a kind of sacrifice? As far as this country is concerned, he might as well be dead. Maybe he sensed what else might be demanded if he stayed. And Bertie began *his* forty-second year three days after he became King."

"Then say that *David* was Bertie's sacrifice for that cycle!" Graham blurted, desperate and sick at heart. "He doesn't need you to be another—not yet in *any* case. Even if the cycles still operated, it's at least three years until the next need!"

"That may be true," William agreed. "It could well be, however, that extraordinary circumstances sometimes require shifting the cycle. That's what our mutual recollections say to me. There is also the very interesting fact that this is the 840th year since the death of William Rufus, and the 770th since the death of Becket—both of which are multiples of seven. That fact alone might well merit an independent sacrifice."

"This is insane. You can't mean what you're saying. You can't actually *believe* it!"

"Can't I? There's this, too: my niece is fourteen. She's the heiress presumptive. Maybe the sacrifice is needed for *her*. Weren't substitutes sometimes given for the heirs in the past, before they came to the throne?"

Fighting down increasing nausea, Graham closed his eyes

and nodded, remembering Wallace and the future Edward II.
He mouthed a tortured "Yes," but no sound came out.

"No, I think it's very clear," William's voice went on softly.
"It's something I have to do. Aside from the fact that I love
my brother and would like to know he'll reign in health and
happiness for a very long time, I'd like for *her* to have the
chance to grow up and lead something of a private life before
she's called to be Queen. If my sacrifice will ensure both of
those things—and incidentally seal the success of what was
willed last night—then I'll consider my life well spent. I can't
think of a greater service I could render my country. I'm asking
you to help me, Gray—as you've done before."

That the logic was inescapable made it no easier to accept.
If Graham believed what he had lived by all his life, then he
could hardly deny what this man who was his prince was now
asking, for it was his destiny—it was both their destinies.
Perhaps the fate of Britain *did* depend on it.

But the idea of being William's slayer was too terrible to
contemplate. How could the fates demand this of him?

"William, I can't!" he whispered desperately, clapping his
hands to his throbbing temples. "Not again. Please don't ask
this of me."

"I have to. You're the only one I'd trust. There's no one
else."

"I can't!"

"Gray, I'm begging you!" William murmured, crouching to
seize one wrist and shake him until he glanced up. "Don't make
it any harder for me, please!"

William's eyes held him pinned for an instant, but the world
was starting to spin as Graham shook his head and staggered
to his feet, half blind with the pain behind his temples, and
dragged William with him.

"William, I can't—and *God*, don't kneel to me! Please!
Ask me anything else—*anything*. . . ."

"No," William murmured. "Only this. *Promise* you'll do
as I ask. . . ."

"I can't," Graham gasped as William's face began to blur.
"I can't, I can't . . . ," and slowly crumpled into blackness.

He was alone when he regained consciousness later that
evening. For the first few minutes, he simply let himself drift

drowsily. Aware that he had been sedated again, he was grateful for the insulation it afforded. Time and the drug seemed to have relieved all but a last dull vestige of the pain in his head, but the ache in his heart remained a heavy, oppressive weight.

He could not sleep again, and the ache changed not at all with the passage of half an hour spent staring at the ceiling. When his stomach began reminding him of its long emptiness, he steeled himself to the inevitable, weakly pulled on his bathrobe again, and went downstairs. He found Alix and the brigadier in the library, obviously discussing him. The brigadier settled him in the overstuffed chair with his feet up and a lap robe tucked around him while Alix fed him tea and sandwiches, explaining that William had returned to London. Graham's appetite seemed to have returned in healthy measure, but he ate cautiously, also hoping to postpone their questions.

When he had finished half a sandwich more than he really wanted and sipped halfheartedly at a third cup of tea, he gave the cup and saucer back to Alix with a weary sigh and laid his head against the chair back. He supposed he could not put it off any longer.

"I assume he told you," he murmured, idly studying the plastered cornices around the ceiling edges.

"Yes," Alix said carefully. "It's a hard logic, but unfortunately a valid one, so far as I can see. What's more important, William truly believes he is called to do this. If so, then you are equally committed."

Graham closed his eyes and sighed dejectedly. "I *tried* to take his place, Alix. It isn't fair. I was ready to die for him."

"Yes, but the sacrifice was not accepted," Alix said quietly. "You survived. There's a reason for that. There's something else you ought to know. Old Gerald came by a little while ago. Dame Emma sent him. Apparently, they had almost as interesting a night as we did."

Graham turned his head to look at her sharply. "What happened?"

"Well, they lost two of their people—one during the ritual and one from aftereffects this morning."

"In backlash from me?"

"I don't think so. Both of them were quite old. They may just have overextended and burned themselves out. That happens sometimes, as you know."

"But you don't think that's what happened," Graham murmured, a sick dread rising in his chest.

"Wesley, why don't you tell him?"

The brigadier sat back in his chair and crossed his legs, his face unreadable as he removed his pipe from his mouth.

"Emma has been out on the Second Road off and on all day, trying to estimate the effect of what was done last night."

"And?"

"And she says last night's working was only partially successful."

"What does that mean?" Graham whispered dully.

"Well, you eliminated Sturm, of course—you and Dieter—but the working against Hitler only set up a potential. It still needs to be triggered. Emma says a final effort is going to be needed to push him over the edge. Her two who died last night—well, she says they intended to die."

Graham's breath caught in his throat.

"Are you saying they—sacrificed themselves?" he managed to get out.

The brigadier nodded. "That's what Gerald implied. It seems we haven't been the only ones to talk about the need for a sacrifice. I shouldn't be surprised if there were others as well elsewhere in the country. In any case, it apparently wasn't enough. Emma said you should be told."

"No. She can't ask that," Graham whispered.

"She isn't asking anything, Gray," the brigadier said after puffing once neutrally on his pipe. "It isn't the place of any of us to ask that kind of thing. But she was there when William put himself in the place of the sacred king. And now he's offered. What comes next is between you and William."

"This can't be happening," Graham murmured, shaking his head in disbelief. "It can't be. It just can't be."

"There's more," Alix said, reaching behind her to retrieve a thin stack of tarot cards. "I did another reading while you were asleep. I think you should see what the cards were. Wesley can assure you that this is exactly how they came up."

As she turned the top card and laid it on the table beside Graham's chair, Graham drew in his breath with a start. It was the familiar King of Wands—the card that had become William's. He shook his head in denial as Alix laid her fingertips gently along the bottom edge.

"The King of Wands covers the situation and influences all else," she said softly. "It is William, as we have seen before, but we must never forget that it is also the King. The possibility of substitution is quite clear. It was there before, when the same King crossed the Knight of Wands, but we simply didn't see it."

"Maybe we didn't see it because it isn't really there," Graham ventured, grasping at any chance of reprieve. "The connection, I mean. Isn't it possible that you're mistaken?"

"Do *you* think I'm mistaken?"

He could say nothing as she turned up the next card.

"Crossing the situation is the Three of Coins," she said. "It is a card of nobility, of skilled workmanship—perhaps even a Masonic card in its literal interpretation—which is certainly apt in this case. The structure of the situation is being worked out by experts—karmic experts, one might even say."

Graham started to sit back in pained resignation at the reference, for he was all too aware of karma just now, but as Alix placed the third card, he raised an eyebrow and leaned forward with more hope. The Ace of Swords was a very potent card of triumph.

"Yes, it's a good card," Alix said, answering his unvoiced question. "It is the most that can be hoped for—and in this case, that is a great deal, indeed. Force and victory are indicated, but you must remember that this may refer to factors far greater than any one individual—even William. It may mean the outcome of the war itself. Also, look at the literal symbolism of the crown pierced by the sword. Keep that in mind as the rest of the cards come up."

Graham set his jaw as he got a look at the fourth card she turned.

"At the root of the situation is the Wheel of Fortune," Alix continued, avoiding his eyes and nervously flexing the remaining cards in her hands. "It is certainly an apt card to describe karma and the working out of intended destinies. Frankly, I would have been surprised if it *hadn't* turned up somewhere in the reading." She sighed. "By now, I don't think there can be any question what we're talking about, though, do you?"

He gave a distracted shake of his head as she turned the next card and dropped it into place.

"In the immediate past, the Eight of Coins—another card of craftsmanship, though this one is more of apprenticeship, of learning—which the past few months certainly have been for William, I should think, as well as for the rest of us. Wesley, how did you phrase your original question when we first did the reading?"

The brigadier puffed on his pipe and gestured toward the cards with his chin. "Basically, it was oriented toward William and his role. Go ahead. I'll comment more when you're finished. I think Gray needs to see the rest of the cards."

With an apologetic shrug, Alix turned the next card and laid it to the right of the others. Graham closed his eyes tightly and slowly shook his head, not wanting to see.

"The Hanged Man, this time in the position of the immediate future," Alix said tonelessly. "The sacrifice moves closer to the King. Insight will be gained and esoteric knowledge revealed in full measure, but he fears—" She turned the seventh card and snapped it down at the top of the scepter. "The Devil Reversed: indecision and weakness—fear that he may lack the courage to carry through with what he feels must be done."

Graham's eyes popped open to confirm the identity of the newest card, and for just an instant, his vision blurred as he fought down the sick feeling in the pit of his stomach. He had not stopped to think before this very instant just what William must be going through.

"The Magician—your card, Gray," Alix said as she turned the next one. "Also, because this position represents his environment in general, I think we must assume that at least some of the rest of us are also bound up in what is to be, if you are.

"And for his positive feelings, we have the Six of Wands," she said, placing the ninth card. "The victor shall overcome adversity despite opposition—and William *is* Victor, isn't he?" she added, smiling a little despite herself.

"But even if William *is* to be *the* victor, the opposition could be read in many ways. *We* are part of the opposition if we do not support him in what he believes must be done." She tapped the card with a fingernail. "The wreath on the wand can be read as hope, at least in the general sense, but it has something of the martyr's crown as well."

When she did not move to lay down the final card, Graham

reached hesitantly across and took it from her hand, breathing out with a sigh as he turned it face up with the others.

"The World," Alix said softly, her voice quite unsteady as she folded her hands primly in her lap. "It is the ultimate success card, but on all planes—*all* planes. In the literal sense, it may mean the real world and, hence, the outcome of the war, but it is also William's own card—and we have already seen the directions in which his personal destiny in this life is being guided." She drew a deep breath. "Unfortunately, I fear that success on a global scale may depend upon William finding his own destiny—and you, yours, Gray. I can't put it any plainer than that."

Graham looked away, all too aware of the finality of what the cards had said. The brigadier cleared his throat and began poking at his pipe with a pipe tool.

"I don't want to raise false hopes, but there *is* a chance— granted, a very *small* chance—that matters might take a turn for the better despite all the signs," he murmured, not looking directly at Graham or Alix. "We can hope and pray that they will, but in the meantime, I think we have no other choice but to go ahead and plan on the assumption that we *will* have to act. Based on the current progress of the war, I should think we have at least a month before irreversible action must be taken."

"I agree," Alix said quietly, turning her attention to Graham. "Gray, I know this is not an easy conversation for you. I hope you realize we neither seek nor desire what is coming into being. If William himself were one whit less adamant, I assure you we would not even be considering it."

"I know that," Graham said dully.

"I'm sure you do," she breathed. "Sometimes it helps, though, to have it verbalized by someone else."

"I suppose."

"You know, then, that we have to mention some other unpleasant things," she went on after a glance at Ellis. "I realize that this is going to sound cold—and that you know it isn't meant that way—but some thought will have to be given to ways and means, and soon, so that things can be properly planned. It will—have to look like an accident or a war casualty to the uninitiated. I know you're aware of the ritual requirements."

As Graham dropped his forehead into one hand and tried to shut out the images her words conjured up, the sound of Ellis tapping out his pipe against an ash tray brought him back to focus.

"Speaking of the uninitiated reminds me of something positive we can do to get us through these difficult times, Alix," Ellis said quietly. "Technically, William is already one of us by birth, since he's of the old line, but I think it might make things easier on all of us, himself included, if he went through a formal initiation and recognition as the sacred king. It would help to cement in all of our minds just why we're even contemplating such an awful measure—and I use awful in its original sense of awe-full, as it most surely is."

As Graham raised his head to stare at both of them in shock, disposing so casually of his and William's lives, Alix rose and brought back a desk calendar, riffling through the pages as she sat again.

"That occurred to me as well," she agreed. "It should be done at a full moon—that's the eighteenth, this month—two weeks from Sunday. We'll delay the other as long as we can, of course, even if we're technically out of one of the sacrificial months, but I suspect it's all going to come to a head before too long. Shall we make it the eighteenth?—provided William concurs, of course."

"I think that's reasonable," Ellis replied.

"Fine. Given William's lack of formal background, I think it best that we keep it very low-key and simple as well, with as few people involved as possible—just the three of us plus him. The others of our immediate group can be told what will be happening, but no one else. Do you agree?"

As the brigadier nodded, sucking shrilly at his empty pipe, Graham finally found voice to protest.

"But what about David?" he whispered, trying to push back the dread suspicion that he knew what was coming next. "Surely you'll want him as high priest."

"He isn't as close to William as either of you," Alix replied. "Besides, he'll be at sea by then—and we don't want to strain our contacts in high places by trying to get him back again so soon. No, one of you can take his place for this."

"Gray?" the brigadier asked, raising an eyebrow.

Aware that he was on the brink of losing control, Graham

shook his head and looked away, blinking back stinging tears and covering his face with one hand.

How could they even suggest it, knowing the terrible price already being asked of him? Could they not see that serving as high priest for William's initiation and sacring almost gave sanction for that other act? If he refused to acknowledge it, perhaps it would not happen. There might still be hope if he did not allow himself to think about it.

As he began to shake, aware that part of his physical reaction was spillover from the previous night, the brigadier rose and laid a sympathetic hand on his shoulder.

"Alix, why don't you see about some fresh tea? I'd like to talk with Gray alone for a while. I'll call you when we're done."

After she left, Ellis sat back in his chair and began filling his pipe, scooping the aromatic tobacco from the pouch and tamping it with his thumb. Graham had stopped shaking at his touch; now he merely felt drained. Mutely, he watched Ellis's hands making a soothing ritual of the commonplace.

"I imagine you're feeling just about as alone and bereft as you've ever felt before," Ellis said after a moment longer. "I don't know if it makes any difference, but I wanted you to know that I understand what you're going through."

"Do you?" Graham whispered.

"Yes."

Ellis sucked on the pipe to check its draw, then struck a match and began sucking the flame carefully into the bowl. When it lit, he tossed the spent match and leaned back in his chair. Graham watched the whole operation in a daze, wondering what the older man was driving at.

"What are you saying?" he finally asked.

Ellis blew smoke over his head and suddenly looked wistful and a little sad.

"Just around the turn of the century—I won't tell you which side—I, too, had a high-ranking friend who was called to a higher destiny. I am bound by a number of oaths not to tell you who the person was. Not even Alix and David know— and no, I can't even tell you whether it was a man or a woman, though for the sake of convenience, you can think of the other person as a 'he.' In any case, I was called upon to function in a role with which I know you're familiar. It was not easy for either of us, but we—did what had to be done. I still miss him very much," he added.

Listening to the old man's confession with growing astonishment, Graham suddenly felt an even greater surge of kinship and affection for this man who had already been father and mentor for so many years.

"*You* were a slayer?" he whispered.

"Well, I wasn't the slain," Ellis said with a kindly smile. "Apparently there are a fair number of us. I simply never realized you were one of them. I—did have a little assistance from other—brothers—though the ultimate responsibility was mine, of course, as it had to be. The point is that I know exactly how you feel and what a difficult road lies ahead for you. The gap between legend and life sometimes seems appallingly wide. Insofar as it's permitted in the greater pattern, I'll do whatever I can to help you."

Graham swallowed and bowed his head, still reeling a little with the shock of revelation. Suddenly, several of the older man's comments over the past few months took on new meaning. He wondered whether Ellis had seen this coming all along— and whether he and his victim had been as close as Graham was to William.

"Were you—very good friends?" he murmured, impelled by morbid fascination to ask.

Ellis averted his eyes and took several slow, studied puffs on his pipe.

"Yes, we were," he said after a moment. "Perhaps even as close as you and William. I know you'd like to know who it was, but I'm not even permitted to tell you when or how it was done. I'm the only one alive anymore who knows the true circumstances." He cocked his head and looked up wistfully.

"I can give you a clue, however. It's up to you to follow it or not, as you choose. Look at the seven-year cycles during that general period. Look at any of the nobility or royalty who seem to have died under—let's say 'unusual' or 'convenient' circumstances. It was a substitute, not a king, by the way. I *can* tell you that. If you look hard enough, I think you'll be able to make some pretty shrewd guesses. You know what to look for."

In that instant, Graham knew the time would come when he *would* want to delve back and seek it out. Somehow the

thought even brought its own sort of comfort: the realization
that he was not the only one called upon to undertake such
terrible duty.

But he would not look too soon. Just now the immediate
ache of the present and near future was too new and raw—the
knowledge that this time *he* was the slayer and William destined
to be the slain.

"How did you do it?" he finally managed to whisper. "I
don't mean physically, but how—how did you find the courage?"

"It was love," Ellis said after a thoughtful pause. "In the
end, it always comes back to that. The link between the slayer
and the slain is best forged by love. What possible value could
there be to a sacrifice made in hate or resentment? It costs very
little to lose something you hate."

Graham screwed his eyes shut and shuddered, knowing Ellis
was right. The words of that other Red William echoed in his
mind from a Lammas morrow more than eight centuries past:
*'Tis not the slaying, but the laying down of life for the land,
the spilling of the sacred blood—yet the dying is better if it be
at the hand of one who loves the victim. Dost thou love me,
Wat?*

"Lord, you know I do," he whispered aloud, catching himself in a sob. "But, *God*, why this cup *again*?"

He could feel his control slipping farther, the weight in his
chest pressing more heavily with every breath, and suddenly
the dread welled up and could be contained no longer. In that
same instant came the clear certainty that the cup would *not*
pass from him this time, any more than it had passed before.

He still might have fought down the physical expression of
his grief, had not the brigadier come and perched on the arm
of his chair, easing his arms around Graham's shoulders in
wordless comfort and holding him when he began to shake.
As once before, when Caitlin died and Graham had been unable
to cry, so now the old man's touch loosed all the carefully held
barriers of bitterness and mourning as Ellis rocked him like a
child, letting him sob out all his grief.

Gradually, the physical reactions spent themselves. As Graham subsided, finally pulling away to drag his sleeve across
his face, trying to regain his composure, Ellis casually collected
his pipe and wandered over to the fireplace, where he made

an elaborate show of cleaning the thing and emptying it into the hearth. When he returned, he had two stiff drinks in his hands and the pipe clenched between his teeth. He said nothing as he handed Graham one of the glasses and sat down again.

"There must be some way to get the same effect without having to taste the stuff," Graham grumbled when he had downed half the Scotch neat and was beginning to feel its benumbing effect. "I know it's from David's private stock, but the bloody stuff still tastes like camel piss."

"I'll tell him you said so," Ellis said, saluting with his glass before taking another sip. "Feeling any better?"

Graham managed a brief, faint smile. "Not so as you'd notice, but at least with this inside, I don't care as much." He tossed off the rest of the drink and made a face as he set the empty glass aside. "Sorry about the scene."

"You're entitled," Ellis replied. "Do you think you can handle things now?"

"You're just going to have to give me some time to adjust, Wes," he answered softly. "One step at a time. I'm not resigned. A lot can happen in two weeks. Maybe we'll never have to do more than we've already done. Emma and the cards could be wrong. . . ."

The brigadier rose as if nothing unusual had occurred and moved casually toward the door.

"If that qualification makes it easier to deal with for now, very well," he said. "Just so long as you realize what else may be necessary—and I think you do."

As Alix came back into the room with the tea, Graham knew he realized all too well.

Graham endured the next two weeks in something of a fog, outwardly cool and efficient but numbed inside, praying that somehow he and William would yet be delivered. He saw little of anyone outside his office, for as the Battle of Britain intensified, his own duties grew heavier, the hours of sleep fewer. Only occasionally was he able to sandwich brief, unsatisfying meetings with William and the brigadier between his own long hours with his intelligence team and William's heavy rounds of royal duties.

Other than to voice quiet acceptance of the initiation plans for the eighteenth, William spoke little of the decision he had made and would not discuss it with Graham at all. Whether that was for fear of being dissuaded or because William himself was having second thoughts, Graham did not know. He wondered whether William, too, felt that if the matter was not mentioned, it somehow would not have to happen.

Those first two weeks of August brought devastating shifts in the emphasis of the war. Poor weather conditions initially prevented any serious German incursions beyond the usual shipping raids in the Channel and an occasional swipe at Dover or one of the other port towns; but by the second week, it was clear that the Luftwaffe was gearing up for a major assault. *Adlertag*—or Eagle Day—had been hinted in secret German ciphers for weeks.

Heavy cloud cover and sporadic rain kept German sorties confined to the usual harassment at the beginning of the second week, but good weather on the twelfth brought concerted attacks on the southeast coastal radar chain: Ventor, Rye, and others. Several forward fighter stations were hit, along with Portsmouth Harbor and two unprotected convoys in the Thames estuary, but at least there were no further raids on the vital radar stations. Oddly enough, the Germans did not yet seem to have recognized the strategic importance of the radar nets.

On the thirteenth, *Adlertag* finally began, though fortunately for the British, it got off to a slow start. Intended as the decisive punch at the beginning of a four-day campaign to knock the RAF from the skies, it was an essential step to the next phase in Operation Sealion—for the Germans could not hope to land an invasion force without mastery of the Channel and the British navy—and they could not master the British navy as long as the RAF ruled the skies above.

But poor weather in the morning led to postponement of the major strike until the afternoon—and because of communications problems, part of the Eagle strike force found themselves over enemy territory early on without adequate fighter escort. In the fifteen hundred sorties flown that day, the Luftwaffe managed to bomb only secondary targets and to bag only thirteen British planes compared to their own losses of forty-five. The following day, attempting to cover their confusion, they confined their attacks to railways near the coast and a few RAF stations. By the third day, however, the German efficiency recovered dramatically.

More than seven distinct German attacks bombarded the length of Britain on the fifteenth. Beginning with a major raid on Lympne and Hawkinge airfields in Kent, just before noon, the Germans next simultaneously attacked the coastal areas of Northumberland and Yorkshire, hoping to draw off fighter defenses so that new waves of bombers might better harry the south. Although the bomber station at Great Driffield lost ten Whitley bombers on the ground in addition to other heavy destruction, and several other lesser northern targets sustained damage, the British radar gave sufficient warning for most of the raiders to be met and engaged while still over the Channel, where Hurricane and Spitfire pilots made short work of them.

By midafternoon, more waves of bombers and their fighter escorts hit Hawkinge again, as well as the airfields at Eastchurch and Martlesham and the vital aircraft factories at Rochester. Later in the afternoon, a flight of eighty bombers attacked the south coast at Portsmouth Harbor and the airfields at Middle Wallop and Worthy Down, though they inflicted little serious damage. An hour later, yet another wave hit the airfield at Croydon, near London. More sporadic attacks continued through the hours of darkness—harassment designed to fray the nerves of the British people.

Pilots of the RAF fought doggedly and effectively, inflicting more than twice the losses on the Luftwaffe than they themselves sustained, but relative losses were of little comfort in light of absolutes. The coastal raids continued to take their toll daily; and though British aircraft production had risen to the point that lost or damaged aircraft could be replaced at the rate of over a hundred a week by mid-August, the fact remained that the replacement of trained pilots could not be accomplished by assembly lines working extra shifts. Fighter Command had fallen more than two hundred below strength by the seventeenth; and as new pilot training programs were cut to the bone and cut again in order to get pilots into the air, the life expectancy of an RAF fighter pilot fell to less than ninety flying hours. Some men were going into their first sorties with as little as ten hours of solo time in Hurricanes or Spitfires and had never fired their machine guns at a target in the air.

It was with this grim awareness that Graham rose on the morning of the eighteenth and drove to Buckingham Palace to collect William. There he and Michael heard Sunday service

in the Chapel Royal with William and other members of the
Royal Family and household, since William asked it, then had
a light luncheon in William's quarters before starting down to
Oakwood. Michael accompanied them, for William had also
asked that he be present that night.

The criss-crossed contrails of distant aerial battles scored
the grey rim of the horizon almost all the way to Oakwood,
underlining the growing need for their journey. Close by, massed
enemy bombers and their swarms of escorts pounded the be-
leaguered airfield of West Malling without mercy. Once, when
the thump of nearby bombs even rocked the moving Bentley,
Michael pulled off the road. Ahead, a disabled Heinkel crashed
spectacularly in a farmer's field and burned.

The sheer physical peril of the drive from London kept the
minds of all three men diverted from the less palpable but no
less real perils of the night and days to come. Alix and the
brigadier were waiting when they drove up the long, tree-arched
driveway of Oakwood just before teatime, and the five spent
a strained several hours discussing the week's war developments and the battle they had seen, waiting for nightfall. By
unspoken agreement, they avoided the real reason for their
coming together.

But as the afternoon wore on, the silences grew longer and
the conversation more forced until, just before dusk, Graham
finally escorted William upstairs and suggested that he nap for
an hour or two while preparations went forward.

"There's no sense getting yourself worked into more of a
state than you already are," he told the prince.

"I wouldn't *be* in such a state if I knew a bit more what to
expect," William replied as he sat on the edge of the bed and
removed his shoes. "Can't you even give me a hint?"

Trying to avoid the searching blue eyes, Graham jammed
his hands in his pockets and studied the pattern in the rug.

"I'll ask Wesley to come up and brief you a little later," he
said softly "For now, you should get some sleep."

"I don't *want* to sleep, and I don't want Wesley," the prince
said pointedly. "I want to know whether I can count on your
support tonight."

Graham turned partially away, forcing back the numb edge
of despair. "I'll be present as a witness. Right now, that's all
I can promise."

"Do you think denying it will change things?"

Graham knew it would not but had no argument to answer William. When he did not reply, the prince laid back on the bed with a perplexed sigh, his eyes never leaving Graham.

"Gray, we have to go through with this," William said. "At least tonight's part. Please don't make it harder for either of us than it already is."

Graham allowed himself a heavy sigh. "Forgive me, William," he whispered. "Simple *being* here is hard enough."

He caught just a glimpse of the hurt and resentment in William's eyes before the prince rolled abruptly onto his side, away from Graham. Stung by that reproach, Graham sat gingerly on the edge of the bed. When he finally summoned enough courage to touch one tentative hand to the prince's shoulder, William flinched.

"William, I'm sorry," he whispered.

"So am I," came the low-voiced response.

"Will you—try to sleep?"

"Yes—for all the good it will do."

Justly chastened, Graham bowed his head.

"William, I told you I was sorry. I can—put you to sleep if you like."

Without warning, William rolled onto his back to stare at him.

"Yes, you can, can't you? But you can't do the one thing I really *need* you to do. Do you think you're the only one who's afraid, Gray?"

"William, I—"

But William only shook his head and closed his eyes, breathing out with a resigned sigh.

"Never mind," he whispered. "Just go ahead and put me to sleep."

Graham had no heart to continue a discussion that he had not wanted in the first place. When William did not look up again, Graham reluctantly brushed his finger tips over the prince's closed eyelids and eased him into kind, undreaming slumber. He wished there were time to make the same sort of escape, if only for an hour, but he feared to dream if he slept. After finishing his own physical preparations, he spent the remaining hour in solitary contemplation, searching his conscience and dreading every step he was increasingly bound to

take. Both Alix and the brigadier tried to talk to him, but
Graham declined their comfort. Wisely, they left him to his
own anguished soul searching.

A few hours later, William sighed and sputtered a little as
he gently surfaced from under his bath water and scooped water
and hair out of his eyes with both hands. Steam rose all around
him, pungent from the herbs the brigadier had run under the
tap when he drew the bath a quarter hour ago. The aroma,
sharp but not unpleasant, lent an odd air of other worldliness
to the ambience of the bathroom, unlike anything William had
ever smelled before. The flickering of the single candle near
the tub softened the white starkness of the tile, but it also gave
free rein to his already active imagination.

Not that the unfamiliar was unexpected under the circumstances. As William had learned in the past two weeks, one
of the principal purposes of an initiation was to cause changes
in the initiate, partially by placing him in an unfamiliar environment. Just what those changes might encompass, William
was not altogether sure. He was not exactly afraid of what lay
ahead tonight, but he could not help a gnawing little knot of
apprehension, for all his trust of those in whose hands he had
placed himself. The hot bath had at least eased a few of the
physical knots and tensions.

He breathed deeply of the scented steam and let himself slip
down in the warm water again until he could rest his head
against the edge of the tub, closing his eyes to drift, wishing
many things were different. Oddly enough, his most urgent
concern for tonight was not himself at all, but Gray, who still
was resisting the decision William had made and could not
seem to make himself a part of it.

It had been the brigadier who had broached the subject of
initiation to William in the first place, while a sullen and uncommunicative Gray sat silently by, contributing only when
questioned directly. Though Gray never again voiced the kind
of resistance he had offered that first time, in the garden—at
least in William's hearing—it was clear that his heart was not
in any of the preparations. William met with him privately
several times after that, but Gray assiduously avoided further
discussion. Not until this evening had William even dared to
bring it up.

Now the part of tonight that William sometimes sensed so joyously in Gray had lost a little of its edge, for Gray refused to be drawn into William's sharing of it. William wondered whether there was any chance at all that Gray might change his mind.

A door opened and closed in the next room, and very shortly there was a discreet rap on the bathroom door. William sat up in anticipation, sloshing water, but it was the brigadier, not Gray, who slipped through the doorway with an apologetic bow, a large, snowy-white towel on his arm in stark contrast to the now-familiar black robe. William hoped his disappointment did not show too much as he put on a tentative smile for the older man.

"How do you feel?" Ellis asked, crouching near the head of the tub and balancing against the edge with one hand.

"Clean?"

Ellis smiled. "And with a sense of humor yet, I see. That's good." He swished his free hand in the water near William's shoulder, apparently testing the temperature, then dried it on a corner of the towel.

"As it happens, 'clean' is what this part is all about," he continued. "The washing away of all impurities and imperfections before one is presented to the gods—psychic impurities as well as physical ones. Fortunately, water is good for doing both. Do you feel sufficiently pure?"

"I'll feel sufficiently waterlogged if I stay in here much longer," William quipped with a ragged smile. "At least physically. Psychically, I couldn't say. You're the expert in that department."

"You'll pass."

"Well, that's a relief. Are you going to brief me any further? Gray—hasn't told me much."

"I'll tell you what I may," the old man returned, standing and holding out the towel sympathetically. "Come and get dry now. I shouldn't want you to grow old and wrinkled before your time."

The prince climbed out and wrapped himself in the towel Ellis held, accepting the older man's assistance wordlessly as he was dried and garbed in a loose-fitting white robe that wrapped across the front. As he knotted a white cord around his waist to hold it in place, he tried not to think about whether he would have the chance to grow old and wrinkled. The possibility got increasingly smaller. Toweling his hair dry, he followed Ellis into the adjoining sitting room, which was also lit only by candles. He studied Ellis furtively in the mirror while he combed his hair. Ellis seemed nonplussed by the scrutiny and only patted the divan beside him when William had finished his toilette.

"Come and sit, son," the old man said, holding up two envelopes. "I have some mail for you: a note from the master of the house and a cable from Richard and Geoffrey. I think you know that all three of them would have been here tonight if that were possible. You've not met my granddaughter Audrey, Geoffrey's sister, but she was here Lammas night, and she also sends her respect and best wishes. She felt you might be more comfortable if tonight's gathering were kept small."

William smoothed his robe over his knees with a restless gesture as he took the two envelopes and sat. Both had been opened, for they were addressed to Ellis on the outside. The first note was penned on the familiar, cream-colored stationery of Lord Selwyn's ship, with its crest engraved at the top in gold.

> *To Victor, with reverence and warm affection. You are in my thoughts and prayers. Your servant, Selwyn.*

William smiled at the "Victor" appellation and laid the note aside, unfolding the cable from Wales. The words printed on the yellow signal flimsy were more informal but also more cryptic.

TO BRIGADIER SIR WESLEY ELLIS, KCB, LAURELGROVE, EYNSFORD, KENT STOP WE WIN STOP TO THE VICTOR BE-LONG THE SPOILS STOP SIGNED YOUR SPOILED GRANDSONS R & G.

"To the victor belong the spoils?" William said, glancing up at Ellis.

Ellis smiled. "Since they had no way of knowing how many nosy clerks might read it, they had to be a little indirect. They're giving you their homage, William, as the sacred king."

William read it again, a shiver of awe gradually overcoming

him as the hidden sense registered. *We win. To the Victor belong the spoils....*

He snatched up Selwyn's note and reread it then, only now seeing his "reverence" in a possibly different light.

"And—Selwyn, too?" he finally murmured, hardly daring to ask it.

As the brigadier nodded, not saying anything, it was all William could do to blink back the tears. He stared at the two messages, seeing the faces of the three who had sent them superimposed over the two very different sorts of paper, then gently folded the cable form around the stiffness of ship's stationery and closed them between his hands, overcome. It was not until he had recovered enough to slip them into the pocket of his robe that he realized he had unconsciously clasped even the written pledges as he would have clasped the hands themselves. He started shaking as he patted the papers in place inside the pocket, and he forced himself to take a deep breath.

"What can I say?" he whispered after he had slumped bonelessly into the softenss of the divan, wishing there had been a fourth name added to the three.

"You don't have to say anything if you don't want to. Are you nervous?"

"What do you think?"

"That's fine. A little anxiety is normal and healthy. There's supposed to be *some* anticipation. I did want to reassure you, however, that nothing terrible is going to happen to you tonight. Even though you've offered yourself in a very worthy cause, we all still hope that won't be necessary."

"I'm not sure I understand what you're saying," William said.

Ellis smiled and produced his pipe and pouch from a hidden pocket, beginning the little ritual of scooping tobacco and tamping it into the bowl.

"I suppose what I'm trying to say is that no one is going to slip in a surprise sacrifice tonight to spare you the anticipation and the worry later on," he said slowly. "What you'll experience out there—and in here"—he touched the side of William's head lightly with a finger tip—"is your's by right of birth, even if it weren't for the other. Granted that in ordinary circumstances it might have been safer for all of us if you never knew about any of this—but none of us, knowing you as we do now, would have denied you its joy, had you come to us in normal times."

"Not even Gray?" William murmured, the words a little bitter despite his best intentions.

"William, try to understand," the brigadier replied. "Gray, of all people, would like nothing better than to share the joy which should go with what you'll experience tonight. It isn't your reception into the old ways which grieves him; it's what seems destined to come after that, and the duty which draws him, out of love."

William glanced down at his hands, at the fingers twined tightly together, and unclasped them with a deliberate motion, laying them flat on his thighs. He supposed it was a kind of love, though the term seemed most inadequate to describe the bond that had bound the two of them across at least nine centuries, and God alone knew how many lives.

"I know that," he said quietly. "Perhaps it wasn't even fair to ask him. I'm not sure I had a choice, though. Has he talked with you about it?"

"Not in so many words. But when you've known a man as long as I've known Gray, he doesn't have to tell you, and you don't have to ask."

"I suppose not." William sighed. "I've laid a terrible burden on him, haven't I? I did have to ask him, though. You understand that, don't you?"

"I understand better than you can possibly imagine, my prince," Ellis said softly.

William glanced up at that, surprised by the tenderness of the tone, but the brigadier was toying distractedly with something on a silver chain around his neck, his pipe momentarily forgotten in his other hand and his eyes fixed on some other time. William longed to ask what he meant, but something stayed the query on his lips. When the brigadier looked up at him again, there was no sign of anything out of the ordinary in his expression.

"Well, I did intend to brief you, didn't I?" Ellis said briskly, dropping whatever was on the chain inside his robe. "I can't give you too many details, of course, since that would detract from the impact of the initiation, but you can expect first of all to be challenged at swordpoint before entering the circle, much as you undoubtedly were for your Masonic initiation.

Then you'll be bound and blindfolded. You'll be presented to the ancient ones and consecrated to their service, your measure will be taken with a scarlet cord which will be marked with a drop of your blood, and you'll be asked to take an oath of fidelity to the old ones, though that does not involve renunciation of any other beliefs you may hold. At this point, you are officially acknowledged as one of us and given a new name. After that, we'll proceed to anoint and crown you as the sacred king. What happens after that, at least ultimately, is up to you."

William managed a queasy smile, and the brigadier laid a fatherly hand on his shoulder.

"I know, son. You have a thousand questions. Unfortunately, I'm not at liberty to answer them just now. I think you'll find that most of them will be answered along the way, however, either by prompting or by experience."

"There's only one question that's important right now," William murmured, looking at his hands in his lap. "Who, precisely, will be initiating me? I—was afraid to ask Gray."

Ellis sighed and gave him a gentle smile. "I know what you want to hear, William. I think you know what I have to say, however. Alix will be principal initiator, as she should be, following the ancient custom that such things must always pass from woman to man and vice versa." He paused a beat. "It looks like I'll be assisting her."

William swallowed, imagining he could hear the sound reverberating through the room.

"Not—Gray?"

The brigadier bowed his head. "This is very, very difficult for him, William," he whispered. "Try to understand. He may yet find the strength to do it, but I mustn't let you raise any false hopes."

"I do understand," William breathed, looking away. "It's just that..."

"I know, son," Ellis said with a sigh. "Believe me, I know."

CHAPTER 24

TWO HOURS AFTER MOONRISE, GRAHAM FOLLOWED ALIX and the brigadier silently along the maze, increasingly aware of a sense of isolation as they wound ever inward.

They had no need of lantern tonight, for the light of the full moon drenched the garden silver. Earlier, several flights of enemy bombers had droned high overhead, obscuring the moon in evil portent of death and destruction, but now only occasional clouds scudded across the lunar face to cast their fleeting shadows. Votive candles in red glass holders guarded the quarters inside the temple rather than the bulkier lanterns used at Lammas, but they were needed less for light than for their symbolism. White-faced in the moonlight, Alix and Ellis mounted the four steps to the temple and entered, leaving Graham alone outside.

As the two set about the business of purifying and casting the circle, Graham bowed his head and closed his eyes to finish centering in, even drawing the hood of his robe farther over his face to further shut out distractions as he felt the betweenness of the place deepen where he stood.

The moment was almost upon them—not for the sacrifice, thank God, for he still held some hope of yet averting that, but another moment just as soul altering in its way. Once William passed through the portal before which Graham now waited and through which Graham had passed so many times, the prince would never be the same, whether or not the sacrifice

was consummated. When William walked the between-path of
the sacred maze and came to stand in this otherness that was
neither of the earth nor of the Second Road, he would feel the
change. Never again could there be a return to the innocence
of the before-times, when he had known nothing of Graham
and his magic.

That alone was an awesome realization. Graham wondered
whether he himself could have made the conscious choice the
prince was making tonight, were he in William's place. For
Graham, the question held little meaning, for he could not
remember a time when he had not known what he was, but
tonight would touch William in ways none of them could guess.

The sense of insulation, of being cut off from the outside
world, increased as those inside wove the circle, until finally
Graham was aware that all was done. There in the stillness
between the world of men and the realms of the mighty ones,
he vowed for the sake of William to set aside his own sorrow,
at least for the duration of the night's work. No hint of his own
anger and resentment at the roles thrust upon him and William
would intrude upon this so-special working and taint it with
mere human smallness. If only at Alix's and Ellis's directing,
he must be an open channel through which the power might
flow.

He was ready when they stepped into the doorway. His
mind was stilled and calm, if a little numb, as he mounted the
steps to face the god and goddess who stood there glowing like
silver in the moonlight. The blade felt hot against his breast as
he paused to answer the high priest's ritual challenge. The tang
of incense smoke was sharp in his nostrils.

"Who comes?"

"*Din*, a friend of the old ones, duly sworn."

As always when the sword fell away, Graham experienced
that slight rush of relief that his answer had been accepted and
he was deemed worthy to enter the circle. The splash of the
water Alix sprinkled on him was less of a shock than it sometimes was, but her kiss was sweeter as she drew him inside.
He slipped off his robe and hung it beside the others pegged
on the wall just inside the doorway, but as he turned, his breath
caught in his throat at the sight. From the dim light of altar
candles inside the gazebo as well as the moonlight without,
both Alix and Ellis seemed limned in silver, a nimbus of light,

both physical and psychic, brightening the crowns of horn tips
and flowers they wore. Graham had expected to fade into the
background at this point, to stand only as witness while they
performed what must be done, but something in their solemn,
sad expressions told him they had other plans.

"Is something wrong?" he asked in a low voice.

"Yes, the name of the high priest," Ellis said softly, gnarled
hands resting lightly on the quillons of the sword. "You know
that, Gray. It is you, not I, who should wield the sword and
wear the horned god's crown tonight."

Graham felt his stomach knot as a chill of dread ran up his
spine. Suddenly, despite the carpet underfoot and the twined
roses and ivy that kept out wayward breezes from the trellised
walls, he felt cold.

"I've told you, I can't," he managed to whisper, the words
tumbling out without conscious thought. "You don't know what
you're asking."

"Ah, but I do," Ellis replied. "I also know that if you persist
in what you intend, thinking it will ease the hurt of what may
later have to be, you'll regret it for all times to come."

With an anguished "No!" and a desperate shake of his head,
Graham turned his back on both of them. Clutching at the
painted trellis grid for support and crushing leaves in his hands,
he trembled. He had prayed Ellis would spare him this.

It was not that he did not long to perform this most sacred
office for William—he would have sworn that before all the
gods who ever were. Reception into the company of the ancient
ones was one of the most precious gifts one being could offer
another. The bonds set at such a hallowing extended even
beyond a single lifetime.

But such bonds already clutched at him from other lives,
and to accept the role as one of William's initiators in this life
was also to acknowledge and condone what was almost sure
to follow. Deep within him, he knew that he would, indeed,
perform that more awful function when the time came—but
could he not pretend for just a little longer that it was not so?

With a soft moan of denial, Graham leaned his forehead
among the cool leaves and closed his eyes, fighting down the
sick fear. He was aware of Ellis moving closer, so close their
elbows brushed, but he could not bring himself to look up at
the face beneath the horned crown. Somehow he knew that

Alix had withdrawn to the other side of the circle to give them privacy.

"Do *you* regret it, Wesley?" he whispered after a moment more.

"Fortunately, there was nothing to regret"—the answer came softly—"though I came even closer than you are now. My friend was at the portal, waiting to be admitted to the circle, before I came to my senses and realized what a precious sharing I was about to deny—for both of us. I've never regretted changing my mind—though I do wish I'd done it sooner and spared us both some anxious moments. It was a very special privilege to be the channel through which the power flowed so that—what had to come later would be the more potent."

Graham swallowed painfully, finally daring a glance at the brigadier's feet and the point of the sword resting between them.

"Do you really think it would make any difference to William?"

"I think it would make a great deal of difference. He told me so."

"He *told* you?"

"A little while ago, when I gave him his final briefing," Ellis said quietly. "He tried not to show his disappointment, but I know he was hoping it would be you. You hurt him when you wouldn't even talk about it earlier this evening, Gray. I tried to explain how you felt, and he *said* he understood, but I think it would mean a great deal to him if he could see *you* wearing the horned crown as he approached the circle instead of me."

The last of Graham's counterarguments vanished clean away at that. He had not considered how his own participation could comfort William and strengthen the bond between them. He had forgotten the force of the bonds forged between himself and his own initiators so many years before, though both of them had long since passed on. How could he have thought of denying that to his prince?

Drawing a deep, shuddering breath, he forced the tension out of his body with a sigh and willed himself to relax, uncurling his fingers from their death grip on the trellis, suddenly aware of pain. His palms were bloody from the rose thorns he had

crushed. He stared at the blood stupidly, for an instant flashing
on the old nightmare.

Alix moved closer as soon as she saw his hands.

"You've hurt yourself.".

His first impulse had been to let the blood stay, but he
submitted to her inspection without resistance, wincing as she
pulled out several thorns.

"It doesn't matter," he murmured, allowing her to bathe his
wounded hands with a cloth dipped in the consecrated water.
"The only thing that does matter is that man waiting outside
the maze right now. I've nearly done both of us a terrible
disservice."

As Alix wiped his hands dry, brushing each palm lightly
with her lips, Ellis smiled and inclined his head in a slight
bow.

"I believe we have a new high priest for this evening, then,
my lady—provided, of course, that you agree."

Alix's face was radiant as she put her arms around Graham's
neck and hugged him, the sweet scent of her flower crown
obscuring even the hint of incense lingering on the air.

"Your lady could not be more pleased," she whispered,
pulling away to gaze at Graham with tears glistening in her
eyes.

She took the sword from Ellis and laid it in Graham's hands,
then moved the horned crown from grey head to brown. As
Graham bent to receive it, he sensed the familiar mantle of
that other, magical identity settling invisibly on his shoulders—
the power of the god surrounding and enfolding him as he
moved into the doorway with Alix, even as the goddess's per-
fume had surrounded him only seconds before.

He rested the tip of the sword on the floor in front of him,
wounded hands resting on the quillons, and raised his face to
the moonlight, inhaling the magic of the night. He seemed to
feel himself grow taller by inches until he loomed like some
great, primal giant bestriding the world—God himself, but also
protector and consort to the one who stood at his side, who
was no longer only Alix and mortal.

A slight breeze stirred, caressing his body and lifting strands
of Alix's hair to partially veil both of them. Its touch was
electric, jolting him to an even higher level of awareness.

His hearing seemed to have turned hypersensitive as well.

Far off, he caught the faint crunch of footsteps on gravel. Turning his attention to the maze stretched out in the moonlight before them, he closed his eyes and eased out onto the Second Road. Far toward the outer edge of the maze, he began to sense ripples in the cosmic pattern: William approaching, Michael at his back, to keep an appointment with the gods.

The moon had retreated briefly behind a cloud, but it returned in full glory as William followed Michael through the library's French doors and out into the garden. The moonlight shone bright and silver-sharp against the inky shadows. The gravel underfoot was cold and gritty.

Just inside the maze, he paused for Michael to close the gate and snap a padlock shut on a hasp. The key hung from a nail close to the ground. Michael's black-robed form was in shadow as he turned to face the prince.

"I don't know whether you've been in this maze before, sir," Michael said in a low voice, gesturing toward the path, "but even if you have, I think you'll find it different tonight. By changing a series of gates, we make the pattern a magical one. Walking it in the right frame of mind produces an effect similar to casting a magical circle, though there will be another circle inside as well. You're to lead. I'll follow along behind. There are no false turnings."

A little taken aback, William gazed at the path stretching away in the moonlight. Out there, something awaited him—he knew not what.

"Just—follow the path?"

Michael grinned reassuringly, his teeth flashing in the shadow of his face. "I think you'll find there's nothing *just* about it, sir. I don't know whether you have sufficient training yet to actually feel a difference, but after Canterbury and Windsor, I shouldn't be at all surprised. If you should find yourself slipping into a light trance, so much the better."

"I'll keep that in mind," William murmured with an uneasy smile.

As William began walking the maze, he could hear only the faint buzz of crickets and other night creatures, the whisper of his and Michael's bare feet on the gravel, and his own pulse throbbing in his temples. He tried to slow his breathing, half closing his eyes and letting his fingertips brush the close-clipped hedges to either side to guide him, and gradually he felt himself relaxing. Just as predicted, he was easing himself into a light, comfortable trance.

He realized as he walked that part of the sound he heard was not his pulse at all but a low throb of drumming, similar to the night at Buckland. Without his conscious effort, his pulse rate and breathing slowed to coincide with its beat. Following the path along its twists and turns, he could feel something that was not quite tension or expectation creeping up his spine, concentrating at the back of his head, at once amplifying and muffling his normal perceptions.

Quite suddenly, he passed from the maze into a flagstoned central courtyard. An old-fashioned gazebo stood in the center, white-painted trellises washed silver in the moonlight, roses and ivy stark against the brightness. A break in the pattern of wood and foliage suggested a doorway toward the left, so he headed in that direction. When he came abreast of the opening, still five or six yards from the steps, he stopped. In that instant, the drumming also ceased.

He caught his breath in shocked wonder, for poised in the rose-framed doorway stood two of the most awesome beings William had ever seen. His eyes flicked first to the woman, slender, nude body partially veiled by hip-length hair that floated a little on the breeze, pale gilt in the moonlight. A silver crescent moon was bound across her brow, a crown of flowers above it. A part of him identified her as Alix, but she was also something far, far more.

And the man—

The relief that flooded over William like a wave was so intense that for an instant he felt a little dizzy, for the man with the sword at rest beneath his hands and wearing a staghorn crown was Gray—but a Gray quite transformed from the taut, grief-strained man William last had seen. He, too, wore nothing save the moonlight and an ineffable mantle of majesty that seemed to make him glow from within.

Magic crackled in the very air. As William's awed glance darted back and forth from Alix to Gray, Gray to Alix, a sense of such joy welled in his chest that it threatened to explode. Suddenly, he thought he understood what Gray had once tried to explain about the divinity in all men and women. Power pulsed from the two, raising the hackles at the back of William's neck in an almost sensual shiver, and he found his hands going to the cincture at his waist and untying it, letting his robe fall into Michael's waiting hands.

He felt no self-consciousness to stand thus before them. Nor was there any real question of multiple gods, though that was a convenient metaphor to explain the many aspects of deity, masculine and feminine in its wholeness. Before such revelation, the shedding of his robe seemed symbolic of stripping away the last vestiges of pretense—a sacramental act. He partook of their divinity with every breath he drew, his longing to be with them a growing ache of heart and very soul.

"You have two perfect passwords: perfect love and perfect trust," Michael murmured close by his ear.

The words registered at some deep level, familiar and new at once, but his attention was centered on what he was experiencing. Robeless, his perception of the power emanating from the two was even more acute, like goose flesh, not unpleasant— merely tingling and strange. Neither of them had moved as he stared up awe-struck in the moonlight, but as he began slowly walking toward the steps that separated him from their realm, drawn by their magic, the drum began to throb again. This time, the rhythm was with his heartbeat from the start: insistent, all-encompassing, compelling his approach.

The two stepped back a pace as he climbed the four wooden steps, and moonlight flashed a warning from the blade Gray raised and poised before his heart. William stopped.

"O thou who wouldst cross the boundary between the worlds, hast thou the courage to face the tests which will be required of thee?" Gray demanded, his voice as steady as the hand that held the sword. *"For I tell thee, it were better to throw thyself upon this sacred blade and perish now than to essay the trials with fearing in thy heart."*

Swallowing, William stared long into Gray's eyes, acutely aware that it was not only the length of steel that separated them in this instant. Instinctively, he shifted his gaze to the more merciful goddess.

"I have two perfect passwords: perfect love and perfect trust," he said.

"All with such words are doubly welcome," Alix replied as the sword fell away and Gray stepped back. "And now I give thee a third password," she continued, slipping an arm around his waist and drawing his head down to hers with her other arm.

Her kiss was leisurely and gentle, but thorough; heady and sweet, but not a lover's kiss despite its intimacy. William was not aware that he had been drawn into the circle until she drew away and released him. As he glanced around, disoriented, he realized that Michael had come in right behind him and that Gray was closing the circle with his sword. Each time the blade was drawn across the threshold, the doorway seemed to become more obscured until by the third stroke William literally could not see what lay beyond save moonlight.

Mystified, he turned back toward the center of the chamber just in time to catch a glimpse of the brigadier crouched on a low stool on the other side, eyes closed as he drummed lightly on what looked like a small tom-tom. Michael stood beside Ellis, arms crossed on his chest, and he smiled reassurance and nodded slightly as he caught William's eye.

Then Alix placed a blindfold across the prince's eyes and tied it behind his head. At the same time, his arms were bound behind his back, Gray knotting the cords.

With his wrists secured at the small of his back, they passed the tails of the cord up around his neck and tied them so that, to avoid pressure on his throat, he had to keep his arms raised slightly by a conscious effort. The ends were allowed to dangle on his chest in a cable tow, and another cord was tied loosely around his left ankle and left free, reminiscent of one of his early Masonic initiations.

Water splashed on his bare chest and face without warning. He flinched a little even though he had been half expecting it, and as he ran his tongue furtively along his lower lip to catch a droplet trembling there, he tasted salt. A faint hissing sound became discernible just above the drumming, and then he was aware of incense smoke tickling his nose and of someone walking around him with a censer.

The cold edge of a blade was laid against the right side of his throat as the incense smell receded, causing him to flinch again. His pulse leaped in answer, throbbing under the steel, and he knew the harsh reality of the threat; for even though it was surely Gray's hand that held it, it was also the hand of a god.

"Men have died for daring to enter a circle such as this,"

Alix's voice said, coming hollowly from slightly to his right. "But because you had two perfect passwords, you were admitted. Perfect love and perfect trust are part of the foundation of all the arts magical, both of them embodied in the sacred kiss which actually drew you into this circle. Without them, to pierce the veil is to perish. Do you understand?"

He thought he did, but he was not sure he trusted himself to speak, so he gave only a slow nod, very careful of the blade pressed against his throat and the cords still binding him.

"That is well. Yet even now your peril is not behind you. Having heard such passwords, I must now ask your intentions in daring to essay this circle. You may answer in your own words."

He did not need to think about this answer. The words came tumbling out, all unbidden, with an eloquence that surprised him, his voice far steadier than he had dared to hope.

"As a son of the old line, I come to claim my birthright and reception into the old ways at your hands."

"And why do you ask this of us?" she persisted.

"That I—that I might better serve," he replied, annoyed at the momentary hesitation.

His inquisitor apparently did not think it amiss, for after a beat, William felt the blade turn flat against his throat—new cold that startled him momentarily until he realized its significance: his answer had been accepted.

"You have answered well, son of the old line," Alix said softly. "Are you aware of the implications of what you ask in offering your life in service, and are you prepared to vow your fidelity to the ancient ones, in whose service you shall be consecrated?"

"I am," he said evenly, though he tried not to think of *all* the implications.

As the blade fell away from his throat, he felt the tug of the cable tow around hs neck. Blindly, he followed as he was led, pausing as Alix paused. Her hand lay on his right elbow, steadying him as they stopped, and he had the eerie feeling that she was addressing someone he could not have seen even if his eyes had not been bandaged.

"O watchers of the east, I here present William Victor Charles Arthur, who comes to claim his birthright as a son of the living gods."

She released his arm and took the cable tow again, leading him to the right a few steps, where the formula was repeated.

"O watchers of the south, I here present William Victor Charles Arthur, who comes to claim his birthright as a son of the living gods."

Twice more she repeated the process, in the west and in the north, returning finally to the east, though she said nothing there. William thought she might have made some sign or salute, but he could not be certain behind his blindfold and was not sure he wanted to know. She drew him back into the center then, and abruptly he was alone.

The drumming stopped. No hands supported him. He could feel the longer end of the cable tow brushing against his belly, the cords pulling against his throat and restraining his hands, and the texture of the carpet beneath his feet. Faintly, he could still smell incense, but he could hear nothing save the night sounds outside. The silence and the sense of isolation set his imagination to working. Suddenly, he was very much aware of his vulnerability as he stood there, bound and naked, helpless to defend himself if they should intend him harm. He could feel his pulse rate rising as his anxiety increased.

What if Ellis had lied? Suppose they *had* set the sacrifice for tonight without telling him? Would they have taken the ultimate choice out of his hands? Was that why Gray had agreed to play the high priest at the last minute, because it was he who must strike the fatal blow? Was William even now the sacrifice, ritually cleansed and bound and ready to be offered up?

As his panic rose, he shivered and then suddenly froze, abruptly aware that the terrifying lightheadedness he felt came from the pressure of the cord across his throat—nothing else. When he lifted his hands slightly behind his back, the pressure eased, and the dizziness passed, and so did his fear.

Feeling a little embarrassed over scaring himself, and trusting them once more, he took a deep, steadying breath and made himself relax, suddenly glad for the blindfold. He fancied it gave some refuge, at least, from the staring eyes that watched from the silence—some of which eyes he sensed were not entirely human. He jumped as he felt something brush the top of his head and tickle down his back and legs.

"Your measure is being taken," he heard Alix say softly

from somewhere behind him, near his feet. "In the old days, the measure would have been kept by the master of the coven and used as a psychic link for punishing anyone who broke the oath which you shortly will be asked to take. It has other uses as well."

He heard the snip of scissors at his heels, the indistinct whisper of her standing. Then an end of the cord was being passed around his forehead and withdrawn, the process repeated around his chest. He assumed it was Gray who took his left hand, still tied behind his back, and straightened out his ring finger.

"I'm going to prick your finger in a few seconds," Gray's voice murmured in his ear as something cold and wet was scrubbed across his fingertip. "It's traditional that a few drops of the initiate's blood be put on the measure to seal the commitment being made. Of course, that also strengthens the psychic link. Nowadays the measure is generally given back—though we can keep yours for you if you like. You don't have to make a decision right now."

William caught a whiff of alcohol as the cord slithered around his waist and was withdrawn and then a quick needle jab in his finger. The cord was passed quickly around his hips, and then, after a slight delay, he felt them fumbling at his back again, his finger being squeezed and something pressed to it briefly. As paper rustled somewhere to his left, his finger was swabbed off again. Then he was standing alone once more. He was no longer at all afraid.

"Are you now prepared to swear the oath?" Alix asked.

"I am."

"Then kneel, knowing that you present yourself before the creative force in all its myriad names, gods and goddesses of many faiths and faces and guises. You are asked to abjure none of them, for all men should have the freedom to reverence deity in whatever form seems proper to them, but you are asked to pledge faith and discretion as a child of the gods."

Slowly, he sank to his knees, awed and humbled, for he had not thought of what he was doing in precisely those terms. Alix's and Gray's hands supported him as he lowered himself, and in their touch he sensed again the mantles of godhood that they had assumed for this night on his behalf and in Their honor. He could feel tears stinging behind his eyelids, and

again he was grateful for the blindfold—this time not for fear
of seeing any unknown watchers. The giving of this oath was
an intensely private thing.

"Repeat after me," he heard Alix say. "I—and state your
full name. . . ."

"I, William Victor Charles Arthur . . ."

"In the presence of the ancient ones and you, my brothers
and sisters . . ."

"In the presence of the ancient ones and you, my brothers
and sisters," he repeated.

"Do of my own free will and accord solemnly swear . . ."

He repeated the lines of the oath with increasing confidence
and in good conscience. Not only the sense but the words
themselves seemed familiar, and he wondered whether he had
said them before in one of those other lives.

"All this I swear by my hopes of a future life . . .

"Mindful that my measure has been taken . . .

"And may all my weapons turn against me . . .

"If I break this, my sacred oath . . .

"So be it."

"So be it," he replied confidently.

The hands that had guided him to his knees now helped him
to rise, Alix pulling off the blindfold while Gray tugged loose
the knot of the cable tow. William blinked in the candlelight
and stared at Gray, uncertain whether the pale, fire-bronzed
being bending to untie his hands was still god or only man
once again, but he caught a faint smile of reassurance on his
friend's face as his hands were finally released and Gray
straightened to wind up the cord. It was then, also, that William
got his first clear look at the horned crown—small branched
horn tips set evenly around a circlet of silver.

Alix undid the cord trailing from his ankle and coiled it
quickly as she rose, taking both hers and Gray's to lay them
on what William assumed must be an altar behind her—a low,
rectangular table covered with a white cloth, a black candle
set to the left side and a white one at the right.

He had no time to study further details, for Alix had taken
up a small vial as she turned to face him again, moistening her
right thumb from it and approaching him with purpose. Sensing
the solemnity of the moment, he drew himself more erect and
stood very still, closing his eyes, his skin twitching a little as

she touched him: right breast, left breast, abdomen just below the navel, right breast again.

"I consecrate thee priest and witch," he heard her say almost in a whisper, opening his eyes with a start as she brushed his lips with hers. "And in honour of this consecration, I give thee a new name before willing thee power. Please kneel."

He obeyed, steadying himself on Gray's outstretched hand as he went down. Michael and the brigadier had come to stand behind him as she spoke. He could feel the hems of their robes brushing against the bottoms of his feet.

"It is customary in most faiths for an initiate to be given a new name at the time of his reception," she said softly. "You received the names of various Christian saints and family members at your baptism and confirmation.

"Because our magical tradition has some of its roots in the mystical Qabala, our forebears chose to use the *sephiroth* of the tree of life as magical names. Within the confines of avoiding duplication, we try to select an aspect which is appropriate to the person. My name is *Binah*, which is the sphere of understanding, of slumbering potentiality, the Mother of the Universe. Gray is *Din*, sometimes also called *Geburah*, the sphere of power, severity, and discipline. Wesley is *Hesed*, the merciful, loving Father, guide and protector. Michael is *Netsah*, which is the sphere of human instincts and emotions, the force of nature."

She moistened her thumb again and touched it to his forehead, splaying her fingers across the crown of his head. He closed his eyes immediately, sensing the power of a name, and felt the spot under her thumb as a warm, pulsing point of energy.

"I name thee *Kether*, which is the crown—the first emanation of God, for so thou shalt be in times to come, as thou hast been in times past."

He stiffened a little at that, for it was the first direct allusion to the ultimate reason for his presence here tonight.

But then, with her right hand still on his crown, Alix knelt slightly to his right, her left hand touching the soles of his feet.

"Relax and flow with what you feel," he heard Gray murmur as another hand touched his head and he sensed Gray crouching on his left.

William did relax as Gray's other hand touched his feet;

and all at once he was acutely aware of kneeling between two poles of incredible power, god and goddess, deity about to act through priest and priestess, dual sacring.

"By this laying on of hands do we will thee power," Alix said, "that all which our hands encompass may be consecrated to the service of the gods: *Kether*, high priest and magus and son of the living gods."

"So be it," Gray responded.

With almost a shudder, William let his mind retreat to the centered comfort of trance, for suddenly their touch began to reach beyond the physical. The sensation intensified—bright, insistent pressure inside his brain and an almost electrical, crawling sensation all over his skin, at once threatening and exhilarating, though the threat was not one of danger, only change. He was aware of other hands being laid upon his shoulders, other minds joining in, and their touch plunged him deeper yet.

No sound intruded save his own pulse hammering in his temples and the breathing of the four around him, which all at once had become one with his. He felt more alive than he had ever been, a vast *something* stirring in places deep within him where no one and nothing had ever touched, though there were flashes of *other-whens* that gave hint that this was not the first time he had felt this way. As the intensity finally began to slack off, William thought he knew where he could find the strength to do what eventually must be done.

And Graham, sensing the ebb of power, knew without doubt that this initiation had "taken." Most did, but a very few did not—though such initiates generally experienced a spontaneous initiation at a later date. Sometimes, too, the ritual was merely a formal sealing of an inner initiation that had already taken place. William's had been neither of those.

Graham watched the prince open his eyes as they all drew back, and he temporarily shed his mantle of godhood so William could see the very human pride and love in his eyes. He let Alix greet their new brother first, as was proper, but then he was vying with Ellis and Michael to embrace and welcome, all rank and divinity temporarily set aside. The five of them laughed and joked like rowdy children, momentarily forgetting the future.

Reality intruded all too quickly, for the drone of aircraft

overhead again wrenched them back—the remnants of the earlier raiders returning east, unladen now, though not so many as before. They froze and listened, none of them moving until the silence had returned save William, who stood in the doorway and stared up grimly at the shadows crossing the moon.

All the weight of Graham's own responsibility came settling back on his shoulders as he hurriedly slipped back into his robe. Officiating with Alix helped, but his heart still twisted in his chest as he watched William thrust his arms blindly into the white robe Michael held for him. Alix finished donning her own robe and tried to put on a courageous smile as Michael knotted a scarlet cord around the prince's waist.

"You may have wondered why your robe is different," Alix said, also putting on a scarlet cord. "White is the proper color for the candidate for initiation, but it is also the garment of the sacred king. The initiate wears the scarlet cord, however—not black or white, because red is the color of life. You're one of us now."

William made no reply to that, though he nodded understanding, but when he bent to buckle on his Garter for the next part of the ritual, Graham had to look away. Though he knew Ellis had been right to insist he take the high priest's role tonight, that knowledge was not making it any easier to deal with what came next. He almost wished someone else could take over the rest, though another part of him knew he would have killed to keep the privilege.

He crouched beside Alix by the altar, glad for the extra hands as Ellis joined them and helped clear it of everything but the cloth and the two lit tapers, black and white like the pillars of the tree of life. He was very much aware of William watching him from the edge of the circle, Michael standing at his elbow.

After Alix arranged all to her satisfaction, she picked up the vial of oil again and glanced at him. Ellis, with a sympathetic squeeze of Graham's shoulder, withdrew to stand on William's other side.

"I realize this part will be especially difficult for both of you," Alix said in a very low voice. "Do you think he realizes you've reconciled your objections?"

Graham turned his head away slightly, to stare into the flame of the white taper.

"*Have* I reconciled them?"

"I think you know you have, insofar as anyone can."

"Then perhaps I have. I've resigned myself to bowing to his will at least. I'm glad you and Wesley made me see how it would have hurt him not to have done what I'm doing tonight."

"No one could ask more, Gray. I don't envy you your choice."

As she touched his hand in comfort, he took hers and pressed it to his lips, giving her a fleeting smile. Sighing, she stood and turned to face the prince, the altar at her back and Graham moving into place at her left hand. At Alix's nod, Ellis and Michael brought the prince forward the few steps where, at Alix's second nod, he knelt. In his white robe, surrounded by their black, his fair hair bright gold in the candlelight, he already looked the young god incarnate.

"William, I am oath bound to ask you once more before we proceed," she said gravely. "Are you certain this is what you wish? It isn't too late to turn back. None of us will think the worse of you for it. No one is forcing you to do this besides yourself."

William's voice did not falter, though the formality of his words might have covered an understandable apprehension.

"My lady, it is not what I would have sought out for my end, but I have come to believe in the past weeks that circumstances leave me no other option. For my brother's sake as well as the sake of the land, I feel it necessary at this time that I at least offer up my *willingness* to stand in the King's stead. If circumstances should change—and I pray they will—then I shall be the first to welcome the removal of this cup. But if that is not to be, then it is meet that I—and he"—he nodded toward Graham—"enter this obligation properly prepared. I beseech all of you to support me in my decision."

The prince's answer did not surprise Graham, though the royal glance touched his soul with ice. To spare both their nerves—since it was obvious there was to be no reprieve from this part—he inclined his head in reluctant submission and backed off a few paces to await his next cue, the crown of the horned god weighty on his head.

"So be it," Alix murmured. "Brethren, let us prepare the sacred king for his anointing."

In numbed fascination, Graham watched Ellis and Michael open the neck of William's robe and ease it back from his shoulders, baring his chest and upper arms. To words hallowed by usage down the centuries, Alix anointed the sacred king.

"Be thy hands anointed with holy oil," she murmured, signing each palm with a circled cross.

"Be thy breast anointed with holy oil."

Her thumb traced the sign bold above his heart.

"Be thy shoulders anointed with holy oil."

She traced the sacred symbol between his shouder blades as he bowed his head.

"Be thy head anointed with holy oil, as kings, priests, and prophets were anointed: and as Solomon was anointed king by Zadok the priest and Nathan the prophet, so be you anointed, blessed, and consecrated King over the Peoples, whom the Lord your God hath given you to rule and govern. *Selah.* Amen. So be it."

"So be it," Ellis and Michael responded.

They helped the prince to rise then, drawing his robe back into place before they led him between Alix and Graham to stand before the altar. There, with the oil still glistening on his upturned palms, he was enthroned between the pillars of severity and mercy, the sacrifice set upon the altar in symbol. A little timidly, his eyes sought Graham once more.

But it was *Din*, the high priest of the ancient ones, who sustained Graham now as he stepped before the prince and paused to bow. All the power and majesty of the godhead he assumed with his office blended with the resigned sorrow of the man as Graham reached slowly to his head and removed the horned god's diadem.

"You are the Sacred King, the God Incarnate," Alix said softly, kneeling expectantly at William's right hand as Graham moved closer to the prince, turning the horned crown in his hands. "You are the fitting substitute for another anointed king who sits a different throne not far away."

Outwardly dispassionate, Graham raised the crown above the royal head in salute and held it there for several heartbeats, hands steady as he gazed into William's eyes, then lowered it gently. William shuddered a little and closed his eyes briefly as the weight settled on his head. He did not seem to notice as Graham bowed again and began slowly backing off, arms crossed on his breast, until his back encountered the trellised wall.

"We acknowledge you as Lord, here in this sacred circle," Alix continued. "Here, before the ancient ones and all the gods and goddesses—who are all but facets of the whole—we pledge you our homage and our service, as our forebears pledged to yours when the land was young." She took off her crown of flowers and laid it at his feet in tribute. "We acknowledge that the sacrifice may be required and that the decision is yours alone. Whatever assistance you may require, we are yours to command."

As though through a fog, Graham watched Alix wipe her long hair over the prince's palms to cleanse them of the sacring oil, then lay the sword across them. William kissed the hilt before resting it across his knees. Graham averted his eyes as Alix placed her hands between William's, but he could not shut out her words.

"In heart as well as hands, I am your servant," Alix said, affirming her own acknowledgment of the oaths first sworn at Laurelgrove. "Faith and truth will I bear unto you, to live and to die, against all manner of folk. And may my powers desert me and my weapons turn against me if I break this, my solemn oath. As you command, so mote it be."

"So mote it be," Ellis and Michael echoed.

Graham forced himself to pay attention as Ellis and then Michael went forward to repeat the homage, drawing unexpected comfort from their example, but when all three of them had retreated to the doorway and knelt once more, trying not to look too pointedly at him, Graham knew he could delay no longer. Awkwardly, he went before the silent prince and eased down on both knees, almost holding his breath. As he held out his right hand alone, William's eyes flicked to it in faint surprise.

"Take my hand, Will," Graham whispered, flinching a little as he caught the prince's gaze again. "Take it as you took it that night you asked to come with me to Buckland and all of this began."

A little puzzled but obviously remembering, William joined his right hand to Graham's as if in handshake, covering its back with his left. Graham relaxed a little and allowed a tiny, wry smile to pass his lips.

"You invoked a feudal bond between us even then, you know," he murmured, feeling his way carefully through what he wanted to say. "I have no idea whether you were aware of it when you first asked your question, but I'm certain you must have realized by the time we'd parted. You knew I was your man and that I couldn't refuse you—even though it took *me* a while to realize that. We'd never talked about it before that night, and we certainly had sworn no formal oaths, but the bond was there. I couldn't even begin to tell you when it started. Perhaps that first day a green young naval lieutenant walked into my office—though I suspect, from what we've both been remembering, that it started long before this life."

William's head dipped in hesitant agreement. "I think you're probably right."

"What I want to do, then, is to make it official, the way it should have been that other night," Graham said, bringing up his left hand to slip it between William's two, palm to palm with his own.

"To you, my prince, I would have given my fealty any time you asked it—even though you never asked. Now that it seems you are destined to be the sacred king as well as my prince and you wear *that* crown, the traditional words of the oath are perhaps particularly fitting: I, John Cathal Graham, do become your liege man of life and limb *and of earthly worship*." He had to pause to swallow before he could go on; he could see William's throat working, too.

"I don't suppose we'll ever know how many times that oath has been true in a literal sense," Graham continued softly, glancing again at the crown he had lately worn, "but it's certainly true now. Your early Garter Knights understood it that way, I feel certain. Incidentally, I don't know how to put this last bit into formal words, but there are no reservations or restrictions to the commitment I've just made to you. I will do whatever you ask me to do for you—*whatever* you ask."

He could not keep his eyes on William's anymore at that, and sensed that his voice would break if he tried to say anything else, so he ducked his head and kissed the royal hands instead. As he rested his forehead heavily against their joined hands, he realized that William was trembling as badly as he was.

"Thank you," he heard his prince whisper as William's head dipped to rest briefly against his own.

Then William drew himself erect once more, and Graham
as well, the two of them embracing in the formal kiss of peace
with a sense of relief that surprised both of them. As William
raised him up, Graham knew that whatever lay ahead, they
would approach it with as much of the joy of tonight as could
be mustered. They were equally committed now. Nor would
the cup pass.

CHAPTER 25

"T HE GRATITUDE OF EVERY HOME IN OUR ISLAND, in our empire, and indeed throughout the world, except in the abodes of the guilty, goes out to the British airmen who, undaunted by odds, unwearied in their constant challenge and mortal danger, are turning the tide of the world war by their prowess and by their devotion," Winston Churchill told a packed House of Commons two days later. "Never in the field of human conflict was so much owed by so many to so few."

Though Churchill was speaking of the RAF and was right to do so, it appeared to an even smaller few in the days that followed that the direction of battle might also be shifting due to other causes. The few at Oakwood had hoped that William's mere act of offering himself as a potential sacred king and going through formal preparations might serve to satisfy whatever fate was directing events. For nearly a week, that did seem to be the case.

Poor weather cloaked most of Britain in rain and cloud until the following weekend, severely hampering enemy reconnaissance and confining bombing to the coast and Channel. Dover endured an eighty-minute barrage from the big guns at Cap Gris-Nez at midweek as well as the usual air raids, but no massed attacks penetrated far inland. With improving weather on the twenty-third, the Germans bombed over South Wales, particularly in the vicinity of Pembroke Dock, but a guarded

communication from Richard indicated that no great damage
had been done.

The twenty-fourth brought clear weather and a tightening
of German air tactics that at first caught the RAF unprepared.
The introduction of "stepped" raids set incoming bombers at
staggered altitudes before they split off in real and feint attacks,
confusing radar interpretation and making fighter interception
far more difficult. The forward airfields of Hornchurch and
North Weald were pounded severely, and Manston was so
heavily damaged that it had to be abandoned. That night, the
largest German bomber force yet amassed was dispatched to
attack the vital factories and supply facilities of the South.

London itself had not been on the night's orders. Up until
then, the Luftwaffe had limited its raids to strategic targets
whose destruction would obviously hasten the demise of the
RAF and clear the way for successful invasion. But ten of the
nearly two hundred bombers sent out that night made a navi-
gational error as they approached their assigned target, east of
London. Instead of hitting the oil storage facilities at Thames-
haven, they destroyed old St. Giles Church at Cripplegate and
other historic and residential buildings in the heart of London.
The very next night, grim, determined pilots of RAF Bomber
Command retaliated with a daring raid on Berlin, with more
following in the days and weeks ahead.

Hitler was outraged, though it took two weeks to feel the
full fury of his anger. To penetrate to Berlin was a gross insult
to a man who had been telling his people for months that
German cities could not be bombed. As he had threatened early
in August when he reserved to himself the right to resort to
terrorist tactics, he unleashed the Luftwaffe for indiscriminate
bombing in the future. No longer would civilian noncombatants
and historic buildings be spared. London, in particular, was to
be singled out for punishment, the morale of its citizens shattered through a war of frazzled nerves, sleepless nights, and
destruction.

"The British will know that we are giving our answer night
after night," he ranted early in September, just before the blitz
began in earnest. "We shall stop the handiwork of these night
pilots."

Meanwhile, as Hitler's rage grew, German raiders continued
to hammer daily at the ring of forward fighter bases and sector

stations defending London—Kenley, Biggin Hill, Rockford, Lympne, Hawkinge, Croydon—massing over France each morning and afternoon to hurl new assaults against a gasping countryside. In the fortnight that followed the fateful London bombing, the Luftwaffe made more than thirty major raids on airfields and factories, seeking especially to draw the last reserves of Fighter Command into the air for destruction. Increasing numbers of fighter escorts came with the bombers—a thousand or more per day—all taking their toll of the dwindling defenders.

The defenders held fast, but the edge was slipping. Though Fighter Command accounted for nearly four hundred German aircraft during that period, they lost nearly three hundred—figures that did not reflect damaged aircraft or the grim statistics of pilot wastage: more than a hundred killed, and as many wounded, from a total strength of little more than a thousand. Training of new pilots could not account for half the dead. Such replacements were green, unblooded, all too easy pickings for German aces. Quickly, they either acquired survival instincts or died.

The pressure was as great on Graham and William and the others of Oakwood as August drew to a close and each day seemed to bring them that much closer to the brink. Some of the personal immediacy of the Nazi menace came through for Graham on the morning after the first London bombing. As he and several of his intelligence team sifted through the smoking rubble of a bombed-out MI.6 office near Cripplegate—drafted to help salvage some of the files—Graham unexpectedly ran across the translation of a Nazi loyalty oath.

By this oath, we again bind our lives to a man through whom—and this is our belief—Superior Forces act in fulfillment of Destiny...

Fulfillment of destiny.... The words flayed him in ironic challenge, a brutal gauntlet flung across the miles from the hated man in Germany, for whose stopping a prince was preparing to lay down his life in sacrifice.

Not for the first time, Graham was seized by doubt, as well as dread—trying to deny the fatal necessity. Were they really doing the right thing? And how did *anyone* ever know for certain?

Then he flashed—as he had so often since that Lammas

night—on the spectre of Hitler's face, contorted with rage as
he approached the dying Dieter and raised a pistol . . . the victim
who looked like William, bowed before the satanic throne with
throat presented to the sacrificial blade . . . the predatory eyes
of Hitler's black magicians watching from behind their
masks . . . the blood of other sacrifices in the photos Dieter had
sent them. And he knew that the man responsible must be
stopped, whatever the cost—even if it meant William must
die. That night, he was more than usually silent as he dined
with William at the brigadier's club, all too aware that a decision must soon be made on the manner of William's death.

Consideration of the subject had been reluctantly under way
since William's intentions first became known, while Graham
still dared to hope he might not have to carry through. From
the beginning, all of them had been acutely aware that a sacrificial slaying must be laid out with meticulous attention to
detail. Though William might be prepared to die for the welfare
of the people and the land as sacred kings had died before, the
circumstances of his death must be such that even Wells's
Thulist confederates—at large once more for want of evidence—would not dare to raise unwelcome speculations about
the King's youngest brother. Just as the King's own name must
be kept immaculate for the sake of the millions of his subjects
who looked to him and his queen for courage and inspiration,
so must any taint of the unconventional or the scandalous be
diverted from William and any of his close associates—or
William's death.

"Thank God I have you and Michael to help me winnow
down the options," Graham told the brigadier later that evening
after William had gone home. "It's a bloody awful tightrope
I'm walking. Part of me is resigned and very coolly calculating
about the whole thing. The other part wants nothing more than
to go gibbering off in a corner to hide. I hardly even know
where to begin, Wesley."

Ellis nodded, sucking at a pipeful of unlit tobacco as he
poured cognac for both of them.

"You begin by discarding the methods that are totally un-
workable, and then you go on from there. Fortunately, the
actual ritual requirements are rather minimal: the blood of the
victim must be spilled, and you must be the active agent of
death—though that doesn't necessarily mean you have to be

present when it occurs." He cocked his head at Graham. "Has William expressed any preferences—or prejudices?"

"No." Graham ran a listless fingertip along the edge of his glass. "He doesn't want to know."

"That's certainly understandable."

"Yes. Well." Graham sighed. "I've eliminated two possibilities at least. No carbon monoxide mishap and no car crash. Our Thulists would have a field day so soon after Wells's death."

Ellis nodded. "That's certainly true. And when the King's brother is involved, one can hardly hope to cover up the evidence with a quick burial at sea. Whatever you choose has to be able to stand the scrutiny of an autopsy—which also eliminates drugs or any kind of poison. Not that you could bring yourself to do it that way, I suspect."

Graham grimaced and shook his head, flashing on the memory of Wells beneath the needle and the hollow look of dread in William's eyes as he became aware of what must be done.

"How about a riding accident, then?" Ellis asked. "Everyone knows William is a horseman. What could be more natural?"

"I'd thought of that," Graham replied in a low voice. "It's too difficult to control the outcome. Riding mishaps are common enough, but not fatal ones. Suppose he were only hurt—or left crippled?"

"Hmmm, there is that."

A few days later, Graham and Michael talked about outright assassination.

"You've had to do it before," Michael noted. "You're bloody good, too. You wouldn't have to worry about botching the job."

Graham buried his face in his hands and tried to massage the tension from between his eyes. He had performed his share of such operations in his rather checkered career with the Service, but sighting down the barrel of a gun with William as his target was quite another matter.

"There are two very practical reasons why that won't do," he told the young agent patiently. "Not only could I never pull the trigger, but I'd almost certainly be caught. What motive could I possibly give that would be believed?"

"Temporary insanity?" Michael ventured.

Graham flashed him a grim, acerbic smile. "It would certainly be that. I shouldn't care to speculate on what else it might be." He sighed. "No, the death of a member of the Royal Family is going to be difficult enough as it is. I suppose it might be different if he fell in combat, like other people's sons and husbands and brothers. But you heard what William said that night at Laurelgrove: they don't allow royals into combat zones."

But death in noncombatant military service of some sort might fulfill many requirements, both civil and sacred. A prince who died in the service of his country would elicit the same kind of martyr's veneration as other war dead, only more so, since his death would bring the whole Royal Family closer to the people in their mutual loss. The notion opened up another entire field of speculation.

"He's a naval captain," Michael offered as he and the brigadier sipped glasses of port late one night in Graham's flat. "How about an accident at sea?"

But as Ellis pointed out, William had not done sea duty for years. Such an assignment now might appear contrived. The most likely kind of military-related death for William, which Graham and the brigadier came to discuss more and more in the next few days, was an air crash.

"In almost every respect, it's an ideal choice," Ellis agreed, walking with Graham in the garden at Laurelgrove one evening late in August. "Planes crash with appalling regularity, especially in time of war. Doesn't he have several tours coming up in the next few weeks?"

"Yes."

"Well, then. There's your answer. It can be arranged without danger of you being associated with it, without you needing to be present, and the results will certainly be swift and fatal."

"I suppose."

Graham continued walking when Ellis paused to light up his pipe, seeing the larger flames of a burning plane in the brigadier's match and not wanting to think about the man who would burn with it. He stopped at the edge of a fish pond and stared at the stars reflected in the water, seeing a hundred Garter stars shine back at him like glittering eyes. He flinched as Ellis laid a gnarled hand on his shoulder.

"What, in particular, bothers you about it, Gray?" Ellis asked softly. "Besides the obvious fact that you don't want to do it in the first place."

Graham hung his head, jamming his hands into his pockets.

"I suppose it's the violence of it—and the terror for *him* just before it happens. Then there's the possibility of fire and—and mutilation."

Sighing, Ellis puffed at his pipe and said nothing for several seconds, his hand kneading the taut muscles in the back of Graham's neck.

"I think he's going to know before the end no matter what method you choose and no matter how carefully you try to conceal it from him," the old man said softly. "There's nothing you or I or anyone else can do about that. He's chosen you; and when he wants to know, he'll know. I suspect that such knowledge somehow comes with the territory—as does the courage to put aside the terror." He puffed again on his pipe before continuing.

"As for the other—well, I shouldn't want this to sound callous, but—what happens to the body will hardly make any difference to William once he's dead, will it?"

Graham sighed heavily. "I suppose you're right."

"You know I am. On the other hand, what happens to the body makes a great deal of difference, ritually speaking. The fire doesn't matter, but it's very important that the victim's blood be spilled on the land. An air crash will ensure that."

Graham could refute none of the brigadier's arguments. The more they explored, the more the air accident began to emerge as the most feasible possibility. The fact that the prince would not be alone in an air crash nagged at the back of Graham's conscience, for he had resigned himself only to arranging the death of the sacred king; but Ellis assured him that a crew could be found who were quite willing to accompany their prince on this all-important final mission, well aware of their impending fate and its significance.

"In ancient times, the sacred king often went to his death in the company of a band of honored warriors," Ellis reminded him. "I think a hand-picked flight crew might fulfill a similar function."

Graham shuddered at the very thought, but he could not spare too much energy worrying about that when he himself must wrestle with responsibility for slaying the sacred king—though he did flatly forbid Michael to volunteer as one of the prince's companions. While he began combing his resources

for the most foolproof and untraceable means to down an aircraft, Ellis started making arrangements for the craft itself and
a suitable crew. As requested, they did not tell the prince their
plans, but they bracketed a one-week span in mid-September
as their potential target period, with several contingency dates
selected to coincide with William's heavy schedule of appearances. As the month began, Graham still prayed desperately
that none of their preparations would be necessary.

But invasion began to appear more and more certain. To
stop it, action must be taken soon. On September 3, four German spies were captured on the Kentish coast who claimed to
be advance agents for an invasion to begin "at any moment
now." The next day, rumors flew that an invasion fleet had
already sailed from Norway, though it never turned up. That
night, Hitler addressed a wildly cheering crowd in Berlin's
Sportpalast in a jubilant mood.

"When people are very curious in Britain and ask, 'Yes,
but why doesn't he come?' we reply: 'Calm yourselves. He is
coming! He is coming!'"

Throughout the German army, leaves were canceled. Fifteen
divisions had been moved to ports facing England by the first
of August, and more were set in position in the ensuing month.
During that first grim week of September, RAF reconnaissance
was able to confirm that preparations for invasion were definitely proceeding in the coastal areas of occupied France and
the low countries. In addition to the landing barges already
noted in August—in Ostend alone, the number of barges and
other landing craft had increased from a few dozen to more
than two hundred in only a week—more bombers and transport
aircraft were moving in from Scandinavia to reinforce the German air fleets in Holland and Belgium. At Calais and other
coastal air bases, support squadrons of the black Stuka dive
bombers were massing, as well as the machines necessary for
ferrying assault troops when the actual invasion came. On the
seventh of September, the invasion seemed imminent.

The seventh was a Saturday and began like most recent days
with a morning attack on a major forward base—Hawkinge,
this time, where Audrey barely escaped injury. Further raids
were expected in the afternoon on other sector stations and
strategic targets.

But the afternoon attackers did not veer off for sector stations this time; they converged on London instead by the hundreds. By dusk, they had dumped more than three hundred tons of high explosives and incindiaries on the Woolwich Royal Arsenal and the eastside docklands, making a second sunset in the east before the defenders were convinced this was not another feint. As darkness fell, more waves of enemy bombers, guided by the raging fires, continued to attack. Surely the invasion had begun!

So strong was the threat on that terrible Saturday that began the blitz that the code word "Cromwell" was flashed to the southern and eastern commands of the British Home Forces— "Invasion imminent, and probably within twelve hours"—for it had always been assumed that the final step before actual invasion would be a massive air assault to break the RAF at last. Some Home Guard units misinterpreted the alert and sounded the alarm locally for actual invasion, the church bells pealing for the first time since the outbreak of the war in mistaken warning. Though no beach assaults or German paratroopers materialized, the Home Forces stood to all through the night, while the bombers continued to drop their loads on London, drawn by the beacon of the burning London docks.

The air raids continued day and night, all through the week. Nearly a thousand Londoners lost their lives in the first two days of bombing alone, but the survivors dug in and dug out with astonishing pluck, fighting the fires, tending their dead and wounded, and trying to restore essential services during the lulls in bombing, while life went on in as normal a fashion as possible. Sunday the eighth was another national day of prayer.

Intelligence information now indicated that the invasion would not be delayed beyond the fourteenth. The British Home Fleet prepared to steam south from Scapa to make a last stand in the Channel narrows. The army, still battered and ill equipped after the disastrous Dunkirk venture, stood by with the Home Guard and other civilian volunteers, women and children as well as men, to repel would-be invaders with pitchforks, pruning hooks, kitchen knives, golf clubs, and even rolling pins if need be, for firearms were still in short supply.

Fighter Command alone, reduced by more than a third from the fourteen hundred-plus pilots flying at the beginning of the Battle in mid-July, licked their wounds and thanked God for the relative respite for men, machines, and shattered airfields, now that the emphasis seemed to have shifted to the barrage of London. The danger was no less to individual pilots, for now they must try to turn back the daily waves of raiders bent on making London an inferno, but at least the air bases and the critical factories and radar installations received less German attention.

Weather gave the defenders brief morning respites for several days, but the nightly attacks increased throughout the week of the eighth. The ninth was as bad as the preceding two days for deaths and injuries. The previous night's bombings had devastated power stations, railways, and the already crippled docklands to the east.

On the night of the tenth, the London barrage finally opened up for the first time, the big guns flinging up a vast umbrella of reassuring flak while the searchlights speared the raiders in their revealing beams. Whether the fusillade did a great deal of damage to the enemy in those early nights is uncertain, but its positive effect on morale was immeasurable. At least Londoners felt that they were fighting back—and the German planes did fly higher. On the eleventh, even St. Paul's Cathedral and Buckingham Palace were damaged, explosions missing the royal residence area by mere feet.

That night, Graham and the prince sat in the visitors' gallery and heard the prime minister address the Commons again in a joint broadcast to the nation:

"If this invasion is to be tried at all, it does not seem that it can be long delayed. The weather may break at any time. Besides this, it is difficult for the enemy to keep these gatherings of ships waiting about indefinitely while they are bombed every night by our bombers, and very often shelled by our warships which are waiting for them outside."

Graham and William exchanged troubled glances as the prime minister went on, for the situation was far worse than Churchill was saying.

"Therefore, we must regard the next week or so as a very important period in our history. It ranks with the days when the Spanish Armada was approaching the Channel, and Drake was finishing his game of bowls." Graham watched the prince's eyebrows go up. "Or when Nelson stood between us and Napoleon's Grand Army at Boulogne. We have all read about this in the history books; but what is happening now is on a far greater scale and of far more consequence to the life and future of the world and its civilization than those brave old days."

They walked back toward the Palace after the speech was over, collars buttoned close against a light mist, ducking into an air-raid shelter once when the sirens sounded and bombs began falling alarmingly close by. William was soon recognized and spent the next half hour shaking hands and talking with the local residents who had taken refuge there, commending them on their courage.

"Do you suppose old Winston knows?" William asked when the all-clear had sounded and they were walking on. "I mean, it seems odd that he should mention the Armada and Drake and Nelson just now, don't you think?"

Graham burrowed his hands deeper in his pockets and shrugged. "If he does, I doubt it's conscious," he replied, wondering whether that were really true. He had met Churchill on numerous occasions and had always sensed just a hint of something well guarded beneath the surface. "He's a well-read man, an historian. I should have been surprised if he *hadn't* seen the historical parallels. Whether he's aware of more esoteric considerations is quite another question."

"Hmmm, I dare say you're right. Still, it does seem odd."

They stopped at Graham's office so he could check the afternoon and evening's signals, but they read nothing there to inspire new hope. William was silent as they walked the rest of the way to the Palace, and he had only two words for Graham after he bade him good night. Chilled, Graham watched the prince disappear through a briefly opened door. He gazed at the closed Palace gates for nearly half an hour before hailing a cab.

"He wants me to go ahead," he said after he downed half a tot of whiskey that the brigadier gave him, pacing the floor of the sitting room in the old man's suite of rooms at his club. "I have the device. Which date do you fancy?"

"I think it has to be the sixteenth, on the flight to Wales," Ellis replied after a slight pause. "The plane will be at Calshot on Saturday. You can rig it that night. I'll make the final arrangements for the crew."

"All right."

Graham slumped into a chair and sipped at his drink in silence for several minutes, trying not to think beyond the present, acutely aware of the old man's eyes upon him. When Ellis lifted the decanter in question, Graham shook his head and looked away.

"Thank you, no. I'll be all right. I don't think the rest of it will really hit me now until it's over. For the present, I think I've managed to convince myself that it's just another assignment."

"That's probably best for now," Ellis agreed, though his expression suggested that he did not really believe it. "How are you planning to cover your visit to Calshot?"

Graham gave a wan smile. "The ploy has been used before, but it's a good one. Michael and I will be installing a new 'navigation' unit. It really *does* contain one of those new, experimental radio altimeters—among other things. . . ."

"Explosives?" Ellis asked softly.

Graham drew a sharp breath and shook his head, trying to shut out the image the word conjured—an explosion, and William screaming. He had not intended to let himself talk much about it, but the words came tumbling out.

"No, too suspicious later on. A very small barometric primer to blow the control cables to the tail when they reach a certain altitude. It will seem like a mechanical failure. When the pilot climbs to cross the mountains—"

"Gray, don't," the old man whispered, looking very pale. "Don't make it any more difficult than it is."

With a shudder, Graham drained his glass and set it beside the brigadier's, shaking his head again.

"I said I was all right, Wesley. I'll do what has to be done, don't worry."

Instead of going home, he went back to his office after he left Ellis. He spent the rest of the night in his chair, with instructions for his night staff to wake him if anything came in that might give reprieve. There Denton found him the next morning when he brought in tea and the morning papers.

The rest of the week was little different from the beginning. Graham and the brigadier dined with Michael and the prince on Friday at the brigadier's club, as was their wont when all four were in the city, and on Saturday, Graham and Michael drove to Calshot and back. Sunday was the worst bombing day yet; attacks began before noon and continued on into the night, with heavy losses on both sides. That night, the prince dined at Graham's flat for the last time.

They dressed formally for dinner. Denton prepared one of his gourmet meals and then tactfully withdrew. Afterward, the two men stood outside the French doors on the balcony and watched the clouds of German bombers overshadowing the moon. Searchlight beams and tracer tracks criss-crossed the night sky, giving glimpses of barrage balloons and an occasional nightfighter. From below, fires lit the London skyline. Ash rained down, powdering the dark mess dress tunics with dust that even William ignored, fastidious though he usually was. The gun batteries pounded steadily, punctuated by the dull-thud of bombs that sometimes detonated all too close for comfort.

Despite the danger, William declined to move inside. Instead, he stood with an uneasy Graham and gazed up avidly into the war-torn sky while they drank Napoleon brandy, in ironic commemoration of the speech the prime minister had made the week before. During a lull, William glanced wistfully at his host and then gestured with his glass toward the moon.

"She's almost full tonight, isn't she?" His tone was light, but Graham caught the brittle edge to the real reason for the question.

"Yes, one more day," he said quietly, watching the royal silhouette against the fires burning all around the city.

William nodded slowly and sipped at his drink, savoring the civilized moment amid the chaos of war, then raised his glass a second time.

"Let's drink a toast to the King's health, shall we?"

As Graham touched his glass lightly to William's, the chime of the crystal cut through all artifice.

"Let's drink to *both* kings," he replied.

William tensed for just an instant, hand clenching around the faceted stem of the glass, then bobbed his head in agreement and drank blindly. After a moment, he turned his face slightly toward Graham again, though he would not meet his eyes.

"It *is* tomorrow, isn't it?" William whispered. "Don't tell me details. Just answer yes or no."

Graham swallowed a mouthful of brandy, which had suddenly lost all taste, and allowed the prince a sparse nod.

"Yes."

"I thought it would be," William breathed, glancing at his glass. "The news has been too grim for the past week. And then Winston's speech about Armada times and Napoleon. I knew it had to be before the moon waned, too."

"It wouldn't *have* to be, but yes, that was a consideration." Graham swirled his drink and stared into the fire-lit gold. The crystal was Waterford and far too civilized for such a moment.

"It still isn't too late to call it off, you know, if you've changed your mind," he ventured when William did not seem inclined to speak—though he knew the hope was futile. "We don't know that the sacrifice will make a difference."

"Don't we?"

With a strained smile, William turned and sank to a sitting position against the wall of the balcony, oblivious to the havoc he was wreaking on his dress uniform.

"Sit," he said, patting the cement beside him. "Let me tell you what I remember, and then you tell me if you don't think it will make a difference."

A bomb screamed overhead, thumping into a building in the next block and raining fine debris almost as far as their balcony. Graham ducked and shielded his head with one arm as he dropped to a crouch beside William.

"Are you crazy? We're going to be killed if we stay out here much longer! At least let's go inside to talk."

"Nope. This isn't how I'm supposed to die. I should think that's quite clear by now. It can't be your time, either, since you have to stick around for me. Sit down."

If Graham believed in what they were doing, then he supposed the logic did make an odd kind of sense, though he was not sure it held for his own safety, since his part had already been done. Nonetheless, he edged a little closer to William and obeyed. The prince stretched out his legs straight in front of him, head resting easily against the concrete wall behind him, and ran a thumb along the rim of his half-filled glass as Graham settled.

"There was sunlight that other time, not the light of a burning city," William finally said, holding up his glass and letting his eyes focus on and slightly through it. "Do you remember? We had dined then, too. You wore a scarlet tunic. You knew what I had asked."

As William turned his glass slightly in the light of the fires and explosions, Graham put his own aside and focused on the glint of the cut crystal, catching his breath as he felt himself drawn into that other life, other mind, other time. He let it happen, seeing the fire flashes of the crystal facets turn to jewels on gold, watching as the cup went to the King's lips and *he* drank deeply of it. He flinched as William put the cup into his hand, seeing beyond the goblet's rim a florid face with redder hair superimposed on William's.

"Drink thou of the cup. I would not have it pass," the sacred king murmured. "Canst thou not recall the good times between us? Who better should I ask to do me this last service?"

The memory was poignant, familiar, the conversation one that had haunted Graham through many lives—the seal of duty set upon one whom the fates knew strong enough to bear the burden without breaking, though it did not make the sadness any less in the final hours.

Cup in hand, Graham let the memory run, then gave his head a little shake and drained the goblet to the dregs. The fiery gold burned his throat far more than wine had done that other time, and he coughed once as he set the empty glass upside-down on the cement next to his own, covering his face with his hands.

"Let be, Wat," William whispered. "I know 'tis not an easy burden to accept, but thou knowest the law. For this was I chosen long ago. The cycle must be observed. The succession shall pass in orderly fashion. I have made all the arrangements. Wouldst have some other hand less loving strike the sacred blow?"

Graham heard himself whisper, "No," for all that the prince was saying was as true in the here and now as it had been in that other life more than eight hundred years before. A sacred king was observing the sacred cycle, a willing sacrifice to ensure the survival of the land. The succession would be assured, at least for a time. Nor would this king find a more loving hand to serve him in this hour of need.

Greater love hath no man....

He raised his head and leaned it calmly against the wall to gaze back at the King in the semidarkness, a great peace filling his soul.

"I recognize the honor you do me, Lord," he heard himself

say, echoing that other man's words so many years before, "and my hand shall not falter when the time comes. It is my mortal heart which aches, heavy in my breast, for I shall miss you. The slayer goes not with the slain."

"Alas, no."

There had been arrows before, Graham suddenly remembered. No—crossbow quarrels. He flashed on a later memory: of putting nock to string and cranking back a crossbow screw. There would be no arrows tomorrow or crossbows or even the sword that had served them both in yet another time and place, but the words they exchanged were fitting. He watched William glance at the cement between them, making the mental adjustment, and he knew what would come next.

"To the best shot must go the finest arrows," the prince said slowly, almost by rote. "I hope that two will be more than sufficient, for I have no more love of suffering than the next man." His eyes sought Graham's in silent plea. "I rely on thee to do the job with dispatch. This—role of God does not come easily, in its ending."

Cold inside, Graham gazed long into the eyes of the two Williams, seeing the device he had installed in the belly of the Sunderland mirrored there. Then he eased roughly to his knees and took one of the royal hands, kissed it in homage, held it clasped in both of his in comfort.

"I shall not fail you, my liege. Only, let us speak no more of this until we must again. I promise, you shall not suffer," he added softly.

With a shudder, William closed his eyes and nodded, then sighed and looked up again. This time, there was only one William looking back, and Graham, in a blink, shed his other self as well. Smiling more easily now, he released the royal hand and retrieved the upturned glass along with his own.

"More Napoleon, my prince?" he asked, ducking instinctively as a burning Dornier screamed past and crashed nearby. "And why don't we go inside? We may well be indestructible tonight, but I think my sitting room is a far more comfortable place to celebrate our godhood."

William grinned at that and let himself be helped to his feet and ushered inside. They finished the bottle that night and stayed awake, talking, until dawn brought respite, at least from the bombing.

CHAPTER 26

THE MORNING WAS OVERCAST, WITH RAIN AND LOW cloud mercifully misting the still-smoking London skyline, matching their mood. They drank strong, steaming cups of Denton's tea while Graham changed from mess dress to service uniform. William seemed a little surprised at the voluntary donning of proper dress, but Graham could tell that he was pleased even though he did not comment. After that, Denton drove them to the Palace so William could bathe and change before leaving on his Welsh tour.

Graham lounged in the royal sitting room and made small talk with Flynn and several other officers while he waited for the prince to finish his toilette, feeling the effects of the sleepless night. He had no stomach for the breakfast a butler offered all around. Half an hour later, an immaculately turned out William emerged in his customary service dress uniform. Uniforms of other services in which William held rank were packed in the valises that Griffin snapped shut on the bed, for many varied activities were planned for the prince's stay in Wales, but Graham knew that this was one time when Griffin's efficiency would never matter. He was silent as he led William down to the waiting Bentley again, Flynn and Griffin following with a footman and the luggage.

Griffin alone, of the five going on to Calshot, had no inkling of the true tenor of the day. They had tried to contrive an excuse not to bring him, but there was no reason they could

425

find that would not have aroused later suspicion, at least on
Griffin's part. Royal dukes did not travel overnight without
their valets, and Griffin had been the prince's man since William was old enough to have a valet of his own. He had served
the Royal Family all his adult life and had no other kin. Kindest,
by far, to let him come.

But for his sake and for other reasons, no one said much
on the drive to Southampton. Nothing more really needed to
be said. William yawned pointedly several times at the beginning and laughingly blamed his seeming lethargy on the late
hours he and Graham had kept the night before and the excellent
bottle of brandy they had sacrificed in the cause of princely
amusement. Then he appeared to doze, though Graham was
certain he was doing no such thing. Sitting there at William's
side, so close and yet so far away, Graham wondered whether
the prince was remembering another drive nearly three months
before when the two of them had made a shorter trip from
Plymouth to Buckland. Even then, life had seemed far simpler.

They arrived at RAF Calshot all too soon, pulling up on the
tarmac near the end of the quay just at noon, right on time. A
guard of honor came smartly to *present arms* as the car stopped.
Denton and Flynn made a brisk show of opening doors and
seeing the luggage taken down to the waiting motor launch
with Griffin. A hundred yards out from the end of the quay,
the Sunderland rode its moorings like a motley, captive swan
in the light chop, straining for flight already, unaware of the
death it carried in its belly.

As the guard of honour ordered arms and their officer started
toward the prince, William signaled Flynn to go ahead and
turned back to Graham, standing attentively beside one open
rear door. A gentle mist was falling, but the accompanying
breeze was quite warm for September. The prince's face was
serene in the shadow of his cap visor, the ribbons of his orders
and medals bright splashes of color against his breast. The blue
of his Garter ribbon seemed brightest of all.

"I'd rather you stayed with the car if you don't mind," he
said quietly. "I don't think I could stand a public good-by at
the dock."

"Nor I," Graham murmured, trying to keep on a brave face
for all their sakes.

He started to make a proper, formal bow, mindful of curious

eyes upon them, as was always the case when Willaim appeared in public; but then William gripped his hand in that familiar, intimate clasp of one hand between his two, grinning broadly, his smile like the sun, which chose that moment to emerge from behind the clouds. Graham thought it was probably the most courageous thing he had ever seen William do.

"Not all *that* formal, my friend, after all we've been through together," the prince said softly, looking him straight in the eyes. "Good-bye, Gray."

To those watching, Graham's bow over their joined hands might have been simply an elaboration of the bow he had begun before. Surely no one besides the two of them heard Graham's whispered "Good-bye, William" or caught the added significance when Graham fleetingly slipped the fingers of his other hand between William's just before they drew apart.

"God bless, sir," Graham said more formally, stepping back a pace to render precise salute to the prince more than to the man.

Then William smiled and walked briskly toward the guard of honor, Flynn falling into place behind him, pausing to take the officer's salute before moving more slowly between their two lines in inspection. As was his wont, he paused occasionally to speak to one or another of the men, exercising that special charm that had always been so much his trademark. Graham was reminded of at least a dozen other leave-takings and tried to convince himself that this one was no different from any of them as William concluded his inspection and headed down the quay.

But as Graham watched William and his party board the motor launch, the Duke of Clarence's personal standard being broken as the prince himself stepped aboard, he was startled to find Ellis at his elbow. The old man wore a service uniform under his British Warm, with a pair of field glasses slung around his neck, but he shook his head when Graham would have spoken, drawing himself to respectful attention as the two of them watched William's launch punch its way through the swells toward the waiting Sunderland. When it was nearly there, Ellis sighed and took off the field glasses, resting them on the car's window frame between him and Graham.

"As I promised you, the crew are all volunteers," Ellis said quietly, though his voice sounded strained. "Each one is of the old faith—families whose names you'd recognize. They feel privileged to be accompanying His Royal Highness on this flight."

Graham stared at the field glasses for a few seconds, not fathoming the reason Ellis was offering them—or why he was even here—then snatched them and jammed them to his eyes, suddenly afraid he knew exactly why. The launch was still a dozen yards from the flying boat, so he had an unobstructed view of the doorway and the officers waiting there to greet the prince. He recognized Geoffrey first, by his red hair, and then his son.

"Richard!" he breathed. "My God, no!"

As he lowered the glasses, sick with shock and anger, he saw that the old man's hands were clenched white-knuckled around the top of the window frame. Abruptly, it hit him that the brigadier's grief could be no less than his own despite the disciplined expression he wore for the benefit of anyone who chanced to look at them. Even were it not for William, both Richard and Geoffrey were beloved grandsons.

The realization deflated his own horror, and he could only take stunned example from the brigadier's outward calm, numbly schooling his own expression to one of only ordinary interest.

"I have to ask why, Wesley," he murmured, when he had found his voice again, though he knew at least part of the answer already. The conversation he had with Richard before the Lammas working came back to haunt him.

"*I love him, too*," Richard had said. And Graham had asked him to serve the prince as he himself had always tried to do.

"They would have it no other way, *Din*," Ellis said in a very low voice, using Graham's magical name to underline the gravity of what he was saying. "I tried to talk them out of it, but they insisted. Richard understood the link between you and William. He was concerned that the link might not be direct enough between you and—the device—so he volunteered to be the pilot. He's your son and a part of you. It will be his hands on the controls when the boat starts climbing over Wales."

"But *I'm* responsible, not—You should have told me!" Graham whispered fiercely. "He doesn't have to do this. And Geoffrey—why *Geoffrey*?"

"I didn't tell you because they made me promise not to,"

Ellis replied. "And Geoffrey goes where Richard goes. You know that. They've been that way since childhood."

"That isn't a reason to die!"

"Perhaps you're right." Ellis sighed. "As for the ultimate why—well, I suppose we just hadn't reckoned on the impression our prince made on the young ones. You know how you had to argue with Michael and finally forbid him to be a part of this. Well, Richard and Geoffrey felt just as strongly, but they were determined not to give you the chance to tell them what they should or should not do. They were afraid that anyone else chosen for the duty might bungle it—might not prove suitable escort for the sacred king."

The sacred king.

As Graham's throat constricted in new grief, his eyes darted to the launch again. It was drawing under the wing of the Sunderland, but he could see William clearly even without the glasses. The prince stood in the stern, watching the flying boat's rigger secure the line one of the ratings had thrown from the bow of the motor launch. He waved a greeting as Richard crouched down in the doorway and tossed off a smiling salute.

Graham watched as the launch was drawn close, raising the glasses to his eyes again as William and then the others climbed aboard and disappeared inside. The luggage was passed up, and then William was back in the doorway with Richard and Geoffrey, bending to peer out from under the wing and raise a hand in last farewell. Graham could see the sunlight gleaming on his hair, and Richard's merry grin, Geoffrey's wave.

Then they withdrew, the door was secured, and the launch headed back to the quay as the Sunderland's engines began to kick over, first the outboard and then the inboard. Graham gave the glasses back to Ellis, but he did not take his eyes from the flying boat as she slipped her moorings and began taxiing slowly away from the quay, out into the roads.

She wallowed there in the long swells, warming her engines for several minutes. Then she was moving slowly forward again, faster, faster, rising up on her step until, with a plume of water streaming off the hull, she came unstuck and seemed to leap skyward, beginning to climb. It was the same perfect takeoff Graham had seen so many times before, with Richard's unmistakable touch at the controls as the boat circled the station and climbed high in the sky, her Aldis lamp flashing *"Ta-Ta"* from one of the dorsal gun hatches before she banked to head northwest.

As the plane disappeared from sight, even with the glasses, the sun went in, and the rain began to fall in earnest. Suddenly, Graham felt very cold.

He spent what was left of the afternoon in his office, reading and rereading intelligence reports whose details he was later unable to remember and which did not matter, anyway, since they told nothing of an invasion halted. He fought to keep his mind from the morning and the stunned, numb return from Calshot.

The brigadier had ridden back with him and stayed the afternoon, ostensibly to assist in a special report Graham had in progress. Michael and Denton were in and out, both of them quite aware of what was going on.

But by dusk, Graham could stand their solicitude no longer, well meaning though it was. He had to get out, away from the clattering teletypes and cipher machines in the next room, whose every new spurt of printing could be bringing the news he both dreaded and longed to hear.

He had Denton drop him off near Deptford, at the high embankment beside the Royal Naval College at Greenwich. Watching the moon rise and listening to the sirens and the thump of bombs and the urgent chatter of the batteries seeking out the bombers, he tried not to think about that other plane or the men who flew her.

Collar turned against the damp and chill, he waited on the same observation platform where, not very long ago, a royal duke had offered him a flat black jeweler's box with a star inside. He closed his eyes to shut out the dockside fires across the river that now blotted out the light of any star, not wanting to remember, but he remembered all too well. He walked some, but he always came back.

The last time, just after midnight, two uniformed figures were waiting for him, one of them smoking a pipe. Denton had a duffle coat for Graham and insisted he put it on before he would leave them alone. After Graham buttoned up the coat, he glanced at the silent brigadier. Ellis was gazing down at the river, elbows leaned wearily on the railing, puffing on his pipe. Cautiously, Graham joined him at the rail, following his stare to the water below.

"You'll find something in the left-hand pocket of that coat," Ellis said, not looking up. "He wanted you to have it, but not until—now. You'll understand when you see what it is."

Chilled, Graham hesitated for just an instant, staring at the smoke curling from the brigadier's pipe, then eased his hand into the deep patch pocket and felt fine linen knotted loosely around something hard and flat, perhaps a little larger than a two-shilling piece. The wrapping was one of William's monogrammed handkerchiefs, he saw, as he drew his hand out into the light, the royal cypher stitched in one corner.

He stepped back from the rail to undo it, fearful of losing whatever was inside. A handsome chain slithered from one of the folds first, cold across the back of his hand, and then he cupped the object in his palm. He stuffed the handkerchief back in his pocket as he tilted his hand to get a better look.

At first, he thought it was one of the link pieces from William's Garter collar, for it was about the right size, with what appeared to be an enameled Garter around the outer edge. Then he realized that it was silver, not gold, and that the center was not the expected red rose. As he canted it toward the firelight and brought it closer, he caught his breath, and his hand began to shake.

It would have aroused no special notice by anyone except himself. The piece was a traditional silver clan badge of the Graham family crest, winged falcon preying on a stork in the center. He had one very like it at home in a drawer somewhere, done as a cap brooch. What made this one unique was that the strap and buckle design around the edge had been filled in with blue enamel. The Graham motto shone bright silver against the Garter blue, the words suddenly taking on a meaning they never had before: *Ne oublie*—"*Do not forget.*"

He closed it in his hand, his eyes closing, too, against the glare of the fires across the river and the silhouette of Ellis standing at his elbow. Afraid even to try to speak, he pressed his balled fist against his lips and could only think of William's hands encircling his own, as the Garter encircled the Graham crest—protecting, cherishing, binding, though all of this would be only in memory from now on, at least in this life.

After a few seconds, he opened his eyes and looked at his hand again, though he did not open it. Now he held William's memory and honor in his hand just as William had held his. It was a precious, sacred trust.

"I—only now realized who gave you the Saint George medal you wear around your neck," he whispered, almost afraid to look at Ellis. "It was *your* victim, wasn't it?"

The brigadier nodded, but he did not speak. When it became clear he was not going to, Graham shook out the kinks in the chain and slipped it over his head. He pressed the badge briefly to his lips in renewed homage before clasping it in his hand again like a protective talisman, remembering how his prince had clutched the Great George of his Garter collar in a room at Laurelgrove. He knew Ellis remembered it, too, as he glanced aside at the old man—and he knew there was one more question he had to ask.

"You have something else to tell me, don't you?" he said softly.

Ellis nodded and pulled some folded papers from an inner pocket with infinite care. Suddenly, even the sounds of war seemed to recede as he opened the first one.

"I have—several items you should be aware of," Ellis said. "Shall I read them to you?"

Graham forced himself to nod.

"This first one ran on nearly all the wire services. It will be in tomorrow's papers," Ellis continued, pausing to swallow with difficulty. "The headline is 'Duke of Clarence Dies in Crash Flying to Wales.'"

Graham closed his eyes and bowed his head, the badge biting into his clenched palm as the brigadier began to read haltingly in the light of moon and fires.

"'The Admiralty regret to announce that H.R.H. Captain The Duke of Clarence, K.G., was killed on active service yesterday afternoon when a Sunderland flying boat crashed in South Wales. His Royal Highness was proceeding to Wales on an inspection tour. All the crew of the flying boat also lost their lives. This tragic news was announced by the Admiralty early last evening."

As the brigadier paused to swallow audibly again, Graham could see William's face behind his closed eyelids, smiling in the sunlight as Graham last had seen him, Richard and Geoffrey to either side. He tried to hold their images as Ellis resumed reading.

" 'The duke, youngest brother of the King, had celebrated his thirty-fifth birthday only two months ago and had distinguished himself in various prewar operations connected with naval intelligence, for which he was made a Knight of St. Michael and St. George. He had become a Knight of the Garter in 1921 and had been created Duke of Clarence only in 1937, shortly before the tragic death of his fiancée, the Princess Caroline-Marie, and as part of His Majesty's coronation honours.' "

The brigadier paused to draw breath. "It goes on to list more of his specific achievements. Then: 'Those of the Duke of Clarence's party were also killed with him: his secretary and aide, Lieutenant James Flynn, RNVR, appointed to that post only a few weeks ago; and his valet of nearly twenty years, Chief Petty Officer Donald Griffin. The crew of the Sunderland included two grandsons of a hero of the Great War: Flight Lieutenant Richard Graham, RAF, captain of the flying boat, son of Colonel Sir John Cathal Graham, V.C., K.C.M.G., and Flight Lieutenant Geoffrey Ellis, RAF, second pilot, both of them grandsons of Brigadier General Sir Wesley Ellis, K.C.B. Also killed were...' "

Ellis went on to read the names of the rest of the crew— eight young men from some of the oldest and most respected families in the country. Graham was shaking his head as Ellis finished reading, too stunned even to cry. He had known it must end this way as he watched the flying boat disappear into the overcast this morning, but the stark reality of the words that the whole world soon would read seemed somehow part of a very bad dream.

He heard Ellis shuffling paper again, and he glanced aside dully, forcing his fingers to uncramp and let the clan badge hang on its chain, rubbing absently at the indentations the medal had made across his palm. High overhead, the drone of aircraft began to intrude once more—wave after wave of new bombers coming in, with the tiny, darting shapes of the defending night-fighters and raiders alike lit by searchlight spears. Explosions jarred the city to the east again, punctuated by the ineffectual but reassuring chatter of the Ack-Ack guns, but something in Ellis's manner with a second sheet of paper made Graham ignore the sounds of war and gaze at him in question.

"I said there were several items you should be aware of," the brigadier murmured, uncreasing a yellow cipher flimsy and flattening it against the heavier teletype paper. "This came in just before I left to find you. Grumbaugh penciled out a rough translation and said to tell you it had been hand carried from Bletchley Park. I suppose that means it's an Ultra intercept?"

Graham found his vision blurring, and he had to brush at his eyes with an awkward hand as he nodded. Grumbaugh would not have entrusted even Ellis with Ultra material unless it were very, very important. Dared he hope that news could have come so soon?

"Read it for me, will you?" he whispered.

The brigadier cleared his throat. "It's from the German general staff to the officer in charge, Air Support Operations, Holland. Usual amenities, etc., etc., *Heil Hitler*. 'As of this date, you are authorized to begin the dismantling of the air-loading equipment at all Dutch aerodromes.' There's more, but that's the crux of it."

It took a few seconds for the significance to penetrate Graham's benumbed mind.

"Dismantling? In Holland? But that's one of the main staging areas for the invasion!"

"That's right, son."

"Then it's off!" Graham murmured. "The invasion is off. We've won!"

"We've won this round, at any rate," the old man returned gruffly. "There will be no invasion *this* season, which was what we feared the most. And if our lads continue to pound the Jerries up there"—he glanced up at the planes and the tracer-filled sky—"it won't come at all."

"Then—was today necessary?" Graham breathed after a long pause. "Tell me, Wesley. I have to know. Did I kill all those people—my prince and my own son and nephew—for *nothing*?"

Ellis shook his head, the old eyes misting at last. "We'll never know for sure, Gray," he whispered. "If today had gone differently for us, perhaps it would have gone differently in other ways as well. Everything pointed toward what was done today. We have to believe there was a reason for that."

"A reason," Graham repeated numbly.

Slowly, he took the last signal from Ellis and read it for

himself, the penciled words slightly blurred in the moonlight, the printed German clearer but hard and cold. He scanned the words again, shaking his head.

When he had read it through a third time and still had divined no answers, he began methodically shredding it into tiny pieces, his mind going back over the past months. When none of the pieces were larger than his thumbnail, he opened his fingers and watched the bits float to the river like faded, obscene confetti. For just an instant, his hands caught the reflection of the burning city and seemed to glow red.

Slayer of kings and slain for kings am I. . . .

He bowed his head then, stifling a sob in his throat, but he did not weep. Clenching his fist to hold the blood he had shed, he paid homage to all the dead who, down the centuries and the seven-years, had given life itself to keep this island safe. With the bombs falling all around and the fires blazing in the nearby docks, he stood arm in arm with another man who had lived the grief and hope before.

Together they watched until the morning light: one warrior old and scarred by other wars, the other man of lesser years, but also, in this leaden dawn, a man no longer young—both, in that brightening moment, worn but faithful servants of the sacred king.

AFTERWORD

THE CHARACTERS DEPICTED IN THIS STORY ARE PURELY fictional, and any resemblance to real people, living or dead, is quite coincidental. However, the historical setting and chronology for the summer of 1940, the months of Dunkirk and the Battle of Britain, are real. So are the secret units of Britain's MI.6 and their parallels in Berlin, which were concerned with utilizing the occult sciences to further the progress of their respective sides in the war. The use of astrology, the Nostradamus prophecies, and pendulum dowsing by both sides is a matter of record. The *Thule Gesellschaft* was but one of the German occult orders that attempted to use black magic against the Allies, though its activities on Lammas night itself are unknown. Hitler *was* an initiate of this group and *was* at the Berghof on Lammas night.

The details surrounding the Lammas working against Hitler are conjectural but are based upon the best information now available, more than forty years after the fact, when nearly everyone who was involved has passed on. At least one New Forest coven did go down to the sea and raise a cone of power for that purpose at least three times that summer. Dion Fortune and some of her associates did engage in an occult operation involving the visualization of archangels guarding Britain. Other groups may have done more or less than that.

Where descriptions of various occult practices diverge from published material currently available, particularly regarding

436

witchcraft, one should remember that before about 1950 and the pioneer work done by Murray, Leland, Gardner, and others, little was written down or otherwise codified concerning native British occult traditions. Thus, it was necessary to construct a suitable background for the Oakwood group based upon what seems fairly universal in present published material on the Old Religion and what was told to me by British occultists of various persuasions concerning what it was like in 1940. To the best of my knowledge, there is no group precisely like the one headed by Alix and David Jordan and no Oakwood Manor with its magical maze. Nor do I know for a fact that any joint gathering of British occultists was held to coordinate a common working for Lammas of 1940—though it seems to me that there should have been and certainly could have been.

Concerning historical precedents for using magic to prevent the invasion of England, I wrote from the section on Sir Francis Drake in Doreen Valiente's *An ABC of Witchcraft Past and Present*, which was one of the early catalysts for this project:

> *Sir Francis Drake is known in all English history books as the man who delivered England from the Spanish Armada. Not so well known is the fact that in his native Devonshire he is reputed to have belonged to the witch cult.*
>
> *During the Second World War, at the time when England seemed in imminent danger of invasion, a large gathering of witches took place in the New Forest, to work a rite to protect the country. It was recalled then that similar rituals had been carried out in past years against Napoleon, and before that against the Spanish Armada. (The ceremony against Hitler took place at Lammas 1940; and the writer has known personally two people who took part in it.)*
>
> *Many legends have gathered about Drake and his defeat of the Armada. That of Drake's drum is well known; and its ghostly beat is said to have been heard during both the First and the Second World Wars. In the West Country, Drake is told of, in winter evening fireside tales, as a particularly active ghost, who has been known to lead the Wild Hunt on dark nights of wind and storm. . . . Other stories say that, because he practiced*

witchcraft in his lifetime, Drake's soul cannot rest. This is why his ghost drives a black coach and four about the Devonshire lanes on stormy nights.

Another version of the story says that Drake sold his soul to the Devil in return for the defeat of the Spaniards, and this is why his soul is doomed to wander. Both tales are basically versions of the same thing, that Drake belonged to the Old Religion.

Regarding Drake's actual involvement and that of the Order of the Garter, I stand by what the characters have said. What they have stated as historical fact is true to the best of my knowledge; where they have speculated, so must we, for no one knows for certain. Similarly conjectural is the material on the deaths of Thomas Becket and William Rufus, which was partially developed from Hugh Ross Williamson's *The Arrow and the Sword*.

As for the theory of the sacred king, I refer the reader to Margaret Murray's *The Divine King in England*. Like Brigadier Ellis, I can only suggest that each must draw his or her own conclusions to decide whether or not the seven-year cycles continue and whether there are still those who serve the sacred king.

ABOUT THE AUTHOR

Katherine Kurtz was born in Coral Gables, Florida, during a hurricane, and has led a somewhat whirlwind existence ever since. She was awarded a B.S. in chemistry from the University of Miami, and attended medical school for a year before she decided that she really wanted to write about medicine rather than practice it. She earned an M.A. in medieval English history from UCLA while writing her first two novels.

Recently married, Miss Kurtz lives with her husband in Sun Valley, California, where she devotes her time to writing.